Predators, Reapers and Deadlier Creatures

Predators, Reapers and Deadlier Creatures

Matthew James Jones

Library and Archives Canada Cataloguing in Publication
Jones, Matthew James, author
Predators, Reapers and Deadlier Creatures / Matthew James Jones

 Canada Council   Conseil des arts
for the Arts   du Canada

We acknowledge the support of the Canada Council for the Arts.

The poem "Gallows Humor" was previously published by In/Words Press, November 2014, in a chapbook called "White Flowers and Landmines."

Issued in print and electronic formats.
ISBN: 978-1-998501-12-0 (paperback)
ISBN: 978-1-998501-13-7 (ebook)

Cover Design: Stefan Prodanovic
Interior Design: Winston S. Prescott

Double Dagger Books Ltd.
Toronto, Ontario, Canada
www.doubledagger.ca

ACRONYMS

9-liner — a request for medical evacuation
AO — area of operations
ACK — acknowledged
Approx — approximately
BDA — battle damage assessment
BiP — blow in place
CAS — close air support
CAT A — a casualty with serious injuries
CAT B — a casualty with moderate injuries
CAT C — a casualty with minor injuries
DBIED — donkey-borne improvised explosive device
DFAC — dining facility
DSR — daily situation report
EKIA — estimated killed in action
EWIA — estimated wounded in action
EOD — explosive ordinance disposal
EOF — escalation of force
ETA — estimated time of arrival
FAM — fighting-aged male
FATA — federally administered tribal area (of Pakistan)
FET — female engagement team
FOB — forward operating base
GSW — gunshot wound
HERON — an unarmed drone
HME — home-made explosives
HQ — headquarters
HUA — heard, understood, acknowledged
IED — improvised explosive device
Illum — illumination rounds
INF — infantry
INS — insurgents
ISAF — international security assistance force
KAF — Kandahar Air Field

KIA — killed in action
LAV — light armored vehicle
Medevac — medical evacuation
NFTR — nothing further to report
NSTR — nothing significant to report
PID — positive identification
POL — pattern of life
PRED — predator drone
PT — physical training
REAPER — a drone with 500 lbs bombs
RFI — request for information
ROE — rules of engagement
ROZ — restricted operating zone
RPG — rocket-propelled grenade
RV — rendevouz
SALT — size, activity, location, time
SAF — small arms fire
SDO — senior duty officer
SIED — suicide improvised explosive device
SIGACT — significant activity
SOP — standard operating procedure
Squirter — someone running for cover
SVBIED — suicide vehicle-borne improvised explosive device
TB — Taliban
TEA — target engagement authority
TIC — troops in contact
TFK — task force Kandahar
TOC — tactical operations center
UXO — unexploded ordinance
VBIED — vehicle-borne improvised explosive device
WU — wheels up
WD — wheels down
WIA — wounded in action

1.

I'D BEEN IN AFGHANISTAN FOR THREE MONTHS when I saw the woman in the marketplace die. Thirty or forty men haggled the price of fruit as she skirted a low stone wall in her burka, stomach swollen in late pregnancy. Our drone was hovering overhead, studying the Pattern of Life, when the woman triggered the bomb, which exploded in a white flash. The screen dimmed; we saw her legs had been severed, nearly at the hip.

Commotion: the men in the market scrambled to aid her, pouring water in her mouth, and we sent a helicopter, which landed in the marketplace a few minutes later. The men formed a protective circle around the dying woman. When the medics climbed from the chopper with their kits and stretchers, the villagers didn't let them get close.

Minutes passed. The medics arguing with the villagers as the woman's mouth stretched into a black 'O' and blood seeped into the sand and we sipped coffee and cracked cruel jokes until she died.

And I didn't even want to *go* here, because you can't make sense of the stupid awful waste of it no matter how you try. But back then I hadn't yet grown wise; after my shift, I stumbled back to the barracks in the pre-dawn fog and sat on the steps outside in the rear of the building to be alone.

I heard a whimper. A muted cough.

Pulled a little sailor's flashlight from my pocket, spun around, and poked my head under the steps. A black cavity yawned   more than large enough for a person to crawl into the building's underbelly. I inched forward, flashlight piercing the darkness, and discovered the Bigfoot.

On closer inspection: this was not a military-issued Bigfoot. It had wormed its way into the corner beneath the shower room where the floor got soggy and sagged. Shining my little light up and down its hulking body, dozens of greasy frogs hopped deeper into darkness. The creature huddled next to a drainpipe, where marks in the fungi suggested it'd been slurping the nourishing scum.

At first I had no idea what I was seeing: a bulkish white man-shape snuffling in the dirt, enormous hands pressed over its brow like the light was a welding torch. Thick fur tufts, filthy and matted with sweat and frog oil. Some kind of tremendous gorilla-bear, eyes glittering with intelligence, whimpering and seeming to mouth language—what other word but Bigfoot applies?

The flashlight nearly slipped in my sweaty palm. A voice in my head told me to run, run far, sprint all the way back to Canada. Another voice said, get your pistol out, fool, and I complied, pulling my rusty 9mm from the holster, and flicking off the safety.

The creature, seated in the cellar's muck, peeked at me through its fingers, big pooling blue eyes, fuzzy eyebrows furrowing low, two great canine tusks jutting over a wolf-like muzzle. It grovelled: the saddest Bigfoot I'd ever seen, yet also the happiest, since it was my first.

I tried to keep my voice steady, but it cracked anyway. "Are you… with the Taliban?"

To my surprise, it responded in a twangy English with a voice deeper than a bear's. "Shit, man. I ain't with anythin' 'cept a hundred frogs, and 'bout four thousand fleas."

"You're obviously not from around here." I was looking at his thick fur, orange and matted, with patches of white, freckled skin peeking out. Summer in Kandahar the heat rises halfway to boiling, and just a bit cooler at night. "How the hell did you get onto the base?"

The Bigfoot hung its heavy head and sighed. "Took a nap on the wrong plane." It picked at a few rags that clung to its shoulders, that might have once been a woolen scarf. "I'm havin' a pretty shitty day on toppa whole stack of other shitty days. I know ya gotta job to do, but please don't shoot me. Please." He closed his eyes, waiting for the bullet, and clasped his hairy-knuckled hands. "I know how I look but I never wanted to hurt nobody." His lower lip trembled.

It could not know that it was pleading for mercy from a drone operator. That in the last month, I had seen eleven people killed by missiles and bombs. I hadn't ordered any of the strikes, but I had facilitated each one by lining up assets and passing information. If I hadn't seen that woman die in the marketplace, I would have wasted the freak. But watching without being able to do anything had been the absolute worst feeling, like a fabric in the chest tearing. Here was a living creature who needed my help, and a chance to prove to myself I was still capable of a good deed.

I took a whole sleeve of Saltine crackers, which my mother had sent me in a morale box, and slid it, and two bottles of water, into the crack at the back of the barracks, where his eyes glittered in the dark.

I felt for him, the big bastard. He was hot in his pelt and chomping the heads off frogs. "Don't let anyone else hear you crying," I said. "I can't protect you. Avoid discovery. Preserve water."

The Bigfoot nodded its huge head in thanks.

I made a promise to tell this story, even if it hurts. There will be drone strikes, monsters, barbed wire, and forbidden love in bunkers. Once I was a giant but now I sit in the wake of strength with the cripples. I have taken innocent life and nearly destroyed myself in grief.

But the story starts with a kindness, and that matters.

2.

TIM HORTON'S COFFEE: obsessed Canadians wait in interminable queues for it, pelted by snowstorms and freezing rain and hail the size of eyeballs. Parents strangle their children for a drop. Fortunately, the coffee comes in paper cups big as buckets. Canadian policy is for civil servants to sprint to work carrying their buckets so everyone knows how busy they are. And why shouldn't soldiers in Afghanistan be as caffeinated as the industrious bees of home? They installed a Tim Hortons in the middle of Kandahar Airfield, about sixty feet from the barracks. Inside, civilian baristas (women, a rarity) had gone squirrely from too many rocket attacks. Each day I waited in line for five buckets that I could distribute among the soldiers in the Tactical Operations Center. That was how I kept them loyal.

So when I walked to work it was always a balancing act. Teetering past the rumbling tanks and jingle trucks and Strykers, crossing the road to stay in shadow. Held my breath as I skirted the poo pond, picturing that Bigfoot squirming in the muck and wondering who I should tell. Concrete barriers blotted the sun. Barbed wire scrawled on top of the thirty-foot walls and coiled in knots along the road. A gray-brown bird landed too close to an anthill; the ants skeletonized it in seconds, scattering the feathers.

No maps, no signposts, no addresses: there was always a chance of getting lost and ending up like the bird. The base was a labyrinth the size of a small town, populated by 30,000 soldiers from many nations who cranked out push-ups in the shade of bunkers, cleaned their weapons, penned letters for big-eyed girls back home, fantasized about the next kill. Always the sound of growling tanks, or minotaurs, somewhere out of view.

I will never forget the smell, always curdling around the corner, a synapse permanently singed. The Canadian compound was upwind of the poo pond, thankfully, but you could never escape the stink of shit. An ever-growing, ever-reeking lake that was basically a huge hole in the ground where sewage trucks dumped the waste from across the camp. I walked past it daily on the way to work. Our compound was a fort within the fort, a mini maze of concrete and barbed wire nestled in the larger base, barred by three locked doors each with their own combination. The colonels changed the combinations every few weeks and you'd find out when your code didn't work and you milled around until someone let you in. No one ever explained why the relatively small Canadian contingent required four full colonels, though rumour was they had mysterious powers, but I knew they were snug behind a fourth or even fifth door, writing shrewd memos, making systems, anticipating problems, lubricating in all directions.

The Tactical Operations Center, or TOC, where I lived twelve hours a day, seven days a week. From the outside you would never guess this was where the magic happened: the medical helicopters deployed, the drone strikes ordered, the artillery blasting holes in poppy fields like the stomping of titans. The TOC was a plywood shack, dilapidated, with holes in the roof from rocket attacks, and thick bundles of cords snaking in all directions. Inside, several rows of computer-laden desks made a U-shape that nearly filled the room, and operators from disparate backgrounds hunched over, turning pale from the glow of computer monitors. Maybe twenty soldiers in the day, withering to eight even-paler bastards on the night shift. The center of the room, about the same size and shape as a pool table, was the map of our Area of Operations, shielded under plexiglass. The wall at the end of the room, the top of the U, was draped with many monitors that showed what the drones were seeing—half a dozen crystal balls we used to spy on our enemies. We were spying on a boy, maybe fifteen years old.

"You think today's the day, Jones?" Bell asked. "Are we gonna kill this little punk?" Bell was the senior Captain, and my boss. He was a gangly troll with a scarred mouth and a tiny, hard potbelly, who talked with his hands while fluttering long, delicate fingers. In another life he'd been a used car salesman and I guess he was pretty good at selling luxury cars to grannies on fixed incomes, since one day he had a pang of conscience so profound that he retired immediately and sought a less questionable profession.

I said, "Well that depends if he shows violent intent, doesn't it?" Bell and I bickered like this regularly—in the TOC, the Rules of Engagement told us when it was OK to strike. But the rules were open to interpretation.

We turned to the black-and-white drone monitor; the boy was standing outside a mud hut. We'd been watching him for several days, so long I'd named him Sahar. Sahar didn't know that he was Sahar, or that he was being watched, or that people were arguing about killing him every day. By North American standards, he was scrawny, a thin wisp painted black and gray by the drone's poor camera. An older woman appeared at the window of the modest hut and spoke to him. Her face was gray and her eyes were two glittering pixels and her mouth was a black pit. He started filling a sack.

Bell rubbed his hands. "Here we go, boys, an IED emplacer. How many missiles do we have left on the Predator?"

"Two missiles!" shouted Crazy Jay, the drone guy.

Sahar kept filling up the sack from the little ditch.

"Any jets? We could level the whole building with a jet."

"I can get a jet in three minutes!" Crazy Jay yelled. He had tendons sticking out of his neck from yelling constantly.

"Oh, we're gonna fuck this guy up," said Bell. "Someone get the Major."

"Bell," I said.

"Yes, Jones?"

"It's potatoes. He's helping his mother fill a sack of potatoes."

Bell peered at the drone feed. It was difficult to see because the screen was very pixelated. The potato-shaped wads of pixels rolled out of the sack a little. Sahar stooped and stuck them back in.

"Call off the jet." Bell grumbled. "Fuckers are getting smart. We'll catch him next time."

The Rules of Engagement (ROE) and Positive Identification (PID)

ROE is about force and when a soldier gets to use it. Comes from on high with the General and other bigwigs telling us when we can launch a missile at someone. When a local puts a bomb in the road we're allowed to strike him. When he takes a shit on the road, he's safe.

PID is about making sure the person you're bombing is an enemy combatant and not a farmer. Staring through a dim-eyed Reaper, it's hard to tell the difference. Sometimes image analysts in the Intelligence cell would determine PID, other times we did. Once we lined up a strike on a man carrying a bazooka wrapped in a blanket. Our missile was nearly in the air when the bazooka pulled back the blanket and waved a tiny brown fist. We'd nearly struck a baby.

It may seem like abstract philosophy but the Major encouraged debate about the ROE and PID, at least to a point. Without them a soldier is a murderer, a general is a warlord, and a TOC is as deadly and fickle as a dragon.

3.

WHEN THE MAJOR CAME BACK, I told her Bell had nearly killed Sahar and she was so pissed she slammed her battered helmet into the filing cabinet. The door never closed right after that.

"Bell, I can't even grab dinner without you trying to blow somebody up! What the hell is the matter with you?"

Bell squirmed and dug his hands into his pockets, shrinking. He always did this when the Major berated him; her leadership both chafed and aroused, despite the fact we all wore the same uniform, baggy clothes with many pockets in patterns of desert and dust, that flattered no one's figure. But the Major was one of the few women in the TOC, athletic even by the standards of the Infantry, with long blonde hair she strangled in a tight bun.

He recovered quickly: "Major, Major, Major—there's no need for anger, we're all on the same team, right? Jones and I were discussing Positive ID, that's all. Let's not get so carried away." Normally, Bell was a whisperer, an underminer, a smoker's pit gossip. But when he and the Major argued, he was the perfect perfunctory gentleman, always using rank, and keeping his body language obsequious. Still, he did raise his voice so the other soldiers in the TOC could hear, as he gestured broadly with his long, supple fingers. Once he had our attention, "We all remember what the General said? 'Keep the pressure up.' And we're good soldiers who respect our General and want to win the war, aren't we?"

She raised her voice as well, accustomed to Bell's jockeying. "Everyone listen up. You do not win the war by killing innocent people. That just makes us more enemies, do you understand? We need strong Positive Identification as well as the Rules of Engagement before every strike." She glared around the TOC at the strange pasty-faced moles we had become. Her eyes were blue, her cheekbones, swords. Bell grovelled under her glare, rooting his hands ever deeper into his pockets. "You can't kill someone for potatoes. You can't kill someone for digging a ditch. You can't kill someone for talking to his mother. We kill Taliban fighters only. Fighting Age Males carrying weapons or showing other hostile intent. Does everyone understand?"

All twenty of us stared at our computers and pretended to write emails: Intelligence specialists; Clay, our helicopter expert; Mr. Artillery; bellicose

Crazy Jay with the drones, a US liaison officer; others. Some sided with the Major—that killing was a necessary evil in war but it needed constraints—and others sided with Bell: everyone we saw through the drone was an enemy. I was in the third camp, a minority of one, a position so contrary with wartime culture it was unutterable. I thought every drone strike was a mistake—each insurgent we killed created a fresh handful seeking retribution. Figure out for yourself if I was the right or the wrong guy for the job.

The Chief, withered minion of the General, yelled "Room!" and we all snapped to attention and stopped moving. Imagine watching a play and all the actors freeze except one; this is why they call it a theatre of war. The only actor permitted to move is the General, who stood in the entrance to the TOC silhouetted, broad-shouldered and narrow-waisted.

"At ease, troops." We relaxed in place, and he marched to the center of the room, the middle of the U, which was filled with the huge map of our AO. He peered through the thick aviator sunglasses he wore habitually, leaning down to the details, and we all held our breath waiting on his words.

"How's the battlespace today? Any luck?" He used to talk like that about killing people, his voice a growl.

The Major appeared at his elbow. "Slow day, Sir. We found some Unexploded Ordinance in the south early this morning and sent an engineering team to dispose of it." She pointed with a pen to sticky notes on the map. "And here we recovered a cache of drugs and Home-Made Explosives." A well-stained coffee pot in the corner belched at this last word.

"Good good," nodded the General. "But did you find any new targets?" He scanned the room; mirrored sunglasses made his eyes blank screens.

The Major opened her mouth to speak but Bell was faster. "Well, Sir, we almost had a target earlier. I'd love to say we had a good strike, but that's not the case." The General swung his head toward the Major, who drew a sharp breath. Bell strained for an extra inch of height. "Hate to say it, General, but the Major has turned one of these insurgents into her pet. Named him Sahar. Yah, Sahar's pretty much family around here—next she'll have him over for a picnic."

A snicker in the room but the General wasn't laughing; a vein in his forehead bulged. Otherwise his expression did not change, tight lips creasing a hard face, his jaw a jutting prow, like a warship. "Major, if there is one thing I hate it is a soft Operations Center. I will not tolerate it. Your job is to sow chaos and keep our enemies on the run." He gestured grandiloquently to the big map. "There are hundreds, maybe thousands, of insurgents here. We could strike one every day for the rest of our tour. Need I remind you that your job is to scour and disrupt the Taliban? You need to get busy, Major. You need to get busy and cold."

"Negative, Sir." The Major's voice cut the air like a bugle. And after this impossibility—saying no to the General—several seconds of silence lapsed before she continued. None of us had the balls for such a thing but that was the Major, infantry and tough as fuck. Rumour was she'd killed a Taliban fighter with her helmet on an earlier tour and gotten a medal. "We cannot kill every day. We must kill Taliban fighters only, not workers, not farmers. When we make mistakes we give ammunition to our enemies and weaken our cause." She didn't blink, staring right at the General. "I always tell my guys, 'We must proceed with our highest integrity.'"

The General stared back, neither face nor sunglasses revealing emotion. He wasn't used to people disagreeing with him. The week before he'd cut off the flow of humanitarian food to a village whose elders refused to stop meeting with Taliban ambassadors. The General had an owlish way of looking at people, with his head tilted slightly, that made us squirm like mice. "Your Major is a smart lady, and I'm glad she's here to guide you through the tough calls. Integrity, of course, it goes without saying." He pointed to the drone feeds. "But these things can also lie to you, I've seen it. You start spending time with your target and you start to think he's like you. You start making things up about his life, his childhood, whatever, and you even start to love the creature you invented. Next thing you know you've got PID and you're dropping a bomb on your best friend."

He nodded to the Major. "Trust me, there's nothing worse than that. Keep the pressure up. Don't make friends with the enemy." Turning to leave, the General shook Bell's hand firmly, the Chief yelled "Room" and we froze again, until the General's footsteps faded and the Major cast the counterspell, stood us at ease.

In the General's wake, the Major tore a strip off Bell right in front of everyone, sentenced him to mopping the TOC for the next month, but he didn't care. He was studying his hand as if it tingled from the handshake. This was partly due to the General's enormous grip strength, and partly to a kind of magic. The General's fingers had twisted knives and gouged eyeballs and lobbed grenades and crushed throats. He had shaken hands with countless world leaders, politicians and other generals, each time self-assessing and improving his technique. His handshake had sparked military operations, christened ships, and built schools—we all wanted one. The entire structure of ranks and codes and layers was built to make that so.

4.

IT WAS STILL DARK WHEN I LEFT work that morning—trudging through Kandahar Airfield, better known as KAF, where the concrete walls and omnipresent barbed wire gave the place a post-apocalyptic feel, just lacked a few dune buggies and thugs swinging chains. Sometimes I marvelled that all these defenses had been erected to protect precisely nothing; our only treasures were the runways and the poo pond, otherwise it was mostly wasteland in all directions. To the south and east of our city-base the hard-packed desert shimmered with mirages until Pakistan. North, the highway stretched three miles to Kandahar City—many-hued and sprawling—where cars, motorcycles and draft horses fought for space on the street. West, about twelve miles, was the Canadian Area of Operations, where we scoured the roads and villages with drones, and packed Forward Operating Bases with combat soldiers. Those soldiers thought it was all frisbees and picnics in KAF. To their credit, we did have a frisbee that first week, but a guy tossed it too hard and it sank into the pond with a schlurp.

Those night-walks were my favorite, though, everything moon-painted blue. I trekked back to the barracks, kicking dust along the edges of the walls that framed the camp—barbed wire and crushed glass on top. Wasn't long before I'd figured the whole base was a cage, or a prison, with snipers in towers scanning the many dips and craters for movement. Outside the wall, a vicious moat of landmines spread for a hundred yards. But during the evening strolls I could say, "I will navigate this strange maze and be home soon," or, "this has all been a dream," and these lies were particularly delicious under the moon, which softened the sharp edges.

Under such a moon, even the concrete walls of a bunker can be inviting. That's where we huddled when the rockets rained down: four big slabs of concrete making a box with another slab for a roof. You could cram ten or twelve people in there, more if you stacked them. But this time I was alone, entering the bunker and sitting on the sandy floor to lean against the concrete wall and feel it, cool, on my back.

The General wanted me to kill Sahar—that was clear. A boy whose crimes were stuffing potatoes into a bag, hoeing the fields, and praying. Fifteen years old and illiterate: this was our bogeyman. What a terror he might be; best to snuff him quickly.

They were dark thoughts. I only signed up for Afghanistan to get away from a woman, anyway, not to kill teenagers. It was one of those break ups that just kept on going: six months, nine months, a year. Her love was like napalm, couldn't scrape it off the skin. But once I got here, I started to believe we could help the people. That we could build roads and schools. Prop up the government we installed. Hold the Taliban at bay while the Afghan Army and Police gathered strength. How does shooting a missile at a goddamn teenage boy help anyone?

Yet I was just a cog, with little control over my destiny. I didn't want to kill anyone, but it was just so damn easy; our enemies were video game blobs on a drone feed.

Will Sahar die in this war? Will I be the one who kills him?

I knew the answers already, and I cried.

5.

MY SORROW TURNED TO WITHERING TERROR FAST when a shaggy hand dropped on my shoulder, heavy as a rocket launcher. Fingers like bananas and long ebony claws and orange curly knuckle hair and the stink of frog piss. I tried my best to scream but no sound came; I just gaped and goggled while fumbling for my pistol.

Yet the warmth and pressure were gentle, and the smell of frog funk familiar. The Bigfoot squatted on its haunches, half-filling the bunker, and stared at me with unfathomable blue eyes.

"Jesus, you scared the shit out of me."

"Ha! This from the guy who came crawlin' into my house with a pistol in his hand two nights ago. Damn near shat myself." The creature slumped onto what seemed to be its ass and leaned back, facing me. "Besides, it's great to have a friend when you're sitting' around, bein' miserable."

A carnivore's teeth with the two major tusks, stalactites descending from the upper jaw, yellowing and sharp and longer than my index finger. The great muscles of the neck and trapezius, awash in orange fur, seemed designed to lock that fearsome mouth in place and tear flesh. *This thing could crack my skull like a pistachio.*

I tried to brush the tar from my shoulders where the filthy fingers had stained my shirt—futile. The monster didn't seem aggressive, but it certainly reeked and who knew what it would do if it was hungry enough. "Look, *Thing*, I'm not your friend."

"*Thing!*" boomed the creature, slapping the sandy earth with its palm. "Ha! We're all things, buddy. Everythin's a thing. And the kind of *thing* ya are is the kind that hasn't shot me yet, which makes ya a different sort than the others." He leaned in a little closer, a flange of fur outlined his face; the end of his black snout drooled as he scanned my uniform. "Jones. Such a borin' name—no wonder ya were cryin'."

The creature chuckled at its own joke. It didn't seem likely to eat me; perhaps it was attempting its own crude version of kindness. Looking at the sheer bulk of him, a mere 9mm pistol would never stop it if things got violent. Usually, it was me making other people feel small.

"What is it you want?" I asked.

"Plenty o' stuff!" said the Bigfoot. "Same as you, prolly. Home. Money. Clean water. A couple plates o' delicious moss every day. A world without pants. A girlfriend who can throw a boulder farther than me—the usual."

"What is it you want *from me*?"

The Bigfoot studied its knuckle hair closely. "Well, some grub would be nice. It's OK if ya got no moss—I can eat anythin'. And, well… I ain't got much of a head for plannin' my big escape, ya know? I'm bustin' outta this joint but I'm gonna need an inside man. That's you." His face split into a vapid grin. "C'mon, didn't you always want someone like me for a friend?"

"You mean a Bigfoot?"

Its eyes flashed in the gloom. "Now wait a second, Mister. I'm a Canadian same as you. Kids at school mighta called me a Bigfoot but that don't mean shit. Call me a Sasquatch if you wanna, but I got me a people birth certificate."

"Well, let's see it."

The Sasquatch made a show of checking his pockets as if I was a policeman who had pulled him over. "Hmmmm… I mighta left my ID in my other pants." With this pantomime the creature did reveal some familiarity with human customs, and it must have learned its scraps of English somewhere. I also couldn't dispute that the Sasquatch was a "he" and not an "it," if the hefty club he was dragging was any evidence. "Nope, sorry boss. Been roughin' it for some time—lost the pants a while back. Never liked wearin' people-pants. I was happy to see 'em go. Used to piss my Mom off back in Wawa. Every time she turned 'round I'd have thrown them up a tree, or flushed one leg down the toilet."

A wary chat, with my tears drying and the creature providing more and more detail about its home of Wawa, a desolate town in northern Ontario I'd visited once or twice, whose chief attraction was a fifty-foot goose in the central square. I had to concede that he knew the town better than I did. Once past the grotesque and fearsome appearance, the creature had a certain charm, a kind of leprechaun magic. After multiple nudges I found myself relating my worries in small words, counting my issues on my fingers.

"I have a Mom back in Ottawa who's sure I'm going to be killed. I had a girlfriend, but she dumped me right before I got here. The General has ordered that people caught having sex, or even holding hands, are sent home in shame. Almost every day someone shoots a rocket at me or I watch a person get blown up." I sighed and looked down at my boots in the dust of the bunker. *And I am constantly pressured to kill people, even when they're innocent.*

The Sasquatch was silent for a long moment. I could just hear the breath whistling in his nostrils. Finally, he spoke: "Shit, I'm sorry, Jones," and patted me clumsily on the shoulder. "Makes you feel any better, I never had no girlfriend. Closest I got was the time I jerked off wit' a squirrel."

"What did you just say?" I looked up in bewilderment.

"Oh, nothing. Uh… girl? Yeah, girl." He avoided my gaze.

Suddenly, a flash of irritation at this clownish creature, at myself for revealing too much. "You need to hide your shits better," I said. "They're all over the place like frigates crashed on the shore. Don't crap near the barracks, and maybe break them up. People will see the size of your stool and figure out there's a monster on the camp."

The Sasquatch did not respond to the scolding as I expected. Instead, he seemed to flush with pride and smiled. "I already did break them up." I could resist no longer, and we laughed. The sound sluiced through the grime of the place, through the weariness of the war, and blasted the shadows back. When he caught his breath, this is the tale he told.

6.

PICTURE IT, JONES. I'm under the tracks outside of Wawa with yesterday's nightmares playin' in my head. Funny thing 'bout the tracks—the train melts the snow underneath, and you gotta clear spot to sleep. Not bad when yer runnin' from home with cops and angry mobs chasin' after ya—yeah, you think ya got it rough, welcome to my world.

Fell asleep under one of them bridges with high walls of snow keepin' the wind out. Woke up wit' human funk up my nose. Some older guy was sharin' the spot with me. Had a ratty-ass jacket, wearin' two pairs of pants, gloves with no fingertips. Dude had 'bout one tooth. Said his name was Jack, and offered me a swig of homebrew from his bottle wit' no label. Jack built a fire—I scrubbed myself wit' snow.

I was done with yer kind—hair on my palms was growin' back and I never hated the cold the way Jack did. He didn't ask no questions when I threw my damn pants and shirt into the fire (because *FUCK CLOTHES*), used the blaze to cook a fox I caught in the woods with my hands. Heh—he gave me a long haul off a grimy joint and after I leaned back in the snow with a smile and the wall between me and the Spirit got real smoky and it was the only time I got a break from all the whisperin'.

Spent a few days there, Jack and me. We'd talk and he'd tell me stories about the long, long fall that was his life. How he always tried his best to do right but it ended up goin' wrong anyways. How everyone always left 'im in the end. How he wanted to be a beautiful person, but weren't. I never told him nothin', since I was still too close to Wawa, was too afraid word would get back to the police somehow. Just needed a bit of time to figure out my next step and stop thinkin' 'bout the shit that went down, though I'd wake Jack up sometimes moanin', so he knew somethin' was up. Still gave me that sweet smoke anyway, and a few days turned into a few weeks, and I think I got pretty close to bein' happy.

Jack had a real raspy voice like he didn't use it much no more. Words comin' out between the only two teeth he had in his head,

GROSS GRAY BEARD SPRINGIN' FROM HIS CHIN LIKE A BALLSACK. SHOWED ME A RING HE KEPT ON A WIRE 'ROUND HIS NECK AND TOLD ME 'BOUT THE WOMAN WHO HAD THE OTHER ONE. THEY'D LOVED ONCE AND GOT MARRIED AND TRIED AND TRIED TO HAVE KIDS, BUT IT NEVER WORKED. EVERY MONTH SHE'D BUST OUT THE CALENDAR AND SAY, "IT'S MY TIME—GET READY." AND AFTER A FEW YEARS THE JOY WAS ALL GONE AND JACK COULDN'T GET A STIFFY NO MORE, AND SHE GOT COLDER AND MEANER. JOB ENDED EARLY OUT IN THE FOREST AND JACK CAME BACK TO HIS CABIN AND SHE'S IN THERE GETTIN' STUFFED BY JACK'S OLD MAN. JACK STILL 'MEMBERED THE GUT AND GRAY CHEST HAIRS AND THE SLIME ON HIS DAD'S DICK. AFTER THAT, JACK WALKED AWAY, OUTTA THE SNOW, AND STOPPED SPEAKIN' TO ANYONE. 'TIL HE MET ME, ANYWAY.

FUNNY HOW PAIN BRINGS PEOPLE TOGETHER, AIN'T IT? SAME OLD SHIT. SO I STARTED BLABBIN' TOO 'BOUT ALL THE REASONS I WAS RUNNIN' AWAY— EVEN TOLD 'IM 'BOUT THE SPIRIT WHISPERIN' IN MY HEAD—AND WE SHARED A BOTTLE THAT NIGHT AND IT WAS LIKE SOME CEREMONY IN CHURCH WHEN ALL YER SINS MELT OFF AND YER HOLY AGAIN.

BUT THAT'S ALL JUST A BUNCH OF DAMN LIES, TOO, AIN'T IT?

NEXT DAY JACK WAS GONE AND I WAS NAPPIN' LATE AND I HEARD BARKIN' DOGS, AND THE SPIRIT HOLLERIN' AT ME TO GET MY ASS IN GEAR. I FIGURE JACK BETRAYED ME. FOR A BOTTLE, I BET.

BOLTED INTO THE SNOW WITH DOGS YAPPIN' AND NIPPIN' AT MY CALVES, POLICE STUMBLIN', FIRIN' THEIR PISTOLS WITH THAT OLD POP-POP. ALMOST REACHED FOR THE SPIRIT, BUT DIDN'T, JUST RAN DEEPER AND DEEPER INTO THE FOREST, UNTIL THERE WAS ONLY ONE DOG STILL FOLLOWIN' AND I LET IT GET REAL CLOSE 'FORE SPINNIN' 'ROUND AND GETTIN' HOLD OF IT. I STILL 'MEMBER THE FEEL OF ITS SPINE IN MY MOUTH, CRUNCHIN'. I WAS SO ANGRY, JONES—YA GOTTA UNDERSTAND. ALWAYS WANNA BE NICE BUT SEEMS LIKE EVERYONE WHO EVER KNEW ME BETRAYED ME IN THE END. 'CEPT FOR YOU, BUT THIS AIN'T THE END.

SOMETIMES I'D CALL FOR MY MOTHER, THE FIRST ONE. LONG NIGHTS, WANDERIN' THROUGH THE FOREST. EATIN' PINECONES AND PORCUPINES. SKUNK. GRABBIN' FISTFULS OF SLEEP UNDER BRIDGES, OR BENEATH PINES, IN OLD SHEDS, BACKS OF TRUCKS. NEVER MET ANOTHER ME. STAYED AWAY FROM YOUS. CHASED BY WOLVES ONCE OR TWICE. TORE THROUGH A DAM AND ATE A BEAVER. ME AND THE SPIRIT SCRAPIN' BARK OFF TREES AND DRINKIN' SNOW.

SPRING WAS OUT THERE SOMEWHERE—I WAS CHASIN' AFTER IT. GREEN THINGS WERE GONNA BLOOM. I WAS GONNA FIND A RIVER WITH FISH THAT JUMPED STRAIGHT INTO MY MOUTH. NICE CAVE WITH MOSS THAT GLOWS AND A SOFT STONE FOR MY PILLOW. OR MAYBE I'D BE A GREAT PLANTER O'

TREES—USE MY STRENGTH FOR SOMETHIN' THAT MATTERED. I CAN PICTURE 'EM, ORCHARDS OF TREES WAVIN' IN THE VALLEY OF A MOUNTAIN, ALL SWAYIN' TOGETHER IN THE BREEZE AND DROPPIN' APPLES. I'LL PLANT A TREE FOR EVERY SASQUATCH THAT NEVER GOT NO AFTERLIFE AND THAT'D BE MY LIFE'S WORK, BEIN' MAYBE THE LAST ONE O' ME, SINCE I NEVER LEARNED ALL THE STORIES, I'D BE A BIG FERRY WHO ROWED ALL THE SOULS OVER.

GAVE UP ON FINDIN' MY MOTHER, ON BEIN' LIKE *YA*, ON FINDIN' SOMEONE TO LOVE ME—MY DREAM WAS A PRETTY SIMPLE THING. BUT I NEVER DID FIND THE VALLEY OR SEE THE SPRING. ONE OF THEM NIGHTS I HID FROM THE COLD AND CLIMBED INTO THE BACK OF A PLANE WITH THE HATCH OPEN, SETTLED IN AMONG THE BOXES, AND DREAMED OF THE VALLEY. WOKE UP NEXT MORNIN', HATCH WAS CLOSED, AND THE PLANE WAS IN THE AIR.

I FIGURED NO PLACE COULD BE WORSE THAN CANADA IN THE WINTER. FUNNY HOW THINGS WORK OUT, EH?

7.

BLINK BLINK BLINK—the story was over and the sun was coming up. That deep bass and the sheer oddness of the storyteller: I could have listened for a few more hours, but he needed his cave and I needed my rack. That's Navy for bed, collapsing face-first on the thin pillow and the squeak of springs. Wasn't sure if I dreamed; wasn't sure what I dreamed—certainly I made no sense of the Sasquatch, nor his backward mysticism about "the Spirit."

Every afternoon after waking, I walked down the hall and rapped on the door of my weightlifting partner. TicTac was my coach and he was also a douchebag, so I called him the Coachbag. He cracked the door with his pecs dancing, six and a half feet tall with his head newly shaven, and every inch of exposed skin crawling with veins, even his face. I met him early in the tour when I was benchpressing 265 lbs and got stuck with the bar in the air three inches above my chest. I strained against it, threw my back into it, but the barbell kept sinking until it was a hair away from my nipples and I squealed like a trapped hog.

Calloused ogre-palms appeared, pulled the bar upwards, but gently, so gently, only enough pressure to get me through the sticking point and then I was abandoned to heave and grunt the full weight the rest of the way. I searched the whole gym for the Prince Charming who gave me the perfect spot, staring obliquely at soldiers' hands, until I found his particularly grizzled set of meathooks, and our friendship formed. He was a jokester, a prankster, a Canadian who inherited his parents' accent. "Home schooled," he said, and would explain no further.

A few quick steps across the hardpacked sand, past the queue at Tim Hortons, and we arrived in a world of clanking steel, a soldier's gym: rusty weights, dozens of machines, neat rows of dumbbells, and the stink of iron, swass and musty towels. The gym-bunker was the size of a mid-range cathedral with a concave ceiling, dumbbell racks instead of pews, a wall of mirrors instead of stained glass, and, in place of an altar, the legpress machine.

I don't have a sacred bone in my body, but the gym was holy. The clanks, thuds, grunts, whirs, squeaks and the rest of the music. The incense of crusted sweat and sprayed testosterone. Sometimes I would think about the weights even when I wasn't in the gym. The potential energy of them, their efficacy as missiles, their patience (for the purpose of weight is to wait), the way they were stowed systematically in rows like sailors on ships, the fact that they remained cold, even in the heat. The rust. The salt. The smell of iron. The taste of chalk.

Arriving in the gym, TicTac's critique of the soldiers' physiques began as we warmed up: "Now check out sad triceps on that one," he observed, pointing a veiny finger. For a man of his musculature, TicTac's voice was surprisingly high-pitched. "Do you think he cries when he looks in mirror?"

Coachbag's Corner: Shoulder Day

You want beautiful muscle, yes? Then you must do eight to twelve reps, and five sets of each exercise. Sometimes we go lower than eight reps but this is more for strength. But never more than fifteen, never, never! Hold your hand like so, on dumbbell. Move thumb a little; open the palm. Is good now.

You notice every workout I make a superset, and my supersets are always different. We take away breaks between exercises and now we use different kind of strength— is good for fighting underwater. Perhaps today we do some negatives for same reason. No, ninety degrees on the elbow, Jones, that is like one-ten. Try to keep control of weight whole time. Focus on muscle you want to work. I am not yoga instructor and this is not magic.

Ah, you cheat so much on last two reps I want to throw up in my mouth but is good. A little cheating is fine on last rep so long as you do last rep. Better to suffer and struggle and fail. People think a weightlifter has huge ego, but no one fails so much. Go Jones. Go Jones   it is a superset, no rest, remember?

TicTac's target was a clean-cut soldier, decently beefy by any other standard, who was fishing through the dumbbells and turning red. "C'mon, Coachbag," I said, "we're here to work out, aren't we?"

"Yes, yes, I know, Jones. I see little drumstick and I start thinking it is dinner time so I get hungry." The soldier blushed crimson. "I am concerned when I see triceps like this that we will not win war."

By this time, I'd jumped onto a bench and hefted dumbbells up from the shoulder. "Maybe you should help him," I gasped between reps, "if it's for the war."

"I don't need to talk to that runt about his shitty triceps. I'm leading by example." "Lead by example" was the Army equivalent to a writer's "Show, don't tell," and TicTac *was* showing. The Coachbag was the strongest man I knew. On leg day, he piled so much weight on the bar that it frowned. Even if you couldn't spot his bald head glowing among the torture devices of the vain, you might find yourself suddenly gasping for breath when his muscles drank all the oxygen.

TicTac took my place on the bench and hoisted a pair of hundred pound dumbbells to his shoulders. "Now that guy's a beefcake," he said, pointing with his nose to a neckless soldier who had been stacking weight on the leg press machine for ten minutes. "Watch this—he'll lift more than you can."

The soldier finished loading—he had thirty 45-pound plates on the machine. Plus the weight of the mechanism itself. "Fourteen hundred pounds?" I said. "Christ, he's about to lift a small car."

There was a ponderous creaking of bones, and the soldier's legs quaked as the wall of iron rose, inch by inch, until the weight was at full extension, the legs were straight, and his quadriceps bloated, until it seemed they must explode.

"Son of bitch," the Coachbag growled. "Nobody lifts more than me in this gym. You know his name?"

"I think it's Johnson. I chatted with him in the line at Timmy's yesterday. Combat engineer."

"If Johnson thinks he's gonna be new freak in town he's got big surprise coming." TicTac threw the dumbbells on the ground with a wall-shaking boom.

8.

ANOTHER DAY ANOTHER DOLLAR, with no place to spend it but the few shit-shops on the boardwalk—I only went on my days off from the gym. The rhythm of the war: nightshift in the TOC, a walk home through the camp just as the world was lighting up, a hard bed and hopefully no dreams, waking in the late afternoon and hoisting weights until the skin on my hands thickened and cracked. Day after day in this sequence with the drone strikes and the dreams and the clanking of dropped barbells, so that it all blurred together and time itself melted and it was like I had always been there, always *would* be there, except for those moments which broke routine. A cracker with peanut butter. A few pages of a book. A wank in a stinking Porta-Potty. A rocket attack. The way the Army cocks looked at me after a good workout, when I had the pump, muscles swollen to their full expression. When I first flew in from Halifax for pre-deployment training and joined the soldiers who would become the TOC-team, they were baffled by having a sailor in their midst. For months it was fag this, and fag that, and how deep could I swallow a cock, and could I pout my asshole like a pair of lips? But when I became strong enough, the jabs stopped.

I hid in my strength like a concrete bunker; I glared; destroyed handshakes; I crushed an empty 120mm illum shell, and kept the hulk on my desk in the TOC. We were strong and power moved around us and through us, too.

"When are you gonna bust your cherry, Jones?" That was Bell. Back in the TOC with the drone feeds and the croaking coffee pot. "That's what all young men want, right?" He snickered.

"Not this again, Bell," I said. He wasn't talking about sex; he was talking about shooting missiles at a teenage boy. He and the Major and I were staring at Sahar through the drone feed again. A black and white world. A mud and sand world. A mud hut with a long ditch and in the yard a leafless tree that looked like a Sasquatch turned to wood. Sahar, under the tree, unfurled a prayer mat, knelt, and bowed deep enough to touch his nose to the carpet.

Bell sidled closer and stage-whispered, "Hey Virgin, don't you wanna get a little of that action? That nice young man there? A Fighting Aged Male?" I hated the way he licked his lips, the tugging on my sleeve.

"I've explained this a hundred times, Bell," said the Major, her voice a frosty blast. "Just because he's a Fighting Aged Male—which is questionable—doesn't mean we have Positive Identification. If we don't have Positive Identification, we don't strike. Ever." She didn't even look at him, just kept staring at the monitor.

Down thrust Bell's guilty hands into his pockets, beads of sweat popping from his forehead. *Was he actually that horny, or I am sprinkling pixie dust?*

The No-Fraternization Policy

Killing was quotidian but touch was taboo. No hugging no holding no petting hair no shoulder nuzzles no back massages no foot rubs no sex no cuddling. You could reach out to your enemy, but only if your fingers were missiles. Even if you deployed with your spouse you were forbidden to share a room: two professionals on a long business trip.

Sure, fraternization happened on the downlow. Two colleagues might snuggle or fuck after watching a man get blown up. Seems a pretty innocent thing to me, but the General was adamant that fraternization was poison; it eroded morale and inspired envy among the troops. As a result, each of us fostered a monster of loneliness which grew more powerful and insidiuous by the day—some were better than others at keeping them in their cages.

"Apologies, Major," said Bell. "If I have said anything to offend, I am deeply sorry." He raised his voice so the other soldiers, twelve sitting in their peripheral desks, could hear. "I was just guiding this young sailor through an important Army rite of passage." He winked at Crazy Jay, who laughed and immediately hid his face behind a stack of papers.

Somehow the Major's steel rod of a spine stiffened by another few degrees. She marched to the front of the room, where she could make eye contact with each of us, where her voice could travel to the corners. Then she waited for absolute silence, for our complete attention, for thirty long seconds where we could do nothing but stare at her. Stare at the few blonde hairs that escaped the helmet she often wore. Eyes like the turquoise runoff of glaciers. Coffee cup in her hand with a little steam. Somewhere buried in that unflattering sack of her uniform was her body, soft curves and hard muscle, dear God it drove us into a froth but all we could see of it was the triangle of pale skin exposed at her throat.

Finally, she spoke in a calm, clear voice: "Gentlemen, I'm a busy woman. I don't appreciate having to go over the same lessons again and again." She glared at Bell, who barely suppressed a whimper. "Quite a few of you think the way Bell does, that killing a person, like getting laid, is a 'rite of manliness.'

Your ignorance makes me want to puke." She sipped from her bucket of coffee. "Thinking that having sex will make you a man is just normal idiocy. But this idea that killing makes you a man? That's perverted."

She set down her coffee and effortlessly leaped onto the waist-high map in the center of the room. It was an eclipse of hotness—none of us could turn our heads, and I caught the scent of vanilla. Behind her half a dozen drone feeds spooled. "Do you really think that killing is sex?" she asked. "Maybe you've been doing it wrong?" Then she laughed at us, a high-pitched and cruel tinkle, suitable for a cocktail party. Blood rushed into my face. "Killing is not sex, troops. Killing is a necessary part of the job, but it isn't a pleasure. We move deliberately with our highest integrity—do you understand?"

Bell opened his mouth, but the Major waved an imperious hand. "Shut up, Bell. Unless you want to spend the rest of your tour with that mop in your hands. From now on, every 'target' we watch through the drones gets a human name. And you will call them by their human names and that's how we will discuss them." Bell, Crazy Jay, and a few others groaned at this—mutters of "hippie bullshit" and "candy-ass."

"Killing is not sex," she repeated. "Killing must be difficult. If this is hard for you to understand, figure it out." With that, she hopped off the map table, and disappeared into her nook at the back of the TOC.

Each of us was mere rope in a tug o' war between giants. On one hand we had the Major, who wanted ethical warriors. On the other hand, something about the bureaucracy, the distance of the drones, the General, Bell, the way none of it seemed real, and the Army culture itself, all pressured us to become killbots.

We stared at the monitors without looking at each other. Bell was sweaty; hearing the Major say the word "sex" multiple times, and the view of her on the table, may have pushed him over the brink. He weaselled up to me, "She's so far above us all. I tell you, if I was a Major it wouldn't be like that. I'd be one of the people," and he smiled that extra wide smile that threatened to split his head in two.

When are you going to bust your cherry? "Bell, if you were a Major, I'd rub my genitals every time you spoke. I'd make you my personal fetish."

He blushed angry. "Fuck you, Jones. The Major is making mistakes and pissing off the wrong people. You should get used to calling me 'Sir.'"

"Lecture me, Sir, lecture me," I moaned, twisting my nipples.

"Fucking sailors," said Bell. "You'll be happy to know there's one of your kind loose on the base. A man was raped last night. He was walking home from work when a guy jumped out of a bunker and hit him with a Taser.

Then he pulled a bag over the guy's head and fucked him in the ass. Does that get you off, Sailor?"

"Holy crap, Bell. Are you serious?"

"Have a nice walk home, Jones."

9.

I MENTIONED THE "MORALE BOX" EARLIER, but I didn't say how important they were. Those boxes from home could boost you for a month. First, there was the social boon of getting a box; everyone knew that you'd have treats to share soon, or potentially, fresh porn. Second, opening a morale box was like opening the brain of the sender: my aunt who runs marathons sent me protein powder and shirts that never got sweaty. My brother's box: entirely packed with granny porn, and books about dwarves questing for a magic axe. But my mother's box (isn't this an awkward place the words have taken me) was my favorite, for two main reasons.

The first is Canada's natural bounty of forests. The way those forests are chopped, and logs bundled into trucks, as creatures scurry from apocalypse, and the topsoil floats away in the breeze. But some of these logs have a special destiny: to become kitten-soft three-ply toilet paper in the most decadent and unnecessary display of Canadian opulence. My mother would cushion the contents of her morale boxes with this rolled-up silk. After months of scratchy single-ply, finally the softness of home.

The other reason was Newfie cheezies: starchy, salty twists that resemble DNA helices, about as long and crooked as a crone's finger. No actual cheese is hurt in the production of these snacks—just strange cheese-flavored chemicals that never turned stale, no matter how tightly I rationed the treat, slurping three of them each night before bed until I could swallow without chewing. I don't know why Mom called them Newfie cheezies, other than the fact she's from Newfoundland, on the east coast of Canada, and whenever she likes something she wraps her identity around it. I never had the heart to tell her Newfie cheezies are made in Nebraska.

The whole walk back to the barracks, after Bell told me about the rapist, I watched my ass, pistol loose in the holster. Would the 9mm work if I needed it? I'd never cleaned the thing and had dropped it in the sand a few times. Shadows of bunkers were the talons of ghouls stretching for the poo pond. Toppled coils of barbed wire leered like malevolent faces with sharpened teeth. Fear drove my feet but there was a sliver of anticipation, too; the day before I'd received another morale box from Mom; it was waiting next to my bunk for a pillaging. The phantom taste of unsavoured Newfie cheezies guided me past darkened bunkers and pyramids of old tires. I felt a shadow flitting behind me but I couldn't tell if it was a friendly Sasquatch or even-friendlier sodomite.

I reached the barracks unmolested, doffed boots before entering my cabin. Cabin is sailor-speak for room, but there wasn't much ocean these days, despite my one photo on the otherwise plain walls of a sailboat lost on stormy seas. There, next to the rickety rack where I slept on the bottom bunk and stowed my crap on the top, was the tin can wardrobe where I hung my uniforms on metal hangers. And there was the morale box, torn open, its contents scattered on the goddamn floor.

Fire sprayed out of my eyes and horns burst from my forehead.

In the scant light of the cracked door, my hands twisted into green claws as I rifled through the plundered box. I found three rolls of superior Canadian toilet paper and clutched them to my chest in one arm, tossing aside meditation CDs, romantic comedy DVDs, and the rest of Mom's morale box padding. No cheezies. *Maybe she forgot them? No, that's impossible.*

In a state of absolute devastation, I slunk to the floor in a fetal position and rested my head on one of the velvet rolls. This may seem like a sensational reaction to the loss of something which doesn't fit into any of the food groups, but when you've been working for months without a day off—these little pleasures get bigger and bigger until soldiers fight with machetes over a Diet Coke or a single stick of gum. Also, if I hadn't been on the floor I wouldn't have noticed the trail of crumbs.

I tucked the asswipe under my pillow and tousled the blankets to disguise the lump. My little sailor's flashlight made a yellow circle when lit. In the back of the room, six or seven yards away, there was another bunk bed and I'd been fortunate to have it empty for the last few months. The circle of light lit a pair of boots, not mine, smaller. A heap on the bunk drew my eye; I peered at a soldier who'd fallen asleep in his combats, just his boots removed. A quick scan: the criminal was a lieutenant, a rank below mine. His uniform had the velcro Canadian flag on the sleeve. Army, based on the color of the name tag, and it bore the name Kool. The stubble on his cheek, as if from a long flight, did little to disguise his youth. Handsome, in a skinny way, and pallid, not sunburnt like the dayworkers. Most important, his face and hands all the way up to the fucking elbows were stained orange with cheezie powder.

The worst had happened: my inner sanctum had been invaded by an Army douchebag.

I sat back on my heels to plot.

The Navy is notorious for riding junior officers throughout their training until they become the crustiest, most sarcastic and evil-minded bastards you can imagine. But having emerged through that, let me state for the record that I am the last one to hate a junior officer because of his rank—that's just stupid prejudice. It never helped me become a better leader, and it never helps anyone else either. What was helpful was learning to make snap judgements, a necessary skill on the bridge of a warship, in the TOC, and now: this guy was a fuckface.

The Principles of Leadership

Some start their careers getting it, and others, like me, have to work at it. I just wanted to make a bit of cash and see fantastical things and drink my beers spiked with rum and get laid once or twice a week—that's why I joined up when I was nineteen, wasn't anything special, wasn't a big calling, didn't come to Jesus, didn't walk on water, but they drilled those principles in my head anyway. Look, I know them still:

1. Be proficient;
2. Know yourself and seek self-improvement;
3. Seek and accept responsibility;
4. Lead by example;
5. Provide direction;
6. Know and care for your subordinates;
7. Develop the potential of your subordinates;
8. Make sound and timely decisions;
9. Build the team and challenge their abilities; and
10. Communicate and keep your team informed.

What an impossible, unfathomable batch of expectations to fling at a young man, a drunk. Those days I wasn't interested in being a leader; just wanted to survive the bizarre maze of military law and norms. Seemed like a system where brainwashed fools advanced as the clever ones gnashed their teeth for years, then turned bitter. The only time the Principles got trotted out was when a senior officer needed to assign tedious labour to a subordinate.

Despite this, there is wisdom in this list that guides me. On better days.

I knew, as Kool's superior officer, it was my responsibility to develop his potential. With this rookie mistake of busting into my morale box, coupled with the other indicators that he was fresh to Afghanistan, I knew Kool needed an intervention and soon. His was the untroubled sleep of an innocent. I developed a plan that required both cunning and stealth. Beneath the plywood floor, a Sasquatch grunted and rolled over in the night. Nobody noticed my smile; nobody heard me drizzling piss in Kool's boots, my first of many acts of vengeance.

10.

WHEN KOOL BLINKED AND SLID HIS FEET into his sodden boots, did I smirk? Well, I'm not made of steel. I expected an apology; the morale box was ripped open on the ground, looking like a bear had pawed it.

"Yo, man, what the fuck is up?" Kool greeted the day by diving onto his hands and blasting out twenty push-ups. "You been here a while, right? Kill a bunch of Taliban?"

I rubbed the grit from my eyes and drily asked, "Did you come here for the war, Kool? Or to eat other people's gifts from home?"

"That was your shit? I thought it was a welcome package from my Unit. Royal Canadian Regiment. Infantry. The hardest motherfuckers in the Army." He stretched his hand for a shake but recoiled when he saw my rank and insignia. "A fucking sailor? Man, I'm not sharing my room with no Navy queer."

Something about infantry training: cuddling for warmth in a two-man tent, nestling your fellow warrior on your back while slithering under barbed wire garrotes and over stake-filled pits, tightening your partner's thigh tourniquet with your teeth, tag-teaming dead-eyed bar skanks on a bare mattress in a barracks—it produced an absolute desperation for soldiers to prove themselves straight.

My eyebrows quivered. "You just introduced yourself to me as one of the 'hardest' people in the Army, and you think that didn't sound a little gay? You're sending me pretty clear signals here."

"Hard for chicks!" he shouted. "I fuck pussies 'til they explode. Hundreds of 'em. Big lines of 'em. I say, 'suck my dick, bitch' and they say, 'mgoorrf.' You wouldn't understand, Fag. What the fuck you doin' here anyway, *seaman*—I don't see any water?" Then he cackled at his own joke, and glanced over his shoulders searching for the ocean, or inviting a posse of fratboys to join in on the laugh. I shook my head.

"Kool, I've been driving warships for ten goddamn years. You don't know shit about this place and you need my help, *Lieutenant*. I've been here long enough to have heard all your stupid Navy clichés twice over." I stood up so he could see how big I was. "Don't wear your damn boots in the room—they drag in the shit-dust. And mop up that puddle next to your bed. Honestly, what the fuck?"

I savored watching the smile bleed off his face. A good little soldier would do what he was told when the order came from a superior. He went to find some paper towels to absorb my piss—what fun. I reached into my toilet paper cache and tucked an indulgent two squares into my pocket, an extravagance; soon I would ration it more closely, but these halcyon days merited a little boost.

We had a brigade run in an hour—the General was keen to keep up our cardio, and it gave him an excuse to get us all together in one spot then rally us with speeches before the torture began. There would be no avoiding this one by hiding under a pile of coats.

About a thousand Canadian soldiers would run, not including a few in the TOC and a couple other spots which needed to be manned. We were just a small percentage of the camp's 30,000 soldiers, all of whom reported to a US general under the umbrella of Operation ENDURING FREEDOM. Once I asked the Major why something so wonderful as freedom needed to be endured. She told me, "You give me headaches, Jones." Well, *my* idea of pain was running in a futile circle through the city-camp, dipping my toes in the poo-pond, and ending where we started. I think the big boss was scared our cushy office-worker lives would make us soft, that our flabby asses would embarrass him in front of the other Generals.

I'm a pisspoor runner even on my best days. I'm blocky, top-heavy, and my thighs are beefy slabs. A forty-below winter? No problem—I'm the only warm person around. But on a 105°F in the desert I sweat like a damn mortar, lobbing buckets, drenching friend and foe alike in my sweat. Running was a mandatory humiliation throughout pre-deployment training, and so it remained. To boost myself I spent the next hour chatting with people, moving from cabin to cabin, asking, "Have you met this Kool kid?" and then regaling my listeners with the fate of the cheezies. I also made sure to tell the guys at the gym, the ladies at Tim Hortons, and the barber. *Fuck that guy.*

Last person I told was TicTac, who was at the opposite end of the building. He never let me look into his room, claiming, "is not finished," and talking to me, instead, through the cracked door.

"You tell me this man-child rob your morale box, Jones? And he didn't even apologize?" The Coachbag chugged a pale, viscous fluid from a water bottle. "We cannot allow Army guys to push us around." As an airman, TicTac had dealt with persecution from toxic Army pricks, too. "Say the word, Jones, and I shall destroy this pipsqueak for you."

That made me snort; I waved my hands dismissively. "Don't worry, buddy. I'm dealing with it. I'm using my *leadership*."

The brigade run was imminent, and all the soldiers were filtering from the barracks or their workplaces in front of the gym-bunker. There was a row of dusty trucks parked against a waist-high concrete wall, a single withered tree, and a tank. The clanking of dropped weights from the gym finally fell silent. A thousand soldiers wearing tan undershirts and gray shorts. And what do soldiers do when they gather in great numbers, other than make massacre?

We bitch. We bitched about how someone had parked the pallets of bottled water directly in the sun, so the bottles were getting frail and thin as the chemicals from the melting plastic leached into our drinking water. We bitched about how the obscene graffiti in the shitters had been painted over again, our creativity supressed. We bitched about the stupid "fun run" and how, when we were *forced* to work out, it drained the joy completely. We bitched about the horrible heat, the long queue at Tim Hortons, the pong of the poo pond, the lack of women in the camp, the sodden floor in the washroom, the food at the DFAC. But mostly we bitched about the Taser Rapist: "Why aren't the police hunting down that bastard and roasting him on a spit?"

We knew it was nearly showtime when the Colonels arrived, all four of them. They always travelled together in a diamond formation, four tough, middle-aged soldiers who scanned in every direction with effortless vigilance. Their confident strides suggested they were the only soldiers on the camp who harboured no deep-seated fear of the Taser Rapist.

The Task Force Kandahar (TFK) Colonels

This unflappable confidence arose because of a daily regimen of butt clenches. Our Colonels would have loved to be in the thick of the action, catching bullets in their teeth, but were sadly seconded to desks. Desks invariably have a way of making people soft, so each day when they sat to write their first memos and check their emails, the butt clenches began. A newly promoted Colonel will set a goal of a thousand, but senior Colonels no longer think about it; they are continuously squeezing and relaxing, and can generate enough electricity to power a warship.

As a result of these clenches Colonels have extremely good posture and can snap branches with their ass cheeks. These senior officers are not victims of rapists; in fact, they are the aggressors, using their claw-like butts to nip and pull the pricks of younger men in the showers. A three-mile run is nothing to a Colonel—just a reprieve from the true work.

When the General arrived with his minion, the withered Chief, all bitching dried up. The two strode to the parked tank, which was the color of a sand dune, boasting a long snout and machine gun turret at the top, and surrounded by grids of rebar to protect from rocket-propelled grenades. The General muttered something to the Chief and the older man laughed like a hyena. Then the General braced himself, clenched brutally, and leaped onto the top of the tank, where he landed firmly on both feet, then turned 180 degrees to face the crowd.

It seemed a little dramatic and unnecessary to me but as a sailor I didn't always have a clear window into these things. I knew in some ways the Army had leadership all figured out. Speeches are better when delivered from the top of something; the Major had taught us that, but speaking from atop a massive, wheeled weapon was best. The General never missed a chance to showcase the spectacle of power and discipline, and to remind us of the fine figure he cut beneath the expressionless glasses: the broad shoulders, powerful jaw, biceps bulging the stitches of his tan t-shirt.

"Troops!" he yelled. "It's great to have y'all in one place so I can take a good look at you. Now I can see who takes fitness seriously, and who thinks this tour is some kind of vacation." He paused to allow a chuckle-ripple to stir the crowd. "Each of you could be stuffed into a chopper any day now and whizzed out to one of the Forward Operating Bases. You might be looking Johnny Taliban in the eyes tomorrow—and he'll look back at you. Damn better make sure you look like a warrior." Beside me, TicTac grinned. Others shifted their feet. A gust of wind flapped the General's shirt, revealing a set of Herculean abs. "It's an amazing time to be a soldier! We have all these new toys, new ways of finding targets, the best gear and training money can buy. So, is it any surprise our enemies are cowards? Digging bombs in roads, cutting off the noses of their locals, shoot n' scoots on our convoys, not to mention landmines?" Angry mutters swept through us; how badly we wanted someone to tell us we were brave. "But that isn't the worst thing. The worst thing is when an enemy pulls out every dirty trick in the book, wants to win so damn bad he commits atrocities that hurt all kinds of innocent people, and still he loses. Then, and only then, does the beaten enemy look up at you with big ol' sad eyes like some abandoned kitten. And he thinks that you're such a weakling you'll forget all about his evil machinations and let him walk away—ha!"

As the General's bark rang over the crowd, I scanned for the Major. Just a single flicker of a blonde ponytail otherwise blocked by two thick necks. The General continued, striding back and forth a few steps each way on the top of the tank. "We are a long way from home but each time you have to make a tough decision I want you to remind yourself who you're fighting for. I want you to picture your wives, husbands, and kids. This isn't about us, and it certainly isn't about Johnny Taliban—this is about our families. *We are their shield.*"

The General dropped his voice lower, even sat on the edge of the tank; we had to lean forward to hear him. "No one said it was easy being a soldier, folks. Sometimes it's damn near impossible. We want to be sound of mind and sound of body so we can make the tough choices. Fitness helps us work without sleep. It makes us resistant to illness and injury. It keeps the brain healthy too. That's why we're here today. We have a nice three-mile run which we'll do as a team. We look down into the battlespace and things aren't clear. We got an enemy who melts away and hides among the civilians. But fitness—now that's something we can see, that's something we can measure. Now get started!" With that, the General's wizened Chief pursed his lips, whistled like a pterodactyl, and the run began.

Since TicTac and I had joined the mob fairly late, and the run began in the opposite direction, I enjoyed a brief moment of being at the front of the pack. That prick Tictac had no problems at all; at 6'5" his stride was immense.

"C'mon, Jones—let's fucking crush this thing," and he loped off on his giraffe legs; I managed to keep up for a full ten minutes at the front of the pack, pumping furiously, firing sweat rockets. The three-mile circuit was one we knew well; it was a lazy circle of the northwest quadrant of the base, with the poo pond marking the halfway point.

Only a one-legged man could understand how much I hate running, especially in the desert. After the last "fun run" my left nipple bled so much it looked like I'd been shot in the heart. Yet every time I took off down that scorching, malodorous road I was sure I'd become a fitter man overnight, that I'd willed myself lean, no matter the puffing nor the heaving as I lurched around with this ridiculous, stocky body.

Stop laughing—I tried. Hundreds, even thousands of hours running in the last few years. Started when I was so big I could only get 200 yards down the road, people rolling down their windows to laugh and throw empty cans. Running that ludicrous fitness test, beep beep back and forth across the gym with copper blood-taste in my mouth. Sure, I threw weights around because I was good at it but always went back to that road, that endless stretching road. Over the years I'd lost 100 pounds, become one of the strongest men I'd met, and developed a passionate, profound hatred of running.

By the time we reached the poo pond's oily sheen, I gasped for breath, inhaling vast quantities of poo dust. I fell behind to the sound of TicTac's tutting, and slowed to a demi-crawl. Too hot—couldn't breathe. Sweat production slowing. Too much weight to move in the heat. Damn office soldier, calling yourself a warrior, weak. I knew exactly what would happen next—well-intentioned encouragement from everyone who passed. My crumb of a soul shrank in anticipation.

The shit-pond burbled.

A rat floated upside down.

Bored soldiers had launched miniature sailboats that floated across the sewage every time the wind changed, a strange mockery of my past life. It was a sweltering day and the poo-dust clung to my sweat. Hisses of escaping gas. The splash of a bursting bubble. The sewage stained the shores with tar. 30,000 soldiers in the camp and we'd all contributed to this vat, our shame and legacy. A septic truck dumped more waste into the pond through a thick, plastic hose. Yet not even those who fed the foul tub knew its depth. Not even the eyeless fish that would flop panting on the shore sometimes, straining for breath.

The General, still wearing his unfathomable sunglasses, sprinted past with the Chief locked in step a half second behind. "Don't give up, Jones! Your will is stronger than your body!" He wasn't even breathing hard.

The Chief spared me a glance, "Work harder."

Fuckers—couldn't they see I was working harder than them, carrying more weight? What about my death rattle suggested I was half-assing it?

"You can do it, Jones! Hang in there!" The Major passed, pumping her arms. She was racing so fast her ponytail was parallel to the ground. Trim, athletic legs, the definition in her calves and hamstrings… Her glutes filling the gray shorts, straining the fabric. Not even my fantasies could spur me to greater speed, as I was near retching from the taste of the pond. I imagined how hideous I must be to her, red as a tomato and soaked in sweat. *Fat sack of shit,* my old Captain used to call me. *Getting so big—you gonna join the circus?* that was my Dad's taunt. So, I reached for that ancient anger and drove the voices away with a snarl.

"Keep your head up, Jones!" yelled an overtaking Colonel. The four of them ran in a diamond formation. I wasn't sure how they'd learned my name but apparently once one of them learns something the others pick it up through the hive mind. They propelled themselves forward by clenching their asses a thousand times a second, like the wings of a hummingbird.

By then even the voice in my head was breathless. I wanted to strangle somebody. Specifically Kool, long, lean Kool, belly full of my cheezies, just a little bulkier than slender, a petite in my books—he flitted past, then spun around to run backwards and pep talk me. "Maybe if you sailors spent less time choking on dick and more time working out, you'd be in better shape right now?" His laughter was interrupted when he stumbled on a rock, and his face flushed with irritation. "What's the matter, Fag? Can't breathe around all that cock in your mouth?"

"Fuck… off… Kool," I growled. He spun around and disappeared.

I had fallen back to midway in the pack, passed by about 400 people. Finally found a pace I could sustain, with half a mile left in the run, and soldiers still streaming by. I counted my footfalls up to a hundred then started again and again. All the helpful clichés were just logs thrown on my rage-fire—they were trying to 'lead by example' and 'develop their subordinates' and I was just the scapegoat of that conditioning, but I still wanted to wrench off someone's head and I had clawed back enough breath to do it. If one more fucking person tried to use their leadership on me…

Oh shit. There was Bell, slowly gaining on me, the cockstand, with his scarred mouth and delicate fingers wiggling loose. I was sure he'd have something choice to say and I prepped a few nasty rebuttals in case. But he didn't say shit, just stared at the ground a few feet ahead of him and fell in beside me.

"I swear to God if you try to encourage me… I will break your fucking arms, Bell."

"Jesus, Jones, you sound like my ex-wives. All three of them."

My laugh came out a snort. "Sorry… too many pep talks."

"Yeah, this running shit's not for me either, man. Couldn't run in Winterpeg, where I grew up, since half the time it was a million below zero. Freeze your nuts right off. Look at these psychos." Another gaggle of soldiers jogged by, and Bell continued, "I joined the Armored Corps so I could drive from place to place, not run. Christ, are we finished yet?"

With Bell as my shadow, nobody tried to encourage me—it must have been another obscure code of the Army. "There's the Tim Hortons… coming up."

"I'm gonna have about twelve cigarettes after this and a twenty-minute nap."

"Maybe puke… and down a bucket of coffee."

I ran with flourishing ball chafe and understanding. Bell was the only person who knew I didn't need to be coached. Sometimes we fail even when we try our best. The General, Colonels, Major and even Kool had never learned that, flying from victory to victory their whole lives. Maybe that's why it was so hard for them to see we were losing the war. But Bell, the retired used car salesman with the three ex-wives—he understood failing. It was the first time he had ever seemed like a real leader, and all he did was talk to me like a person—is that one in the principles of leadership anywhere?

Crossed that finish line and thudded to a stop, all the chafe and the promise of a stinging shower. Last quarter of the pack and a time of 40 minutes. Goddamnit—a cripple could do better.

11.

BACK TO THE TOC, the brainstem of the war—we knew everything that was happening in our Area of Operations except the stuff we were clueless about. Sure, we saw a lot through drone feeds, and other HQs (a few subordinate, but mostly other nations) sent us constant reports and radio traffic. Yet most of the info came through the combat chat: scrolling lines of text explaining everything, displayed on big-screens in the TOC, side-by-side with drone feeds. Infantry, drone operators, hospitals, artillery, headquarters: everyone was plugged into the combat chat. You could use it to let people know you were under attack, or beg for assets from a higher HQ, or deconflict operations that might overlap, or ask Santa for a new baby brother. Sometimes the chat messages were easy to read and other times they were so packed with acronyms they looked like formulae. It was a dense, fast way of passing info to each other; it probably saved lives and made us better killers but language itself was one of our victims.

This particular day, Bell, the Major, and I were staring at a blob of pixels. It was Sahar. The pixels made Sahar look blocky and gray-colored, barely human. The Predator carried four missiles but the resolution in the camera wasn't clear enough to show delicate facial expressions—Sahar's face was a shifting mask with the mouth of a jack o' lantern.

He sat on a mud wall, kicking his feet. He was staring up and down the road, and occasionally at the sky. Every few minutes he nodded as groups of locals passed on motorcycles—five or six adults could and did ride on the same bike, no problem.

"Do you think he sees us?" I asked.

"Unlikely," said the Major. "It's more likely he can hear this bigger drone, though."

I asked, "Do you ever worry we'll scare him into joining the insurgency?"

Then Bell piped up, "Who says he hasn't joined already?"

I didn't know how to answer; surely there was a reason the Intelligence folks had us monitoring this guy in the first place.

Targeting

Might have been some rumour, some rumination, an intercepted signal, a spy's report, or an image analyst's careful study. Might have been who he knew. How do you systematize assassination anyway?

Network-based hunting and pre-emptive strikes: in the great web of human interactions, are you a hub or spoke? The logic of counterinsurgency. Kill enough hubs and the whole web falls apart.

It was easiest when we sent a drone to help pinned-down troops, or caught an IED emplacer red-handed. At least then we knew who we were killing.

Sahar was staring right at the drone; he could see it for sure, floating in the air, a bomb-toting raven. I wondered how it felt to have missiles aimed at you—worse than being in the crosshairs of a rifle, I imagine. But Sahar's face was impassive and unreadable. Like an insect.

Don't do anything stupid, Sahar, and you might make it through the war alive.

Crazy Jay shouted, "We got Troops In Contact!" He had been watching the combat chat on one of the big-screens, and the report came in from the troops in the field. When I stretch out all the acronyms it looks like this.

Situation: Troops in Contact. Improvised Explosive Device and Small Arms Fire. 5x Taliban.
Action: Bravo Company returning fire. Request Close Air Support.
Location: 41R QQ 392 409
Time: 1915Z

These SALT reports were one of the few things that could get everyone moving, fast—our fellow soldiers were under attack, pinned down by five insurgents. They needed our eyes, our teeth. Bell typed ACK, short for acknowledged, into the combat chat, then yelled out the grid reference and I hustled to the big map to plot the location. It was northeast of Zangabad, along the Panjwa'i river, a few miles from Sahar.

"Send over that Predator, Jay!" yelled the Major.

"On it, Ma'am."

What other weapons could we line up? Did we have any jets nearby, could we borrow one from another headquarters, from our American allies north of the river? Was it too soon for artillery, was another drone closer, how about infantry? Sometimes we could scramble a combat helicopter in a few minutes, or send snipers from another Unit, do something other than chew our nails to the pink, our friends were in danger and no one, absolutely no one, wanted to see that big nasty report, the one that sometimes followed that first report. It came anyway.

MEDICAL EVACUATION REQUEST
Location: 41R QQ 392 409
Radio frequency and name: 179.144550 VHF, Bravo Company
Number of casualties and severity: 1 critically injured, tourniquet applied
Special Equipment required: Hoist
Patient requires litter or ambulatory: Litter
Security of pick-up site: Insurgents in area, proceed with extreme caution
Method of marking pick-up site: Smoke, green
Patient nationality and status: Canadian, military
Chemical biological or nuclear threat: None

"Fuck," Bell cursed for us all. A crushing feeling. *It's my fault—could have moved faster, done more.* A Canadian soldier wounded, likely someone I know. A roadside blast and desperate first aid with bullets whizzing overhead.

"We can still save him if we move now," said the Major. She turned to Clay, the helicopter guy. "Line up a helo and medical team; we'll launch as soon as it's safe."

"Yes, Ma'am," he said, phone against his shoulder, fingers tapping into his own specialist chat.

The Predator flew east over the Panjwa'i river—through the drone's camera we entered a gray world, gray clouds, gray fields, gray enemies, gray friends, a world where the riverbed churned the same monotonous gray as the fields of poppies, their blooms the only spot of white in a gray world, rolling fields dotted with huts and crude walls, the darker streaks of roads. Over a road pockmarked with old explosions, toward a plume of smoke, a Light Armored Vehicle with two wheels blown off, a soldier hunched over and tightening his comrade's tourniquet. A dying soldier. The leg-pixels stopped beneath the knee, a black puddle spilling on the road. Arterial blood is brightly colored, but a severed limb will still ooze the grayer pixels. Three other soldier-shapes crouched low against the side of the vehicle, firing their C7s in quick bursts of white sparks. They'd been in this firefight for ten minutes, their only shelter from the bullets was the burning vehicle, packed with explosive rounds.

"Who are they shooting at?" asked the Major. "Move the drone to the trees."

There. Gray shapes hiding in the rows of chest-high poppies. Just vague darker outlines against the flowers and twisted shrubs. Eventually the hard lines of AK47s emerged, and the flare as they were fired, brighter pixels at their snouts.

The Major's voice was getting icier. "That's Positive ID, Gentlemen. We have confirmed the insurgent's violent intent. We're clear to fire in defense of our soldiers as per the ROE."

A growing excitement in the room. Bell thrust his wizardly hands into his pockets, and half the TOC-moles left their seats to crowd the drone feed. The drone's reticle was exactly atop a gray man-shaped blob at the edge of the opium field. A baggy-shaped humanoid with a vague face, a glittering black pixel for a mouth.

"Fire the missile," said the Major.

The moment dragged, as it always did. First the Major relayed the kill-order to Crazy Jay, who sent it to the drone pilot in his cockpit which was wedged into a shipping container on base. A tiny room of monitors and blinking lights. Then another half second for the "fire" message to get to the Predator. Then another fraction of a second when the missile was actually in the air. It all added up to a multi-second delay that felt much longer.

A flash. All the pixels turned white for a second. The screen rippled from the smoke. The missile must have burst right at the man's feet because he didn't look like a man anymore. More like a child's toy dashed and shattered on the ground, with burning patches on his body and in the field—this is why the missiles are called Hellfires. There were gray blobs and darker patches everywhere, pieces of the man, scattered. The largest piece convulsed, threw up a darker patch of gray on its chest, and stopped moving.

Task Force Kandahar responded to Bravo Company request for Close Air Support and arrived on scene with a PRED at 1923, conducted strike at 1926, resulting in 1x insurgent Killed In Action.

The Predator was searching, sniffing. "Another, they're still fighting," said the Major in a flat voice. The reticle of the camera lined up with another blob-shape, another person. He was farther back in the poppy field, retreating, standing straight to fire a few shots, then ducking and backing away. She stared at the screen with her arms folded across her chest, inexorable: "Fire the missile."

A second flash. We willed another lightning bolt to strike our enemies; we were gods. But the missile was not on target, exploding five yards away. The man-shaped blob was flung out of the opium field with darker pixels on his clothing from the shrapnel. He was on his back, rocking to and fro. Maybe he was praying. I'd pray.

The third man disappeared into the poppies. Bell asked the Major, "Aren't we gonna finish the job? We've got two more missiles?"

The Major spun to me, "Jones, launch the medical helicopter—there's no time. You'll need to line up a second helo for the wounded insurgent, too."

"Aye, Ma'am," I said. I yelled to Clay, "Launch the first helo for the injured soldier. We need a second helicopter in the air immediately, with an armed escort."

Bell whispered urgently, "Major, you're gonna let him get away? Let's finish the job."

Her glare was as vicious as her drone-work. "We *have* finished the job, Bell—how many times do I need to explain this to you? When the threat has been neutralized, the fight is over. Our soldiers have been protected. Now we will proceed with our highest integrity."

"Major, we can't run like chickenshits and call it heroism. First you blow the shit out of the guy, now you want to save his life?"

She turned to face Bell, but everyone was eavesdropping; Mom and Dad were fighting again. She strained for an extra inch of height. "That's correct. As soon as he was injured, he became a non-combatant. And now he has useful intelligence that we can extract. This isn't the first time we've recovered a wounded insurgent—why are we having this conversation?"

"This guy was shooting at us five minutes ago! Now we have to spend millions of dollars healing him, and guarding him, as he tries to escape and sends info back to his terrorist bum-chums? We can't let them *bleed* us."

"The first helicopter is on its way," I reported. "The second will fly soon. A military policeman is providing the escort for the wounded insurgent. In accordance with your recent direction, Major, I named the insurgent Hamid."

Bell flinched. "Goddamnit, Jones, the Taliban are not your pets."

I met the Major's eye, and it softened for a second with gratitude, I think—to have someone in her corner, to not be completely alone. She had killed a man a minute ago but I wanted her anyway. Maybe I wanted her more. I hadn't forgotten that I was a hulking brute who could barely run three miles, that she was a soccer champ in another life. But the loneliness monster is not a reasonable beast.

Update: Medical helicopter Wheels Down at Kandahar Airfield surgical hospital at 1934 with critically wounded Canadian soldier.

We all breathed a sigh of relief, and the tension melted like fog. The wounded Canadian soldier was out of our hands—nothing we could do to help him more. We'd moved swiftly and defended our people. We made difficult choices with limited time and scanty information, but still wrought destruction on our enemies while maintaining a code that kept us from being savages. That's who we were.

"I need you vigilant, Bell," said the Major. "Keep the Predator on site in case those fighters return. Stay sharp. Scan the area." She patted his shoulder, and he shuddered at her touch. "Jones, keep working Hamid's medevac. Let me know if there are any issues."

But the fighters didn't return, and the second helicopter made it back safely, too. We had killed a man, but also saved a man. We saved a second man, but he was only dying because we launched a missile at him in the first place. Seemed like the kind of day that the Major would be proud of, with even enough blood to please the General. But to me, it was difficult to tell if we had made a difference.

I'd been looking through drone feeds too long. Everything was blurry.

12.

Dear Mom,

Wonderful to get your letter; I'm sorry I haven't been in better touch. I've fallen behind with work and weightlifting, but I'll try to keep the turnaround to a day or so. ☺

I know you're worried, but that explosion you mentioned was old news—happened a month ago. Must have been a slow news day in Canada. Also, that vehicle detonated in Helmand province, and I'm in Panjwa'i. Super far away. It reminds me when I was playing rugby in high school and you'd watch the games, and a kid would get hurt and you'd start crying thinking it was me. The funny thing was that the hurt kid was always on the other team, and I was usually the one that broke him.

Don't worry, Mom. The camp is huge and full of soldiers. We've got walls that blot the sun. We've got moats of acid, and acid-proof alligators. We've got snipers in towers scanning twenty-four hours a day for anything that comes close. We've got giant juggernauts and robots and artillery that can launch rounds into space. We've got a General who rappels out of helicopters and can bench press a tank.

Mom, I'm safe—I'm going to be fine. Yes, I can hear you now, "That's what every son who went to war said." Sure. But this is a new kind of war, with different rules, where people fight from offices—no trenches or D-day landing parties for this guy. Last week the coffee pot broke down for an hour and *that* was a crisis. I'm not a combat engineer; I'm not infantry; I'm not taking apart roadside bombs. I'm really just a juggler, same as I was on the bridge of a ship.

So. No more sniffling. No more watching the news with a whole tissue rammed up your nose, OK? Maybe just change the channel back to Dr. Phil. And if you get really worried, just send me an email and I'll tell you that I'm OK as soon as I can.

I love you, Mom. You have no idea how important your letters, cheezies, and toilet paper have been. <3

Matthew

P.S. Please send extra peanut butter for my new friend, the Sasquatch.

13.

WOKE TO TAP TAPPING at the cabin's darkened window; we night-owls always slept through the days. "What the fuck is that?" groggy Kool asked. Through the window, I could see the silhouette of a monstrous, hairy hand.

"Go back to sleep, dude, you're dreaming."

"Bullshit I'm dreaming. I know I saw something." A pistol materialized in Kool's hand—maybe he'd stowed it beneath the pillow. Maybe he slept holding it, like a lover's wrist.

Looked like he was going to charge out there, naked and shooting. Wasn't he in for a surprise. "You're right," I said. "Slipped my mind. I asked the internet guy to come by today. I'm having some trouble with my shit." You could pay civilian contractors for an internet connection, but the company was deeply religious and censored the porn sites. Thus, the black market of crusty porn mags and burned DVDs.

Kool stared at me with a deep, suspicious frown. "Coulda sworn I saw a big fuckoff hand."

"Fine, Idiot. If you hate the internet that much go shoot the guy. I'm going back to sleep." But of course I didn't sleep, just watched Kool through one heavy-lidded eye as he grimaced at the window, shot a baleful look in my direction, slipped the magazine from the pistol, and crawled back into his rack. One of the things I admire about soldiers is the ability to fall asleep in thirteen seconds—wasn't long before Kool's snores rattled the room, and I stealth-scurried into my boots.

Kool was my curse, attached to my ass like a fetal twin. The Major made him my understudy in the TOC—I was training him to do my job. We shared the night shift but he was still goddamn useless to me, fingers twitching for that pistol, wishing our problems were concrete enough to shoot. All the shit that happened the day before—he'd just stood there gaping. Caveman stares at fire and thinks it's magic.

Certainly, I didn't trust him enough to mention the ape-beast who slept beneath us. What the hell was the hairy bastard thinking, tapping on the window in the day, wandering around the side of the building where anyone could see him and shoot him with a rocket launcher?

Our room was the last of twenty-four in the barracks, right across from the showers and the rear exit; just outside were those steps where I sat the night I met the Sasquatch. Since then he was doing a better job, mostly, of hiding his frigate-shits, and sweeping his footprints with a willow branch. There was still the musk, strong enough to twist Kool's nose, but I'd pointed to the showers, the accumulated fluids, the rotting floor. The funk was shocking at first, but eventually became mundane, and then you barely noticed, like watching strangers die.

I crept outside to the creature's nook, where his wide cheekbones, glittering eyes, and flanges of orange fur poked from the basement crack under the stairs.

"Jones," he tried to whisper, but it was still too loud. I put my finger on my lips to quiet him. I wasn't going to scramble in the frog slime with him, so I crept to a nearby bunker, scanned for soldiers, waited for a gaggle of four spitting grunts to pass, and waved the brute over.

Was I going mad, or was the Sasquatch getting bigger? Seemed the latter as he slumped against the opposite concrete wall, and nearly filled the bunker with shoulders TicTac might have envied. His tongue lolled from that ursine muzzle.

"Jones," he repeated, "I can't take it no more, man—I'm losin' it. I'm always sweatin', always thirsty, and if I have to eat one more damn frog…" I scanned his face for a hint of a threat, but it was missing. All I noticed were his eyes: blue, wet, pinched. "Not that there's many frogs left. Shit. I destroyed the whole civilization, brother. Maybe I was foretold in the frog prophecies—some sort of hairy doom." He paused to rake his sides with long, black nails. I spared a glance for his slime-covered and festering body. He was losing patches of fur in great tufts, revealing cirrhotic flesh underneath; his skin was peeling and itching. He had scratched hard enough to draw blood, and there were other scars, older ones, poking through, too.

"Look at me, Jones. I'm a hot mess. I can handle the bugs but I gotta get some food, a real meal. You ever heard of a skinny Sasquatch? Last night my stomach growled so loud it woke me up." He trailed off, staring wistfully over my shoulder at the outer perimeter wall, our cage. "This ain't home, Jones. You've helped me lots but I need proper food and a way outta here." He reached for my shoulder, imploring, but I shrank from his claws.

The outstretched hand dropped. Didn't say anything more, just stared at his lap, as a tremble ran through him. I could foresee all the obstacles; he didn't know about the snipers, landmines and circling drones. Not to mention the more pressing issues of his hunger, thirst, and the growing legion of parasites infecting his fur. Even if he passed the defenses, he'd find himself in the middle of a scorching desert that bristled with IEDs and was packed with guerillas and soldiers. Meanwhile, his tremble increased to a full-on shake; he was holding onto his own arms, hugging himself and moaning.

"Stop that goddamn racket," I chided. The creature looked up, a snot bubble expanding at his snout. He hiccupped loudly. "I'll bring you food from the mess hall. Don't try to climb the wall—they've got snipers watching. You say you got here on a plane? Start looking for another one and stow away. Search the base at night; it'll be quieter. A plane with a maple leaf on it might take you back to Canada, but anywhere is better than here."

He clasped his hands together in a disturbingly human show of thanks. "Thanks—hic—Jones. I owe you big time."

I noticed a stone about the size and shape of an ostrich egg. "This guy here, you see it?" He nodded. "We'll call this the Speaking Stone. When we need to chat we put the stone on the step. Otherwise we keep it in the bunker, OK? No more thumping on the window."

"Speakin' Stone—hic—got it."

And then I asked the unthinkable question.

"What should I call you?"

His eyes brightened.

"Noah. That's what my foster Mom used to call me." He smeared the snot from his nose with the back of his hand.

"Pleased to meet you, Noah," and I patted him on the right triceps. My hand came away sticky. "I'll be back in a few hours, OK?" He nodded and I left him to wallow.

It was a kind of infidelity; I was cheating on hardness itself. The day before I'd watched men explode. But this day, in a bunker, a furtive meeting where the brutes took off their masks and were gentle—a forbidden club with its own secret rune of entry. The idea put bounce in my step as I trudged the mile to the base hospital, on the far shore of the poo pond. One of the little boats had tipped over in the sludge and the murk was sucking it down—Abandon Ship, Abandon Ship!—no, that was my other life.

Italians, French, Romanians—it wasn't a far walk but it covered half of Europe, with the barracks lined side by side. There were other flags I didn't recognize, lots of them, plenty of countries answering the call to war, sending troops of all races, all clad in arid-pattern fatigues, with their hair buzzed, or cropped short. Some troops were paragons of discipline, with their laundry crisp, stretched taut on the line. Others were slovenly soldiers tossing dice in raucous packs. I breezed past both sorts, but paused at the Romanian drill square for respect. There were a hundred soldiers or so standing still and proud. In front of them, six soldiers marched with deliberate and jerking steps, carrying a coffin draped with a flag: blue, yellow, red. A casualty of the last rocket attack.

The Ramp Ceremony

We dreamed of going home but not in a box. Doesn't matter to the dead anyway, how much we polished our buttons and blackened our boots. Doesn't matter how straight the lines of soldiers, perfectly dressed at an arm's length from each other, how long they stood at attention while the padre mumbled a few words into the microphone. How the bagpipe pierced the ear, or swamped it with its drone. Whether it was a good man or a bad one who died, whether it was a heart attack folding blankets, or a bullet in the teeth, or a shabby grenade that burst too soon, or an IED that chewed off his legs. Didn't matter if was a warrior's death or a suicide or an accident—someone would stitch us back together, rest our bodies in the coffin, and drape a flag over top for a bit of dignity before packing us into a plane for the long flight home. From there, the hearse drove us from Trenton to Toronto, along the Highway of Heroes, as solemn Canadians watched from overpasses.

I stayed at attention until they'd stuffed the coffin into a fat-bottomed plane, a cargo of tears. Afghanistan was a major exporter of those. Each one drained the communal will to fight. In some ways Bell was right—the insurgency was winning through pinpricks designed to *bleed* us. If we were smart, we wouldn't have ramp ceremonies at all. Just throw our dead into the poo pond and write fake letters to the families until after the war.

Made my way to the hospital, which was indistinguishable from the other bunker-like buildings, except for the red cross in front. This symbol was supposed to protect humanitarian workers and medical crew from targeting by hostile groups. But the Taliban considered doctors and aid workers another limb of the invader and sometimes cut off their heads on video.

The hospital rooms themselves were sterilized by constant scrubbing, shielded by heavy curtains that kept the sand and shit-dust outside. Nurses and doctors in light green scrubs and rubber gloves were too harried to worry about me; just a soldier visiting a friend. But the man I was visiting was not a friend, just a pixelated blob with one leg. A line of anti-poetry, the combat chat—this was the Canadian soldier we'd medevac'd.

I'd thought that if I visited the casualties, saw them for myself, I might make them *real*. Here he was in the flesh with tubes running into his nostrils.

His hairline was receding a little but he was only my age, thirtyish. There was a bag of fluids going in and another going out. I remembered his leg as trailing-off pixels, one shade of gray bleeding into another. Now it was a bandaged stump, sutured and saturating its wrappings. Bandages on his stomach, chest and arms as well—his tour was over, the lucky bastard. Acrid stink of blood and shit and stained sheets. Drool pouring out of his mouth. Shoulda seen the way his good leg was twitching, like he was running in his dreams.

Remember flipping through the file at the foot of his bed. A laundry list of injuries on top of the obvious missing parts. Corporal Crispin was his name. Scanning the scorched and torn flesh: *more like Corporal Crispy.*

Crispy

And who'd have thought I'd end up roommates with the guy, on the other side of purgatory, him birdfrail with his stump, learning to walk again. His cough in the night for my strong arm and a lift to the john. Me on my knees, lacing up his one good boot, before his arms got better. If I'd done a better job, got a faster chopper from another HQ, he'd still be whole.

"Shut the fuck up," he says. "I ain't wrecked."

Crispy's jealous because I still have both feet on the ground; thinks I owe him something since he cut me down from the rafters, army crawled up my pant leg with a knife in his teeth. But my neck was too thick to break anyway, during the slow spin, as my specters clapped and hooted, same way we used to cheer for a drone strike. One-legged bastard won't even give me my grief—now I owe him double, too in debt to die.

"Shut the fuck up," Crispy insists. "Just tell the truth."

There was another casualty: Hamid, the Taliban—the one I'd named in the TOC.

He lay naked, on a bed down the hall, having tossed the sheet on the floor in the night. They didn't know his real name, so "Hamid" was written on the dossier at the foot of the bed. Bandages all over his chest, belly, and covering one eye, the shrapnel had torn him plenty. He was unconscious and handcuffed to the bed. Morphine medicated, as well, it seemed he knew he was a prisoner, for he strained against his fetters in his sleep. A male nurse scowled and changed his bandages. A military policeman, wearing a red beret, guarded this most helpless of detainees from near the door.

The Major was there, too. It was always a surprise to see her outside the TOC, an icicle in the desert. She was sitting on a chair in the corner with her head in her hands, but she looked up when she heard my footfall.

"Come to gloat, Jones?" she asked. So hard, the way she hit, edge in her voice like a battle axe. It left me chewing the air for a full ten seconds before words emerged.

"Major, mind if we have a little break from it?"

"From what?"

"The stupid Army bullshit where we try our best to bruise the other?"

"You're not used to that yet, Jones?"

We fell silent; the Major's face sunk back in her hands. I leaned against the wall to watch the nurse finish tending Hamid, sponging blood that had leaked from beneath the bandages on his belly. Still scowling—no one wanted to heal a terrorist. The nurse kept glancing up at the Major and me as if he was embarrassed, then fled the room with a self-conscious air.

The silence stretched. The military policeman remained; cleared his throat twice. The nurse had left Hamid exposed, with the sheet only pulled up to the thighs. And he was a sad bastard, tiny by North American standards, with a neck as thin as my wrist, and his penis showing.

Finally, I spoke, "When we hit him with that missile, he wasn't a person at all. But now look—he's a man. Or maybe a boy."

The Major looked at me with one eyebrow turned up, as if I were a puzzle. Her gaze drifted to Hamid and stayed. Her whisper: "I always look, Jones. After every strike, whenever it's possible."

"This is my first time," I said. And we were quiet again, long minutes punctured by Hamid's groans and the policeman shifting from foot to foot. The ticking of the clock on the wall. The Major's breath through her fingers. Somewhere under the scents of blood and antiseptic, a sprig of vanilla.

"It's not your fault," she said at last.

"What was that?"

"The strike. I ordered it. I was the Target Engagement Authority, not you. Hamid is my fault." As if recognizing his fake name, Hamid coughed and tried to turn over in his sleep, but couldn't. She was staring at me, eyes like two crystals. "You don't have to deal with this."

"Do you want me to go?"

"That's not what I said. I said it wasn't your decision."

Watching the policeman, the way he had been squirming during our conversation, like he was trying to bore straight through the floor, was causing an inappropriate grin to creep onto my face.

"Well, why do you get all the blame, Major? You didn't push the button. You didn't tell Hamid to take up arms. You told a guy to tell a guy to push the button. Anyway, it was the General who gave you the Rules of Engagement and ordered you to use them."

She growled low in her throat. For the first time I noticed the dented helmet beneath her chair. "Damnit, Jones, how did I ever get stuck with a sailor in Afghanistan, anyway? What do you want me to say? We're all to blame? It's true. Happy? I swear, Jones, I'd rather deal with Bell than you any day."

I wanted her to look at me, but she didn't. I wanted her to apologize, recognize she was lashing out at me unfairly, but she didn't. I closed my eyes and fell into a deep well where the sun got dimmer and dimmer. I was numb to a lot of things: not to her.

"If there's nothing else, Major. I'm going to excuse myself. I've got an appointment."

She sighed. "Oh, don't go like that, Jones. You know I didn't mean it." She held her helmet in her hands, flipping it over and over. "You've never killed anyone—I've killed dozens. I don't even know how many. You can go and have a normal life after this. I can't."

"Thank you for your insights, Major. I will consider them closely next time I grieve a life. Is that everything, Ma'am?"

And didn't she seem small and alone when she looked up at me that time? My loneliness beast was beating its head against the bars. Hamid, the Taliban, strained against his manacles. Failed. Gave up.

"Yes, Jones. Dismissed."

14.

A LONG WALK HOME with plenty to mull over and a hungry Sasquatch to feed. An American soldier spat desultorily from the top of an idling tank and his hork nearly struck me. *I'd rather deal with Bell any day than you.* The dust was thick that day; I blew my nose and a stone came out.

Dining Facilities (DFACS)

Plenty of cafeterias in Kandahar Air Field, perhaps ten or fifteen at least, all of which sucked, but we had our favorites. The Canadian DFAC was just as shitty as the rest of them, but they served omelettes throughout the day. A dextrous Indian wearing a turban crafted them using two metal spatulas and a jug of egg paste.

Most of the food came teetering from Pakistan in convoys along IED-laden mud roads. Maybe half the shipments never showed up—we were feeding our enemies. Sometimes the truck would arrive and the logisticians would crack open the trailer and it would be packed with bodies. After, we'd wonder what comprised the meatloaf.

Egg-man and the other workers detested the soldiers and assembled the meals with the same pride you'd have brewing a pig's slop. This was fair; we were in Afghanistan to kill Muslims. Only the cucumbers were safe to eat. Everything else was booby-trapped with sharpened bones, even the tomatoes.

I munched a grim omelette in the middle of eighty cursing Canadian soldiers. Laughter wasn't forbidden but it was pretty scarce sometimes. Picked up a to-go Styrofoam container heaped with enough dodgy meatloaf to choke a wildebeest, could barely close the lid.

Vicious ants patrolled the stunted bushes and bouquets of barbed wire on the way back; the meatloaf pheromones kept them at bay. A treat: two women in gym clothes, wearing pistols in shoulder holsters, walked past deep in conversation. At the rear of the barracks, Noah the Sasquatch had placed the speaking-stone on the steps. I checked for privacy, then parked myself in the anti-rocket bunker with the yard-thick walls, where we'd spoken earlier. I knew the meat-scent would lure him.

There was a snuffling. A shuffling. A brute rooting. You could smell him before you saw him. He slunk into the bunker nose-first, face inches from the bare earth, stomach rumbling like artillery bursting in faraway villages.

"That for me?" he asked, slobbering into the dust, a flicker in his blue eyes beneath the protruding brow.

I couldn't help but snicker despite a stab of pity. "Yes, Man. Eat something quick!" He didn't need much encouragement. One quarter of the container was cucumbers, one quarter canned corn, and the rest was the meatloaf heap; the gray tongues of meatloaf slimed down Noah's throat like oysters. I edged a bit further away to avoid losing a finger, or worse. Noah feasted with one arm circled around the meal, the other hand shovelling. Little snarls and gasps for breath—the wet flapping of the meatloaf, a rain of white Styrofoam crumbs, and the glug of a water bottle draining down his throat. At first, I thought the nearby mountain was erupting but, no, it was just Noah's supersonic belch, a note so low it sounded tectonic, or glacial, which for some reason made me dizzy.

"Feel better?" I asked.

"Oh my god, so much better," he said, plopping down beside me, and trying to catch his breath. "I owe you big time, Buddy."

There he was with a vacant, dumb grin on his face, leaning back against the wall, eyes closed, smug as a sailor on his first solo watch. He muttered, "A fine loaf, Jones, a fine loaf," as he licked his fingers.

"Don't fall asleep here," I warned, as Noah's eyelids drooped. "Almost everyone on the camp is armed; anyone might shoot you."

That snapped his eyes open. "Goddamn, I hate this cage."

"Then let's get you out of here. I've had two ideas since we last spoke, but both are terrible."

"Bet they're better than what I got."

"OK. First, I'll lend you an extra uniform. I don't expect it will fit, but I am one of the biggest guys on the camp. Might help you blend in. From a distance."

"Fuck clothes," said Noah.

"Second, well, if you're ever desperate because people are chasing you or something, and you can stomach the idea, you could probably hide in the poo pond."

Noah recoiled, snorting. "That's the worst idea I ever heard."

"It's a desperate move, but no one will ever go in there. If people are chasing you, jump in and hold your breath for as long as you can. When you surface, just stick your nose up and nothing else, as close to the surface as possible. It will be the worst thing ever. But you will live.”

“That’s the nastiest shit. What the hell is wrong with ya?”

“Could save your life some day, Buddy. You’re welcome. Anyway, I warned you they were bad ideas. Like I said, you need to do your own reconnaissance. At night. Carefully.”

“I’ve been tryin’,” sighed Noah. “You know there are patrols of men runnin’ around with flashlights all night? They’re lookin’ for something. You think it’s me?”

“Nah. You’re not the only freak on the camp, Noah. There’s a rapist who hits guys with a Taser. He strikes every couple nights and no one ever sees his face because he pulls a bag over their heads.”

Noah’s lips curled in disgust, showing more of his long, yellowing canines. He even spat into the dust. “No, no, no—that’s too much. You made that up, didn’t ya, ya sick bastard?”

“Wish I did.”

Noah couldn’t look at me anymore. “My whole life. Ever since you humans took me in, when I was a boy. A big stupid boy who couldn’t speak good. That whole time people sayin’ I was a monster—showed me pictures in their books of blurry ape-people—‘Look, Noah! It’s you!’ People usin’ laughter like bullets. People usin’ bullets like laughter.”

He stared at his vast pale palm, the thick fingers, long claws caked with mud and frog-scum, then clenched his hand into a fist—a hard fist, a great boulder of a fist. “Monster,” he repeated. “This place is a factory that only makes killin’. My best buddy murders people from the sky with robots. And there’s a pervert on the camp who buggers soldiers. And you say I’m the freak!” The look on his face hardened, his lips pulled back, and his eyes slitted. The bones in his fist started grinding and popping. Seeing Noah’s muscles swell with rage made my mouth run dry. Needed to remind myself he was no damn garden gnome dancing around the mushroom ring or pixie shitting vials of magic dust. Intelligent creatures weren’t supposed to be as big as rhinoceroses; he forced words through his teeth, “Nothin’ drives me crazier than a bully; got fuckin’ Wawa to thank for that. This Taser-perv better not try anythin’ when I’m around, Man. You got no idea—I’m way stronger than I look.”

It was easier to be his friend when he was the one afraid of me, like when we met. Fortunately, we Canadians have developed certain “pacify the giant” impulses that get us out of a lot of shit with our southern neighbor when we’re not being too smug about health care. Still, I couldn’t control the climbing of a single skeptical eyebrow—I mean, Noah made Hercules look like a little bitch. How could he be stronger than he looked?

"Oh, you want me to prove it, I see." Noah cracked his knuckles—the anger draining from his voice, the showman remaining. "You want me to lift this wall up?" He pointed with his thumb to the concrete slab that served as the "door" of the bunker. "That's nothin', buddy. I could throw it. No prob."

I was accustomed to every kind of man-posturing and gym-banter. TicTac's smack talk made sure of it. But that concrete slab was lodged in place by a crane, and weighed at least 4000 lbs. It looked like one of the obelisks of Stonehenge, except with a fat, extra-heavy bottom.

"You're full of shit, Noah," I said, half-laughing.

Noah peered outside the bunker to scan for nearby soldiers—we were clear. "Maybe there's a little bit of shit," he admitted, sizing up the stone. But then he stood and braced his shoulder against it. He squatted low and gripped the sides of the obelisk for purchase, his ratty orange pelt threadbare against the straining of enormous quads, the broad back, and the shoulder muscles clearly delineated into three separate "heads." He grunted and shifted his stance. The stone shimmied a little. Noah farted poisonously, and I frantically wafted the smell from my face with my sleeve. The stone rose.

"Jesus suffering fuck," I said.

Three shocked centipedes scurried out from underneath, where the dirt was damp. Noah's muscles were taut enough to explode—a Sasquatch version of "the pump"—veins peeking through the hair in the bald patches of his arms, thighs, and neck. The obelisk jutted over his head, casting me in shadow.

"Want me ta throw it?" asked my tremendous friend, grinning.

"Noah, you're gonna get us busted. Please put it down." I poked my head from the bunker, to make sure no soldiers could see us. He obliged with a thud and wasn't he pleased. A couple pieces of dirty meatloaf and suddenly he had a strongman act.

"Impressed, Jones, impressed?" Noah asked, literally dancing within the limited space of the bunker, a goofy grin plastered on his face. "Don't worry, buddy. I won't eat ya."

Was it impossible? Was it magical? Thousands of hours I'd spent at the gym to only achieve a fraction of what Noah could do. I had figured he was stronger than me, but…

"Ah, stop lookin' at me funny, Jones. You just dunno Sasquatch. Do a Google or somethin'. I had my first puberty when I was three, and I think now I'm gettin' my fourth."

I kept looking at my hands, cracked from all the weight training, then at Noah's gloating mug, back to the displaced stone, with the wet earth breathing.

"Wanna join my fan club?" he asked. "Play yer cards right and you could make it to president."

15.

DON'T MATTER IF YA PINCH YERSELF—Sasquatch strength ain't no dream. Don't be shakin' yer head, neither. Bein' strong ain't the problem for us. Problem is stayin' alive.

Maybe tomorrow I get killed by a rocket. Tomorrow I get shot by soldiers. Tomorrow I get blown up by a tank—we dunno the end! Where do all the stories ya never told go when ya get killed? Do they just float up in the air, like the soul? Do they soak into the sand like blood? Shit, Jones, I don't wanna die but bein' forgotten's the real death, ain't it?

I was justa kid, maybe six or seven, when my first Mom dragged me up a mountain. Nothin' could really stop that lady once she got goin', strong as one of yer tanks. Top of that mountain there's this huge log cottage with six or seven graybeard Sasquatch, all holdin' bigass books and starin' outta sunken eyes with avalanche voices. The graybeards trapped me up there with 'em for three whole days, tellin' stories, readin' from the bigass books with squirrely tracks on every page.

I think they wanted me to be like them—to keep our stories goin', but back then I couldn't take all the pressure. Kept escapin', runnin' down that big ol' mountain. Once I even set the teacher's robe on fire with a burnin' stick. Well, Sasquatch are pretty hairy folks as you can see and it took less than a flat second for his fur to go up in a sour-smellin' cloud and so did the bigass book in his hands. Burntbeard was most upset about the book, moanin' "That's our history," over and over as he cuffed me upside the head.

Never did become a real storyteller, just a bit by accident from the books I found wit' the most pictures. So now, ya listen to yer buddy Noah and I'ma tell ya 'bout the secret of strength—since yer so damn busy breakin' yer back to figure it out—and maybe after ya can shut yer hole 'bout it, for once.

In the old days Sasquatch had six gods but now we only got four. We had a god for the river and a god for the wind, a god for stories and a god for tasty moss, a god that guided dead souls and a god of

STRENGTH. USED TO BE THAT WHEN A SASQUATCH DIED THE SOUL WOULD GO INTO THE GROUND AND START A NEW LIFE AS A TREE. BUT THE GOD WHO MADE THAT HAPPEN WAS KILLED BY THE STRENGTH GOD AND NOW THE TREES IN THE FOREST ARE ALL EMPTY AND SASQUATCH DIE FOR REAL. SO THE FOUR GODS TEAMED UP ON THE KILLER AND THREW HIM DOWN TO THE EARTH, WHERE HE CRASHED IN A BIG OL' FOREST AND WOKE UP WITHOUT HIS MAGIC. MAYBE THAT WAS THE START OF THE ENDIN' FOR US—MAYBE IF WE HAD ALL SIX OF OUR GODS, WE'D ALL BE TOGETHER IN THE FOREST AND NOT DEAD, DYIN' AND SCATTERED ALL OVER.

WITHOUT HIS BAG O' TRICKS THE BROKEN STRENGTH GOD STARTED LEARNIN' REAL FAST ABOUT OUR WORLD—HOW THE EARTH DRAINS YA WITH ITS AGEIN' AND HUNGER AND SICKNESS. HOW DO GODS DIE? THEY START TURNIN' SLOW INTO STATUES AND LOSIN' THEIR VOICES. TRAPPED IN THEIR OWN HEADS WITH ALL 'EM THOUGHTS. THE GOD REACHED OUT IN A DREAM TO A YOUNG SASQUATCH, MACK, FAMOUS NOW, A REAL HERO, AND TOLD 'IM THAT HIS GOD-POWERS WERE LOCKED IN A GREEN STONE ON THE OTHER SIDE OF THE WORLD. YOUNG MACK WAS STRONG—AFTER THE DREAM HE USED A WHOLE TREE FOR A CLUB AND STARTED WALKIN' THE WORLD, NOTHIN' HIS PARENTS OR SISTERS SAID COULD SWAY 'IM.

MACK SPENT A LIFETIME SEARCHIN' THE WHOLE EARTH FOR THAT ONE GREEN STONE. STARTED IN OUR HOMELAND WHERE THE WIND'S COLD AND THE STARS HOLD UP THAT BANNER OF WHITE LIGHT. EVERYWHERE HE WENT PEOPLE THOUGHT HE WAS CRAZY, WALKIN' 'CROSS GREAT PLAINS, FIGHTIN' HORRIBLE HORNED BEASTS AND CREATURES WIT' PITS O' TEETH FOR MOUTHS. HE SWAM RIVERS FULL O' ANGRY FISH GNAWIN' HIS JUNK. HORRIBLE SKINNY-ASS CREATURES FELL ON 'IM FROM TREES IN THICK JUNGLES AND SANK THEIR FANGS IN 'IS NECK. IN THE MOUNTAINS HE MET OTHER SASQUATCH WHO TOSSED BOULDERS AT 'IM, BUT MACK CAUGHT 'EM ALL AND THREW 'EM BACK. ONE BOULDER HE HUCKED HIT THE SIDE OF THE MOUNTAIN AND THE MOUNTAIN ROARED LIKE A SEASICK DRAGON AND 'BOUT HALF OF IT CRASHED DOWN, MAKIN' A CLOUD O' DUST THAT LASTED THREE DAYS. WHEN IT FINALLY BLEW AWAY THAT OL' MOUNTAIN WAS JUST A BROKEN FINGER, AND THE VILLAGE, THE WHOLE TRIBE, EVEN THE LITTLE ONES, WERE BURIED 'NEATH IT ALL.

MACK FELL INTO A BLACK GRIEF AND TORE OFF 'IS BEARD. CLIMBIN' OVER THE RUBBLE TRYIN' TO DIG EVERYONE OUT FROM 'NEATH THE STONES. SPENT A WHOLE YEAR OF 'IS LIFE DIGGIN' AND THE GRIEF TURNED 'IM OLD. BALLS DROOPIN'. HAIR GOT THIN AND WHITE. THE WIND CUTTIN' AND SPEARIN' 'IM SO MUCH HE WRAPPED 'IMSELF IN A LONG ROBE AND 'VENTUALLY EVEN 'IS CLUB GOT TOO HEAVY TO CARRY. HE LEFT IT WHERE TWO RIVERS MET LIKE OLD FRIENDS, SPLASHIN' AND LAUGHIN'. TOOK UP A WALKIN' STICK INSTEAD, AND

CARRIED IT WITH 'IM TO A DRY LAND WHERE THE GROUND ITSELF'LL BURN YA, AND WHERE YOU CAN WALK ALL DAY NEVER FINDIN' SHADE. VILLAGES, AND VULTURES CIRCLIN', EVERY NOW AND THEN HE'D TRIP OVER A SKELETON THE SUN HAD PAINTED WHITE. WAS A LAND JUST LIKE THIS ONE, JONES.

MAYBE IT WAS HERE WHERE MACK FINALLY FOUND THAT OL' MAGIC STONE, BURIED UNDER A MOUNTAIN, WHERE THE ANCIENT GODS HAD HURLED IT. GROPIN' HIS WAY IN THE DARK THROUGH A CAVE-MAZE FOR SO LONG HE NEARLY WENT BLIND 'TIL HE SAW A GREEN, SHIMMERIN' LIGHT. MACK REACHES OUT FOR THAT STONE, WHEN THE MAGIC JUMPS OUTTA THE ROCK AND HITS HIM IN THE FINGER. THEN HIS BODY'S TURNIN' YOUNG AGAIN, GRAY HAIR GROWIN' BACK BLACK, THIRST QUENCHIN', BALLS LIFTIN' UP TO THEIR FORMER GLORY, AND HIS SKIN BECOMIN' TOUGH LIKE BARK. IN HIS HAND HE FOUND A WEAPON O' THE GODS. A SPIKED BALL OF MIGHTY IRON ON THE END OF A LONGASS CHAIN. THIS WAS THE PICTURE THE GRAYBEARDS SHOWED ME O' MACK, FREAKIN' INVINCIBLE, NEARLY FILLIN' THE PAGE WITH HIS MUSCLES, SWINGIN' THAT CHAIN LIKE A COMET, SKIN HARDER THAN THE BOULDERS THAT KILLED THAT VILLAGE, AND A GREEN GLOW IN HIS POCKET. BUT IN ALL THE PICTURES, HE ALWAYS HAD AN OLD FACE, LIKE NO AMOUNT OF GODLY REBIRTH MOJO IS GONNA MAKE YA FORGET THE SHIT YA DONE. I ASKED THE ELDERS, "WHY DIDN'T THEY MAKE HIS FACE YOUNG AGAIN?" THEY SAID, "MACK LOST HIS INNOCENCE, BUT HE LEARNED WHAT STRENGTH WAS FOR."

HE DIDN'T WASTE IT NEITHER, HIS STRENGTH. USED IT FOR GOOD— SMASHED THE FORTS OF EVIL MEN AND SASQUATCH, FREED PEOPLE FROM CHAINS, AND DISAPPEARED BEFORE THEY COULD EVEN GET HIM DRUNK. WENT FROM VILLAGE TO VILLAGE SOMETIMES AND JUST TALKED. TALKED ABOUT STRENGTH AND HOW PEOPLE USE IT FOR VIOLENCE AND PRIDE. HOW IT FEELS TO LET STRENGTH GO, SEE THAT SHIT FADE. HOW, WHEN IT CAME BACK, HE KNEW THIS TIME HE WOULD USE IT TO PROTECT PEOPLE AND BRING AN END TO VIOLENCE.

THEY WROTE HIS WORDS DOWN IN A BOOK AND MAYBE THAT WAS THE ONE I BURNT BUT THE STORY STUCK ANYWAY. MIGHTY MACK STOPPIN' WARS, TOPPLIN' TYRANTS—THEY SAY HE COULD EVEN STARE DOWN STORMS. WITH THAT GREEN STONE'S POWER MAKIN' HIM IMMORTAL, MACK BECAME A GREAT CHAMPION OF THE PLANET AND IT LASTED FOR THREE HUNDRED YEARS, A TIME OF SWEET PEACE WAY BEFORE YOU HUMANS STARTED FUCKIN' IT UP.

MY HERO IS MACK. HE NEVER RAISED HIS FISTS TO NOBODY UNLESS HE HAD TO. HE FIGURED OUT WHAT STRENGTH WAS *FOR*. AND YEAH, EVERYTHIN' WENT TO SHIT AFTER THAT, BUT I TRY TO THINK 'BOUT HOW AMAZIN' IT WOULD FEEL TO BE A HERO LIKE THAT, EVEN FOR A SECOND, WITH ALL THE PEOPLE CROWDIN' ROUND. A *CHAMPION*, JONES, CAN YA SEE IT?

16.

LATER, WHEN I REACHED FOR TICTAC'S DOOR at the end of the hall, animal grunts and snarls echoed from his room. I rapped my knuckles and he cursed a muffled word like 'titfuck.' Then the sibilance of something heavy being dragged along the floor.

"You're late, my friend! We go to church today?" he said, cracking open the door. He wrinkled his nose, "Jones, we have worked out many times and I know you are not flower. How do you smell so bad before we lift?" Shirtless and corded, today the veins on his shoulders and traps seemed thick as worms. We hadn't even worked out yet: I stank like a Sasquatch and he already had the pump.

"That's the testosterone," I said. "You wouldn't understand. This is how *a man* smells."

He chuckled and waved me in, the first time I'd made it past the door. "Is finished now, look."

TicTac had wallpapered his room entirely in pictures of naked women. In a curious display of discretion, sticky notes covered the genitals.

"Why did you hide all the crotches? That's the best part."

He shrugged his titanic trapezius. "They look like axe wounds to me."

We worked our way down the back, as TicTac badgered and bullied the other men in the gym, using them as props, pointing out their weaknesses. He scolded one man for not mopping up his sweat from the weight bench. Another, for not returning his dumbbells to the rack. Six foot five and colossally ripped: not even the infantry would fight back in this space, so obviously his temple.

TicTac was a brute and he got meaner when he worked out. He had a few reasons for enduring my company: I'd learned the secret of the zero-help spot; I was lifting heavy enough that we didn't have to spend too much time changing weights; and with my bulky appearance I slightly boosted his ability to dominate other men: a pet ogre. And that day he was particularly savage—deep in the throes of M-KRAK, that potent poison and combination of twenty-seven testosterones, a whole Noah's ark: giraffe, shark, scarab,

Coachbag's Corner: Back Day

Is one of my favorite days, Jones. Yours too—you have hump like camel. I am glad you are not douchebag who builds chest at expense of back. For chest is muscle of coward. Is designed to push away. With back, we pull people close and bite nose, yes?

Back day is hardest on hands and this is good. They will hurt at first then turn into beautiful leather. What is point of having nice, soft hands? Are you hand model? Are you touching nice soft breast anytime soon? No. Me neither.

Look at Tiny over there with weak forearms. Do not be like him, Jones. In order to save his pretty hands he use wrist strap. So weight hangs off wrist, instead of fingers. Now his fingers are not getting stronger, and you see forearm suffer, too.

A weightlifter must develop relationship with his fingers. No, is not masturbation, Jones. Every single set there is failure. Every failure there is muscle weaker than others. You do bent-over rows, which is for back, strong muscle. But when you lift, bicep fails, or fingers fail—only the bodybuilder wants to fail, to fail with strongest muscle! And that is reason fingers must be strongest of all muscles. You must have gorilla grip. If you learn one thing from me, Jones, is this: anyone who uses wrist strap is pussy. Never bring wrist strap anywhere near me—I don't want to see them! I would not wipe my ass with such a thing.

anaconda, bald eagle, grizzly bear, and those fish from the depths with the bioluminescent eye stalks. The Russians briefly experimented with giving M-KRAK to soldiers during the Cold War, but the soldiers, so contaminated, became impossible to control, throwing off their military discipline and folding iron bars into origami. During the bent-over rows I lifted five pounds more than TicTac and he shrieked, "Go, Jones! Go, Jones!" inches from my ear. It seemed he required no rest at all, and couldn't focus his eyes.

When it came to bodybuilding, I believed everything TicTac said. He was always tweaking the workout, maximizing it; I was a mess of lactic acid somewhere in my body at any given time. And I was getting stronger.

But when we got to the deadlifts, all I could think about was Noah lifting that stone.

I knew TicTac was the greater freak: faster and stronger in the arms, chest, abs, traps, forearms, shoulders, and hands. But the Army guys still fucked with him sometimes (sending him spiralling into conniptions) because he was Air Force, and it was common knowledge that the Air Force was stuffed

On Strength

Don't think I've figured it out—we're all blind and I'm weak and washed up now, no matter what you say; back then I was strong, proper strong. I was always aware of it: when I met a person or shook a hand or spoke.

I wanted to roll back time and bring my strength to ancient playgrounds, those lessons of grubby fists, where all I learned was to hide in books. Send me back to my big brother when he beat me with the baseball bat—watch I'll break it over my knee. Biggest bully was my Dad, the sot, with hands hard as tree branches, smashing bottles on me in the haze of cigarette smoke. Look, I've outgrown them all.

That was until I started this Army shit with the queer jokes, moronic, thoughtless. So yeah, it was satisfying to shake a man's hand for the first time and feel his tiny bones click. To see the flicker of surprise and pain on a tough soldier's face was tops.

So here it is: nothing is more important than strength. Nothing at all except gentleness. But not everybody hits the lottery on that second one.

with nearly as many queers as the Navy.

Kool strutted into the gym slicking his hair and wearing a towel like a scarf. He almost walked past a mirror, caught himself, then returned for a leisurely session of self-admiration and duck-lips.

"Douchebag alert," I mumbled. I'd been sore about the Cheezies for a couple weeks.

"Oh, that clown," muttered TicTac. We were just finishing our deadlifts; the barbell was on the ground, loaded with about 550 lbs. That much weight doesn't want to be moved—it doesn't roll when you kick it or behave like something on wheels. It's structural, part of the building.

"Hey, Ladies," said Kool. "Mind if I work in for a set?" He gestured to the laden bar like it was a sack of feathers. He was wearing a tight tank top, and staring over his shoulder at his arms in the mirror.

"Christ, Man," I said. "Are you here to work out or jack yourself off? Aren't you ashamed to show those things in public?" I pointed my nose to his scrawny triceps.

"Ashamed?" His eyes flared. "I am a goddamn force of nature. I make women wet and men shit themselves. You fucking jealous bitches."

TicTac scoffed. By his eyes he was immersed in M-KRAK-fueled fantasies of violence. "Who is this little man, with big mouth? Perhaps it is too soon for boasting, yes? You need basics, Pipsqueak: bench press, squats, and yes, I agree with Jones, major focus on triceps."

"You keep your tips to yourself, you little bitch," Kool answered. "I'm a goddamn infantry officer. I didn't have to suck dick for my commission the way Jones did it in the Navy." He glanced at TicTac, "Or take a shot in the ass the way they do it in the Air Force."

TicTac went supernova.

He roared like a goddamn warlock. Time slowed. The Coachbag grabbed the barbell in an overhand grasp and pulled explosively. The weight swung up until the whole 550 lbs barbell was over his head. As the howl echoed off the walls, my mouth gaped for words of warning. Kool's eyes widened. Then, like a Sasquatch hurling a boulder, TicTac heaved the barbell at Kool.

The weight was in the air, flying. Gravity moaned in betrayal. Words emerged from TicTac's howl, "Fuuuuuuccccckkk yooouuuuu, Koooool," and the other gym rats gasped at this spectacle, this meteor entering the atmosphere. Kool's eyes got bigger and bigger; he lifted his hands to protect his face.

"Looooooook oooooooooouuuut—" I tried to yell as the second stretched, as the meteor flew, then crashed into Kool, his feeble arms swept up in the destructive path. His legs buckled under the weight of it, the breath blown from his lungs with a noise like puking.

He crumpled. The barbell thudded onto the ground, on top of Kool, too heavy to bounce. The weights on either end of the barbell were high enough to absorb the impact, and the bar was poised two inches above Kool's lean chest, his hands flapping like two shocked birds.

Being a scrawny bastard saved his life.

Kool curled helplessly beneath the bar, trying to suck air. I started pulling the weights off the barbell. "Help me, you goddamn animal," I growled to TicTac, but he stormed out of the gym, slamming open the double doors. Nobody tried to stop him.

17.

THE DAY OF THE SPARK: I woke and reached for my dreams but they had become starchy pages that crumbled when turned. When leaving the barracks, I always half-expected that the world would have turned soft and green since I slept. Imagination painted a unicorn's glade of trees and vines, but it was always a manticore's heath of blowing sand.

Avoided TicTac for two days after his meltdown, and the sun was a vicious bastard too; I pulled my bush cap low over my eyes. On the walk to work the stench of poo pond and meatloaf had blended and swept over the camp. Paused at the mess to eat an omelette and found a tasty treat inside: a cigarette butt. Just outside the cafeteria I stopped. There was a drone.

I was so used to looking *through* them, but never *at* them. On the other side of a fence, the drone idled on the tarmac in front of a bunker. It stood as tall as I did. Shark-like, with two pectoral fins that extended from its sides like a traditional plane. Yet the stabilizing fins at the tail pointed down in an inverse 'V'. Gray. Gray with white patches: a camouflage of cloud. The most disconcerting thing was its eyelessness. Easy to imagine planes with cockpits and windows and WWII pilots mummified in looping scarves. Not these flying robots, piloted by science and logic. The drone seemed to have a face, but without eyes, it was blank, expressionless. Instead, it "saw" through hypersensitive nodes on the back of its neck, and chin. Drones have no agency; they obey the voices in their heads, clutching close their clusters of bombs: four in each armpit. This type of drone was the Predator, little brother of Reaper. I met its unblinking gaze for a moment. Truly it was a predator, as unfeeling as they wanted us to be. Its job was to hide in clouds or the glare of the sun. To lurk behind bunkers with a Taser. When Predator was a child he was never invited to picnics. His hands were full of missiles that he thought were flowers. He was a strange boy, too quiet. Always muttering to himself and wanting to be older so his bombs would drop. Always rubbing his node on the legs of teachers. No one wants to be your friend, Predator. The only thing *you* know how to do is assassinate people. You think, because you're unmanned, you can cross borders and kill in other lands, and no one will think that is war. You're on the wrong side of history. You could be so noble, flying into radioactive areas, dumping water on thirsty crops, detonating yourself in the eyes of sharknados. But you were seized early, by powerful men, and made a weapon, same as the rest of us.

"Fancy meeting you here, Jones," said the Major. "Dreaming of using one of those soon?" She sipped from a bucket of coffee, and had a take-out meal under one arm. "Ah, sorry, I keep forgetting you don't like the Army banter."

"Afternoon, Major," I said, heart skipping faster. Turning to face her I noticed a few droplets of sweat on her brow but she was otherwise unwilted. "It's true, I prefer smart banter to Army banter."

"Oh, you cheeky sailor," she said, smiling. "So what were you doing?"

"I was imagining what the drone would have been like as a kid in school."

"What an unusual thing to say," she blew on her coffee. "What did you decide?"

"I think he was lonely. Why did we take the people out of planes, anyway?"

"Well, I can answer that question, Jones, but you have to promise not to storm out on me like you did last time. You'll give me a complex."

"Major, your mental health is my highest priority." We shared a smile and our eyes connected for a second before she returned to her coffee and heat rose in my cheeks.

"Walk with me, Jones, and I will share my sweet sweet gems of wisdom." Hard to tell if we were flirting but ego says, *yes*. Perhaps it was just nice to talk to someone who wasn't a giant, hairy dude, for once. "When we send our lonely friend into combat, we don't risk a human life—that's one advantage. And it's cheaper and safer to train a drone operator than a pilot. But perhaps you're interested in the real reason? The true reason?" She glanced conspiratorially over the rim of her coffee cup.

"Major, you promised me gems."

"So I did. It's all about distance, Jones. We started out with swords and spears," she stabbed me in the belly with the corner of her take-out container, "but it was too messy. Far too intimate. We invented crossbows and rifles and now drones, and killing just keeps getting easier."

I couldn't help but glance at her battered helmet, which she always wore, even on the hottest days. She noticed and said, "Yes, Jones, there's nothing saying we can't also do it the hard way, but generally it's getting easier."

This was too dark for me—I wanted to bring us back to the banter. "Maybe in the next war you'll be shooting people with lasers from orbiting space stations."

She grimaced. "I hope this is my last war, Jones. If I can get the Female

Engagement Team off the ground and hand it over to someone competent, I'd be happy. I've done the soldier thing long enough—I have a kid. People keep telling me I should go be a mother."

I looked at her in astonishment—I'd had no idea. Wanted to ask her more but a siren drowned me out. There were loudspeakers dotted all over the base-town. It took a second for the noise to "warm up" and build to full volume and you were never sure what you were hearing, until the sirens were deafening, mewling like dinosaur babies. ROCKET ATTACK. ROCKET ATTACK.

The Taliban were firing rockets at the camp—we threw ourselves on our bellies and covered our faces—shrapnel blasts upwards, slain soldiers take it above the crotch. The Major was scanning for the closest bunker. I was scanning the Major, all the way up from the properly bloused pant legs, past the bulge of her pistol holster, the curves of her helmet.

WHOOOMPH of the rocket as it crashed into the camp and exploded nearby: a deafening roar overhead and the ground swelling like waves. A tinkling rain of falling gravel, and its feel, like hail, on our backs and legs. Even the Major gasped—I cursed with a sailor's eloquence, palms dripping sweat.

More rockets coming down—a storm. "Stay low, Jones, and follow me," said the Major, tugging at my arm. She'd spotted a bunker across the road; we sprinted and dove in, for a second a tumble of uniforms and helmets and pistols and our bodies beneath all that. More booms, more bangs, rumbling and secondary explosions and more raining gravel and the siren screaming ROCKET ATTACK—ROCKET ATTACK and the bombs kept on coming, maybe this was the Taliban's lucky day, the happy bomb tumbling through a DFAC's chimney, a massacre on the boardwalk, but we were safe, we were alive, with nothing to look at but each other in that bunker with all the world going to hell on the other side of the concrete, with her hair loose from her helmet and her lower lip just a bit swollen from our desperate dive.

"Are you all right, Jones?"

"Yes, Major, I'm fine. Are you OK? You're bleeding."

"I'm sure it's nothing. My dinner's out there getting cold, though—who knows how long we'll be stuck in here now."

"Let me look at your lip. I have a certain… fabric… which has amazing properties." I extracted a single sheet of Canadian toilet paper from the dwindling roll I carried in my pocket.

She saw the roll and laughed, "I don't need your toilet paper, Jones, I'm fine."

"Major, this is no time to be tough—you're injured. If you keep laughing, you'll split your whole lip right in half."

Finally, she stopped smiling, sat still and let me dab the blood from her lip. A taboo territory, almost fraternization, with only the flimsiest pretence of an injury.

"Am I gonna make it, Doctor?" she asked.

"I hope so."

You might be thinking this was all going really smooth but don't get it twisted. Wasn't five seconds later when the Major remembered who she was and cleared her throat. And that reminded me of who I was, and the main difference wasn't that she outranked me, it was that she was beautiful and I wasn't. Some wizard cursed me and stuck my essence in this golem's body, blocky and heavy with stone columns for legs and hands carved into fists. I blushed so hard I'm sure it showed through the sunburn, then sagged to the ground across the bunker from the Major, staring at everything but her bright, curious eyes.

With so many bombs crashing onto the camp, and the sketchiness of those Russian-made munitions, there were invariably rockets which landed but didn't detonate: unexploded ordinance. Soon engineering teams would arrive to BiP, Blow in Place, the duds. Considering there might be casualties and fires across the base—hell, we might be stuck together for an hour or more. She called the TOC to let them know we were marooned until the "all clear."

After a few minutes she spoke, "Got any food on you?" and I tossed her a small bag of pistachios, which she ate and washed down with a bottle of water.

After a few more minutes she spoke again, "You're not angry."

"What's that?"

"You're not my first bunker-buddy, Jones. Most of the guys take it pretty personally, to have rockets fired at them. They start swearing, froth at the mouth a bit, you know?"

"I'll work on my froth."

She frowned and threw a pistachio shell at me. "Stop hiding. We're trapped, you might as well talk. Why aren't you angry?"

I flicked the shell off my collar. "I'm not angry because I paid attention to the Int briefings. We know the people firing the rockets aren't Taliban. They're just poor and need a few bucks. I hear the Taliban offer them a year's wages— somebody offered me that, I'd take a few cracks at Kandahar Airfield myself."

"Don't let the General hear you say that, Jones."

"Course not. Yes, Sir! HUA, Sir! Three bags full, Sir!" I clicked my heels together in a mock salute; the Major hid a smile, or a frown, behind her hand. Yes, I was never a true believer; the long war had made us decadent with compassion.

Sometimes the rockets hit home. They crashed into the boardwalk, in the center of KAF, where sutler-shops and crap-restaurants catered to the soldiers, and sometimes the troops played ball hockey when the sun dimmed, though I was always on shift for that. The rockets often landed, curiously, onto the relatively small Romanian section of the base. Sometimes the duds would detonate before they could be properly BIPed and take out an engineering team. Sometimes the munitions would not strike the earth, but plop and splash into the poo pond, metal turds settling to the bottom.

"It doesn't make me a bad soldier," I said.

"Say again?"

"I'm not angry because I see that it's more complicated than good guys and bad guys."

"Of course it is. Only an idiot comes to Afghanistan thinking that things are black and white. The same idiots who think that we can win the war with one glorious charge. Unfortunately, these are the people running the show." Things had gotten spicy again—now we were critiquing our leadership. She unholstered her pistol to inspect if it had gotten dirty in our tumble. "We're yesterday's soldiers, but this is today's war."

At this exact moment, a curious robot, about as high as my knee, rumbled past the bunker on little wheels, thin arms outstretched. It had an antenna on its head, like a feather. When the Major saw the robot, her face lit with a shy grin, and for a second, as in that moment when I dabbed her lip, she seemed like a girl. The smile melted away quickly; I needed it back.

"What's so funny? The explosive disposal robot?"

"You ever see that movie, Wall-E, Jones? I just remembered the time I took my kid to the theatre and he clapped and cheered for the hardworking robot every time he came on the screen."

"It's a pretty cool little robot, helping us not get blown up. If I had to guess, I'd say when it was in grade school it had all sort of friends, and even kissed the teacher once."

She suppressed a giggle and it sounded like a windchime of icicles—I wish I had recorded it so I could listen to it on a loop. "You and your robot school, Jones. Spend a lot of time thinking about that?"

"Every waking moment."

"Is that what you scribble about in your journal?"

"You know about the journal?"

"I have my eye on you, Jones."

"Are you watching me with drones?"

"What's in the journal?"

"It's embarrassing."

"Tell me, I'm bored."

"It's personal—"

"Really, super bored."

"Poems."

In that second the whole base fell quiet, the poo pond stopped bubbling, even Wall-E paused as he puttered toward a nearby dud. The Major gaped like I'd grown a second head—classic Army reaction. I blushed again, worse than the first time.

"Read me a poem, Jones."

"They're ugly,"

"I don't care."

Gallows Humor

She wanders the marketplace
whispering to her swollen belly
when the roadside bomb explodes

wrenches her legs off below the knees
her blood turns the sand to mud
hangs in the air like a shroud

We sent a helicopter for her
the men of the village
didn't let the medical team
get close

I made jokes to ease our impotence
"she's a gusher all right"
"check out her O-face"
as she screamed
her life away

"Oh, I remember that day—that was the worst day." The Major closed her eyes and wrapped her arms around herself. "We'd been here for about a month. All of us watching, but nothing we could do."

"I told you it was ugly."

We were both quiet for a second. When the Major spoke her voice was hard and angry. "This is exactly why we need initiatives like the Female Engagement Team. All the men in that village making the choice for the woman, letting her die. We need to talk to women more—I say it every damn day but no one's listening. Send teams of female soldiers into the villages. Talk to the women—hear what's actually happening. Get them the medicine and the fabric and doctors that they need."

"Hey, don't take it out on me. I like the idea—I could see you running one of those."

"I did run one of those teams, Jones. The first Female Engagement Team. I was a Captain. It was my second tour, about four years ago."

"Holy shit, it's story time, isn't it? I love story time."

"Listen up, Jones, this one is close to me. I stopped talking about that tour. It's like the war becomes this thing you have to perform for people and I get tired of it."

"Sounds like I'm finally going to get some of those gems of wisdom you promised."

"My second tour I was chosen to be the section commander of the first Female Engagement Team. I was so happy when I heard I'd been picked. I threw the baby at the husband and jumped right on the train—I was going to fight for *women*. I had a team of absolute *femme fatales*. We patrolled in Dand district, at the village level. When we rolled into a village on the back of a LAV, bristling with guns—should have seen their jaws drop. Women finally had someone to talk to! They weren't allowed into the shuras, they couldn't speak unless spoken to first, and they couldn't travel without a male relative. Jones, you should have heard them open up, once they started going—the translators could hardly keep pace. They wanted medicine. They wanted schoolbooks. They wanted cloth to make clothes—it was all so fucking *reasonable*!" The Major gestured wildly with her hands, like she wanted to dig her fingers into men's throats.

"Well, what the hell happened, Maj? If the FET was so awesome why don't we have a bunch of them now?"

The Major flipped her helmet over and over in her hands. "It was great for a couple of months. We made real progress in the villages. The men called us witches but the women sneaked us into their homes, and organized private women-only shuras, and let us hold their children. Then we started hearing reports that women who met with us were getting beaten by their husbands afterwards—one guy cut off his wife's breasts. Another woman came back from a woman's *shura* and someone had killed her baby, cut off his fingers, and stuck them in his mouth. You think Afghanistan has been at war for a long time? Women have been at war *forever*. Don't ask me why I care more about these women than I do my own family; that's a stupid question. What matters is that we inspired a few of them to fight for themselves. What matters is we brought the medicine and the fabric and the schoolbooks—hell we even found a teacher for one village, and a place to hold lessons for girls." She dropped the helmet in the sand. A few hundred yards away, an adorable robot laid a satchel of explosives next to a smoking rocket. "And then it all went to shit."

"Another one of those worst days, I'm guessing."

"Yes, a terrible day." Her voice had dropped an octave and gone cold, like we were giving an official report, or reading lines from the combat chat. "It started when a government official invited me to his home for a *shura*. I left my section on the street in front of a walled compound with guard towers. There were men patrolling the tops of the walls with AK47s. I didn't like the defensive position but we were there on good faith, building trust. It was customary to go unarmed to these meetings, and remove your helmet, to show courage, which the Afghans respect—this was back before they started swinging axes at our bare heads in *shuras*. I was a bit suspicious when a servant led me to what looked like a bedroom. That's where the official met me wearing a loose white robe. He was the only Afghan I'd seen with a gut, and his beard went all the way down to it. He ran at me and tried to grope me through my body armor, smacking his lips at my face. I looked around for my translator, but she was gone. Later I learned she'd been shot. I pushed the official away and yelled at him in English. That made him angry."

Beneath the cold tone, an undercurrent of rage. "Are you sure you want to hear the rest, Jones? You look pretty uncomfortable."

"I want to know the rest."

"Good. After I yelled at him he spun around and backhanded me and I crashed into the wall. I could figure without the translator that he was trying to fuck me. His robe had opened up and his dick was poking through the hair. I grabbed this helmet right here," she held it up so I could admire the dents, "and started swinging. I kept swinging too, no matter the crunching noises, until he was dead and ugly and smashed and I heard the sounds of gunfire. The village had turned on us."

"Holy hell, Major. Remind me not to piss you off."

"Never ever piss me off, Jones. I ran out of that room, and out of that compound, and the FET was pinned down with small arms fire from the guard towers. I pulled out my pistol, jammed the bloody helmet on my head, and charged up the stairs to the outer wall and shot two men. I rejoined the team and we started exfiltrating from the village, and radioing for help, but men kept shooting at us out of windows. Once we saw a group of women in burqas and we called for them to help us, hide us. They pulled AK47s out and started shooting—they were men, disguised. It got real bloody—I lost two of my sisters in that attack, before we flung a grenade into the middle of them. I don't know how many we took out. A lot. We fought our way to the edge of the village where the helo was coming. We were carrying our dead."

She stopped for a long minute and was quiet, head slumped forward on her chest. "You got a cigarette on you, Jones? I could use a smoke."

"Sorry, I don't."

"Goddamnit." She sighed and pressed her cheek against the cool concrete. "Those were the toughest women I ever knew, Jones. Warriors. Friends. I think about them every day. The Colonel gave me a fucking medal. I was on the promotion track after that. But the real trophy was this." She kicked at her helmet where it nestled in the sand. "I grieved, Jones. My dead sisters, that village's betrayal, and the whole idea of the Female Engagement Team, which our *leadership* dismantled after the attack. They said we tried to change things too fast." Then, in the saddest, loneliest voice I'd ever heard from her, "This place has broken my heart so many times."

I wanted to hold her but this was forbidden. I tried with words, instead, and said simply, "I believe in you." She nodded, but seemed done with speaking for now, back in the past with her dead Valkyries.

A dull, percussive thud. The engineers had blown the dud. They would need to investigate again to make sure the work was complete, but this kind of disposal was routine. Soon the "all clear" would sound; we would return to the TOC and put our faces on and be strangers again.

After a moment I asked, "Do you think, after the war, when we look back at it, that we'll remember how lonely it was?"

She looked up at me and said, "Yes, Jones, we'll always remember."

The Major and I stared right into each other's eyes. Some defenses had slipped and her monster was glaring through the pupils, too. It was trapped in a small cage, a bear-shaped creature with the head of a fierce owl, screeching and growling even louder than mine, more frantic. In the background the sirens were warming up, the sirens were shouting ALL CLEAR, the sirens were saying go back to work, you lazy bastards, the war hasn't stopped.

But neither of us moved.

18

BELL HAD TRACKED THE TRAJECTORY of the rockets back to their launchpads, but the rocketeers hid in a busy marketplace and we lost PID. This upset him terribly. When the Major and I found him, he was slumped over his desk, cradling his head in the nook of his elbow, hiding his face with his delicate fingers. Half his five monitors had gone to screensaver.

"They got away again," he moaned, fresh bags under his eyes. Performing grief for not killing someone was a classic Bell move. This one time, he was *sure* that someone we were watching with a drone's infrared camera had a rifle. Turns out it was just a splash of warmth on a car seat. He'd been inconsolable.

"I'm sure you'll get another chance, Bell," I said.

"You don't get it. Those ragheads were in my sights."

"You wanna talk to the padre, get some counselling?"

"Fuck you, Jones." He buried himself in his email.

"You've got assets doing nothing, Bell," said the Major. "Pass the Predator back to the Battle Group, and send the Heron to check out Sahar. Brief Jones on your shift; I'll get someone to grab you a meal."

Bell grumbled, and transmitted the Major's direction to Crazy Jay, our drone-man with the shouting problem. Crazy Jay was crestfallen about the bloodless afternoon as well; mutters of "ragheads" and "*hajis*" echoed from his corner. Jay had once told me about a dream he had where he slept on a mound of dead Afghan.

The drone floated over mud roads and dry riverbeds. Bell met me at the big map (Kool, my shadow, lurked nearby) and briefed me on each Significant Activity of the shift. The rocket attack, two shoot and scoots in Panjwa'i, and a curious event in Dand.

"You're gonna love this SIGACT, Jones. This stuff is why I get up in the morning." Bell rubbed his hands. "We had a medical evacuation for a wounded Afghan policeman near FOB SHOJA. We got him to the hospital here in KAF at 1334 this afternoon, and he was stable. What happened, you wonder?"

I did wonder.

"This guy was a policeman working with the Afghan Army. They searched a compound here," Bell pointed to the map, "and our man sneaks into the women's quarters. He finds a chest of clothes and starts digging." Bell acted out the motion of digging into a chest of clothes, his earlier grief gone. "Well, one of the soldiers caught our guy rubbing the undies all over his face. That didn't go over too well. They dragged the panty sniffer into the street and held him down. One of them grabs a rocket launcher." Here Bell paused dramatically. "I know what you're thinking, Jones. We're about to see some good old Afghan justice here, but why a rocket launcher when you're surrounded by your own soldiers? You gotta think outside the box on this one. What do you imagine happened? Any guesses? C'mon, Jones, I need this."

"I'm drawing a blank here."

"You got any guesses, Kool?"

"Not a fucking clue."

"They clubbed him with it! Yes! Clubbed the shit outta him. Broke his ribs and his femur. Then they called us for a medevac. Great, eh?"

It was one of our better handovers, hit me in the funny bone. "Sometimes the war gives us these little gifts."

"Damn straight."

Pattern of Life (POL)

We watched for people digging in the road, too many FAMs with guns on the same motorcycle, mobs with pitchforks and rifles. But we often watched for change.

A market that bustled yesterday is quiet today. A normally trafficked bridge is empty. All the cars on the highway push to the extreme edge of the road, despite lack of construction. Sometimes the locals knew where the bombs were, if we were clever enough to see.

We thought we were. Yet how can you watch POL without disturbing it, when your camera is buzzing like a lawnmower in the air, and covered in missiles?

Meanwhile, the drone arrived at Sahar's hut. This time he wasn't in the field, he was perched on a stone wall that ran along the street. He wore one of those white robes that we always called "man-jammies." This unarmed drone had a better camera and we could see details, short-cropped brown hair, the sad first few pubes of a teen's beard. He had eyes, lips, ears—all the parts. Last time I'd seen him he was just a blob of pixels with a dark hole for a mouth. This time he glanced furtively up and down the street, and sometimes at the sky. Right at us.

An older man with a better beard arrived on a motorcycle and stopped next to the wall in a cloud of dust. He handed Sahar a small package, which Sahar tucked into his shirt. More surreptitious glances. The older man drove away.

"What do you think, Jones?" asked the Major.

"He's networking," I said.

"He's conspiring," said Bell.

"Niner this is Charlie Foxtrot, over," came a voice over the radio, after a screech of static.

"Charlie Foxtrot, Niner. Go ahead, over." A signaller, Alice, a reservist who studied Sartre on tedious night shifts, answered back on our behalf.

"We have a report of a disturbance at the village of Mushan. Request Close Air Support, over." The metal voice grated a grid reference and Alice jotted it down.

"See ya later, Sahar," I said. We wheeled the drone en route to Mushan; the Major joining Bell, Kool and I at the map table, as we stared at the main screen.

Infantry guys like Kool prefer it when the enemy is right in front of them, clearly labelled, wearing a different uniform than theirs. But this was a gray war; the Taliban weren't all bad. I mean, sure they toppled the buddhas of Bamiyan, and there was the time they took a dozen road-workers and chopped off their ears and noses in the middle of the marketplace. But still, not all bad—listen for a second. If you were an Afghan, and your neighbor stole your goat, you don't have a lot of options for justice. The court systems were corrupt and inefficient, and the Taliban's shadow courts, practicing Sharia law, might be the way to go. Don't underestimate the value of a little stability—something we never gave to Afghanistan with our drones and Special Forces ninjas.

In Mushan, they were stoning a woman.

There was an open space for market stalls in the center of the village. One of the largest buildings had a long wall, which marked the end of the communal space. The crowd was thirty-five or forty people, and they were spread in a semicircle. There was a woman in the center, with her back to the wall. Her hair was loose, long and black. She was young and strong.

It was difficult to see the stones in the air—they were too small, moving too fast. The human eye was a little quicker than the drone's. But we could see flecks of black for a frame or two as the stones flew. And we could see the stones clatter and bounce off the wall behind her. This drone's camera had color—there was blood on her face.

"Adulteress," muttered Bell. "That's the only crime that leads to stoning." Many of the soldiers in the room had wives. Most worried about their fidelity.

"Sometimes they stone women for getting raped," said the Major, grabbing the radio, her voice metallic: "Charlie Foxtrot, this is Niner."

"Charlie Foxtrot," responded the signaller at the other end.

"You will send troops, at least a platoon, immediately to the Mushan village square. A crowd is killing a woman with stones. Prevent it and report on the casualty. Niner out."

"Major, are you serious?" Bell protested. "You can't intervene. This is their culture."

I haven't heard this fight before. The Major wasn't budging. "We *can* intervene and we will. We have the Rules of Engagement to use force to protect civilians."

"Protect them from who, Major? Their own government? Themselves? I mean, just because we have the ROE doesn't mean we have to use them."

"Shut up, Bell," said the Major. "This coming from the guy who wanted to kill Sahar for hoeing potatoes. You don't think I can make a judgement on this 'cultural practice'? Watch me."

What was astonishing was the rage on the faces of the crowd. It was mostly men but there were women in there, too, even some crones. The young woman was defiant, dodging and deflecting projectiles with her hands, and yelling back. But they didn't let her leave the circle—someone always threw her back against the wall.

"You're gonna lose the whole village," Bell muttered.

"Fuck this village," said the Major.

The stones were getting faster; the young men were getting into it. They would sprint up a few yards away then hurl the stone as hard as they could. Too fast for the camera: we were lucky if we could see a single frame with the stones in the air. But we could see her stagger.

And because we couldn't see the rocks anymore it was like her wounds were springing from nowhere. Like she was being eaten from the inside out. A blow to the pelvis. The kneecap. The temple. And after that last strike to her temple, she couldn't dodge the same; her face was wet and streaked with tears.

"Looks a bit like a gangbang doesn't it?" snickered Kool.

"Killing is not sex," said the Major, automatically.

The mouth. That was the worst to watch. One second we were looking at a beautiful, harried woman. The next second her mouth was a bloody gash and all her front teeth were smashed out. She tried to yell again but her mouth was a different shape, and the words came out as bloody bubbles.

The problem with pity is that it happens too late. It should have happened before the first stone was thrown. But the crowd was feeling it now. That rock to the mouth—it made the killing *real*. The mob's tosses were getting lazy. Her beauty was despoiled, maybe that was punishment enough? She was crawling through the sand, collecting her teeth.

But she was too dazed to protect herself. Sometimes when people are dying they get caught in a simple, repetitive action. *I have to keep hoeing this field. I have to take my boots off. I have to touch my brother's hand. I have to find my teeth.* All other concerns melt away and we are reduced to our bare wiring, our circuits corroded and sparking.

Pity is a bastard the way it turns on you. The few stones still in flight were hitting home. One of her eyes went dark. A wound in her scalp appeared and the scalp bleeds more than anything. Now pity demanded that the execution be finished. The exhausted crowd had screamed and hurled all their rage away. They were just normal people after all, fruit vendors and farmers, mostly. Even the cruelest had lost their appetites for violence. So it was the kindest who picked up stones.

"About time," said the Major. She looked as cold and hard and lonely as a mountain.

She'd noted the Canadian soldiers who arrived in a Light Armored Vehicle and drove it right onto the square. Soldiers leaped from the vehicle, ten of them, burly in their body armor, helmets, webbing, weapons. They ran toward the woman and made a wall of flesh between her and the villagers. This foreign intrusion provoked the young men; they threw a few stones at the soldiers. Black streaks bounced off helmets and body armor. The soldiers gritted their teeth when a stone struck, but none of them fired.

Heroic restraint, they called it. There was a medal for this sort of thing. The platoon commander picked up the shattered woman in his arms and carried her gently to the armored vehicle as soldiers circled, making a wall of broad backs and chests. With the entertainment gone, the crowd began to break up, flinching away from the soldiers' stares. Maybe the executioners were afraid of the C7s, but the shy way the farmers and fruit vendors started dropping their stones, as if surprised to find such foul objects in their hands, made it seem they were ashamed.

But for all the pain and tension and ugliness of that moment, I was damned proud of those soldiers, though if they had been ten minutes earlier… They filed back into the LAV and the nine-liner came.

MEDICAL EVACUATION REQUEST
Location: 41R QQ 385 457
Radio frequency and name: 179.144550 VHF, Charlie Company
Number of casualties and severity: 1 critically injured
Special Equipment required: Hoist
Patient requires litter or ambulatory: Litter
Security of pick-up site: Area secure
Method of marking pick-up site: Smoke, green
Patient nationality and status: Local National
Chemical biological or nuclear threat: None

"Let's get that helo in the air," said the Major, her eyes burning with maniac intensity. "Halima. Yes. We'll call her Halima."

19.

I RETURNED TO THE BARRACKS and Kool had made it back to the room a few minutes before; he was standing in front of our shared mirror, staring himself in the eyes. Some flicker crossed his view and he snapped the pistol from its holster, grabbed it with both hands, and pointed it as his reflection while pumping the trigger. Had the magazine been loaded, he would have wasted the mirror and blown his reflection's head off. Instead, he cocked his head to the side with a hard look on his face. He was practicing his watching-someone-die face.

"What's up, Jones?" he said over his shoulder.

"Is that shit necessary?" I asked him.

He turned from his practice to scoff. "Of fucking course it is. Quickdraws are one of the core infantry skills."

"You look like a goof."

"Fuck you, Jones." He turned back to the mirror.

Army guys keep saying that to me for some reason. "Kool, I'm turning out the light in ten minutes so I can sleep for a few hours. Go to the bathroom if you want to keep wanking it."

"This isn't *wanking*, you fucking pillow-biter." Another imagined foe perished in the mirror. Kool experimented with a sneer. "Tell your friend if he lays a fucking finger on me, I'll shoot his nuts off."

I laughed and sat on the edge of my bunk. "Is that what this is about? Feeling a bit inadequate? I have to admit my heart went out to you when you were pinned under that bar, your little hands flailing, as you squealed like a piggy."

Kool's face flushed an ugly purple, "Yeah, you guys are strong but can it stop a bullet? I'd fucking kill you all." He shot the mirror in several places, like enemies were leaping from windows.

I laughed again. "Poor Kool. Got his ego bruised and now he wants to kill someone to feel better." He glared at me, but I continued anyway. "Man, they fed you Army guys a lot of horseshit, didn't they?"

"They taught us to Destroy, Clear, and Neutralize, not to suck dick. We achieve the fucking mission with maximum destruction. You fags will never have my respect." Kool holstered the pistol, bristling. "And what the fuck you talking about? I ain't bruised. I'm immune to pain." I noticed Kool wasn't wearing his boots (as ordered) and that the legs of his combat trousers had bunched around his socks—like a kid who borrowed his Dad's uniform. I remembered when I was his age, maybe ten years ago, how badly I wanted people to admire me.

"Immune to pain? That must be handy," I said.

Kool frowned. His ears stuck out too far. "That shit today. The woman in the village. That was pretty fucked up, right?"

"Halima. Yes, it was horrible."

"You seen a lot of stuff like that?" I got the impression he wanted me to say something tough and muscular like a grizzled sergeant might. *It gets easier* or, *skank had it comin'* or, *focus on your mission*. He wanted me to shore up his crumbling tower of lies, years of Army propaganda, exercises, ugly banter, man-posturing, gruelling physical training. Take him back to a pre-grief world where a soldier could do the good work of killing without reflection, proper little killbots.

But Kool was my ward, and it was my job to educate his ignorant ass. "I'm going to visit Halima in the hospital tomorrow. The woman from the village. You can come if you like."

He goggled. "Fuck that. You're fucking sick, you know?"

"Ten minutes, Kool." I grabbed my towel and walked across the hall to the showers.

Just because you have a roommate doesn't mean you have someone to talk to. I craved the Major's company, but she was in a different, women-only barracks, with a slightly less raunchy shower. Otherwise, there was my Sasquatch pal, but he was getting eaten alive by his own worries. Literally, as the clumps of orange hair around the back step indicated. And there was TicTac, the Coachbag, huggable as a cactus; I hadn't spoken to him since he'd crushed Kool under the barbell.

The next morning when I knocked, a bloodshot eye appeared in the crack of the door.

"We working out, you giant bastard?" I asked him.

TicTac edged the door open, enough to reveal a grin and a smattering of pornstars on the walls. "Jones, there you are, friend! You are here for church, yes? I asked lesser man yesterday to be spotter and was terrible. He kept trying to help me. I wanted to bite his hand off."

"I never help at all, even if you're struggling," I said. "Secretly, I want you to crush yourself."

"This is pressure I need from workout buddy." We laughed, but it trailed off.

"You almost killed Kool the other day, Man." I ran my fingers through my short-cropped black hair, stiff as boar bristles. "That sort of stunt could get you sent home."

TicTac cleared his throat; his look was almost sad. "Yes, like good little soldiers we are supposed to hate idea of going home. What could be worse? Sleeping in queen-sized bed, air-conditioning, supermarkets with proper food and whole milk. I have almost forgotten how beer tastes, Jones." His upper lip twitched, twisted as he opened the door a little more. "Every day I wake up in barracks and is assholes everywhere. I have been called fag at least thousand times, often by puny douchebag. And if I give beating I am punished, sent home, which they tell me again and again is shame."

I waited. I needed more. An apology, or something.

"Shame got me here in first place. War was going on for eight years and all men in Unit had gone but me. Walking around in dress uniform there is big bald patch where medals should be. If you have not served you are not a *man*. And now I stay here eating poo pond and enduring jabs of lesser men because of fear of shame. Perhaps tomorrow I go home and have bad nightmares and tell no one because of shame. If I was killer in war I hide because of shame. If I was not killer, I also hide because of shame. I am tired of it, all of it, is horseshit as far as I can see."

TicTac was grinding his teeth. I said, "This may not make a lot of sense to you but I get enough violence in my life already—I don't need it in *church*. Not to mention, Kool is my subordinate, and we don't get to pick them. We work with the shit we're given and protect our subordinates, even the dickheads." I breathed deeply. "You know what I need."

The grinding continued. TicTac seemed to be weighing me, eyes flickering over my shoulders, arms, neck. Eventually, he spoke, "You want me to promise not to crush your little peon? Fine. For your friendship, Jones, I will endure insect." His face grew very hard and strained. "To a point."

"Now go down to my room and give him a hug."

"What? You serious, Jones?"

"Of course not. He'd shoot you for sure."

TicTac leaned in closer, a sudden grin lighting his features. "That Kool kid is very annoying. For some reason he thinks I am homosexual—he has not seen my room is shrine to beautiful women." The dead-eyed women on the walls and ceilings had evolved since last time. Now not only did sticky notes cover their nether bits, but he had x'ed the eyes with black marker.

"Why'd you kill all the eyes?" I asked.

"I am not some pervert who likes to be stared at, Jones. Don't you find photos little bit creepy, how they never blink?"

"Well, now they look like dead bodies."

"Oh, you poor man, got drones on brain." By the end of the workout our arms were busting through the skin. "One more exercise," said the Coachbag, and he led me to the back of the gym, an old, ruined boardwalk with piles of tires and heaps of chain. He walked about twenty yards away and hucked a medicine ball at my head. A leather pumpkin, stuffed with sand.

When the ball slammed into my hands my whole skeleton shuddered. TicTac's laugh boomed. I was standing in yesterday's marketplace, in the crowd, considering the stone in my hand. "What, can't make it this far?" TicTac taunted. I growled and heaved the ball straight at his face.

TicTac was knocked back two steps. He wasn't used to being pushed around. I called, "C'mon, Nancy—you resting already?"

Blowing sand and testosterone on the boardwalk: inflated egos and masochism. We threw overhead, arms chopping like battleaxes, to nail the triceps more. Dust rose from our scuffling feet. Dropped balls banged boards. We would throw the medicine ball until one of us relented, or our bodies failed.

After a few dozen tosses an exasperated TicTac gasped, "What's gotten… into you, Jones?" and fired the ball at my neck like a rocket. Sweat and dust had turned to mud streaking down his face.

I caught the ball with a snarl and hurled it back. My hands were starting to bruise. "I watched a woman… get stoned yesterday."

The ball smacked his chest, driving out the air. "What… she smoked some hash or something?"

"No!" I howled, catching the ball. "Villagers threw rocks at her." I sent the boulder back.

"I see." The ball caromed off Tictac's chest into his larms. "Did she die?"

Our pitches were getting weaker. After each throw we took a step closer to one another. "Troops showed up… at the last minute." I threw and took another step.

He caught and lurched closer. "You should be happy, right?"

"I don't know… Bell thought we should have let them finish." A step closer.

"What do you think?" The mighty Coachbag was flagging.

My arms were well past burning, almost through inferno, approaching numbness. "I think Bell… can get fucked."

TicTac nodded, the sun beating his bald head. "Agreed." We tossed the ball a few more times, getting closer and weaker. "Did you see her eyes?"

A step closer. "Her eyes?" My breath was ragged; the air was thick with shit-dust. I wasn't in that crowd anymore; I was no longer chucking stones at a woman, at Halima. I was too exhausted to be angry. My hands were throbbing and bruised black.

TicTac took a step closer and threw the ball. He looked ready to collapse. "I saw my father's eyes… after he died. He looked… afraid."

I caught the ball. "I saw her eyes," and took another step. We had finally reached each other. I handed TicTac the weight and he let it drop to the ground then clasped my shoulders instead. "They were like that," I said.

20.

THE CAMP REEKED LIKE A PIT OF BODIES. Give me a field of flowers, potpourri, a sizzling steak. On the way to the hospital, I paused at the bank of the poo pond and enjoyed the little signs soldiers had posted: "Area Fifty-Poo," "Lifeguard on Dootie," "Willy Wonka's Chocolate Factory," and "Lake Shitticaca." Across the road, sixteen Romanian soldiers sat in a circle cleaning their rifles, pulling wads of cotton through the barrels with metal rods. They had lost yet another comrade in a rocket attack; there was an air of siege. This close to the shit-lake, they kept a meticulous camp; they shepherded the sullied cotton balls with vigilance. I was exhausted from the workout, with swollen hands, but that wasn't the reason I dragged my feet.

Oh, yes. The pelted lady. I felt her pain radiating, like plutonium, as I ghosted through hallways of green scrubs and sanitary gloves. At her doorway, I paused. There she was, the lady from the drone, a mess of tubes and bandages. I remembered seeing her long, black hair in the wind. But it was shorn to treat her injuries, which crisscrossed her face like the stitches in a scarecrow. The stitches ran from her eyes like tears and disappeared into her mouth. She was too weak to whimper, under the sheet, an opiate coma.

"The doctors don't know if she'll live," said the Major in a flat voice. She was sitting on a stool in the corner, helmet under the chair, spine stiff and hands on her knees. I didn't answer, just sat on the floor beside her, close enough to touch. It was enough to be near her, the scent of lemon.

Finally, eyes closed, I said, "Would you say we did our best to save her?"

"Yes, it just wasn't good enough." I glanced at her and it seemed she was holding back.

"You want to tell me it's not my fault?"

"No, we're past that. Besides, I didn't see you throwing any stones." She leaned closer. "What the hell happened to your hands, Jones?"

Yes, I suppose they were in rough shape, swollen and bruised, with callouses peeling off and pain in the wrists. But it felt ridiculous to complain in front of Halima, whose only evidence of life was a rattling breath.

"It's nothing, Major."

"Looks like something to me. No macho stuff. Give it here." She pulled my hand close to her face to investigate; her touch made me shiver. Tiny wrinkles near her eyes spiderwebbed. "You need to take better care of yourself, OK? We can't afford any injuries. How did this happen?"

"Throwing a medicine ball with TicTac. I was upset." An expression flickered over her face, but it was gone too fast for me to read it. She still had hold of my hand. "I'm fine, really."

She released her grasp and her voice was stern again, the Major from the TOC, "Perhaps you boys have taken this far enough? The military doesn't look kindly on self-inflicted injuries."

"It helped." Then we were quiet for another moment, as I savoured the way her fingers felt on my hand, the two of us staring at Halima, the shallow rise and fall of her chest as she breathed. "What happens to her now?"

The Major sighed. "Assuming she lives? We've made some inquiries through the Afghan police. "Her hometown, her husband, they all consider her dead. No other town will take her." She massaged her temples. "She might beg. She might try to sell herself."

Halima was under a thin sheet. Her perfect, dainty feet were exposed. A young woman's feet. Beyond that, a ruin of bruises and welts. But I could only stare at her feet. Flawless. Ten little toes and a delicate ankle. A whisper of tendons. A freckle.

On Kindness

The Major always said we should act with our highest integrity but never mentioned the price tag. Turns out Bell was right—the village never welcomed our troops again. I remember when our soldiers arrived to stop the stoning, how proud I felt.

But all we'd given her was a nasty scrap of her old life. Maybe death was better.

Halima, the mutilated woman with the human feet. A casualty of that other older war, Halima the scarecrow—the first of my specters. Halima whose crime was loving, whose punishment was life. She taught me hard wisdom: sometimes kindness is cruelty.

"You're crying," said the Major, and her voice was choked. I was shaking too hard to answer. "Stop it, Jones, or you'll get me started." Her eyes were welling, a blink away from tears. She slid from the chair to face me—we were both blurry to the other—and touched my cheek, saying, "Please stop, I can't—" in a kind voice but I couldn't stop and she blinked and the tears rolled so fast and hot from her eyes, I thought they might scald us both.

The Major plunged her face into the hollow of my neck. She was my superior but, in a way, I'd given her permission to weep. I wrapped her in my arms and pressed my face into her soft hair. We grieved hard and lonely, leaving damp patches on the other's uniform. Shipwreck and a midnight storm—the sea tossed. Only two survivors, clinging on a driftwood raft.

We held hands, adultery of the fingers. We wiped each other's tears. Had a strong wind pushed us closer, we might have kissed. When she looked up, her eyes were clear. "Let's go, Jones—someone might see us." We had crossed a line, had fraternized, a forbidden thing. I knew all the reasons it was wrong; I didn't give a shit about any of them.

From her bed a few feet away, Halima's breath rattled. I slid the blanket to cover her feet. Here was a woman who had lost everything for forbidden love—would she bless us?

21.

Dear Cynthia,

Apologies for not writing. I'm still in Kandahar, and
not sure if I'll even send this letter, but if I do,
I hope it reaches you well, that you are happy, and
dancing.

Last time I saw you, we were like two drunks whose
passion was a poison. Pure masochism, on both our
parts, a six-month slog of trysts in public restrooms
and laundromats. I wonder, sometimes, if I hurt you
more than you hurt me. I wonder, sometimes, if I came
to Afghanistan to get away from you.

I am trying to remember us in our finest moments. When
we would endure the snow on Tuesday nights and meet
for a Salsa class; you would chuckle at my bumbling
and I was still laughing along with you, then. For I
was always clumsy footed in all angles but this one.

Remember when we toured Boldt castle? He built it for
his sick wife, but she died before it was finished? You
wanted to twirl in the ballroom, but it was behind
the velvet rope? So we broke in, and I held back the
security guards and you danced in your yellow skirt?

Or I was learning a song for you on the piano, and
playing those notes over and over, like a person
trapped, like a person dying? You were dancing with my
roommate, and I knew you liked him more, but I thought
if I could get the notes just right…

We were best when we let ourselves be a boy and a girl.
We were never very good at being two adults together.
So I brought her along, the Cynthia-girl, in a barracks
box I keep on the top bunk. Each day after finishing

my shift I lie in bed and wiggle my toes—this is the sign. The girl pops out of the box and climbs behind the sheet I use as a sun-shade.

"Who are you tonight?" she asks.

"A pirate," I answer.

"Well, where are we?"

"This is my pirate ship," I say, looking around at the metal bunk. "It needs a little work."

You giggle and I say, "Would you like to be a pirate with me?"

"Can I be a ballerina-pirate?"

"Of course. Those are the best pirates."

Because when we were kids with each other it was the only time we were gentle. And in the last few months I've been a knight and a skydiver and a dragon and an astronaut, even a sailor again. Everything but a soldier. And you were with me, and it was innocent, and that was a comfort.

But now I am ready for something new. Tonight the box stays closed. My griefs have compounded; I am letting this one go.

M

22.

MY RELATIVES GREW FANGS and became vampires. Each wanted to suck the last reserves of my energy stockpile, which was already strained by the TOC, the workouts, the Sasquatch, the extra-curricular visits to the hospital. Another helicopter crashed in Helmand, 500 miles away, and I knew that within days a Mom-email would fly into the window, a hideous bat. "Please write soon, and tell me you're OK. I'm worried." I usually tried to be kind to my Mom but the idea of spending a single calorie on her, or any person, made me grind my teeth. *Leave me alone; I've worked nonstop for five months straight.*

The goal was to get into such a rhythm that a week or two would disappear. Just pad the routine of work/gym/sleep enough to kill the hours. Sometimes I'd get a little surge of juice and write a letter or two, like the one above, never sent. Sit with a bucket of coffee in the Canada House bunker and challenge a stranger to a game of chess. Argue about killing a teenage boy. Wander to the boardwalk and eat a soggy pizza at TGI Fridays. Crush a book on the e-reader. On Sundays, there was a bazaar at the edge of the camp where Afghan entrepreneurs sold chipped jewelry and pirated DVDs. Crack the laptop and watch the same-old Arnold Schwarzenegger movie: muscleman battles giant snakes, decapitates wizard.

Perhaps five days blurred by before I noticed the speaking stone: this time when Noah placed it on the back stoop it felt like another email burning in the inbox—each day I dropped off Styrofoam containers of omelettes and cucumbers and the occasional meatloaf outside his stinkhole, what more did he want? *A friend, maybe? A favor?* Damnit.

By midnight the wind had swept the stink out into the desert, and the moon was bright. I left Kool in charge of the TOC for the first time (he hooted and cracked his knuckles) and joined the shadows. No tanks rumbled down the streets, but a breeze from the *ghar* actually felt cold. Occasionally, snipers, in their towers along the walls, scanned inside and outside the camp with their floodlights, blasting the shadows into long, lean forms. We had only started searching inwardly, like this, since the Taser Rapist arrived.

At the engineering compound the gates were not locked—who would be crazy enough to steal one of these vehicles, surrounded by soldiers? Like many in the desert I was only a thief of water, as I crept past the main engineering bunker, and between rows of vehicles that carried bridges on their backs, others that could unfurl instant roads, the occasional armored bulldozer. At first, I thought Noah hadn't made it. "Stood up by a goddamn Sasquatch," I muttered. "Fucker couldn't figure out the time…"

The moon was getting higher and twice the spirits bolted when the searchlight passed over the compound, but eventually one of the shadows of a Stryker coalesced into my friend.

"Sorry I'm late," said Noah.

"Shhh," I responded. "Whispers only, if you can." He nodded. "We need to find a hose."

Should have been a funny sight: he was bent nearly in half, sniffing the ground like a bloodhound, while scratching his ass with one hand, but I wasn't laughing; the consequence of getting caught was getting shot. Whenever the searchlight passed overhead, Noah froze like a statue, often in a strange pose, mid-scratch with one paw in the air.

"Noah, what the hell is that move?" I hissed.

"They can't see me if I ain't movin'," he rumbled back.

"Stay in the goddamn shadows."

"Found it," said Noah. He held up the end of an industrial-sized hose like a strangled snake. I tossed him a bottle of liquid soap.

"I'll hose you down, then you soap up, and I'll hose it off, OK? Get ready, Noah—I'm going full blast."

"Born ready," said Noah.

Noah may have been born ready, but his parasites were even more so. They'd laid anti-tank mines and IEDs on his inner thighs. Lice loaded AK47s and crouched behind the knocked-out windows of his balls. His anus was an anti-air missile silo, hurling buckets of flak. And his armpits were two castles with the drawbridges pulled up, the boiling oil ready to pour, armed with arbalests of flaming bolts.

Noah's insects didn't give a shit what century of warrior was flung at them—they were anachronistically ready. Small moths had scrambled and were circling around Noah, an air-wall. I could hear one little bastard, the cockroach General, *what the fuck makes one life better than another one? Does it matter if it's a human being, a Bigfoot, a scabie?*

But I will not be lectured by micro-organisms, even if they have a point. "You do not get to live at the expense of another creature. Compassion demands I destroy you."

"Who you talkin' to?" asked Noah.

Hypocrite, hypocrite squeaked the roach. *He kills for a living! He eats meat!*

"Eat mother nature, bitches." I growled in my Rambo-voice, blasting the hose. I started with Noah's gnarled feet and their long, yellowed nails, worked my way up the thick calves, quads, and battered the balls. Noah started giggling a little bit at this, *hehehehehee,* but I persisted. Noah's ecosystem was disrupted by that barrage, the bug-corpses splattering against an armored bulldozer.

"Turn around," I said. Noah pirouetted; I fired a jet into the missile silo. *Heheeeheee!* And kept spraying up his back, into his armpits, even the top of his head.

That all you got? snarled the drenched bug-General, as he and his comrades floated away on macabre streams. *Your Momma* spat one hardened lice, his carapace helmet pulled low.

"Use the fucking soap, Noah. Now, it's personal."

He lathered and slathered. Biological warfare rained down on those fucks, a nuclear winter of murderous blue froth. "Who's laughing now?" I demanded of my micro-enemies. "Does that sting your eyes a little bit?" Stung a bit more than the eyes, I imagined. "Scour those ass-ants right out of existence, Noah!"

Noah was frothing himself and laughing the pure joy of winning. *Heheheheeheee!* He flushed the silo in a spray of shrapnel, besieged the armpit-castles with foamy trebuchets, bombed the battered ball-village to rubble with a soapy barrage.

But that one hardened lice, with the helmet, coughing up green blood from a thorax injury, still had the venom to spit and snarl, *You can never defeat us, you fuck. You have only delayed us. Our rise shall be swift and merciless and you shall be suckled, over years, from a trillion tiny wounds!"*

"Get ready, Noah," and I blasted the hose again, the blue foam dissolving from Noah in rainbows of dead bugs and loose hair and frog scum. Noah was laughing and clapping and spinning around and around and that's when I noticed it.

He had a tremendous erection.

A missing piece of the puzzle clicked into place. 1) His terrible personal hygiene; 2) his lack of aptitude for planning; and 3) this moment. Of course, my friend the Sasquatch… was a teenager.

I shut off the hose. Noah spun one more time *hehehehee* and turned to face me, and *it* turned to face me, Cyclopean, unblinking, bearded. It waggled.

"I am *so* happy right now," he said. And didn't he look majestic, wearing nothing but a scarf of foam, the hair slicked down to show his broad back and shoulders, the deep drum of his chest, rivulets of water dripping from his body. He looked every inch the hero from the stories, Mack the mighty yeti, god of Strength.

"Yes, Noah, I can tell." I indicated the cockstand with a sideways nod.

It was hard to tell if he blushed in the dark, "O', Jeez. You gotta towel?" But at that second the searchlight passed over us and seemed to linger.

"No time, Buddy. Let's get out of here before it gets weird."

23.

I RETURNED TO THE TOC, another endless night shift, scanning the highways for IED emplacers, writing the Daily Situation Report, and listening to Ke$ha on the unclassified computer, no matter the groans of the soldiers.

That morning the sun never rose, suddenly shy, hiding behind a veil of clouds. A thrumming on the metal roof, the marching of mini-soldiers: rain. I wanted to stand in it and feel it on my face. Even more unusual than the weather, Bell didn't show up for his shift—he was never late. Crabby? Yes. Bloodthirsty? Yes. A bullshitter? Oh, definitely. But never late, not since I'd met him. Normally Bell arrived in the TOC at 0700, I turned over to him, then he briefed the Major when she arrived at 0800.

"Kool, when you get back to the barracks, check for Bell," I said. Kool was still technically my bitch, learning the ropes, and I could free him when I wanted.

"Want me to beat the crap out of him?"

"If you don't mind."

Damnit, where is that prick? After twenty minutes I started to prep the Major's brief myself—the show must go on. I guessed even the crustiest, most diligent soldier could sleep through the alarm. I had done so the week before, despite setting two clocks. The duty cell phone buzzed on my desk— It was Kool.

"Jones, shit, listen up. Bell isn't in his room, man. Nobody's seen him since last night." That was unexpected.

"Roger, Kool. Thanks for checking."

"Well, what are you gonna do?"

"I'll phone the Military Police, I guess, and get people searching. Offer to help them when they get there."

An audible gulp over the phone. "Do you think… he's alright?"

I was quiet a second, thinking, "It's too soon to panic. Keep the phone on you and call me with updates when you can."

"Roger, Jones." He sounded small and young on the phone. "You should know the roads have turned to shit. I almost lost a boot in the fucking mud."

"Thanks, Kool—I'll let the police know."

I put the phone down; I picked another one up, "Yes, I'd like to report a missing person…"

The Major strode in a few minutes later. Muddy boots, wet helmet. She met my gaze, "Where's Bell?"

"Missing," I said. "I've just called the Military Police and they're arranging a search party. They'll send us updates through the combat chat. Kool is helping and has a cell phone."

She computed—no emotion flickered on her face. "OK. Give me the morning brief and then stick around to handle the search." She handed me a cup of liquid gold, Bell's coffee, presumably. "Thanks for volunteering."

I briefed the Major at the big map, while the night-shift owls turned over to the day-working weasels. My shift clicked over the thirteen-hour mark. Flicker from the big-screen monitor on the wall, the omni-present combat chat.

Update: Missing person report received at 0728 from Task Force Kandahar. Search party assembled consisting of 25 military policemen, with 15 other Canadian soldiers. Outside barracks, signs of struggle. Playing cards scattered, plastic table knocked over. Search ongoing.

Sinking feeling. The Major's face was a grim mask.

She raised her voice, "Listen up, everyone. One of our comrades is missing. Unless you have essential duties here, get down to the barracks and join the search." Soon it was just her and me, Alice the signaller, and Crazy Jay the drone guy. The Major and I worked the phones like a two-headed squid, convincing other units to send soldiers to the search, calling our superiors and briefing them. The rain swelled and trampled the roof. Kool called.

"Shit man. They say if it ain't rainin', it ain't trainin', but fuck this."

"Any news, Kool?"

"It's a shit sandwich, Jones. There's a fuck-ton of people looking, but the cars are all stuck in the mud, so it's mostly happening on foot."

"Any sign of Bell?"

"Lots of signs of where he's not. Not at any of the messes, or the gym, or Canada house. Door was unlocked in his room, and his uniform was folded, ready to go. People are starting to say maybe it was the—"

"Enough of that shit, Kool. Out."

I didn't want Kool's fuckboy fantasies poisoning the searchers. It had happened just like this the other times, when the Taser Rapist struck foreign soldiers, Americans, mostly. A nibbling in my entrails—the rat of worry, gnawing. Sure, Bell was a toxic bastard, a bloodthirsty bully, who wheedled, undermined the Major, and asslicked the General. He was also a pervert with a number of nasty habits but I didn't wish harm on him, did I? After all, he was the only guy who wasn't a condescending dick on the "fun run." Uncle-like in a certain light, charming in his own way, a relic of a different age. Like a lot of people with a dead father, I kept my eyes open for a replacement. The worry-rat burrowed deeper.

On Tasers

Jumped on the unclassified computer during a lull and Googled the shit out of them. Turns out, a Taser is a little gun that shoots two darts with a blast of nitrogen. The darts are connected to the mechanism by spools of wire. These darts are sharp, barbed, so they can rip right through clothes, and stick in skin like fishhooks. And once the barbs are rooted the electricity streaks down the wire—the affected muscles seize. Watched a line of police officers under training get zapped: some people fishflop. Others sink to their knees, growling. A few stayed standing, hands clenched and jaws grinding. One guy shot his gum out of his mouth, another shat his pants. Paralysis and agony: none of us are immune.

Update: Police search expanded with approx. 100 Cdn soldiers assisting. Time of abduction estimated at 0035. Half-pack cigarettes found by attempted message in mud, illegible. Search ongoing.

"Damnit," cursed the Major. Muscles in her jaw and neck stretched taut. "You can't have another one of mine. I won't allow it." Her eyes were blazing again—she wasn't talking to me, but I spoke anyway.

"Bell is tough," I said. "Tough as a Winnipeg catfish."

"They all were," she said, staring at the combat chat.

Another hour of the worst kind of waiting, the rain beating on the roof—all the drones were grounded. I stoked the coffee pot and thought of the woman in the village who struck the IED and died when the men of the village turned away the medical team. Held hostage by a waterlogged searcher up to his knees in the mud, or waiting for Kool to call, or another line of combat chat, hating it, dreading it, but wanting to see it all the same so the waiting could stop and we could act again, do something.

Update: Victim located at 1112, in shock, blood loss, repeated use of Taser, condition unstable. Identity confirmed. Medics on site conducting evac by litter. Area cordoned by police.

Crazy Jay broke the silence, "Shit, do you think—"

The Major's face was a shade paler than usual. "We'll wait until we have more information. Understand?"

Crazy Jay swallowed and nodded.

The air had gone soupy, from the rain, from the dream-like quality of things. A disassociated quality—watching yourself from a distance, from a drone, wondering when that poor bastard would wake up.

Kool called; I picked up the phone. "What's the SITREP?"

His voice was edged, almost a snarl. "I saw fucking everything, you sick piece of shit. Saw Bell tied to the hood of the car with the goddamn bag on his head. Saw his fucking pants cut off, his bare ass, and the blood. But did you see the time he was kidnapped, didya Jones?" Kool was even more shaken than the rest of us, it seemed.

"0035—Yah, I saw it. Hey, you alright?"

His voice got real low. "I know it was you, Jones, you fucking queer. You fucking sailor." The phone clicked off, and I set it back in its holster, reeling.

"Was that Kool?" asked the Major. "What did he say?"

I met her gaze for a second. "There's going to be some drama, Major. Kool thinks I'm the rapist."

A muscle in her cheek jerked and her hands sought each other, tangling. "We'll sort out this confusion as quick as possible, Jones. I've got one soldier out of commission today and I don't need a second."

Wasn't long before pounding echoed through the room. Half a dozen policemen, wearing red berets, marched into the TOC. Kool was among them, soaked to the skin, leaving puddles on the ground. He pointed at me, "That's the fucking guy there."

"What is the meaning of this?" demanded the Major. "Take care of yourself, Jones," she whispered.

"I didn't do it," I whispered back.

My palms dripped sweat—I clenched them into fists. For a brief, ludicrous second, I considered smashing the nearest cop with a computer monitor, the second with the filing cabinet, leaping over a line of desks, landing on Kool's scrawny neck with the satisfying crunch of broken branches. At the peripheries, vision blurred, but Kool's face got clearer and clearer.

No. She was there, watching. *Go back in your cage, Ogre. You're just afraid.*

"We need to take you in for a few questions, son," said a grizzled old cop with dark crescents under his eyes. The other five policemen formed a wary semi-circle around me. "Hand over your pistol to me or the Major and put your hands in front of you." I made the pistol safe and gave it to the Major— funny, I hadn't even thought of using it.

Click click—the handcuffs snapped over my wrists.

24.

POCKETS PLUNDERED. The long bench with splinters was too narrow to sleep on and awkward with the handcuffs, anyway. A wet stain on my collar where Kool had spat on me, drying. A metal cage with silvery bars, the rain still gushing outside. It was now over twenty-four hours since I had slept and like any good sailor I could sleep through the apocalypse. But every time I started to nod off, a loudspeaker in the cell blared a mundane message, "Could the person responsible for the truck with the licence plate AMYL 644 move their vehicle now. It's blocking a delivery lane," and "A reminder that this Friday is casual Friday. Donate your two dollars to the Military Family Resource Center, and you can earn an extra hour of gym-time." Just those two messages, repeated back and forth.

Not sure how many hours ticked by, but no food arrived. Missing a meal or two wasn't the end of the world, but when you're nailing the body at the gym and it's trying to rebuild, hunger is real. Urgent. I wanted *meat*—my stomach was a cornered bear, digging its claws into my temples.

No, it wasn't torture—Canadians are not torturers; we pat our dainty mouths with handkerchiefs when our friends in the Afghan Army pull out the car battery and nipple clamps. Canadians are interrogators and softeners. They were softening me.

But I can drift away. *They cannot touch me, the places I go.* Eyes closed or eyes open, stomach snarling or sated—this clumsy body cannot follow anyway. I blink, and I'm another man, with a slender face and the toned muscles of a dancer. She is there, too. The Major. When we clutch hands our grips are soft, without callouses—we have taken a different path, a peaceful path, and found each other earlier. She is wearing bangles on her wrists. I am kissing up her arm with a long-eared puppet. A shaggy creature, with floppy front arms and ticklish whiskers. She is a kindergarten teacher and I am a poet; we have filled our home with books and sundresses. Dream catcher on the window. Through its net, a garden: a little toil in the soil, baskets of fresh tomatoes. Always, always, I chase her laughter. I am a clown for it, a slave for it. Her laughter has sunk into the wooden floors, the ceiling beams, the puppets, the racks of spices, the dangling crystals, the bean bag chair. It has sunk into me, too.

Deep within Kandahar Airfield, in a prisoner's cell, sat a sad-eyed brute with serial-killer hands bound in cuffs. As the hours waned a tiny smile crept onto my face.

25.

ODE TO A CHEESEBURGER: two thick patties, just a bit of char, with juice streaming out every bite. Slightly too much cheddar, the correct amount. Above, a token lettuce leaf drowned in a puddle of mayonnaise, ketchup and mustard. Two slices of tomato crowned the condiments, adding their own juice and holding aloft a single sliver of pickle. Yes, every ship needs a hull—a sesame-seed bun, fresh and light as dandelion down. From a white ceramic plate with roses along the edges, the burger exuded the smell of barbeques and faraway summers.

My drool ducts reacted, flooding the mouth. Eyes grew wide and lost. Stomach snarled.

"You'd like one of these, wouldn't you, Big Guy?" asked my interrogator. A man in his forties sitting behind a plain metal desk, bare lightbulb swinging overhead. We were somewhere in the depths of the prison; there were no windows to gauge the time.

"I don't think I can get it all into my mouth at one time. I'll have to cut it in half." He took a huge bite that squirted juice over his chin and Navy-blue blazer.

"Oh, look at that." Mopping his face with a handkerchief, he said, "This might be too much for me."

I was handcuffed with my hands behind my back. My stomach thundered. "Can we get on with this, please?"

"Harold," said the cop, extending his hand. I stared at it coldly, and he grinned. "Ooops! Forgot about that. I'll be right with you, Big Guy. I just got so busy with work—forgot to grab lunch." He tore the double-decker burg with his teeth; the napkin could barely cope with the stray juice.

The beautiful burger (where had they found it?) shrank, disappearing into this goblin's gut. He apologized the whole time, ruining three napkins in the meal, smearing juice almost up to his round-rimmed glasses. Finally, a quarter-burg remained, and Harold slumped in the chair with his belly stuck out. "Jeez, Big Guy, I just can't handle it." He belched and threw the last quarter, the juiciest part, straight into a garbage can.

"Now, where were we?" he asked, leaning forward, grinning.

"I didn't rape anyone."

Harold's smile slipped. "Well, it's my job to figure that out, isn't it, Big Guy?" He affected a huge, clown-like frown.

"My name is Jones."

"I know, Big Guy." Perhaps something flickered on my face. "Ooooh, does it make you angry? Big Guy, doesn't like being called Big Guy?"

On Naming

Yes, it made me angry. That's what my Dad used to call me when booze lowered him to a snake. The voice was the venom, twisting into an effete flourish for the name. "Do you think your face is tougher than a fridge, Big Guy?"

I stood in the corner of the kitchen, by the sink, thirteen years old. He was punching the shit out of the fridge door with sickening wet crunches. Rorschach patterns of butterflies in the bloody knuckle prints. The fridge door buckled and dented, even along the metal seam. Important lessons of strength were being taught—something let go and trickled down my leg.

The cop wanted me angry—he was searching for a rapist. Like everyone else on the camp, he was convinced he was protecting people. I smiled my best, most pleasant, most Canadian smile, and choked the urge to loose my bladder. Harold smiled back. The silence stretched like oozing maple syrup.

"Hey!" shouted Harold. I jolted awake dripping. He'd splashed his glass of water on my face. "We're having a conversation here."

"Terribly sorry," I mumbled, blinking away water drops, and blowing them off the end of my nose. My head was full of fog from not sleeping. Like early mornings in Halifax, leaving the harbour, with the sun too weak to burn the mist. "What was the question?"

"Are you a homosexual, Jones?"

"No, I'm not." I thought for a second. "But…"

"Yes?" Harold reached for a notepad.

"Are we sure the rapist is gay?"

He tapped a pen on his teeth. Scanned me. A clock on the wall ticked the seconds. "Are you fucking with me, Big Guy?"

"No, Harold, I am not."

"Well, obviously, the rapist is gay because he is a man who rapes other men."

"But is he attracted to the men he rapes?"

"You tell me."

"I don't know." Sweat trickled down my back as I cursed silently. Harold sized me up and down, leaned back far in the chair and flung one knee over the other.

His voice again, "You obviously lift, Big Guy, but are you strong enough to rape a man?"

"It depends on the man, obviously."

He slid his glasses to the end of his nose. "Could you rape *me*, do you think?"

"No."

"Why not?"

"Because I'm handcuffed, you have a pistol, and I don't have an erection."

Another long pause. I could still smell the burger from the garbage can, and was fantasizing that he might leave me alone with it and I could root in the basket with my face like a hog.

"Where were you yesterday between midnight and 0100 hours?" The tide of sweat trickling down my back became a river. The truth would not save me—I'd been hosing down a flea-ridden sasquatch. "Well?" Harold repeated.

"Midnight meal," I croaked.

"That the best you got, Big Guy? Midnight meal? We know you usually get take-out and you're back in the Operations Center in fifteen minutes. Something special about this day?"

"It was a slow night," I said, thoughts churning in the fog. "Sometimes it's nice to sit and enjoy the meal like a day worker." None of that was a lie.

"Yes, Big Guy, yes—I agree with you. Nothing better than a fine meal." He kicked the garbage can, jostling the burg. "But no one saw you there until 0050. So I ask again, what were you doing between midnight and 0100 hours?"

"I was sitting in the smoking pit."

Harold chuckled. "Nice one, Big Guy. But we didn't see any cigarettes when we cleaned out your pockets." He laughed again, eyes narrowing.

"I didn't say I was smoking, I said I was sitting."

"So what the hell were you doing, Jones?"

"Writing a poem. You'll find a small journal among the items you confiscated. The ink is fresh." I kept my face expressionless.

His face was pallid and sallow under the dangling light. He cracked a briefcase by his foot and extracted the journal. "We," he paused, "haven't had time to peruse these notes."

"Go ahead, read it," I said. "It could be a window into my *perversions*."

<u>Out of Reach</u>

We watched it all, circling round in drones
When Halima to her bloody fate was wed
Don't look at me, I didn't throw the stones

That was her choice and *those* her moans
Halima, as she was dragged from her lover's bed
We watched it all, licking lips in drones

The crowd was made of faces: children, adults, crones
Black hair, black dress—they'd torn her veil instead
Don't look at me, I didn't throw the stones

At first defiant, subsiding into groans
Halima, who blinked a rock as her eye went dead
We watched it all, vultures who wheeled in drones

Allah, villagers, some soldiers, Christ and Jones
As Halima searched for pearls on rocks stained red
Don't look at me, I didn't throw the stones

One drinks of pleasure first, then atones
Halima dying, curled in a heap with legs spread
We watched it all, panting hard in drones

Now the princess holds court amongst her bones
Crowned—a smashed and baggy scarecrow's head
We watched it all, circling round in drones
Halima, I wonder, was it worth the stones?

Harold was silent for a long moment, chewing on the end of his pen. Finally, he looked up, "It's ugly."

"Writing helps me process."

Harold shifted in his seat, and his tie slipped out of his blazer. Sunflowers. Huge ones, overlapping. A gag-tie, or the clumsy gift of a child. "I've written a few as well," he muttered, almost under his breath.

In a flash, I understood him. The theatrical jacket, the loud tie, the antics with the cheeseburger. Here was just another misplaced artist, washed ashore in a war. I imagined Harold wearing a cape, a proper spoken word artist, with a corny stage-name like Legion, rocking a packed bar and talking over his glasses, a beer in one hand, upraised. My sleep-deprived brain embraced the idea.

Legion flipped through my journal, glancing at me occasionally. I said, "You won't find any rapes in there, Man. Kool—the guy who turned me in— he's got issues about the Navy and a bit of small-man syndrome."

The cop didn't speak, kept flipping. He answered a knock on the door and spoke briefly in an urgent whisper to another man I didn't see. When he returned to the table he tucked his sunflowers away and spoke. Something pinched around the edges of his eyes. "We got a guy raping his way through the camp and you're in here playing games with me. Why didn't you just say you didn't do it? Would have saved us a lot of time." Legion rubbed his temples. "I'll be damned if we can get any kind of DNA evidence with this Neanderthal equipment in the middle of a downpour."

"Jones," he rolled the name around in his mouth. "We just got a report from the hospital that the victim has regained consciousness and vouched for your innocence." Relief felt like a cool breeze on my soaked back. "But I'm almost positive you're hiding something."

I said nothing. Turned my face as impassive as I could. Anything else would endanger Noah. The urge to piss came back, stronger.

Legion continued, "You're not the guy I expected but you're not as smart as you think. A mistake that seems small can have a big impact. You hear anything, anything at all, write a memo up the chain and put me on CC, got it?" He produced a key from his blazer pocket and clicked open the handcuffs.

"Best of luck with the rest of your tour, Jones," he said as I reached the door.

"Thanks, Legion," I mumbled sleepily, earning a puzzled look.

26.

A MAN WITH A RED BERET led me down a long hallway with many closed doors and twists. Another cop returned my journal, wallet and other personal items, including my roll of triple-ply polar-bear-soft Canadian toilet paper. I stared at the bored cop suspiciously—the roll seemed a bit smaller, had he poached a square or two?

Outside, another day in the mud puddle, though at least it wasn't raining anymore. I had no idea how many days I'd been in there, how long I'd been awake, or when I last ate. It was a mile to the TOC, a weary trudge with the muck slurping at my boots; I nearly fell asleep on the march, catching myself an instant before toppling. *I need to see her, let her know I'm OK, innocent.*

Door to the TOC, but I kept losing the code in the fog, had to input it six times before the door unlocked. Aware of a sour smell: me. Curious moment of homecoming, even the drone feeds were welcoming, the bubbling coffee pot, the taste of dust, the fibreboard desks holding their monitors, slumped-over gophers, tangles of wires. Rays of light penetrated the roof where shrapnel had ripped it, a dozen spotlights that crisscrossed the room, transforming floating dust specks into glittering creatures that flitted and swam. There was life in here, and she stood in the middle, the warrior-woman wearing the halo of swords, the light piercing her like silver lances.

She spun, saw me at the door, and her eyes softened. "Welcome back, Jones."

"Reporting in, Major," I said, which was almost smooth, except I stepped forward and stumbled badly, catching myself on the dented filing cabinet, which betrayed me with a loud boom. All the moles looked up. "Apparently, I'm innocent."

"I had no doubt, Jones," said the Major, stepping closer, off her pedestal, the lances slipping woundless from her body. "You were interrogated?"

I nodded. "Tortured me with a cheeseburger." I searched the swamp for words. Important words, words that needed to be strung. "But… they cannot touch me where I go." I stumbled again, the other direction, but glanced up at her, to see if she understood, to see if she imagined that cottage where she was a kindergarten teacher and I a poet, the bangles on her wrists, if she pictured it as clear as I did. But all I saw in her eyes was worry. And something stern over top.

In her loud, clear voice: "You're no good to me like this, Jones. You need a full night's sleep. Report in tomorrow night at 1900. I will have strong words for Kool, and I'll get one of the signallers to give you a lift back to the barracks." Then she whispered, "I'm glad you're back."

Was it the Major who said those last words, or the version of her I made up? I honestly don't know but the signaller had to shake me awake to get me in the truck.

27.

TWELVE HOURS OF SLEEP without needing to set a clock: luxury, but I dreamed of Halima. Kool was fast asleep when I got in and gone when I awoke, little bastard; I was brewing strong words for him, too. A hot shower burned away the fog, and I slipped into a clean uniform. Tying up my boots, I found myself whistling until I remembered the rapist was still out there, among us.

After a coffee, I'd be whole.

I waited in the Tim Horton's queue, up to my ankles in mud, with the rain pouring down. The cops had gone batshit crazy—police sirens wailed all over the camp, many in foreign tones. Hoarse shouts echoed over concrete barriers.

"What the hell is happening?" I asked another drenched soldier in the line, a crusty old warrant officer.

"Didn't you hear?" he rasped. "They're arresting all the strongmen in the camp, looking for the rapist." He eyed the width of my neck and kept a hand on his pistol.

I must have been the first in a campaign of arrests. "That's insane," I said. What were the selection criteria? If you could bench press 300 lbs you were a suspect, but 250 lbs didn't suffice? Were they setting up spycams in the gyms? Since Bell's rape, strength had become a crime.

As the coffee queue inched forward, the rain thundered harder. I turned when I heard shouting from the gym. Five policemen were trying to haul a handcuffed soldier into a police car. But the suspect was a huge fucker with totem poles for legs—he had three cops on his back, one pulling on the cuffs, another slipping into the mud. Hard to tell at the distance, but I would have bet it was Johnson, that soldier who leg pressed more than I did.

The whole pack stopped abruptly. A shout, "I didn't do shit!" and the three cops on Johnson's back flew into the mud. Only the officer holding his irons was left standing; the cuffs quaked as the ogre strained, looming overhead, rage and hunger on his face.

Two muddy officers pulled out Tasers, aimed. Sparks flashed on Johnson's back and shoulders. He fell to his knees growling, muscles convulsing around the darts.

"See how he fucking likes it," grumbled the warrant officer.

This was happening all over the camp. Fourteen rapes, three of them fatal, and Bell had been the last straw. Not a single pube as evidence—only the reports of irresistible strength, a man who made soldiers helpless as children. And now all the neckless brutes chained and caged, thick wrists distending the handcuffs. The surliest bunch of bears, the proudest, stomachs growling like leopards. Many of them arrested right at the gym, the regret: "Shouldn't have added that extra ten pounds to my shoulder press." They were all sentenced to splintery benches, sleep deprivation, bizarre interrogators, and the torment of the cheeseburger. For the soldiers of many countries, it would be even worse: thumbscrews and testicle clamps.

Balancing two coffees, I knocked on TicTac's door—had they taken him as well? No answer. I called out, "You in there, Coachbag?" Something beyond the door lurched.

"Is that you, Jones?" TicTac's voice, haggard.

"Last time I checked."

"No one is with you?"

"Just me."

The door cracked an inch. TicTac's bloodshot eye appeared, bulged, darted. Behind him, the wallpaper of porn stars, their genitals shielded by sticky notes, stirred in a slight breeze. He didn't move from the door. Or blink.

I said, "If you opened the door a little wider, I could pass you a coffee."

"They said you were rapist, Jones. Your little friend Kool—with tiny triceps—he was very convincing."

"Jesus, TicTac, do I have 'rapist' tattooed on my face?" The bulging eye flickered over my face as if determining exactly that. "The cops already questioned me."

A bead of sweat trickled down TicTac's forehead, following the bulge of a protruding vein. A little note of warmth crept back into his voice, "Oh, you must tell me all these stories, Jones. One second—I'll come out. We lifting?"

"Why else would I be talking to you, fuckface?"

The eye retreated; the door closed. A minute later, TicTac emerged wearing gray sweatpants and a huge, baggy sweatshirt. The logo on the shirt was a velociraptor dribbling a basketball. So swathed, TicTac's physique was invisible—a sweaty dumpling of a man. I chuckled a little.

"What is so funny, Jones?"

"You look like a nutsack." I handed him his coffee and we stood, sipping, in the hallway of the barracks.

He grinned, glancing at himself. "A bad day for flexing in mirror, no? You are aware what's happening?"

"Yep. I saw them arrest Johnson a few minutes ago. Apparently, it's the same all over the camp."

"They arrested you, Jones, right? How did you talk your way out of it?"

I smiled enigmatically. "Poetry."

His right eyebrow climbed to the top of his head. "You are very surprising man, Jones."

"I have a rich inner life."

We sipped our caffeinated ambrosia in silence for a second. TicTac seemed to be wrestling with something in his head, the way his brow kept furrowing. Eventually he spoke, "This is such bullshit. We work out in gym right now, we cannot go heavy. We won't let them defeat us, Jones." He chugged the rest of his coffee, crumpled the cup. "Today we take workout outside. The tires behind gym."

"You're aware that it's pouring rain, right?"

"You afraid of little mud, Jones?"

On Mud

I wasn't afraid. Brought me back to football fields and rugby scrums, muddy ball squeaking from the fingers like a watermelon seed. Elbow smashes and the wet thunk of headbutts—I was the storm. Bite marks in the scrums, claw-marks of cleats. The mud slowed the agile players, the dancers, to the speed of the brutes. The great reckoning. Skinnies dragged from the field on stretchers. The heavies cackling during penalty minutes, lightning zapping the field posts, puddles in the end zone—it was never about the score. Waiting for Dad in the rain, after the match, he could never meet my eyes. Pain fades. Bruises heal. Mud cakes.

We slogged to the rear of the gym via a roundabout route—TicTac scanning furtively. Arriving at the old ruined boardwalk where we threw the medicine ball, by the barber shop and the graveyard of tires. Great rubber fuckers as tall as the waist settling into the mud. A few sledgehammers leaned against the back wall of the gym. Usually, this area was dusty and empty; that day the mud frothed as the rain poured down, my shirt slicking to my body, nipples poking through like daggers.

The whole workout TicTac kept glancing at the road, watching for something, nearly cost him his footing once or twice on the box jumps; the tire was a slick prick. It wasn't like him to be distracted—I might have said

Coachbag's Corner: Tire Workout

Yes, is not perfect—we do not always have good gym, with right weights, not too busy, and lots of energy. Sometimes gym is crawling with police officers or, I don't know, alligators, and then we, how you say, improvise. Everything is equipment, Jones, everything is weight. You are weight. That tank is weight. Barrel of water is very good weight. A log is weight. A rock is excellent. Men have been strong for long time, and many place become church.

Ignore mud—is no big deal. Just little resistance on feet. We start here on big tire, and we jump on top. Let's see if you can do twenty reps of this one, but is not over, is superset. No rest, remember. Hop into tire, grab onto edge, and stand up, and now you do farmer's walk all the way to tank—very good for forearms and traps. Is OK to wibble wobble like drunken sailor. Five supersets of that one.

Now is not swordfight—we grab sledgehammers and we smash tire. You will see, good burn in forearms. Is big help to shout dirty word as you swing. Picture face of every bully, everyone who put you in cage, call you homo, or threaten to cut out eyes. Bullies with strong hands or clever bullies with little jokes—we club them down. Dick! Cunt! Ass! Fuck! Pussy! Asshole! We smash all dirty parts of body.

You must become one with rubber, Jones. You see how raindrop hit tire and jump into air? That is like bodybuilder. Each day we fail but we always bounce back. Catch breath, Jones and we finish with big tire. Flip to failure, that is plan.

something, but lifting this heavy frame into the air took all my breath.

Just after TicTac's sledge splintered, the metal head twirling down the boardwalk, we'd grown an audience. Two military policemen in red berets, behind the wheel of a police car, had stopped to stare as I flipped the tire.

TicTac's turn. He strutted to the tire, a wet rat in his baggy sweatshirt. Crouched, and gripped the tire in both hands. The muscles in his arms, legs and back tensed, grew thick with veins and blood; the tire quivered. It rose an inch, then splat into the mud. The unthinkable had happened: TicTac had failed a feat of strength.

"Sorry, Jones," said the Coachbag, stretching his back. "I must not have eaten enough."

"Try again," I said.

He nodded, dropped low, slid his fingers under the rubber rim. Again, his body contorted with effort, but the stubborn tire stayed rooted: another failure. TicTac sat on top of it with his shoulders slumped. The police car continued down the street—he watched it go.

I had the sense the workout was over—I sat on the other side of the tire, back-to-back, and pulled my feet from the mud. It was quiet for a moment with just the sound of the rain in the puddles, drumming on the tire.

"You hid your strength," I said. "You hid behind me."

He seemed to mull his words. "Yes. Is true. I do not wish to be put in cage today, or any day, by little bullies who call themselves police. They cannot make strength illegal—is great injustice. These are *our* bodies. This strength is *mine*."

My eyes drifted to the shards of splintered wood that had broken off the hammer. TicTac continued, "Today you learn important lesson from Coachbag. A bodybuilder must be stronger than his ego. Is pride that push us to injury, or make us train before we are healed. Is good to challenge limits, but wise to know them."

TicTac slid around the tire, so we were side by side. "People will look at our bodies, or hear my accent, and think we are stupid. Let them. Sometimes is great advantage to be invisible." His hand squelched on my soggy shirt when he squeezed my shoulder. "Come, is cold, we done with this one."

28.

BLASTED OFF THREE POUNDS OF MUD in a scorching shower, the water running off black. Since Kool decided I was the rapist, the little room I shared with him was no refuge—he'd moved his locker to make a screen between our bunks so he could change in privacy. Sometimes I'd see his paranoid eyes peeking around the edge.

I grabbed a quick meal and a take-out container, head down in the drizzling rain, placed the speaking stone, and settled into the bunker—someone had carpeted it with a few layers of cardboard.

A waft of bear den, and the Sasquatch was upon me, squeezing me to death. My spine cracked in three places as Noah lifted me from the ground in a colossal hug. "You were worried about me?" I croaked, when I could croak, but he didn't answer. Was flinging an omelette down his throat with his bare hands.

Better shape, though. The pelt was starting to grow thicker in the bare patches, the pink of new skin poking from previous raw gashes. I noticed, in the places crisscrossed with scars, the hair grew white. And despite his hunger, he seemed in no danger of wasting away—he was still building mass, particularly in his shoulders and quads. He swallowed, belched, and spoke, "Hell yeah, I was worried when ya didn't come home—had four-hundred soldiers crawlin' up my butt too." He reclined, as much as he could in the bunker, sprawling on the cardboard. "What happened to ya?"

"Arrested. They thought I was the Taser Rapist."

Noah shot me a horrified, concerned look. Or perhaps he was still hungry—it was tricky to read his emotions with those two jutting fangs. "Jeez. Glad you're OK." He patted me clumsily. "They found that pervert yet?"

"I don't think so." *Sometimes is great advantage to be invisible.* "They've been arresting all the beefcakes on the camp for questioning. The last victim was a guy I work with—he's still in the hospital."

"I hope he gets better," Noah said, frowning. "And I hope they find the pervert. They got guys with guns roamin' the camp all night now, but I still managed to snoop a bit. Pretty tempted to jump onna plane I thought was goin' to Italy—can you imagine me there, slurpin' noodles?—but I wanna get back to Canada, maybe find my Mom. Seems like the planes with the leaf on 'em only come once every week or so, and there's been too many guys to sneak past."

"Here—maybe this will help." I tossed Noah a duffel bag of my most worn uniforms.

He wrinkled his nose. "Fuck clothes."

"At least try them on."

Noah held up my baggy arid-patterned combat shirt and sniffed it. He made my XXL seem puny.

"It's got the nametags and everything. Deep down, Noah, everyone's a Jones. If you get challenged at night just tell them you're Captain Jones. There must be 400 of us on the base."

The boots were impossible—not even attempted. Noah managed to pull the pants halfway up the quad before giving up, bitching constantly. It seemed the shirt would work: he couldn't get the top three buttons fastened, and it looked like his biceps were wearing tourniquets, but the name Jones was emblazoned invincibly on his chest. He might have gotten past a casual inspection, late at night, with a groggy guard and a thick fog. Until we heard a sound like a thick canvas sail being torn—he'd ripped the back right open.

"Fuck clothes," said Noah, throwing the tatters in a heap. "If I gets in over my head I'll call on the Protector Spirit. Ya don't need to worry 'bout me."

"Your stories aren't going to save you, Noah. Let's see how well your stupid 'Protector Spirit' does against a city's worth of soldiers."

Deep regrets stirred his whisper, "Oh, the Spirit is real, Jones. He talks to me everyday, tellin' me how easy it'd be for me to get outta here with his help. He says I should kill ya for yer meat."

I made my voice light. "You tell your Spirit I'm quite attached to my meat."

Noah grinned. "He'd have to go through me first, Jones."

29.

A FEW THINGS YOU GOTTA KNOW TO BE IN THE FAN CLUB, JONES. I'M LEANIN' ON YOU TO ANSWER QUESTIONS FROM REPORTERS AND CHICKS. WHERE'S HE FROM? HOW'D HE LEARN TO SPEAK SO GOOD? MOST IMPORTANT, HOW'D HE GET SO DAMN HANDSOME?

ALRIGHT, JONES, IMMA PAINT THE PICTURE. MOM AND ME HAD A NICE HOUSE IN THE WOODS MADE OUTTA LOGS WITH EVERGREEN BRANCHES FOR A ROOF AND ONE WHOLE WALL FULL O' HER BOOKS. I REMEMBER BEIN' A BOY, SIX YEARS OLD, PUDGY LITTLE BEARCUB, GAZIN' UP AT MY REAL MOTHER, THE ONE THAT LOOKED LIKE ME. IT WAS LIKE LOOKIN' UP ATTA PINE TREE. SHE HAD A THICKASS BLACK PELT, ALL OVER, 'CEPT SHE NEEDED TO SHAVE HER FACE AND LEGS EACH DAY 'FORE SHE WENT TO WORK. TRUCK STOP, ON THE SIDE O' THE HIGHWAY, MY MOM WEARIN' FLOWERY DRESSES WITH HAIRY ANKLES PEEKIN' OUT UNDERNEATH, HANDIN' OUT PLATES O' TATERS AND BACON. TRUCKERS DROVE FROM THE ENDS OF THE EARTH TO SEE MY MOM, FAMOUSLY UGLY AND STRONG, BUT QUICK TO LAUGH ANYWAY. AND IF ANY OF THEM HAD THE STONES TO GRAB HER ASS WHILE SHE WAS BENT OVER THE COUNTER THEY'D GET A PLATE O' EGGIES SMASHED ON THEIR HEADS.

MY MOM SPOKE A BIT O' ENGLISH TOO, BUT AT HOME WE ONLY SPOKE SASQUATCH. YOU'D HEAR A BUNCH O' RUMBLES AND GRUNTS—NOT LIKE THESE HIGH-PITCHED BIRD SQUEAKS YOU PEOPLE MAKE. MOM'D GET BACK FROM THE DINER, BALL UP HER APRON, AND FLING IT IN THE CORNER WITH THE BOOKS. 'FUCK CLOTHES,' I'D WHISPER, DOODLIN' ON THE WALL, OR BURNIN' SOMETHIN', OR TUGGIN' ON MYSELF, SHEDDIN' CLUMPS OF ORANGE HAIR.

I REMEMBER MOM, WEARIN' A DRESS IN THE HUMAN STYLE, TAKIN' MY HAND AND LEADIN' ME TO THE FOREST. THE WORD MEANT FOREST BUT IT ALSO MEANT GRAVE—SHE SAID THAT'S WHERE OUR PEOPLE WERE LAID TO REST. COULDN'T STICK A SASQUATCH IN THE GROUND FOR TWO DAYS BEFORE A PLANT BURST OUT, LEAFY AS A MOTHERFUCKER AND THIRSTY FOR LIGHT. WHOLE GROVES, JONES, WHERE ALL THE TREES ARE THICK-SHOULDERED AND SHADY, PLANTED IN CIRCLES, LIKE THEY'RE STILL 'ROUND THE CAMPFIRE SWAPPIN' STORIES. MOM SAID SHE COULD HEAR 'EM, AND I BELIEVED 'ER, CUZ I COULD HEAR 'EM MYSELF—I MEAN, EVEN THE WIND SOUNDS LIKE WORDS SOMETIMES, DON'T IT?

"YOU'D BE A BEAUTIFUL TREE, MOM," I TOLD 'ER, AND IT MADE 'ER SMILE

SADLY.

"Help me gather these pinecones."

Yes, Jones, we ate the shit outta those cones. Could go for ten or twelve of those crispy pricks! Or maybe a heap of blue-glowin' moss, that grows in caves. Handfuls of seeds straight in the shell, for more interestin' poops. Scrape me some o' that soft whiteish wood-paste that grows just under the bark. Slap a log on the kitchen table and I'll suck the bugs outta their holes, or chase 'em down with this long tongue—don't get any ideas! But it all came from the forest, and when my Mom wasn't around to teach me, I learned at the roots o' 'em trees. Chattin' with 'em. Nappin' on 'em. Climbin' up 'em. Hell, first time I gotta boner, I didn't have no Dad to tell me what to do, so I wrapped my arms around a tree trunk and ground my hips against the bark 'til I made a mess—Ha!—why do you think they call it a "woody?"

Whenever she could, Mom dragged me to the corner of our cabin with all her books. Used to trap me on her lap and read to me no matter how hard I squirmed, and believe me, Jones, I could squirm my way up an earthworm's asshole when I was a kid—no kiddin'. "Please stop fighting," she'd say, "If you'd only try a little it would make me so happy." She never forgave me for screwin' it up with 'em graybeards, had to teach me all my words 'erself, at least while she still had 'er voice. Figure she might've reached out to some of 'em other Sasquatch, and sure at the start we had plenty o' bullshitters 'round the campfire, but in time, the circle got smaller and smaller, 'til it weren't no circle, just me and Mom passin' a bucket o' rainwater back n' forth. Whenever I asked where everybody went she'd say they went south for the winter. But after a year or two, I figured that was a lie. Finally, she told me the Protector Spirit came for them and never let go.

"Is the Protector Spirit gonna come for me, too?" I asked her.

"Eat your moss."

Then one night when I was snoozin' in my little bunk near the book-wall, I woke up to Mom shakin' my shoulder. 'Fore I knew it, she was wrappin' me up in a blanket and carryin' me outta there even though I was squirmin' my best, sayin' the forest was haunted, and she was snifflin' deep in her throat and tryin' to hide it. I waved bye to the forest and cried for Muffles, my teddy bear, after that we were always runnin' from somethin', or searchin' for somethin'. Maybe there were a few rumours at the diner that my mother wasn't entirely *human*.

Slept on a log that night, under a bridge the next night, on

A PILE OF LEAVES THE NIGHT AFTER THAT. ATE BARK AND RAINWATER AND SOME DRIED FRUIT MOM HAD IN A SACK. DUNNO WHERE WE WERE GOIN' BUT IT WAS ALWAYS FARTHER AWAY FROM THE CITIES, EVEN THE LITTLE PISSANT TOWNS. LOOKIN' BACK, WE WERE PROLLY SEACHIN' FOR A HOME. WE WERE PROLLY RUNNIN' FROM YA.

I CRIED. I CRIED FOR MY FRIENDS THE TREES, FOR MOSS, FOR MUFFLES, FOR MY BED, FOR BLANKETS. MAYBE YOU THINK FOOD CAN'T GET PLAINER THAN PINECONES, BUT YER WRONG. YA NEVER SLURPED SHINY-WINGED BEETLES FROM HANDFULS OF MUD, OR CHEWED BIRCH BARK RAW, OR ATE FEATHERS. MOM TRIED TO MAKE IT FUN AT THE START, TALKIN' 'BOUT IT LIKE IT WAS SOME BIG ADVENTURE, EVEN CALLED ME MACK A LITTLE BIT SO I'D FEEL LIKE A HERO. BUT THEN SHE STARTED SPACIN' OUT. STANDIN' THERE LIKE SHE'D DIED AND TURNED INTO A TREE AFTER ALL, BLINKIN' AT NOTHIN' LIKE IT WAS THE STARS. CHEWIN' HER LIPS, MUTTERIN', EVEN A GROWL EVERY NOW AND THEN. SLEEPIN' IN LATE WITH BLANKETS PILED ON 'ER HEAD. SOON IT WAS ME PULLIN' ON 'ER HAND AND *THAT* WAS A SAD DAY. I DUNNO IF YOU EVER HAD SOMEONE SLIP AWAY FROM YA, JONES. SOMEONE THAT YA LOVED AND WANTED TO HELP. THE BODY IS THERE—RIGHT NEXT TO YA—BUT THE MIND IS AWAY WRESTLIN' WITH SOMETHIN' AND YA CAN'T DO ANYTHIN' BUT WAIT AND SEE WHO COMES OUT ON TOP.

"NOT SURE HOW MUCH LONGER I CAN FIGHT HIM," SHE TOLD ME.

"FIGHT WHO, MOM, WHO IS IT?" AND I LOOKED UP AT THE TREETOPS, AND DOWN BY THE ROOTS, BUT DIDN'T SEE NOBODY.

WINTER CREPT UP ON US AND I DON'T GOTTA TELL *YOU* HOW COLD IT GOT, WITH THE MAPLES EXPLODIN' WHEN THE SAP FROZE. WE HUDDLED CLOSER, ME PUSHIN' HER HALF THE TIME, HIDIN' UNDER A PILE O' SKINS. STARTED EATIN' SQUIRREL AND OTHER LITTLE FURRY GUYS—FOR THE MEAT, FOR THE FURS—AND MOM HAD A PRAYER SHE'D SAY EACH TIME WE ATE AN ANIMAL. ONE NIGHT WE FELL ASLEEP IN THE ROOTS OF A BIGASS PINE. COLD AND HUNGRY AND SHIVERIN' AND HOLDIN' ON TO EACH OTHER WHILE THE SNOW WHIPPED AROUND ON THE WIND. WOKE UP AND MOM WAS GONE AND I DIDN'T KNOW WHAT THE HELL TO DO. I WAS ONLY SIX OR SEVEN... I CRIED FOR A BIT AND THEN FOUND SOME WOOD AND CAN YOU PICTURE ME TRYIN' FOR HOURS TO MAKE A FIRE BY BANGIN' THEM STICKS TOGETHER? AND I WAS WORRIED 'BOUT MY MOM OUT THERE BY 'ERSELF, AND I WAS SCARED OF WOLVES, AND I THOUGHT MAYBE MY TOES WERE GONNA FREEZE OFF.

SPENT THE WHOLE DAY PEEKIN' OUT FROM 'NEATH THE TREE, SCARED. NEXT NIGHT I DIDN'T HAVE NO TEARS LEFT. I WAS SO HUNGRY I WAS 'BOUT TO EAT THE TOES OFF MYSELF. MOM SHOWED UP, NAKED, BUT IT WAS LIKE IT WASN'T 'ER. SHE'D GONE ALL... SHADOWY, LIKE SHE WAS WEARIN' AN ARMOR MADE O' BLACK MIST. HER CLAWS HAD GROWN LONG AND WICKED

AND SHE SEEMED EVEN BIGGER THAN BEFORE, WITH HER HAIR WISPIN' IN ALL DIRECTIONS. BUT THE WORST WAS HER FACE—HER SMILE STRETCHED INTO AN UGLY SNEER PACKED WITH TEETH, AND HER EYES TURNED INTO RED PINPRICKS. THEN SHE THREW A DEAD BEAR AT MY FEET, HER NAILS STILL DRIPPIN' WITH ITS BLOOD. YAH, SURPRISED THE SHIT OUTTA ME, TOO. "WHAT HAPPENED TO YOUR DRESS, MOM?" I ASKED, BUT SHE ONLY GRUNTED, NUDGIN' THE DEAD BEAR WITH HER HEAD TO SHOW ME I SHOULD EAT IT. AND THAT WAS IT—ALL GRUNTS AFTER THAT. COULDN'T GET A WORD OUTTA HER. EYES GONE BLANK. WE MUNCHED THAT BEAR UNTIL WE WERE STUFFED AND IT WAS FROZEN SOLID, THEN WE CURLED UP AND SLEPT, AND HER SHADOWY SKIN FELT LIKE COARSE BARK, AND I WAS TOO AFRAID TO SLEEP.

AFTER THAT SHE WAS RIGHT IN FRONT OF ME BUT I MISSED HER ANYWAYS. SHE RAN ON ALL FOURS, SCAMPERIN' OFF INTO THE FOREST AND COMIN' BACK WITH A BROKEN-NECKED DEER IN HER MOUTH. IT WASN'T MY MOM—IT WASN'T 'ER! MY MOM WAS GENTLE. THIS ONE… WELL. THERE WERE TIMES I FELT 'ER STARIN' AT ME, WEIGHIN', AND MY SKIN WOULD GO GOOSE-BUMPY. BUT I WAS JUST A KID, WHAT WAS I SUPPOSED TO DO? RUN OFF INTO THE WOODS BY MYSELF??

THERE I WAS, RUNNIN' AFTER 'ER IN THE TRAIL SHE BROKE IN THE SNOW, JUST TRYIN' TO KEEP UP, WHEN I HEARD SOUNDS OF FIGHTIN' UP AHEAD. SNARLIN' AND GROWLIN'. I STUCK MY HEAD OVER A SNOWBANK AND SAW MOM SCRAPPIN' WITH FOUR BROWN BEARS, YAPPIN' AND JUMPIN' AND RIPPIN' THEIR CHESTS OPEN WITH HER FOOT-CLAWS. BLOOD WAS BRIGHT RED IN THE SNOW. TWO O' THE BEARS WERE TRYIN' TO RUN OFF AND I 'MEMBER THIS WAS THE WOMAN WHO HAD TO SAY A PRAYER AND APOLOGIZE TO THE SQUIRREL FOR EATIN' IT. SHE STARTED GOIN' AFTER THE LAST BEAR, SLASHIN' AT THE HAMSTRINGS, AND I RAN AFTER 'ER CRYIN', "STOP, MOM, PLEASE STOP," AND SHE SPUN AROUND AND HISSED—I WAS LOOKIN' STRAIGHT INTO THE VOLCANO, JONES. DEATH COMIN' RIGHT AT ME, BLOOD DRIPPIN' FROM HER MOUTH AND FROM ALL TWENTY CLAWS, AND I SHAT MYSELF.

THOUGHT SHE WAS GONNA SLICE MY HEAD OFF, BUT IT WAS LIKE THE CLAW HIT A WALL, BOUNCED BACK. SHE WAS FIGHTIN' WITH SOME HUGE FORCE, MOANIN' AND WITHERIN', WITH HER TEETH AND NAILS SHRINKIN'. THE SHADOW LIFTED OFF 'ER LIKE SOME KINDA HUGE BAT. IT TWIRLED THREE TIMES IN THE AIR AND DISAPPEARED. AND WHEN IT WAS GONE, MY MOM WAS BACK. SHE SAID, "I'M SO SORRY, DARLING. I'M SO SORRY." AND WE BOTH CRIED AND SHE LICKED THE BLOOD FROM MY FACE AND I DIDN'T EVEN KNOW HOW LONELY IT WAS WITHOUT 'ER UNTIL SHE WAS BACK.

THAT NIGHT SHE MADE ME PROMISE IF SHE EVER GOT TOOK BY THE SPIRIT AGAIN, I'D RUN FAST AND FAR AS I COULD. SHE MADE ME PROMISE THREE TIMES.

30.

EVENTUALLY WE SAT IN SILENCE, listening to the rain. It was a downpour that started the night of Bell's rape and soaked all November. I had only ever known the Panjwa'i river as a dry bed, hardpacked, an alternative road for insurgents. We used to drone-stalk it like a road, anyway. In November, the river flooded, coursing southwest from Kandahar City along the spine of horn-shaped Panjwa'i district. Suddenly that porous and annoying border was tight, secure. Insurgents could no longer tickle our scrotums with their back-and-forth antics, crossing between the zones of control between us and our American homies north of the river.

Wherever the river went, it brought green—the banks bloomed; wasteland turned paradise, with wild sheep drinking at the shore, and men watering their donkeys. No longer did our drones hunt over a cracked wasteland of sand and clay, but over green fields and flowering thistles.

Bell in the hospital, and the river acting like a wall in the north; the desert to the south suddenly a mud pit that dropped to freezing at night; our own roads turned to swampland: the war was on hiatus. We hunkered, stared at the sky in amazement, scraped mud from our boots with a stick, skirted the edges of the bloated poo pond as it strained against its banks, the reflected moon an angry brown eye, trapped.

Sure, there was still violence. Those fields were half-packed with unexploded ordinance and landmines. Much as we pretend that drones are a new special thing that kill from a distance, it's bullshit—landmines have been exploding since 1300 AD, often decades after they were planted. We sent engineers to blow up bombs unearthed by the rain, deployed helicopters for people who stepped on yesteryear's mines.

The peace of the off-season. The Taliban smeared honey in their wounds and trained new fighters. Mostly, it just drove us crazy. Especially Kool. Banging his head off the desk, cleaning his pistol obsessively, mourning the slow pace, "I could be out in the shit right now! Kicking some fucking ass." I didn't let him forget that he'd had me arrested. I revenged myself through various humiliations and passive-aggressive acts of sabotage. Correcting him while he was briefing the General. Throwing his clean laundry bag straight into the garbage. Refusing to give him time off work to get a replacement uniform. Then, after a week in the same shirt, haranguing him for his body odour.

How did our straight-laced Major feel about my little campaign? I suspect she was of two minds. Many smiles hid behind hands in those days. Quite a few involuntary snorts, followed immediately by a clearing of the throat. Once or twice the mask cracked and a nightingale flew out and danced around our heads: her laughter, flitting off the plywood desks, hovering over bowls placed to catch the rain, whizzing past the monitors of drone feeds.

We left a chessboard on the rear-most desk in the TOC, and moved our pieces when the other wasn't looking. Once or twice we talked about books. Then, even as my knights badgered her king and queen into a bunker of impotence, she let me know she wasn't fooled.

"Jones, how long are you going to keep messing with Kool?"

My eyes grew wide in hurt innocence. "Major, what an outrageous accusation. I—"

"No bullshit, Jones. Look, you've won." Kool was slumped at the front desk, his pistol dismantled into all its component springs, his face mashing his keyboard. "I was pissed off about the arrest too, Jones. But he's beaten. The guy has requested to be sent to the FOBs three times, and we need him here."

I nodded, bit my lip. "One more prank?"

Her eyes twinkled in shades of iceberg blue. "Make it a good one, Jones."

It was a happy time, believe it or not, that month. Bell's rape was the best thing that had ever happened to me—it was lovely not to hear his bloodthirsty whisper, or see him thrusting his hands into his pockets whenever the Major raised her voice. To hear his insinuations to Crazy Jay and Clay, undermining, painting bloody rainbows, the pandering to the General. I only liked Bell when he was frail and exposed.

I liked him a lot that month. Three times I visited him in the hospital with two buckets of Tim Horton's coffee in my hands.

"God bless you, Brother," he said, taking that first sip. Bell was alone in a four-person room—not enough injuries in the rainy season to fill the racks. He was a bit thinner, aged, having lost a bit of the bulk from his chest, shoulders and waist, and his triceps sagging in the sleeveless hospital gown. Wrinkles around his eyes and mouth were carved a little deeper.

"How you holding up, Bell?" I asked, settling into a wheeled office chair.

"King of the world, Buddy, king of the world. Three good meals a day, ten hours of sleep, I don't even need to wipe myself—a guy could get used to this kind of treatment." He laughed, pointed to a nightstand. "Look, they even gave me flowers. How long have I been on this planet? And this is the first time I get flowers." A bouquet of desert thistles with nodding yellow faces colored the otherwise bare room.

I grinned. "You Army martyrs love suffering, don't you?"

"You call this suffering? Shit. Try growing up in Winnipeg in 40 below. That'll put some hair on your nuts. This is a vacation, Jones—better than a vacation because now I don't have to put up with my wife."

I couldn't tell if Bell was in a fine mood or putting on a brave front. "Is that why you stayed? To avoid her?"

"Honestly, they tried to send me home. Had two dude-nurses tugging on my robe. I crossed my arms like this," he folded his arms across his chest and stuck out his chin stubbornly, "and said 'No. My tour's not over.'"

"I knew you were Superman in disguise."

"Better believe it, Jones. On that note, you're welcome."

"Welcome for what?"

"Wasn't for me, you'd still be rotting in a jail cell. Who knows what they'd be doing to you in there." Curiously absent was the normal jab at my being a sailor—the customary, "but of course you would have liked it."

I raised my cup for a toast. "Greatly appreciated, Bell. I'm quite fond of freedom." We talked like this for a few more minutes, light banter that skirted the edges of the incident, until I plunged: "Hey, I know it's none of my business, but the guy who attacked you… did he have a strange accent?"

Bell's eyes grew wide and his mouth worked silently for a few seconds. "You with the military police now, Jones? Ha! No, my *friend* never spoke, thanks for asking."

I stood. "Sorry about that—just had a wild thought. I'm going to run and grab a workout before my shift. Anything I can do to help you out?"

"You know there is something, Jones. Worst thing about what happened? I lost my deck of lucky cards. Might be nice to pass the time with a few hands, you know?" A muscle in his face quivered, and for a half-second he seemed a haggard creature with pinched cheeks and haunted eyes. Then he swallowed and grinned.

"No trouble at all," I said.

Too stubborn to die. Nobody wants "fucked to death" on their tombstone, I guess. I'd heard the story of Bell refusing to leave the hospital bed. *His* version didn't include the part about the screaming down the halls, kicking the nurses so hard he tore his stitches open, or how they knocked him out with a tranquilizer. It was hard to hate a guy on a hospital bed, who was tougher than a damn honey badger, and who held his head up straight despite the shame of the rape. But I am a sucker for strength.

Second visit: Bell was thrashing deep in dreams. The flowers on the nightstand were wilting. I stood and watched in the corner of the room while the sheets twisted tighter and tighter around him like an anaconda. He whipped his head from side to side. Tore an IV out of his arm—even that didn't wake him. I was wondering if I should go, just back out of the room now, leaving the coffee on the end-table. Bell tensed, bolted upright, and bellowed "YOU CAN'T DO THIS I'M A PERSON." His eyes shot open and he panted in ragged gasps.

Coffee trickled down my hand. I was squeezing the cup too hard.

"What the fuck do you want, Jones?" said Bell, leaning back into his pillows.

"Just dropping off a cup of joe, Buddy. Checking up on you."

"Well, I'm obviously fucking fine, aren't I? Not like I need a bunch of assholes gawking at me like I'm in the zoo."

Canadians have an expression to fill awkward moments like this one: "I'm sorry." I put the coffee on the end-table. "I'll take off. Get well soon, Bell."

"You think you could have done better?" Bell's weary voice from the bed. He was staring at the ceiling. "If he'd put the Taser into you and strapped that bag over your head. You think you could have done better, Jones, you goddamn prick?"

Probably, I thought. "No," I said.

"Have a seat." Bell gulped coffee, his face a hard mask. "First thing's first, wipe the goddamn pity off your face—I've shat guys like you for breakfast my whole life. You got no idea what it was like for me growing up, no idea what tough looks like. But lately I've been thinking, Jones—been thinking a whole lot."

Then he told me this ugly/hard Winnipeg story, interrupting himself with self-pitying chuckles as the bloodshot eyes protruded and the coffee disappeared down his throat.

Sure, we broke the rules but that's the point of having a gang. We were bad men but that girl loved us even if she couldn't say so. I remember in those days having a bandage on my arm where I had tattooed "Bell"—so I don't forget, I said. A blurry job even when it was fresh, you see, Jones?

If I'd been more sober I would done it proper, but that was Frank the Tank's fault. He kept slipping me drinks and making me laugh. He wore white shirts with the collar open and could make flowers appear out of thin air for girls. Never explained the mystery to me. With the girls, he used his cheekbones and ass-shaped chin like a boxer uses his left and right: jab, jab, cross—they couldn't get enough of him. But with men he used his fists and nobody could fuck with him, except maybe the Bear.

I got on with the team because of my decent right hook and because of that time I got arrested for stealing a car from the police impound. I led six cops on a chase across ruined dockyards and old train tracks and the roof of an old factory and spun circles in the dump and finally wrapped the car around some tree, like a scarf.

She touched my face, that blind, mute girl. When she felt my scars from the crash she snatched her hands back like she'd been burnt. *Muh muh muh* she said, but that was all she ever said. Her eyes got big and wet like a cow's, even after the Bear grabbed her by the hand—it was his turn.

You didn't want to get between the Bear and something he wanted, Jones. He was twice *your* size, a giant who'd had too many beer bottles smashed on his head. His hair was all patchy in places from the scars. You always wanted him in your corner, especially if there was a scrap—he made grown men shit their pants, and he only had one move. He'd just grab a hold of the guy by the arms and start eating him. That's why they called him the Bear. The other guy'd be clubbing and swinging around and begging for someone to save him but the Bear didn't feel a thing.

Every Thursday the three of us'd get into the car—I was always the driver because of my rep'—and pick up our *girlfriend* from her parents' place. They'd always try to stop her, but she'd bolt out the back door or shimmy out a window soon as she saw the headlights. We'd open the door and she'd fling herself in the car and Frank or the Bear would catch her and we wouldn't even have to slow down, the parents chasing after us on the lawn, screaming about calling the cops.

She'd greet us with a *muh muh muh* and that was the sign for Frank to start tearing her dress off. The four of us and a bottle in some field with the moon making everything *shine*. The feel of the hood of the car when it was still warm. Corn waving in the field like thin soldiers. Sirens of police cars. Feel of mud under the knees and the sound of *muh muh muh*—we never hit her, Jones, not once. We were softness and hardness together and everyone was happy, I think.

By the end of the night, we'd all be drunk, even the girl. We'd roll her out onto her parents' lawn without stopping and she'd stumble and fall into the grass with her ripped dress, her face bruised from kisses. And in the rear-view you'd see the parents come out in their pyjamas and wrap a robe around her. I imagine they'd quiet her crying, and clean her up, and sew the dress and maybe call the cops, but there's nothing anyone could do—the girl was willing. The next week she'd be climbing out onto a branch and swinging down a rope and jumping in the car again.

I grew up, Jones. Had a knack for selling people cars they couldn't afford, lasted about half a career, least until even I started feeling like a piece of shit getting granny to sign away her retirement on a Bentley she didn't need. Joined the Forces. Now that tattoo on my forearm's just an ugly smudge. But the people I remember best were the Mom and the Dad of that mute girl, the way they took her in their arms and stared at the car until the taillights disappeared. It must have made them crazy to think there were people like us in the world. It must have hurt them something awful to know their daughter was so lonely she'd want to get used like that.

I never thought about how she felt at the time. Only started thinking about it now.

"Jesus, Bell."

"Some days I feel about a thousand years old, Jones." He had shut his eyes, sunk deeper into the pillows. "Just leave me alone for a while, OK?"

"I got your cards—you want them?"

"Put them on the table and leave me alone."

Third and final visit. The flowers on the nightstand had all dropped off, leaving a bouquet of thorns. Bell was awake, turned onto one side and playing solitaire with those cards I bought him. I put that day's bucket of coffee beside him and settled into my chair.

"You came back," he said, not looking up.

Sometimes you just need someone to run next to you without judgement. "How are the cards treating you?"

Bell flipped one. "I think they got me on some strong stuff, Jones. Sometimes I flip a card and stare at it and next thing I know four hours have passed."

I said, "Same thing used to happen to my Dad after inhaling a quart of rye."

He looked at me, then. The lines on his face etched ever deeper, pouches around his eyes sagging to his cheeks. When I met him, I thought Bell must have been near my age, thirtyish. But now…

"Sorry for last time, Brother," he said, hazarding a weak laugh. "All new territory for me."

Shrugged, "I get it, man. I mean, if you'd been shot you'd at least have a story to tell over beers at your unit."

He was quiet for a long moment. When I looked up, tears glinted on his cheeks, but they ran too fast for him to scrub away. I stared at my shoelace.

After a minute of composing himself, Bell spoke again, and this time his voice lacked that false bravado of the first visit, and the grit of the second. "Been on a journey, Jones. I'm getting through it, but every day I wish I never signed up for this fucked-up war."

"So why didn't you go home when you had the chance?"

Bell reached for the coffee. Gulped. "The cash, of course. Couldn't stand the thought of going back to my wife after all the shit we'd been through. Her begging me not to go and me saying, 'think of the swimming pool I'll get us with all that danger pay.'"

We shared a very dry and mirthless chuckle. When it dried up, I said, "Kool's been taking jabs at you since you left. His big joke is that you liked it."

A glimmer of the old Bell sparked on his face, and he grinned. "I'm not worried about Kool. If I can handle getting tasered twelve times and almost bleeding to death, I can handle that little punk. I'm not superstitious, Jones, but I been thinking. I was tied to that truck for hours, and it started to rain. How long had we been here? Six months, seven? Never seen a single drop of rain. Sweating my balls off this whole time. But *then*? In *that* moment, it rains? I didn't believe it at first. I thought maybe I was getting pissed on."

He searched for words, swallowed something, continued, "But now maybe I think I was getting *washed clean*. Those words "washed clean" keep popping into my head. Is that crazy?"

Oh hell, Bell has found religion. "Doesn't sound crazy to me," I said.

"I don't think I'll be the same after that, Jones." He glanced toward his crotch, toward his injuries. "I'll be better."

31.

OTHERWISE, THAT MONTH WAS THE GOLDEN AGE of the TOC—no one dies in this whole chapter. Sometimes war is funny and once or twice we laughed so hard we nearly pissed ourselves. Like the time a soldier complained he'd grown tired of masturbation and I advised him to use his feet. And that worked out great for a few weeks, at least until he got a fungus. Life was as stressful as it needed to be. We spent less time prowling the skies, and more time waiting, reading, and talking. I had a case of CDs which was ancient tech even then but it was the only music we could play on the unclassified computer. For some reason, Ke$ha, raunchy pop princess turned country star, kept making it into the rotation.

Clay, from his computer a few yards away, threw up his hands. He was an Air Force Captain in his fifties who had long squashed his dreams of promotion. With a short buzzcut, his head seemed a perfect cube. "I can't take these contradictions anymore."

"What's the matter, Clay?" I asked.

"In one song, she says she hates old guys like me, and tells a guy who's hitting on her 'you should be prowling around the old folk's home.'"

"Yeah, so what?"

"Well, in this song she says she 'kicks them to the curb unless they look like Mick Jagger,' and that guy's a hundred."

"Yeah, what the fuck's up with that!" shouted Crazy Jay, the cords on his neck jutting from all the yelling.

Clay was on a roll: "Is it too much to ask for a little consistency in our music? Is that impossible?"

"Stop toying with our feelings, Ke$ha!" Crazy Jay hollered.

I changed the CD. That was a quiet night.

Another: we projected a Pacman game onto one of the main screens, where normally the drone feed played constantly. *Nom nom nom nom*—the yellow head munched dots and ran from a rainbow of ghosts. "Kinda like Bell running from the Taser rapist," Kool joked. *Wah wah wah*—the scream of ultimate agony, a melting into a puddle, soul sucked out. Kool had lasted twenty seconds and died two dots away from the power-up.

"Suck at the game, just like you suck at life," I said. Because Bell would have a hard enough time coming back and because chirping Kool remained my chief joy.

But eventually I turned the game off and people grumbled a bit but I didn't want to watch the little man snuffing it over and over. Soon it would be real people dying on that screen.

Another: around suppertime, our drone hovered over a mud-walled compound—suspicious fighters lurked inside, according to intelligence reports. A rare moment when the sun shone that month, warming the skin, setting the mood for… romance?

Kool saw it first. "Is that guy fucking a goat?"

We turned. The Major's hand rose to her mouth. A pen clattered to the floor.

Riddles abounded. What foreplay? What investment of time? What history of passion? What forbidden love? What murmured words of anguish, of poetry, were slipped into that hirsute ear? No one knows what passed between the Fighting Aged Male and his goat before the carnal act began, but the goat had no reservations, syncopating and heaving with all the wildness of nature.

"Maybe the goat's fucking him?" said the Major, from behind her hand. We crowded around the screen: privacy is just another casualty of war.

The man's loose robe was pulled up over his hips, his stance imperial, pelvis a blur. The goat bucked and heaved, pressing its ears flat and low against its neck. It bared its teeth in a rictus of ecstasy, whinnying and pawing the air.

"That's fucking disgusting," said Kool.

"You're just jealous," I said, "of the goat." Even Kool laughed. Afterwards, the goat and its paramour cuddled in the shade of a lean willow, the goat resting its head on the man's forearm, and staring into his eyes. In moments, the man was snoring; his lover inched closer.

But after, I thought of Bell and the strange episode made me sad, the long-suffering goat with its ears pulled back. Is it possible to break a feeling, the way we break a bone? Or is that just going mad? I didn't know when it was appropriate to feel compassion; it was coming out at strange times. I pitied Pacman but thought a violated goat good fodder for jokes. I visited Bell in the hospital, brought food to Noah in his cave, but tormented the living hell out of Kool. I sympathized for those shooting rockets at us, for the victims of our drone strikes, but spat scorn at our leadership, their regimen of ass clenches. *I have forgotten how to human.*

Another: you know how kids sometimes send letters to soldiers? Well if you ever wonder where those letters wind up, it might be at a TOC pored over by pasty-faced moles, killers and desensitized bastards like me. And it was all the same shit like *thanks so much for your service and for fighting the bad men* and it was endearing the way the war was so uncomplicated for the children, good versus evil forces, lies they had been told. The crayon-drawings of Mum and the dog were always sweet, and I responded to a few of these letters with pictures of warships and Sasquatch and sweet, simple narratives.

One evening we received a package of letters from a school—I read a whole stack of them. Stick-figure men holding rifles in the margins, shooting fat bullets and shouting *bang*. Since the Major asked me to ease up on Kool, I'd stopped fucking with him, mostly, even got him moved back to the dayshift for a more "normal" life, since Bell was away. Sure, I stomped Kool verbally whenever possible, particularly when he threw up his hands moaning, "I should be out in the shit, not surrounded by you pussies!" like he did every damn day. But the Major had blessed one final prank, the culmination, final revenge for getting me arrested, for the Cheezies, the gay jokes, the moaning that our tour wasn't hard enough, and all the other chafes. The other soldiers probably thought I was going crazy, reading those sad letters, an evil snicker growing into a mad scientist's cackle.

Now you will see me at my most petty. For there was one child who never got a response back from a soldier. Who watched all his classmates get soldier-letters, heard the teacher read them all out, admired the pictures of warships and drones and tanks and Sasquatch, who waited as the teacher called out all the names and is perhaps still waiting, will always be waiting. If you're reading this, I'm sorry, Danny. You seem like a nice person. You deserve to know what happened.

First, I steamed the letter open with the mist of an iron. Then, I copied the letterhead and studied Danny's spelling and grammatical errors. I wrote a fake letter for Kool and carefully resealed the letter in its original envelope.

Early morning, end of my shift; the Major arrived early with a coffee in her hand, yawning. She knew something was up, "What's that smirk for, Jones?"

"We received a batch of letters from schoolkids last night, Major."

"Ok. Put them on my desk and I'll distribute them today. Is that all?"

I handed her the false letter. "Can you make sure Kool gets this one?"

"Is this what I think it is, Jones?" A crooked smile.

"The last one, Major."

0800. My shift had grown with Bell in the hospital, so I'd been giving the morning brief to the Major and TOC-moles. It was a quick one, nearly meatless. Afterward, she distributed the letters to all assembled. Kool snatched the letter from her hand, sneering and rolling his eyes, reminding us that he should be "out in the shit." I knew his letter by heart.

> *Deer solder in Afhganistan,*
>
> *My nem is Danny. I am grade 5. My Mom seys I am verry specal.*
>
> *I want thank you for yor service. I heer you fite bad guys and sav people. This vary incredible.*
>
> *I also heer some solders are office solders that hid frum the fiting. If you r that tip of solder, pleaz pass my lettr to a reel solder, a reel man?*
>
> *I hat the idee that my lettr might end up in hands of coward office solder.*
>
> *Thank you fer fiting and doing the hard werk of a reel solder, and not beeing a derty coward.*
>
> *Danny*

We drifted away, after the briefing, to read our letters, but we kept an eye on Kool. He held that letter for five whole minutes, like he was reading it over and over again, shoulders slumping lower and lower. He shook his head from side to side, glaring around the room, an ugly scowl on his face.

His mutters were loud enough to hear: "That little bastard. This little fucking punk thinks he's better than me. Let's see him do Phase 3, the pissant." After a final read-through, a furious look seared onto his face, Kool grasped the paper as if to tear it to pieces.

"Kool!" shouted the Major. "Are you tearing up one of the children's letters?"

Redhanded. He actually blushed. "Ma'am, this little peckerwood deserves worse than that. In fact, I'm going to visit him, once I get home, and beat the ever-living shit out of him."

"You are not going to beat up a child, Kool. Don't be ridiculous." Kool blushed a deeper shade, purple. "Well, now you've got us all curious—read the letter loud enough so we all can hear you."

He started, "Deer solder in Afhganistan," in a small child's voice. The Major's hand flew to her mouth. By the time Kool got to that third paragraph, I was straining so hard not to laugh I nearly shat myself. By the fourth paragraph, all the TOC-moles were cackling. At the fifth paragraph the Major herself started to giggle, a tiny shake of her shoulders, a miniscule bobbing of her bun. Tiny quivering of her breasts, a muscle tensing in her forearm. Last paragraph, the whole TOC was roaring, myself included, the

Major unleashing her full laugh like cages of doves.

"Shut up, you fuckers!" Kool screamed, which only made everyone laugh harder. Clay was dabbing tears from his eyes. The Major had collapsed against a desk, holding her sides, and I tried to memorize her completely in that moment, she seemed so happy.

In the midst of the din, understanding dawned in Kool's eyes. "Which one of you fuckers wrote this?" He demanded—we met him with a chorus of hoots and howls. "I'll tear his goddamn eyes out!" Kool snarled, showing his incisors.

"Take it easy, Office Soldier!" Clay wheezed.

"Yah, keep your pants on, Office Soldier!" That was Crazy Jay.

Kool stormed out. When I left, my shift over, twenty minutes later, he was rage-smoking in the smoker's pit and kicking the chain-link fence.

After that he was a snarling beast for a full week. And it didn't take him long to figure out who wrote the letter, either—things were even more tense in our shared room, with many a glare, redoubled quickdraw practice and polishing his handgun. After the public reading everyone called Kool "Office Soldier" from then on, at least until he was renamed, and I don't think he ever forgave me. Not that I apologized. I never felt bad about it—not once. Every time the guilt started to creep up, I remembered the Major bracing herself against the desk and laughing so hard it was noiseless.

I'd do anything to make her laugh like that again.

32.

MOSTLY SHE WAS TOO EXHAUSTED FOR LAUGHTER. Literally fell asleep with her eyes open once or twice, rousing for a coffee and the gentlest of shoulder pats. Sixteen-hour workdays, at least, often twenty, attending briefings, giving briefings, a quick work-out during her lunch, and hours, countless hours, poured into upcoming operations—specifically the Female Engagement Team. She was most alive during the "emplacement window," dusk, when insurgents boobytrapped the roads with IEDs. This was the start of my shift and it was always packed—the Major wanted as many people in the TOC as possible during the window in case we needed to strike.

But that month, we didn't. Not once. We had four Colonels clenching their asses a thousand times a second in sweaty anticipation of the next strike—the static electricity was growing. And without killing, where does all that power go?

Stupid speeches. Napoleon was wrong when he said armies march on their stomachs. Stupid speeches are all we need.

A gruff voice called "Room!" and we snapped to attention for the General. There he was, the magnificent bastard, unfathomable behind his sunglasses, his aura of awesomeness causing a lightbulb to burst.

"Listen up, troops!" He snapped his fingers, a whipcrack. "Figured I should say a few words after what happened. Always a sad day when one of our warriors is injured. We got cowards on the other side of the wall trying to blow us up with IEDs, and a coward inside the base waiting to zap us with a Taser—it's the only way our enemies know how to fight." *Because sniping someone with a drone is so heroic.* Kool must have been thinking something similar—he blushed more easily since we dubbed him Office Soldier.

The General's mirrored glasses reflected our pasty faces back as he strode the room, up and down the computer-aisles. "I suspect the reason we've been suffering these kinds of attacks is because people have been in breach of the no-fraternization policy, am I right? One person starts messing around, getting some action, and then another person gets jealous and, before you know it you got perverts in bunkers and heroes in the hospital. That's why I made the policy—to keep y'all safe.

"Best thing to do? Stay focused on bringing the war to your enemy. This so-called Taser Rapist is helping the Taliban by sowing discord on the camp and making us doubt each other. It's normal to feel fear. To feel alone. To feel confused. And your job is to take all that energy, turn it into missiles, and send it back into Johnny Taliban's face. Y'all need reminders about why you're here and bringing the fight to the enemy will do that. So keep the pressure up. Take inspiration from Bell, the sacrifice he made, and the courage he showed after the attack. That tough prick refused to be sent home, you know that? He told me himself, he said, "My work's not done here, Boss."

"I want you all to know that we are doing everything in our power to find this rapist and bring him to justice. In the meantime, buddy system. Keep your pistols loose in the holster, and oiled. Keep your head on a swivel…" The General began to string familiar military expressions in such a continuous stream of encouragement that I'm afraid I began to zone out a little, and I'm not sure if my memory will do it justice, but I'll give it a shot.

He sounded something like this: "Roger that, this gongshow will go pear-shaped, if it ain't raining we ain't training, a goddamn dog's breakfast, bravo zulu troops, not another dog and pony show, take a bite of that shit sandwich, hurry up and wait for the clusterfuck, useless as an asshole on the back of my neck, get that shit squared away, over and out, take a knee folks, figure out who's who in the zoo, unfuck yourself shitbag," and it seemed he would go on like that for days, channeling his repository of Army clichés, head tilted back and his eyes blank. But it was comforting, in a strange way, to know where each word was leading, and to be able to finish his phrases for him in your mind.

A nine-liner showed up on the screen. A local, injured; we needed to act.

MEDICAL EVACUATION REQUEST
Location: 41R QQ 385 511
Radio frequency and name: 179.146750 VHF, Charlie Company
Number of casualties and severity: 1 critically injured, scalded genitals
Special Equipment required: None
Patient requires litter or ambulatory: Litter
Security of pick-up site: Secure
Method of marking pick-up site: Main gates of Forward Operating Base
Patient nationality and status: Afghan, infant
Chemical biological or nuclear threat: None

I didn't make this up—someone had scalded a baby's genitals. An angry mutter ran through the assembled soldiers, but the General was still duck-speaking, staring down at us through those glimmering mirrors. A series of polite coughs—the Major cleared her throat. Then, as the seconds ticked on, the courage to interrupt, "Ummm, Sir," and frantic nods toward the screen. But the General's mouth raced, "We say HUA early in the morning, zero dark thirty, in accordance with the battle rhythm, good time to send rounds downrange, and he said don't call me sir I work for a living, so I throatpunched him right in the nuts, just full-spectrum operations, close with and destroy the enemy—"

"Sir!" The Major shouted loud enough to pierce the General's encouraging babble. He spun around and saw the 9-liner; he could read the anti-poetry same as the rest of us.

"Get to it, troops," he said, and a leather-throat called room and we all ran to our computers and phones. I jumped on the combat chat to confirm receipt of the 9-liner with a resounding "ACK," and ran to the big map to doublecheck the coordinates—they made sense.

"South of Bazaar-E-Panjwa'i," I yelled.

Clay nodded his brickish head. He was sending messages down his own helicopter-specific chat, searching for an available bird. "Major, all the helicopters on the camp are out on mission. I'll phone and try to cancel a less urgent one."

"Move it, Clay," said the Major. "We got a kid with scalded genitals, critical condition."

Kool's voice from the front of the room, near the monitors. "Who the fuck scalds a baby's genitals?"

The Major whirled and, in a firm voice: "Get angry after. Now we react."

Sure there were people, faces, monitors, keyboards, phones. But what I remember most is that combat chat scrolling down, black ink, black news, burying everything that came before. The war, sterilized; you had to remind yourself it was real.

I passed the 9-liner and other info to the hospital chat. They needed to prep to receive another patient, with special considerations for the child, and send their medics on the flight we were trying to book.

"Shit shit," said Clay. "All six of the base helicopters are on CAT A missions. We need another option."

"Talk to Regional Command South," said the Major. "We'll borrow a combat helicopter."

What the hell are you doing with our medics? asked the hospital
Why do you want a combat helicopter for this? asked Regional Command South

"Can't send a helicopter right now anyway, we got a Restricted Operations Zone," said Crazy Jay.

"Who authorized that ROZ?" asked the Major.

Fuck you, here's another 9-liner, said the war.

MEDICAL EVACUATION REQUEST
Location: 41R QQ 376 437
Radio frequency and name: 179.444600 VHF, Alpha Company
Number of casualties and severity: 1 critically injured, scalded genitals
Special Equipment required: None
Patient requires litter or ambulatory: Litter
Security of pick-up site: Secure
Method of marking pick-up site: Green smoke
Patient nationality and status: Afghan, infant
Chemical biological or nuclear threat: None

"Jesus," said Clay." Another one."

ACK I wrote into the combat chat, then ran to the big map. "About five kilometers south of Mushan."

"Ack," said Clay.

"Get that fucking ROZ down, Crazy Jay. Whose fucking ROZ is that?" said the Major.

"Can't," yelled Crazy Jay. "We got American troops in contact north of the river. It's their ROZ."

Here's another 9-liner, I said to the hospital
What the hell, said the hospital. Is this the same 9-liner as before?
No, I said, this is a separate event
Ack, said the hospital, where's the helicopter?

Working on it, said Clay

Fuck it I'll phone RC South myself, said the Major
Second 9-liner is outside the ROZ, said Crazy Jay
We need a goddamn helicopter, said the Major
Fuck you, said RC South, use a medical helicopter we got troops in contact
Hey we fucked up the grid reference on that second 9-liner, said the troops
Fuck, I said, but wrote ack
Here's the correct grid reference, said the troops
OK six kilometers south of Mushan, I said
That's still outside the ROZ, said Crazy Jay
Fuck you, said the war, here's another 9-liner

MEDICAL EVACUATION REQUEST
Location: 41R QQ 387 436
Radio frequency and name: 179.76640 VHF, Bravo Company

Number of casualties and severity: 1 critically injured, scalded genitals
Special Equipment required: None
Patient requires litter or ambulatory: Litter
Security of pick-up site: Secure
Method of marking pick-up site: Designated Landing Zone
Patient nationality and status: Afghan, infant
Chemical biological or nuclear threat: None

You can't be goddamn serious, said Clay
Ack, I wrote
Fuck yourself, yelled the Major
Just south of Kandahar City, I said
Here's another 9-liner, I told the hospital
We got three critically injured now, Clay wrote
You gotta be shitting me, said the helicopter people
What the hell's happening, said the hospital, is this the same as the other injury?
No, I said, three different events, same injury
Who the fuck scalds a baby's genitals? shouted Kool
Fuck you, said the war, ROCKET ATTACK ROCKET ATTACK
Third 9-liner is outside of the ROZ, said Crazy Jay, from under his desk
I'm phoning those pricks, I said, under mine
Boom, said the exploding rocket
I'm bright and shiny, said the spray of sparks
We need the helicopter for the rocket attack, said RC South
We got three critically injured, yelled the Major
We're coming into your goddamn ROZ, I said
I got a helicopter, said Clay
Send it to the second 9-liner, I said
Ack, said Clay
Boom, said a second rocket
I'm loud as fuck, said the siren
Take the damn helicopter, said RC South
You're goddamn right, said the Major
Send your medics here and here, I said
Ack, said the hospital
Sorry, grid reference wrong again, said the troops
We're taking off now, said the first helicopter
Ack, I wrote
Wah wah wah, cried the baby with the scalded genitals
Ack, I wrote
Now we're taking off, said the RC South helicopter
Send the RC South helicopter to the third incident not the first, I said
What the fuck is going on guys, said the RC South helicopter
Shut the fuck up and do it, said the Major
I'm landing on the ground now, said the first helicopter
Ack, I wrote
Did you ack my new grid reference, asked the troops

Ack ack ack, I wrote
OK we're landing now too, said the second helicopter
ROZ is down now, said the troops in contact
Our baby died, said the first helicopter
Send the helo to the first incident, I said
Go get the first baby, Clay wrote
We're landing at the hospital with our baby, the second helo said
This baby died too, the first helo said
Ack, I wrote

33.

ALMOST FORGOT THAT PART ENTIRELY, about the babies.

Breath fogs the window on a rainy day, staring out onto Toronto streets with the gray cars chugging past. I never saw the babies so they aren't as bad as my other specters—haven't taken shape. Can't taunt, no words, just words.

Still.

I would have rather not remembered.

I will write no more today; the pen shakes.

34.

Mom,

Just got home from work and saw your message. Today was difficult and, frankly, a blast of shit about my poor correspondence rate was the last thing I needed.

I get that it sucks, having a son in the war. That you worry a lot, that watching the news is torture. You know what's worse? Being in the war. When you get upset you can grab a coffee with Sue, or drive down to visit your sister. Hell, you can buy a bottle of wine and cry to pieces on the kitchen table. You can go for a hike in the woods or to a yoga class. I can't.

Here's what I think is fair: when you see on the news that some soldiers were kidnapped, check the date of the kidnapping, and make sure it was in the right province. That incident happened in Camp Nathan Smith and I'm in Kandahar Airfield. It was a month ago—I've emailed you since. Had you done a scrap of research—how hard is it to Google something?—you would know I wasn't kidnapped, you'd have saved yourself all that pain, and you wouldn't have splashed it all over me.

Stop putting extra crap on me; believe it or not this is my best.

35.

Dear Mom,

Just woke up and read that last letter over—sorry for the harshness. I've been tired lately, tired all the way to the bones. Yesterday was a bad day. I understand that your emails are coming from a place of love and worry but sometimes they drain me.

Truth is there is beauty here, Mom. When the mountain eclipses the dawn. Flowers blooming in the Red Desert, starlings in the thistles. The Panjwa'i River, when it runs, gardens sprouting on either bank. Farmers hoeing the irrigation trenches, mules pulling furrows. Mostly, it has been a quiet month, a mopping up, with the rains drenching a world of mud. They never depict the beautiful parts of Afghanistan on the news. They're always going for cheap sensationalism, crashed helicopters and whatnot. But the day-to-day is much more mundane. Please stay suspicious of the news and try not to worry so much.

Beyond worry about the kidnapping two things emerge from your last letter: 1) a request for feedback on the morale box; and 2) skepticism about the Sasquatch. As for the former, those morale boxes, particularly the kitten-soft rolls of pressed silk and crispy cheese-flavored twists, are treasured, and will be remembered my whole life. Not only by me, but by Noah, the Sasquatch, who slobbers with excitement when I receive one. You should see him scoop out the bottom of the peanut butter jar with his long tongue, delight shining in his eyes (please send more peanut butter).

Noah is a story-telling joker—he's been telling me the tale of his life. He's also the strongest creature I've ever met. Noah has made the following boasts, all true. He can:

- crush stones into diamonds in his armpits
- dropkick the world tree
- belch the entire alphabet
- tame a herd of rampaging hippos
- bulldoze bulldozers
- straighten a perfect circle
- wrangle whales
- and choke PI until it surrenders its final digit

Amazingly, Noah has flourished on a diet of frog heads, dubious meatloaf and <u>infrequent</u> peanut butter doses. He continues to gain height and mass. How strong will he be when he stops growing, I wonder? What will he do with all of it, his strength?

So you see, my dear mother, with a friend like this, there is no need to worry: I am safe and well protected. Please send me light updates from home—I particularly enjoy the tales of the cat and the kids at school—I'll respond when I can. <3

Love you.

M

36.

SURE THE WAR WAS FUTILE. The Taliban made killers a crop that sprouted every year in the deserts of western Pakistan. They intimidated, coerced, lured and brainwashed youth, training them to shoot AK47s and build roadside bombs. Handicapped youngsters, kidnapped by Taliban, were groomed to be the next generation of suicide bombers—we're all just trying to make a splash, aren't we?

Until we thumped Bin Laden, we never got near the sophisticated spine of international terrorists; we were only ever fighting fodder. Pakistan denied knowledge of the camps, slipped money and weapons to the Taliban, accepted billions of aid dollars, and released an official protest whenever our drones hunted down an insurgent within their borders.

An impossible war, but so was the one the General and Colonels, higher brains of this whole noble effort, had been waging on the common soldiers: the Battle of the Toilets. The back and forth of the guerilla graffiti, the black and blue and red of it.

This is how it was my first day in Kandahar, a fresh-faced soldier parting the curtain of fumes, pawing at a roll of Canadian three-ply velvet silk toilet paper, rationing himself a single square, swinging open the washroom door… to disaster. Shit all over the walls and bootprints on the toilet seats.

The next day, the mess was cleaned, but words had flowered in the night, penned in marker on the stall walls. Words like, *Kilroy was here* or *there is no magic in Kandahar.* The next day, a carnivalesque diagram: a Colonel blowing a man wearing a turban. Two days of silence, and then, on the third, more words: *I am the Taser Rapist* and *killing ragheads gets me hard* and *my friend died—I felt nothing.* The words had gotten larger, more urgent, and spread from the walls onto the door. Then it was as if a cork had been unstopped—the artwork bloomed. More words: *all ragheads must die* and *my wife just had a miscarriage* and *Charlie Company is hard as fuck* and *the General fingerbanged my sister.* More artwork: a man in a turban impaled on a spike, the General fucking a Colonel while flexing his biceps, the body of a beautiful naked woman. I began to detect distinct voices, and imagined which of my comrades might have scribbled which lines. A three-day lull, then the artwork entered a self-subversive phase; *C Company is hard as fuck for little boys* and the sentence *all ragheads must die* was scratched out in a different pen and the new sentence read, *we all must die.* The naked woman had grown a giant phallus, a fertility god. One of the rules of the graffiti war was we never talked about the graffiti war, even when the artwork crawled onto the ceiling, and our necks grew stiff from craning upward. A philosopher made his mark; I suspected Clay. *Why are we here? Is this war just? How do we know we're right?* And there was a picture of a cottage by a lake with ducks and the words *I miss home.* But the vulgar poet still boomed in giant letters: *Ragheads have tiny dicks. The General fingerbanged my sister* grew an appendage *in the ass until she cums.* I began to understand—this is where we splashed our fetishes and caprices: *Bell liked it* and a picture of a man with a bag on his head tied to the trunk of a car. The next day a goat with a huge schlong fucked a turbaned man. *Fingerbanged* had been crossed out and replaced with *fistfucked. Cums* had been crossed out and replaced with *died.* A confession: *I am unbelievably lonely.* A man in a turban melted in a pit of acid. Four Colonels stirred a cauldron wearing pointy hats. The naked woman with the giant meatstick wore a Major's rank. In life the Major was powerful and aloof, over our heads. In the toilet, she was a plaything, willing or tied up, her body imagined from four hundred different angles, long queues of lovers with monstrous, inflated cocks. Her face in ecstasy. Her face in agony. She was our boss; we stripped her, disgraced her, and fucked her back to the earth. Perhaps because of this, when the inevitable day came when the General took a crunch in the troops' toilets, he was so offended he spun the wheel of power, issued threats. "Should the graffiti continue we will remove the doors of the washrooms," and I learned even this modicum of privacy could be taken away. By the peak of the cycle, the shitters were works of degenerate art, with countless artists contributing to the conversation, with absolutely no pretensions or claims to loftiness. Crisscrossed and scratched-out words, misspellings, masturbatory fantasies, lampooning of leadership, many hands contributing to each picture: the whole goddamn room inked, even the toilet seat. You could not sit in peace amongst the words without being amused, moved or outraged. In this strange, silly war, it was the height of the fighting season.

Finally, I went in and it was all whitewashed; a few faint afterimages were the only record of our achievement. The blankness was blinding but I was glad the stuff about the Major was gone. A smirk: *soon the cycle will begin again.* After washing my hands and checking for ink, I left the toilets and encountered the soldiers' primary muse.

"I didn't see you at the hospital today, Jones," said the Major. She stood in line at the mini canteen that served flat diet cokes and chocolate bars, with about five soldiers ahead of her.

"Good evening, Major."

"You forgot our date, didn't you?" she asked, quiet enough so the surly Sergeant ahead of her couldn't hear. "Stood me up so you could go lift weights with your man-friend, probably." She dipped her head to one side, battered helmet tilting.

Oh, to be far away from here, on an asteroid belt, just the two of us. "Shit," I smacked my forehead with a palm. "The baby. I didn't go to the hospital to see the baby."

She leaned closer, "Guess you weren't tough enough for that one, eh? Didn't want to hear her little cough?" She had such an easy, bruising way to her.

"You win, Boss—I wasn't tough enough. I had tricked myself into believing it was just words on the combat chat."

"She was real," said the Major in a faint voice. "But not tough enough either, turns out."

We were silent for a moment as I absorbed what that meant. The line moved forward and we let it go.

"You win this round, Afghanistan," I said, gesturing to the walls, the barbed wire, the mud puddle.

"I was trying to say that I missed you, but I fucked it up." Her fierce bravado slipped further; she stared somewhere at the ground. "It's tough being the only one who seems to give a shit."

"I'll be there next time," I promised.

"There's really no one to talk to, is there?"

"You said we would always remember how lonely it was."

She laughed: a cold and bitter sound. "I hate being right all the time."

"I'm sorry about the baby," I said. My fingers twitched; I wanted to stroke her cheek. She looked up, and our eyes met, and hers were turquoise pools of melted icebergs. The owl-headed loneliness monster was staring out of her again, reaching through the bars. Mine was howling.

37.

STARTED AS A NORMAL NIGHTSHIFT and kept getting stranger. First it was the Military Policeman's call, a murky story about a disturbance down at Clothing Stores, with a promise of a full report in the morning. Then it was me: horny and irritable. When the Battle Group, a subordinate headquarters, called to borrow a drone to survey a routine vehicle recovery, I damn near snapped the Lieutenant's head off. "You princesses can't even take a crunch without a fucking drone." But then I handed it over a few minutes later—it had seen nothing but a long, empty road all night. Most of all, I remember that bloody handprint, the one splashed on the door of my cabin when I got back to the barracks at 0830. Twice the size of a man's hand, and smeared.

A selfish fear gripped my spine—the blood was still wet—had anyone seen it? All the dayshift had already left for work; I could picture them gaggling around the door and gossiping about the stain. *Noah's in trouble.*

First step: find him. I burst through the back door of the barracks into the dawn; blood was splattered on the ground and porch, even the wall of the concrete bunker. It was almost like the aftermath of a drone strike, except with trails of enormous bloody footprints. He wasn't in the bunker. I kneeled to look into Noah's crawl space. It was dark and reeking, with shower ooze glinting on the walls and faint-glowing moss. From within, a wheezing burble.

My knees sank into the muck as I crawled into the gloom. Hands slid into the bloody mud while insects danced on my knuckles. Stink of compost, unwashed beast and toilets. In the gloom, things came into focus: a mountain of Styrofoam containers and empty water bottles; one crude shelf with a jar of peanut butter; and a carved wooden mouse. There, near the glittering shower-corner, was Noah in the southwest corner, the great bulk of him, lying on his back with the ceiling about a foot above his face. I scurried over.

"Noah, Noah!" I hissed. "What the hell happened? Where are you hurt?"

His fingers clutched his chest and blood seeped through them. Muzzle contorted in a grimace, his two long fangs exposed. The burbling noise was his breath. "Got shot," he rasped. "Searching for… home."

"Two seconds, and I'll get help—you hang in there."

Noah grabbed my arm with his free hand, "They called me… T-Taser Rapist. Shouted at me. Called me… m-monster."

"Let go, Noah, you fucker—I'm trying to help you. We both know you're not a monster."

He chortled and his laugh expired in a hacking cough, followed by a moan. "Might… find h-home… anyway…" and his hand fell limp on my arm, and his blue eyes rolled back, showing white.

"You're not gonna die, Noah."

Everyone I try to help dies. Panic rising as I beetled from the basement. Second step: find a medical kit. I sprinted into the barracks. Grabbed the red-crossed medical kit off the wall, and, from my room, the sailor-flashlight, a canteen of water, and, in a moment of blind impulse, my last roll of Canadian toilet paper. Another night shift guy, Clay, was brushing his teeth—he raised his eyebrows at me as I ran past with my medical gear and muddy knees.

Dove into the cave, with the equipment clutched close, slipping in the slime. At Noah's side I switched on the flashlight, banishing the gloom. He was covered in blood from his neck to his knees; his fur was matted and dark and his breath was coming out a wheeze. Third step: find the wound—tucking the flashlight into my mouth I frisked Noah from his knees upward, pressing my fingers into the hair and slimy skin, losing precious time where the blood pooled between his muscles. When I got to the top of his chest, he moaned again—on his anterior deltoid, the front right shoulder, about a hand-width apart, two bullet holes oozed.

There was no exit wound. Must have been a pistol; a rifle would have pushed the bullet through. "Where's your goddamn Protector Spirit now, Noah?" But he didn't answer as I opened the medical kit, fingers slippery from the slime, the air almost too close to breathe. Wiping my fingers cost me three whole sheets of toilet paper. I wanted to enter that cold efficient zone like I did in the TOC arranging the evacuation of the infants, but it was harder to be cold when you had blood on your hands. I rinsed the wounds with hand sanitizer, and dabbed them clean to see. Noah tossed his head as I probed with a ginger finger the edges of two dark and seeping holes, about as big around as pennies.

Fourth step: get the bullets. Noah's breath getting fainter and fainter. No pliers or forceps in the medical kit, just rolls of gauze and tape and triangular bandages. One bent pair of scissors for cutting the gauze—no help. My panic rose in a stream of curses, and I muttered, "Not strong enough to stop a fucking bullet though were you, ya goddamn bastard."

I had to operate or lose my friend. I didn't have any painkillers, even. I looked around for something to ram into Noah's mouth, so he could bite down, at least. A half-second's hesitation, then I plunged my last and most precious roll of Canadian three-ply velvet toilet paper into Noah's mouth. He clenched on it reflexively, the paper tube bending, but the roll stayed true.

I plunged my finger into the bullet hole.

Noah groaned. That moment of closeness, that awful rooting into his shoulder, the spurts of blood, the tricky little bullet way down there, me gritting my teeth around the flashlight and Noah squirming and grunting and mashing the toilet paper. He kept knocking me out of the hole with his spasms and I'd begin anew, burrowing. "Stop fighting me, Noah, you son of a bitch—you're going to fucking live, do you hear me?"

The bullet clinked as I tossed it into the medical case. I rinsed my fingers for the second go. Noah had started to whimper, the noise distorted by the toilet paper. "Stay with me, Noah," I pleaded. "I've got a big jar of peanut butter I've been hiding—it's all yours. I won't touch any of it, ok?"

The second bullet was an even trickier bastard than the first, lodged into the shoulder bone. Whenever I touched it, Noah would whimper harder, and I'd babble faster, "I'm not trying to hurt you, Noah. Just a few more minutes. Hang in there. I gotta plane ticket for you—you're going back to Canada. Your mother is waiting at the airport. And I'm going to visit your family and we'll be friends until we're gray. Just hang in there—a few more minutes, ok?" and I rubbed my eyes dry on my sleeve so I could see.

Finally, I tickled the bullet free and tossed it into the case where the two bullets clung like magnets. Fifth step: bandage him. Stuffed the wounds with dressing, then wrapped the gauze around him—I lacked the tools or expertise to stitch him. Extracting the tattered shreds of toilet paper from his mouth was a strange and dangerous chore; after, I poured the rest of the canteen down his throat. Noah swallowed and his eyes fluttered and he started to snore. *Hang in there, buddy.*

Step six: hide the blood. It was all over my hands up to the elbow, sticky. It was splashed on the door to my room, smeared on the back step, and trailing to the spot Noah was shot. Outside the cave, the sun was fully risen—the police would be investigating the shooting in the morning's sober light. I had a nightmarish vision of a pack of police, led by my old buddy Legion, following the trail straight to Noah, who lacked the strength to fight *or* flee.

Ran back into the barracks—the nightshift were all passed out. Stripped my bloody uniform and stuck it in my metal locker. Scrubbed the bloody handprint off the door (how many had seen it?) with a pair of Kool's clean underwear. And how many had heard Noah's desperate stumbles, his attempts to summon me, before crawling into his pit to die? My mouth was pasty, an ashtray.

Out back. Noah's willow branch for sweeping footsteps was tucked into his cave—it worked on blood stains too, breaking up the dried puddles and mixing the crusty bits with sand. The blood trail skirted the edge of the barracks—mostly gravel on the ground there. I broke the trail by kicking the gravel and to hell with the nightshift workers sleeping on the other side of the wall—we'd learned to sleep through rocket attacks. The whole time I was sure the cops would show up and slap me in cuffs again. Front of the barracks the trail connected to the road, then passed near the gym. The laundry bins were out there, in front of the building—I splashed a few water bottles onto the road-blood under the pretence of grabbing my laundry. But when I saw three military police coming up the alley next to the gym, I disappeared back into the barracks. This was all I could do. The rest was fate.

The adrenaline was wearing off. Step seven: fall the fuck asleep. But before that I entered the frog-cave one more time to tuck a blanket around Noah—the blood was soaking through his bandages—and drop off five or six bottles of water. His eyes flicked open. In a faltering whisper: "Did you save me?"

"Not yet."

Noah coughed and the stain on his shoulder grew. "Are they coming?"

"Try to get some sleep."

38.

FINALLY FELL ASLEEP AFTER AN HOUR of fretting to the background purring of tanks. When I woke, about six hours later, I stumbled to the toilets for the "morning" leak. I met Clay scrubbing his teeth again. "You alright, Jones? Seemed in a bit of a state yesterday." I didn't feel awake enough to start managing yesterday's crisis.

"Oh, I'm great today. Just needed a band-aid—thanks for asking."

Clay gave me a shrewd look and spoke with his mouth full of paste. "Looked like you needed more than that. I mean, I was there the day with the babies, remember? We've dealt with some serious shit and this was the first time I could see it on your face." *Because Noah is real, and the babies were just words.* I reminded myself that Clay was no slouch, no matter the shape of his brickish head.

"You're right. It was more than a band-aid." I reached into my seemingly endless font of bullshit. "It was a dog."

"A dog?" Clay's eyebrows rose. He spat into the sink.

"Yep. Mangy little fucker. Had blood all over his leg, running around out back. I tried to help him, but when I got close with the medical kit he bit me and ran off, little bastard."

Clay chuckled. "Shit. So it was your handprint on the door?" I said nothing. "I gotta dog. Why didn't you tell me that in the first place?"

Shrugged. "I don't want word to get to the Army guys that I'm going soft." Clay was an air traffic controller, Air Force.

"Ain't nothing soft about loving an animal. Especially not an Afghan wolf, probably eaten about twelve bodies. You tell me next time you see that little punk and we'll fix him up, all right?"

"Thanks, Clay—appreciate it." I washed my hands and turned to go, congratulating myself for my well-timed bluff.

"Oh, and Jones," I looked back. "You see this gray in my stubble here? I been around the block a few times." He slathered shaving cream on his cheeks. "You don't gotta tell me everything. Just stay out of trouble. You get sent home and I'll have to work for that Kool clown. You got me?"

"I got you. Thanks again," I said.

When I knocked on his door for the daily workout (Arm-ageddon), TicTac had questions too. "Very strange. I see you running around with a branch yesterday—is this some new exercise? You are cheating on me, Jones?"

"No, not exercise. The branch was for… pleasure."

If TicTac had hair, his eyebrows would have disappeared into them. "Pleasure. With a branch?"

"Pleasure." I repeated, voice stony.

TicTac's guffaw blasted out from him. When he caught his breath, "I should have joined the Navy. You sailors are kinky bastards."

So it went. Four other soldiers approached me that day with questions about the handprint, the blood, the muddy boots, and the branch; I deflected each with my dog story and kinky banter. Hated feeding into the Army's homophobia, but they were low-hanging jokes, easy to reach. Thought I'd spun a decent web of lies by the time I made it to the TOC that night—not everyone was as skeptical as Clay. Maybe a few people thought, even then, that I was losing it.

"Didya hear they shot the fucking rapist?" That was Kool, during the handover.

"Really?" I let nothing show on my face but the usual contempt. "Because you've been so great at identifying the rapist so far."

My barb bounced off. "Yah. He was prowlin' around the runway. Maybe he wants to fuck some Air Force fags, eh?" Kool's fingers slid to his pistol. "They said he was a huge naked hairy fucker. They plugged a couple rounds into him and he jumped over the goddamn fence."

"Unbelievable," I said, willing my face expressionless. "How did they know it was him?" *Huge naked hairy fucker sounds like Noah, all right.* I should have never suggested he check out flights home—too well defended. A gurgle of guilt in my guts.

"Who else is running after queerbait? I betcha he's still fucking alive though, whaddya think, Jones?" For a second, Kool's furrowed eyebrows relaxed and his eyes grew a little wider.

"Hard to say." Certainly, I didn't want to encourage a search for Noah, even if Bell's assailant was still at large.

"Anyway, the guy I talked to said the rapist has a dick like a sledgehammer. I'm sure you'd like to get your hands on that, eh Navy?" Kool was back on safe ground—he snickered. There was no getting to him—my leadership wasn't working. He'd continued to be an arrogant little shit even after TicTac crushed him with the barbell, my daily verbal thumpings, and the prank war.

"You go around asking people about the size of the rapist's dick, and I'm the one who's gay?" Kool's mouth worked soundlessly for a moment, settled into a scowl.

"Fuck you, Jones."

"You know it's OK to be gay now, times have changed? Read the memo, Office Soldier."

"I said fuck you."

39.

YES, I BADGERED KOOL REGULARLY; but for Noah I was tender, I swear it.

For about two weeks, the last of the rainy season, twice a day I brought a container of meatloaf or omelettes into the slimy cave and spooned bits into his maw. The moments I was gentle were the ones I liked myself most. After every shift I changed his bloody bandages and shovelled his crap. Sometimes he'd wake up long enough for a single sentence: "Home home, I just wanna go home," or "I promise I ain't doin' it again, Mr. Richards." I spent a lot of time scurrying back and forth into Noah's smelly dungeon, hustling to faraway bins to dispose of his bandages and the rags with which I scrubbed him every few days. I'd developed a twitch from the effort of disguising my furtive antics with bullshit excuses.

The Major wasn't fooled. "You look tired, Jones. Have you found yourself a girlfriend?" It was funny because it was forbidden. Her half grin. She was the only one whose teasing stung. Our chess games continued: my bishops bludgeoned her king; my rooks battered her walled defenses; one lone pawn reached the end of the board, detonated his suicide vest, and was reborn without boundaries.

She used to stand too close to me, which was not nearly close enough. Unnecessary touch of the fingers, the forearm, the shoulder, the elbow. The brush of her uniform as she strode past, one day the scent of lemon, the next vanilla. The curve of her hip under her combats. Whispers under her breath: "Oh, you sneaky devil, you thought I wouldn't see your little ploy?" and once, husky and so close I felt her breath on my ear, "You're going down this time, Jones. I can feel it." I groaned in longing, skin flushing into goosebumps, and I'm sure she heard.

We played the game well, though—never flirted in front of the troops; when the Major asked me into her office to critique her Female Engagement Team correspondence, we never closed the door. When the requests for medevacs streamed in through the combat chat, we submerged our little spark beneath cold professionalism, acronyms, the lonely and loveless lingo.

"Jones, what's the ETA for the CAT B?"

"ETA for the WIA at KAF is minute 1823 in 7 minutes, Ma'am."

"Roger," or even, "Ack."

Meanwhile, the Taser Rapist was active again. A Pakistani laundrywoman discovered a US medic strung face-first to a tree, with a dozen darts jutting from his back, a puddle of blood at his feet, and a black bag over his head. Under the bag, his eyes had been mutilated: the rapist had slashed X's into them. When military police cut the rope, the medic collapsed lifeless on the ground.

The day it happened, Kool started staring at me the second I arrived in the TOC. "It wasn't me, Idiot."

"That's exactly what the rapist would say," he snapped back.

"We went over this already—remember when you had me arrested, jerkoff?"

Kool gritted his teeth. "Hey, I'm not the only one who thinks you've been acting a little fucking strange."

I folded my arms across my chest, so he could see the bulk of my forearms, and planted my feet. "If you really thought I was the rapist, would you be calling me out? What if that pissed me off and I decided to target *you?*" I leaned closer.

Kool chewed harder, eyes narrowing to slits, "You can't fucking threaten me, Jones, cocksucker."

"I don't think you think I'm the rapist. I think you're just showing off for your little boyfriends."

He roared, "I AIN'T NO FAG!" and lifted his fists as if to swing at me.

"You're gonna punch a senior officer now?"

"Stop this immediately!" shouted the Major, running up from the back of the TOC. "Kool, behave like a goddamn officer—put your hands down." He relaxed from his warrior stance and I chuckled. Said the Major, "You're done today, Kool. I don't want to see you until tomorrow. We got enough going on without this extra bullshit."

Kool stormed from the TOC, slamming the door behind him. The Major rounded on me, blazing. "What the hell are you laughing about? Not a day goes by where I don't have to deal with some alpha male bullshit from someone."

"Sorry, Maj'," I said. "But don't hate the player, hate the game."

"What the hell are you talking about?"

"The man-game. It's the one where the wolves constantly nip each other's balls."

In her official voice: "Did he hit you?" I shook my head.

In her private voice: "I like you better when you're not an ogre."

That one sent me tumbling down a mineshaft, bouncing off the jagged walls. It had never occurred to me that *I* was the bully. I willed her to apologize to me. She didn't. As if I enjoyed the man-posturing day after day? Did I ask to be a brute or was it imposed, the end result of many cruelties? Haven't I come by my bit of viciousness honestly?

I stared at the ragged callouses on my hands where the weights had torn them. "Me too," I whispered.

Soon enough, Noah started to regain strength—wasn't long before he didn't need spoon-feeding, could even handle a little chitchat when I arrived with his meals. Still whimpered, though, when I changed the bandages, and once a fat tear rolled out. I bought a package of sticky fly strips from one of the shops on the boardwalk and hung them in the cave so Noah's wounds would be pestered less. I brought in more cardboard to lie on so he wasn't right in the muck. The woolen blanket I'd wrapped around him when I found him injured never left—he clung to it like a doll, named it Lumpy.

Sometimes I'd hear him crooning to it as I entered the cave, "Any day now, Lumpy, and we're gonna get out of here. Don't ya worry. We'll find a nice stream to wash ya in." I'd tell him to keep his voice down.

Other times, in his sleep, it was all moans about yesteryear's harassers: some guy named Mr. Richards, particularly. Noah was a tormented bastard inside that ugly melon but physically he was remarkable. Despite the moist environment of the cave, the drips from the ceiling, and the near-constant attention of insects, his wounds were healing, and quickly. In the blur of weeks, he regained the energy to scratch himself in his sleep. His snores were getting deeper and more regular—it seemed very much like the healing comas that I've read certain high-level monks and colonels can enter. Except with Noah, it had nothing to do with discipline.

I had to repeatedly remind myself he didn't play by the same rules as us. For example, despite the lack of exercise he even managed to gain weight; the muscle didn't grow slack. I was starting to think he was sturdy even by the measure of his own kind. That fourth puberty he mentioned might have been agonizing even without the GSW. Gunshot wounds, sorry—the combat chat has a way of sticking in your head. Once, one of his joints popped with the pressure of his growth, and I jumped, thinking it was a rocket.

But mostly, Noah was quieter after he was shot, his whispered stories more urgent.

40.

YOU GOTTA KEEP ME ALIVE, JONES—don't lettum erase me. Yer people wiped the Sasquatch right off the map, just a few blurry videos of a naked lady-yeti, a sitcom or two where a white family keeps one of us as a pet—fuck that. Turned us into a joke because you didn't wanna admit we were people with music and stories, squeezed us until we turned into the animals ya wanted us to be. When I think how much I hate ya, it makes me *shake*.

Face it—ya'll love killin'. Does yer little pink cock wiggle when yer missiles drop?

Wasn't for you soldiers, I wouldn't be here in the first place. Mom and I were walkin' on the edge of a frozen lake, when there's these three crackin' noises, but it weren't the lake. Mom growled and her muscles bunched up, and I got splashed in the face with her blood. Lookin' 'round for the sound—there ya were. Four of ya. Human soldiers, with twigs comin' outta yer helmets, and yer rifles blazin'.

She growled and started lopin' toward the hunters on all fours again, the shadow streamin' outta 'er and wrappin' 'round like a cloak, the claws stretchin' long toward the ground. I caught a look at her eyes and they were red pinpricks, just as dead as before and I didn't need to be told twice, just ran, ran across the ice, with her howls, two more gunshots, the soldiers' screams, and the sound of bones crunchin' all chasin' after.

Don't call me no coward—I ran just like I promised. Never stopped missin' 'er neither.

Now I don't mind a bit of cold but I ain't no penguin. Snow swirlin', bare feet slappin' and slippin' all over the ice, face twisted up. Made it far enough that the evergreens on the shore were small as pinecones when my foot went through a slushy bit and I plunged into the lake. Too cold even to think—icy fingers squirmin' up my butt. Had to club the ice open with my face, see the scar? Damn near drowned haulin' myself outta there and I 'member that first breath tasted like shards o' glass.

Got to the shore and Mom was nowhere in sight. Wandered up and down, freezin' and callin' her name. 'Til I heard a few more rifle cracks—that got me movin' right quick, plungin' on into the forest. Spent a few days in the brush stoppin' only to eat pinecones. Every time I thought it was safe to stop, I heard the shots again. Ran so hard I slammed into a wall of hedges—thorny bastards. Reached so-called civilization without realizin'. Had icicles comin' out my eyes like extra fangs. Those branches held me up the way my mother used to. It was warm enough and I was tired and scared—I slept.

Woke up to some unstoppable force haulin' me outta that bush. Spat outta the forest and into the human world. Lookin' up at furious eyes and shoulders like a grizzly. A barkin' rumbly noise. She'd grabbed me by the ankle. My first human touch.

I started grabbin' for the hedge and tryin' to squirm outta there. Spirit in my ear, "You want me to kill her for you?" But Donna, turns out that was her name, had a grip on my ankle like a bear's bite. I was too weak to kick free. I guess I whimpered a bit. The hard lines in her face went soft.

Still thought she might have been tryin' to kill me though. Stuck me in a bathtub first thing. Kept plungin' my head under water—bit too soon after the lake; think I pulled out a handful of her hair. Short and gray. Took a small mountain o' dirt off me anyway, this woman. This woman who first looked at me like maybe I was retarded. Then got even more confused when it turned out I weren't. Ran a comb through my hair and I got real poofy. Then she kept lookin' at me with a little smile on her face and I thought, *maybe it's safe here.*

Seemed to think I was her teddy bear, Mom #2. Not sure why she took me in, or what kind of paperwork-hell it took to keep me. Buncha doctors comin' by to shine their lights in my ears and nose—I bit a guy who tried to poke a stick into my mouth. Books, more books. Books with big bright letters and pictures of apples and bananas and cars and deer all the way down the alphabet. Different language though—pain in the ass after almost learnin' the last one. Donna teachin' me each morning: English, numbers. And more basic stuff too. Clothes. Hate 'em. Had a way of makin' 'em disappear, flingin' 'em over the wall, up into a tree, over the power lines. Nothin' ever fit—nothin' was ever comfortable. Always felt like some kinda cage I'd been trapped in. Not sure how you feel,

Jones, but I say, *fuck clothes*. Yeah, you heard me. *Fuck clothes*. I wanna cannonball into the lake with no swimsuit. I wanna stand naked at the top of a mountain with the sun comin' up.

I learned some words but I ain't no poet. A few other lessons never took—Donna was always buffin' this little silver cross on her chest, whisperin' to it. If you grew up in Wawa—that's the shitty little town where I got stuck in the hedge—you were either a bible thumper like her or a banjo-playin' pervert. Guess it's no surprise where my name came from—I'd say, "I don't need no God, I got the Spirit," and then envy would fill up her whole face. Maybe it was envy that Sasquatch got real Gods and humans gotta make theirs up that led to yer people killin' my people.

But I never transformed into the Spirit in fronta Donna. That lady deserved better than what I gave her—than what that shitty town gave her. One drunk-ass ex-husband who knocked her up early. One tiny white dress never been worn in a trunk I shouldna opened. Hard hands from swingin' an axe, my second mother the lady lumberjack, rubbin' her cross, crushin' a beer on her head sometimes, rockin' that flannel. Strong woman. Arms like yer legs. Hands made outta stone. She could strike like a comet comin' down from space but at least she never carried me 'round by the back of my neck in her teeth, like my first mom. Shoulda seen her, Jones. Tryin' to fit my huge foot into a tiny human sock. Scoldin' me for eatin' the dog. Combin' the lice outta my hair. Lettin' me lick the chocolate off the spoon. One day, after they figured out how old I was, she said I had to go to school with the other kids. Had all the paper in her hands—the ones with my human name. Too young to hold a razor, she said. So she shaved my face, neck, and hands each mornin'.

But still I gave her hell because she weren't my real Momma. Sometimes I think *she's* gotta be out there still lookin' for me, trapped in a winter that never turns, searchin' for me. Or maybe she got a bit o' the old magic, twisted 'er roots into the earth, grew a thousand leaves, and now she's a weepin' willow that looks out over the water, birds livin' in her hair.

41.

THE TIME WARP OF THE WAR, squashing a whole year of my life into a bundle of memories: sometimes I can hardly believe it was real. At some point the rainy season ended, or seemed to. Stagnant puddles dotted the roads on the camp, some of them driven a yard deep by tank treads. Eventually Noah climbed back to his feet—we could stare at the sky together. One day the clouds had been shredded by the sun. The next, they swirled in an angry maelstrom.

In the TOC we sensed the end of the season as well, the inevitable return of the fighting, fiercer than before. Still the drones surveyed a world of mud and flooded *wadis*. The river raged. A bored drone operator zoomed in on a floating stick. The Major drilled us on our emergency responses, so they didn't rot. She strode up and down amongst the monitors, clear voice ringing.

"What do you do when we receive a SALT report? How do you respond to a crashed helicopter? Who do you need to inform when there is a vehicle crash? What are the different categories of casualties? If any of you do not know exactly how to respond to the crises you will encounter in the following weeks, you are a liability to me and the team."

"Yes, Ma'am," shouted the soldiers as we pored over instruction manuals, guidelines and *aides memoires*.

"You've really won them over, Major," I said, in the privacy of her office, late one night when the dayshift had already left. A tiny office, really, six feet by six feet, with a crappy wooden table, computer, and filing cabinet wedged in.

"Yes, it's amazing what happens when people focus on the job instead of my tits."

"Extra homework *and* a bucket of bitterness," I joked. "Why shit on me when I'm helping you?" I handed her a folder stuffed with her documents I'd edited. All of them concerned the Female Engagement Team: emails to staff officers in other countries; letters to Army bases seeking the names of likely candidates; draft operations in which the FET played a pivotal role; and funding proposals.

She grimaced, took the folder, and began to rub her temples with her thumbs. I noticed a tiny triangular scar beneath her left eye and memorized it. "The only time men are nice to me is when they want to fuck," she said.

"And what about when they're mean to you?"

"They want to fuck too."

"What about when they treat you with respect?"

"No one's tried that yet."

"Aye, Ma'am." I turned to go. The tiny office made me claustrophobic—I nearly filled the whole space.

"Open your eyes, Jones," she said, before I could reach for the door. When I turned, her gaze was blue concrete. "Stared at all the time, guys rubbing themselves when I talk to them, the General himself leering at my ass in a briefing? Not to mention the goddamn rape-factory that was the military college. You've got no idea how difficult it is for a woman in the Forces."

"No, that hasn't been my life," I said. "But I know what it's like to never be stared at. To train myself to never show that I like someone, because there's no chance she feels the same way. Women have been scared of me since I was a boy. My whole life they've crossed the street at night to walk on the other side."

The Major scoffed. Leaned back in her chair and folded her arms across her chest. "You think I wouldn't choose that? Were you not paying attention about the guy who tried to rape me on my last tour?" She gestured to the battered helmet on her desk.

Haven't you heard the Taser Rapist prefers men? "Will that be everything, Ma'am?"

"Close the goddamn door, Jones."

Damnit, I'd earned a scolding; I clicked the door shut.

But she spoke in our private voice. "It would be so much easier to get respect if I looked like you."

"It would be so much easier to be loved if I looked like you."

We were quiet but for the yowls of the loneliness beasts. She leaned back in her chair, crossed her legs, tapped her fingers on the desk and gave me an appraising look.

"We have to be discreet. We reveal nothing, to anyone, ever. No notes, no pet names, no public displays of affection, no social outings."

"Major, I'm not sure I'm following?" My skin was tingling.

"Do I have to spell it out for you, Jones?" She raised an eyebrow. "I'm tired of being perfect and watching life go by. I'm tired of the hypocrisies and the double standards—I know for a fact the General is sleeping with his Master Corporal. This is my life and my body and I'm tired of men trying to control it. Now do you the understand the rules or not?"

I waited for the jokers to pop out from under the desk—some cruel counter-prank from Kool? Bell to appear in a gameshow host's garb, laughing and telling me it was all on camera.

Does she actually want me? This ogre's body?

My eyes stung in gratitude, and I nodded.

She stood, played her fingers upon my upper chest, and kissed me on the mouth. Soft lips, hard kiss. An IED burst in my brain stem. My cock instantly responded—yes, it was forbidden; eight soldiers waited on the other side of the door. I wrapped my arms around her waist, pressing her uniform tight against her body, our tongues tangling in the taste of vanilla. The scent of lemon and the feel of her back where it curved. She pushed me against the door.

We stopped to breathe. Her cheeks flushed and lips wet, the blue eyes still fierce and commanding, hips slanted. Blood surging in all my muscles. Tingling down my back. The pressure of eight months of war-time loneliness straining against my pants.

Still, I couldn't believe it was happening—but if it was a dream of my madness then let me wallow. Leave me there with that first kiss and all the possibilities unfurling before us, and none of the grief.

"I need to finish these emails, Jones, but you can walk me home tonight. Now holster that thing—" she grabbed it— "and go do some work."

Ever since Bell was attacked, night-shift workers walked home in pairs. This had never applied to me because my shift ended as the sun rose. But I was accustomed to sending an escort with the Major when she worked late. Usually one of the signallers, well-armed and equipped with a radio, who would call in on arrival at the barracks, then walk back via the most well-lit routes. And tonight it would be me. A rare moment: I didn't want to be someone else.

At midnight she emerged from her nook at the back of the TOC, stretching her neck. "Shit. How am I gonna get home?"

"I was planning to step out for midnight meal, Major. I could take a detour."

"Don't forget the radio." So far, it seemed, we were perfectly convincing. The eight other men in the TOC didn't even look up at us. Alice the signaller gave me a thumbs up as she flipped pages of a thick tome. *Does she know?*

The Major set a brisk pace, scanning the shadows of tire stacks and pyramids of empty crates. Her hand rested on the butt of her pistol, not in an ostentatious display of hardness, like I might expect from Kool, but rather a habit developed over years in war.

We were fifty yards from the bunker where we had sheltered from the rocket attack. There was an enormous grumbling—so loud we looked around for artillery, half-expecting to hear the siren. But it was the sky. The cauldron of clouds had brewed all day, stirred by mysterious goblins, and the concoction was ready: a storm-spell. The rain didn't come in droplets; it came in sheets, splashing and thundering—so much force we were soaked straight away, so hard it was astonishing, baggy uniforms drenched and pulled taut, shivering cold down the collar.

We scrambled for the bunker, the Major pulling on my hand *she touched me she touched me,* our fingers sliming together, our boots sucking into the mud. The whole nasty city-base was drowning, and we stood in the bunker, dripping; I had forgotten to let go of her hand. No, I would never let go of it. A part of me holds it still. I will hold it until this body withers and the spark fades from my mind. I will hold it even as the water rises, a great desert tsunami, and washes clean this base, scrubbing it from the earth, flotsam of old IEDs and unexploded ordinance churning in the wake.

"Ever seen a monsoon before, Jones?"

"No, but I felt one once."

Jesus, Jones, what the hell is happening here?

Crispy, you can't just jump into my book like this—

Yer damn straight, I can. I got shit to say. You gotta beautiful woman there and it seems like you're about to do the nasty and you're talking about hand-holding?

What's your point?

That ain't the truth. I wanna see these two perverts go at it and you're throwing poetry at me. You can't stick your dick into poetry, man.

This is the truth—I felt love. How crippled are you?

No one's gonna read your book if it don't have titties in it, Jones. That's just logic.

Crispy, you're a goddamn abomination. I had one moment in the war, maybe in my whole life, that was holy and you're trying to make it ugly.

Jones, you owe me—I saved your life. Can't they just shit on each other a little bit?

We're done here.

She smiled, slipped her hand from mine, and took off her helmet to shake out her hair. A blond cascade tumbling over her wet shoulders in the bunker. The rain was drumming so loudly, we knew we were alone, standing inches away—I stepped closer and her lips parted. Our loneliness monsters shattered their cages. I wiped a drop of water from her cheek and she kissed me.

"Are you sure about this?" I asked.

"Not remotely." She laughed, a wild noise, and bit my shoulder. A fire rose. Doubts melted. Warm lips and the feel of the cold bunker on my back. Strong fingers and the roaring of the rain. We couldn't tear at each other's clothes fast enough to be warm.

"Just tonight, just this one time, call me Jen," she whispered as I slipped the holster from her shoulder and kissed the freckle on her collarbone. We wrestled with wet buttons—one of hers came off in my hand. Under the uniform shirt she wore a sports bra and a second pistol and I was hauling on her belt and kissing her breasts, running my claws down her back. Her boots would have to stay on—for the mud, for the extra seconds.

She was on top of me and I was alive. Rubbing against me through thin cotton panties. Her body luminous in flashes of lightning. My hands around her thin wrists. Her tongue slipping in my mouth. A tearing sound—she had torn off her underwear. A clutching. A grasping. She crouched over me, her guiding hand holding my cock at bay, sudden worry on her face.

"We shouldn't," she said.

"We shouldn't," I agreed.

But we did.

The war winked out like distant stars. The rain pouring and the sound of splashing. Jen pressing down hard in the lightning flash with her hands on my shoulders, her long low moan growing fiercer and fiercer. Her nails digging in my shoulder—we were killers but we weren't dead yet. She was grinding, and rocking her hips back and forth. I was memorizing all of her, the blonde hair nimbus in the lightning, the squelch of her boots in the mud, the freckle on her collarbone, another on her right breast, my supporting hands on her thighs—she leaned back, stiffening and squeezing, perfectly quiet, concentration on her face until the taut muscles of her abs contracted and she called wordlessly into the air three times, as if we had won a victory over the war, as if we could bring them all back to life, and I could endure no more, squeezing her thighs and pulling her deeper and moaning.

We clutched for a few more minutes listening as the downpour faded to a patter of droplets in the puddles. She was warm against my chest and I wrapped my arms around her, sinking my nose into the softness of her hair. As she buried her face into my shoulder she began to cry. I held her tighter as I softened inside her, feeling utter confusion, shocked by her tears.

Stroking her hair, I tried to comfort her with soothing words. She was far away already. I was as lonely as before.

42.

WE WALKED HOME IN THE PETRICHOR. Clear, fresh. Just a hint of diesel. The rain had slackened to steady dripping in the puddles. Flickers of a furtive moon. The Major strode a few yards ahead; we did not walk hand in hand. We did not steal kisses in shadows. We did not act like lovers at all.

"We need to get you back to work before people start asking questions," said the Major in her flat, professional voice. "Make sure to scrub yourself for the smell before you return to the TOC."

Automatically, the professional response first: "Aye, Ma'am." Then, after a pause, "Are you alright?"

She halted and, without turning, "I haven't been alright in a long time, Jones."

"Were you crying because I was awful?"

Her shoulders shook—it took me a second to realize she was laughing. "You boys and your egos."

Then she turned, saw that I was standing bewildered in a puddle, and she softened. "I needed that," she said. "All of it. I hope we can do it again." And she kissed me on the mouth, squeezed my hand, and disappeared into the women's barracks.

I had a lover. I had another secret. I had the Major's torn-off button in my palm. My loneliness monster wheeled three times around a soft, shaggy carpet, curled into a ball, and fell asleep. A deep sigh burst from my mouth as if I'd eased into a hot tub, and a knot of pressure in my trapezius dissolved. I began to dream: waking, sleeping, always in color, sounds, smells, memories, creatures, home. Suddenly, I could think about the future, what awaited me there, what would I do next, would I go back to school, would I leave the Forces, would I grow my hair long, would I write books, would I wander the earth? Would she be with me? The barbed wire twisted into smiles. The taboo of touch: the military made love illegal but some things cannot be taken away.

Before we were lovers I hid my loneliness in books and jokes and lifting steel. After we became lovers, I hid my joy. Even from her.

In other ways I was slipping. Since I was arrested, I kept seeing red berets—the kind the military police wore—in the mess hall, in the queue at Timmy's, even in the damn gym with TicTac. The Taser Rapist was still at large and, I suppose, my attempts to cover for Noah's injuries had only increased my dodginess. Maybe I was getting paranoid, checking for hidden cameras in the shitters and wondering if soldiers in their PT gear were really plainclothes police. Certainly, I couldn't afford a mess-up like the following.

"What the fuck is this," said Kool, holding up the bloody bandages.

Shit. I had meant to throw those out—the last truly sullied batch from the Sasquatch's wounds. They were in a garbage bag in the room, but the bag wasn't tied. I should have known that Cheezie-munching fucker would root through it. Think fast—

"I meant to tell you, when you're asleep sometimes I fist myself in the ass. Leads to a bit of tearing." *Yes, yes. Hit him in the homophobia. Harder.*

"You're full of fucking shit, Jones."

"Not anymore, I'm not." *Oh, this is going swimmingly.*

"You're the most fucking disgusting person I've ever met."

"You're the one contracting AIDS right now."

Victory. He dropped the bandages in a hurry. But not without a parting volley, "People are talking about you, Jones. They say you're losing it. I still say *you're* the goddamn rapist." He slammed the door on the way out. Kool's stupid prejudices against the Navy would only protect me so long—the strength of my deflections waned even as the size of my secrets waxed.

Three weeks, maybe four. My entire love affair, titillating, transformative. The Major kept working late on her Female Engagement Team project, and I escorted her home a few times a week. How many times did we make love—eleven, twelve? I wished it was every night; I wanted to spend a whole evening with her, like a proper lover. But this was impossible. We worked opposite shifts. And I had a douchebag roommate.

Instead, we only made love in bunkers, in half hours shaved from midnight meals. Lonely nights I rubbed that stolen button until it gleamed. The bunker was everything, my whole life.

"You don't understand, Jones," she said one night, pinning up her hair, her taste still in my mouth. "Senior officers, the men, fuck their subordinates all the time. It's one of the perks of the job. But if they ever got wind that I was doing it? It would be like Halima getting stoned in the village all over again."

I tried to put my arm around her shoulder and she shook it off. "It's not a goddamn joke. You've never seen how the machine can turn on someone, especially a woman. And if it turns on me it'll turn on the FET, too. And I'm not letting anyone *near* my baby—you understand?" She stiffened, alert, one ear cocked. "You hear that? Shut up."

We stood there, silent. Straining to listen, framed by the cold walls of the bunker. The wind moaned through the barbed wire. A distant rumble of a generator. Satisfied, she faced me and whispered, "Now say the rules again."

"Major, you know I know them."

"Say the rules, Jones, it's not a debate."

"No hickies. No notes. No pet names. No public affection. No social outings. No eye contact. No yearning. No blushing. No inappropriate hard-ons—am I missing anything?"

She grinned a little, face ghostly in the starlight, but then her smile evaporated. "You know this is a mistake."

I knew, but the words hurt anyway. I did my best to please her but when her six-pack pressed against my soft belly we knew we were different. That she had a hard-bodied husband at home who ran marathons with her kid on his back. That she could have any man on this camp, even the Special Forces ninjas who invaded people's homes like Santa, through the chimneys.

A few times when I walked her home, we didn't make love. Instead, I held her and stroked her hair and kissed the warm spot behind her ear. Sometimes she would press my great thick palm into her cheek or rub lotion into my callouses. Once, she dozed on my shoulder for a full ten minutes and these were the best moments of the whole war, no matter the hard world outside the bunker, nor the flitting of dangerous shadows.

I remember so clearly those ten minutes; she was muttering a little in her sleep and plucking at my sleeve. I permitted myself to dream. We were young lovers picnicking in parks, or hiking through hills. Socialites, with the war scrubbed off, attending soirees with champagne. "Aren't you gonna jump in?" she asked, skinny-dipping in the neighbor's pool. Even in my fantasies I was too shy to join her. For her, I crammed these awkward feet into skates, slipping and stumbling, arms windmilling, down Ottawa's city-long canal, while she raced along. And we looked at the ice sculptures and I had ideas about the art and she laughed at me for them. I drew shapes of Sasquatch and giant octopuses on her back as she fell asleep. We put the killing behind us and had some kids of our own…

I felt her warmth on my shoulder and knew, with a jolt, I was deluding myself. That whatever we had, could only happen here, in Kandahar Airfield, in the ugliness. On the street in Ottawa, she wouldn't look at me twice. Doubt, worry, even a stewing rage: their tentacles tickled the lizard-level of my brain.

She felt me shift, both her arms wrapped around one of mine.

"Thank you," she murmured.

"For what?"

"For being human."

"That word doesn't mean anything," I sighed, staring over her head at the concrete wall of the bunker.

She squeezed my arm. "Of course it does." Today her eyes were a lighter blue, almost the gray of a warship's hull; I felt her breath on my face. "If it didn't mean anything why do we give them names?"

I didn't want to say more—I've been around the block enough to know that arguing ruins the mood, even so, letting go of the fantasy of being with her, truly with her, left me feeling chafed and hollow. "The Taser Rapist is human. Mother Teresa is human. If all behaviour is human, what good is the word?"

She clucked her tongue in irritation. "No, the word matters. It means having the basic scrap of compassion you need to connect with people." She stroked my cheek.

"It means weak."

Her hand froze, slipped from my face, and she turned away.

<hr>

On Love

Sometimes you try your best to love someone and it fails anyway. Sometimes love is a sword and we are sliding down it. What I felt for her I will never feel for another person again, not like that. Love that quakes from collapsing mountains. Love that sleets, that blows fierce with wintry blasts and spears of ice. Love with its trestles and tumults, its lurches and its exclamations. Love where I stifled moans in long, blonde hair. Love where we clutched and lurched and sighed. Love like cold concrete pressing on your back. Love that promises not to leave a mark, but does. Love that circles itself, a spinning vulture, a drone. Love like two dragons soaring over green-spun valleys, cattle in their teeth; love like falling face first in a volcano; love like your molecules detonating; love that breaks the cage and *is* the cage. Love, where I kissed her trembling body and rubbed my whiskers on her bare breasts. Love, where she came hard with a yelp and wept desperately into my shoulder. Love stolen from a cuckolded husband. Love reclaimed from the jaws of sharks. Love that burst the cobblestone like a stubborn flower. Love which was its own insurgency, its own war. Love whose ivy shattered walls, whose roots stretched and cracked the pot. A love that let us grieve the people we'd seen die, then snared us in its inexorable logic: if our victims are human than maybe we are too.

43.

AT THE BARRACKS THAT DAWN, the back door was propped open by the speaking stone. Noah's shining eyes did not glint from the depths of the frog-cave, so I checked the bunker. Scrawled into the dust was a map sketched with a fat finger.

Course the bastard had no sense of north, so I had to look at the map from all angles before it clicked—good thing he had the poo pond splat in the middle. Once I was oriented, it made sense—there was a picture of a Sasquatch flexing in the north-west corner of the camp: the old junkyard where they found Bell after he was raped. I scrubbed the map with my boot, grabbed a sleeve of crackers and a jug of peanut butter (another shipment from home had arrived, complete with rolled-up silk), checked to see I was unobserved in the waking camp, and trudged over.

Skeletons of cars, covered in scorch marks. The raw ridges of steel, glinting where the metal was torn by IEDs, the hulks hauled here and dumped. Coils of barbed wire too rusty for safe handling. Over there—the truck where Bell was tied, the trunk dented. A stray dog, mangy to the point of leprosy, barked twice and disappeared into a heap of 155mm shell casings. The way the car-husks had been nudged aside to make a path, certain damp marks in the soil, suggested the nesting of an indomitable beast. Sand and earth fountained upward—I followed the spray to an inner cloister where the smashed cars and trucks were piled high. Around a corner, Noah. Back in his prime, new pink skin on the shoulder, standing in a hole up to his waist, bending and scooping the earth with his claws, then hurling it overhead. A sunburn was blooming in the bare patches of his orange pelt. A flicker of nostalgia for shovelling snow from the driveway back home.

"Tunneling to freedom, like in a movie?"

Noah paused, turned, panted. "Ya saw what happened when I tried to catch a plane. I figure if I can get under the wall—"

"Then you'll find yourself in a minefield, Noah. With a shit-ton of barbed wire, and snipers in all the towers. Even now…" I glanced at the skies. "It's not safe. They have a drone circling the camp. You shouldn't be doing this in the day."

"Dude, that's why I stacked the cars. I ain't as dumb as I look." Noah pressed a filthy cloth to his forehead to wipe the sweat: Lumpy the blanket.

"It's a bad idea," I insisted. "You get past the mines, the barbed wire, the snipers and the drones and what? You're still in the fucking desert, man. Maybe you can make it in the forest, but this is different."

Noah sat on the edge of the hole, facing me, not talking, head tilted, as if listening to someone else. He spoke in a quiet rumble, "Gotta go, Jones. Ya don't understand all the shit I'm dealin' with. Gotta voice in my head keeps tellin' me ya'll need justice in the form o' death. I can do less damage out there." He pointed to the wall, what was beyond it.

"Noah," I sat on the other side of the hole, "I don't believe in magic."

"Spirit says the best way to kill ya would be to slash ya right now across the neck. He says I could do it so fast ya couldn't stop us. But if ya rolled backwards I should spit in yer face so you couldn't aim yer pistol. And if ya kept backin' up I should huck this at you." He rested his hand on what looked like a carburetor and raised his voice. "These ain't my thoughts, Jones. *Where* do ya think they comin' from?"

I looked at him flatly. "Just because I don't like the idea of killing doesn't mean I'm incompetent at my job. But you're not going to find your mother out there, buddy." I pointed to the wall.

Noah's face twisted into an ugly snarl. He swung his arm overhead, claws coarse and packed with earth. In the air, his hand trembled, one force pulling it down, another, resisting. He growled, "Spirit says my mother is dead. Spirit says I should kill you for mentionin' 'er. Spirit says you killed 'er."

For an instant, the whole earth fit in that hand. The dirt-filled claws drank all the light of the sun; the mighty arm with the patchy orange fur reached halfway to the stars. My bowels tossed like a stormy sea, but I was too shocked to move, defend, resist. Just went pale and waited, even closed my eyes.

The blow never fell. When I heard Noah snuffle, I opened my eyelids a crack.

"Ya see, Jones? I barely got my shit together." His muddy face was streaked with moisture. "I'm sorry for scarin' you. All I ever wanted was to be gentle, but look at me now." He crushed Lumpy in a suffocating hug.

I waited for my heart to slow. "It's OK, Noah. I don't think you'd hurt anybody."

He squeezed tighter, shook his head, eyes suddenly lined and weary. "It ain't me who hurts people, Jones. It's the Spirit."

44.

YA SAY YOU DON'T BELIEVE IN MAGIC BUT YA GOTTA LISTEN ANYWAY, JONES. I KNOW THE ARMY KILLED YOU A *LONG*, LONG TIME AGO BUT YOU KEPT WANDERIN' 'ROUND LIKE SOME ZOMBIE, THINKIN' YOU WAS ALIVE. I SAY, 'DUDE, THE PROTECTOR SPIRIT GRABBED HOLD O' MY MOMMA,' AND YOU SAY, 'WELL, I'M NOT SURE I BELIEVE IN THAT.' ARMY GOT THEIR SCREWS IN YOU, AND MAN, THEY'RE SQUEEZIN' 'EM TIGHTER EVERY DAY. MAYBE YOU STILL REMEMBER THE TIME THEY SQUEEZED SO HARD YER IMAGINATION POPPED OUTTA YER EAR, FISH-FLOPPED ON THE GROUND A FEW TIMES, AND DIED?

YA STILL REMEMBER MACK, THAT INDESTRUCTIBLE CHAMPION OF MY PEOPLE, WHO HAD THE GREEN STONE THAT MADE HIS POCKET GLOW? HE'D GONE ON A QUEST TO FIND THAT FUCKER FOR THE STRENGTH GOD. WHEN HE HAD IT, HE BECAME THE GREATEST HERO, JUST LIKE ALL 'EM BOOKS SAID.

WELL, MACK NEVER FORGOT 'BOUT THE GOD-STATUE IN HIS HOME VILLAGE. KNEW ONE DAY HE'D HAVE TO GIVE THAT GLOWIN' STONE BACK TO THE GOD BUT THERE WAS ALWAYS MORE GOOD TO DO. AFTER THREE CENTURIES OF SWINGING THAT MIGHTY BALL O' IRON HE HAD, I GUESS HE GOT TIRED, WENT BACK TO HIS VILLAGE, WHERE NO ONE KNEW WHAT TO SAY TO 'IM, AND VISITED THE GRAVES OF HIS SISTERS AND PARENTS.

NEARBY, THE DYIN' STRENGTH GOD HAD TURNED TO STONE COMPLETELY AND LOST HIS VOICE—THE VILLAGERS BUILT A SHRINE O' HUGE LOGS 'ROUND 'IM. MACK STOOD IN THAT SHRINE, SAW THE FLICKER IN THAT STATUE'S EYE, AND TOLD 'IM EVERYTHIN' HE'D LEARNED ON 'IS ADVENTURES. TOLD 'IM THAT THE ONLY THING HE EVER REALLY FIGURED OUT IN THREE CENTURIES OF QUESTIN' WAS THE RIDDLE OF STRENGTH. APOLOGIZED FOR KEEPIN' THE STONE SO LONG BUT COULDN'T HELP IT, ON ACCOUNT O' ALL THE GOOD HE'D DONE. SAID HE WAS TIRED OF BEIN' THE CHAMPION BUT HE'D KEEP ON DOIN' IT FOREVER UNLESS THE STRENGTH GOD AGREED TO TAKE HIS PLACE.

THAT STATUE'S EYES CHANGED FROM GREEN TO BLUE. FINGERS TWITCHED OPEN BY A HAIR.

MACK NODDED, THEN PRESSED THE GREEN-GLOWIN' STONE INTO THE STATUE'S FINGERS. THE IRON BALL GREW HEAVY IN MACK'S HAND, CLUNKED TO THE FLOOR. MACK'S GREAT MUSCLES SHRIVELLED AND HIS SKIN PITTED LIKE VOLCANIC STONE. SLUMPED TO HIS KNEES, SKIN GROWIN' BAGGY WITH GRAY

BONES JUTTIN' OUT. LET OUT A LONG MOAN AS HIS BODY STARTED TURNIN' INTO ASH, ALL THE POWER SUCKIN' OUT OF HIM, FILLIN' THE STONE WIT' A LIGHTNIN' WHIRLWIND. AFTER THE STORM PASSED, MACK WAS A PILE OF BONES AND GREEN DUST ON THE FLOOR.

THE GOD'S POWER CAME RUSHIN' BACK, BLUE MAGIC BLAZIN' FROM HIS EYES, THE MOUTH CRACKIN' OPEN AND A SCREAM TEARIN' OUT. THAT GODDAMN STATUE, A GOD'S PRISON, EXPLODED, SENDING CHUNKS OF STONE IN ALL DIRECTIONS, BLASTIN' THROUGH THE SHUTTERS O' BARK AND RIPPIN' THROUGH THE LOG-WALLS.

VILLAGERS HURRIED TO THE RUINED CHURCH, SAW THE STATUE WAS GONE, AND COLLECTED MACK'S ASHES. THEY ALL AGREED, THE STRENGTH GOD HAD LOST ITS BODY, BECOMIN' A SPIRIT THAT COULD ONLY ACT ON THE WORLD THROUGH US. STILL, IT KEPT ITS PROMISE AND, FROM THAT MOMENT ON, AND LISTEN CLOSE, JONES, WHENEVA MY PEOPLE GET THREATENED, THEY CALL ON THE PROTECTOR SPIRIT TO GIVE 'EM STRENGTH. A MAN 'BOUT TO BE MURDERED, A WOMAN 'BOUT TO BE RAPED, EVEN A CHILD WHEN HIS PARENTS WERE FIGHTING—EVERY SINGLE, LIVIN' SASQUATCH CAN REACH OUT TO THE SPIRIT AND TRANSFORM INTO A GIANT GLOWIN' MACK-LIKE SUPER-WARRIOR.

WELL, FIGHTIN' PRETTY MUCH DRIED UP AFTER THAT, AND WE GOT GENTLE. TEN THOUSAND YEARS OF PEACE, SASQUATCH RULIN' THE EARTH. WE SPREAD ALL OVER THE PLACE, SPITTIN' OUT BABIES AND THUMPIN' OUR DICKS ON HOLLOW LOGS. THE WHOLE WORLD TURNED, TWICE. BIG ISLANDS CRASHED INTO EACH OTHER AND MOUNTAINS ROSE UP OUTTA NOWHERE. VOLCANOES PUKED FIRE INTO THE SKY THEN MELLOWED INTO LITTLE ISLANDS WITH BRIGHT-WINGED BIRDS. ICE CAME. ICE WENT. YOU HUMAN PRICKS SHOWED UP IN THE THAW. THE SPIRIT FOUGHT IN BATTLE AFTER BATTLE, AGAINST AND WIT' ALL THE WEAPONS OF THE DIFFERENT AGES, AND IT WAS STARTIN' TO GROW OLD AND ANCIENT TOO, SAME WAY MACK DID, BUT IT WAS BOUND BY ITS PROMISE, GOD-MAGIC: TOO STRONG TO BREAK. TRAPPED INTO AN ETERNITY OF KILLIN, WITH EACH DEATH HURTIN' HIM A LITTLE MORE.

THE SPIRIT KNEW IT WAS CHANGIN'. GLORIOUS GOLDEN WARRIOR BECAME A SHADOW-MONSTER. FORGOT 'BOUT MACK AND THAT SECRET OF STRENGTH—WHENEVA THE SPIRIT TOOK OVER THE BODY OF ONE OF OUR PEOPLE IT DIDN'T WANNA LEAVE, LEFT HORRIBLE BLOODY RAMPAGES, WHOLE VILLAGES WIPED OUT AS IT CACKLED AND ATE THE FRESH SHIT OUTTA PEOPLE. WHEN HUMANS STARTED PUSHIN' AGAINST US, SPIRIT'D SHOW UP AND KILL EVERYONE ON BOTH SIDES. MY PEOPLE STARTED TO FADE, PRETTY SOON WE LEARNED TO STOP CALLIN' ON THE SPIRIT, SO IT STARTED WHISPERIN' TO US. ALWAYS PUSHIN' KILLIN'. BLOOD'S THE ONLY ANSWER. GOT SO BAD, PEOPLE

STARTED UP A COLLECTION OF THE THINGS THE SPIRIT WHISPERED AND WROTE IT ALL IN THE SECOND BOOK OF MACK, WHICH I ONLY SKIMMED TO SEE THE PICTURES. IT WAS AN ENCYCLOPEDIA O' KILLIN'. "WHEN YOU TEAR OUT AN EYE, YOU'VE ALREADY WON." "HE'S HAD AN OLD INJURY IN HIS LEFT KNEE; STRIKE HIM THERE." "YOUR OPPONENT IS STRONGER THAN YOU—YOU MUST STAB QUICKLY AND DEEPLY." WHISPERS, WHISPERS, ALWAYS THE WHISPERS. NOW I THINK BACK TO THOSE CAMPFIRES WHEN I WAS A SPROUT, I REALIZE EACH ONE OF 'EM WAS FIGHTIN' AGAINST THE SPIRIT THE WHOLE TIME, THAT MY MOMMA HAD BEEN FIGHTIN' IT FOR YEARS. AND NOW, I THINK MAYBE IN THE MAD LOGIC OF THE SPIRIT, THE ONLY WAY IT WOULD BE FREE OF ITS PROMISE WAS IF EACH OF US WAS DEAD. OR ELSE, ALL Y'ALL.

"THIS MAN HAS ACCESS TO DANGEROUS WEAPONS. KILL HIM IMMEDIATELY." THAT'S WHAT THE SPIRIT WHISPERED TO ME FIRST TIME I MET *YOU*, JONES. THE SPIRIT'S BROKEN. IT SPEAKS TO ME EVERY DAY AND ALL NIGHT LONG, WHISPERIN' THAT I CAN UNLOCK ITS MAGIC. BEGS FOR ME TO REACH OUT FOR IT—IT KNOWS I'M STRONG AND COULD HURT A LOTTA PEOPLE. BEEN SO AFRAID OF LOSIN' CONTROL THAT I BEEN STAYIN' 'WAY FROM YOU FOLKS, WANDERIN', LIKE MACK. UNTIL NOW.

I AIN'T NO FAN OF THE SPIRIT. I MEAN, SURE, THE SPIRIT LOOKED AFTER US, BUT THEN IT STARTED PREYIN' ON US AND NOW WE GOTTA HEAL IT AND FORGIVE IT AND SET IT FREE.

BUT I'M SCARED, JONES—I NEED TO GET OUTTA HERE. I'M SCARED OF WHAT I'LL DO WHEN IT *TAKES* ME.

45.

WHEN BELL STRODE INTO THE TOC his first day back, he toted a teetering stack of coffees: my own morale-boosting tricks turned against me, but I was helpless to resist the offering, two milk one sweetener, just a hint of bitter brew, the tar still warm from the pot.

"There you go, Brother. Really appreciated your visits," as he handed me the bucket of caffeine. He looked leaner and sallow, with sunken cheeks. His eyes were more lined.

"Got one for you too, Major," he called, and she appeared from her nook to accept it.

"Thanks Bell, and welcome back. It's been pretty quiet."

"Well, I didn't want to miss any of the fun," Bell grinned. Absent, conspicuously absent, was the pocket-plunging routine of yester-month. He no longer grovelled under the Major's gaze, or wiped drool from his mouth when he looked at her. Even as she ordered me around, she kept her eyes on Bell; *no glancing.*

"Jones, help Bell get up to speed."

"Aye, Ma'am."

I shook his hand, and Bell and I walked to the big map, sipping our coffees. He had developed a limp, and walked stooped forward, like his head was too heavy. I started briefing him on the day's SIGACTS, eventually unfurling events from previous days, the big ones, the ones I could remember. He smiled and nodded amicably, the car-salesman charm smeared like camouflage face paint. What surprised me was a growing contempt—I wanted to spit in his eyes, slap his baggy cheeks. I was fine visiting him in the hospital, but now he held his rape under our noses, forcing us to smell. *You should have gone home, or died, like you were supposed to.* Even though I didn't say that he blushed at the exact second and averted his gaze.

"Hey Bell," Kool called. "You didn't get enough action, eh?" The younger man stood at the back of the TOC, with his arms crossed in front of him, a drone feed behind showing the river.

Bell gritted his teeth, turned, and squared his shoulders. Wounded honey badger bracing for the molestations of a young lion.

"Come here, LT," growled the honey badger. Kool sauntered forward, similar to his strut in the gym before TicTac squashed him. "Closer. Look me in the goddamn eye."

A muscle stiffened in Kool's jaw. He seemed about to ram Bell with his head, stopping short by an inch. Nose to nose, the LT was a hand taller, and Bell's previous advantage of mass had withered on the sickbed.

Scorn dripped from Kool's voice. "Is it true when everyone is saying? That you came like a rocket when you got assfucked?"

Staring contest: Bell didn't blink, though his fingers twitched convulsively; he let the silence drag. New lines had been etched around the eyes and the scars were deeper along the edges of his bullfrog mouth. That fierce gaze now with the hint of sadness locked inside.

Kool's handsome face, to contrast. Skinny with the long nose, jaw clenched. He wanted so badly to be hard, and he gets there in the end, but not yet. In the meantime, everyone else in the TOC, maybe twelve people, less the Major, who'd returned to her nook, had leaned in to listen. I was standing a few feet away, scanning from face to face, incredulous about the extent to which soldiers measure dicks.

"We are not doing this, Kool," Bell finally rasped. "I've been through enough shit already. If you had any fucking idea what it's been like to be in my head, this body, over the last month you would salute me twice as hard as you do the General."

Bell raised his voice for the benefit of the eavesdroppers. "Well, it's no big secret, is it? I got raped, tasered and left for dead—you all were probably out looking for me. The doctors say that the first week my fever was so bad I nearly died three times." Mutters from the soldiers—Kool had taken a step back. "Twice the General visited and offered me my ticket home, back to my family, and I said no. I chose to stay here, full of tubes, wearing a diaper, two doors down from the poo pond. You know why?" Bell spun around, beseeching the crowd.

Kool blanched. I opined, "The General said you weren't done yet. You wanted to finish your tour."

His eyes, when they met mine, showed immense relief. "That is what I told him. But do you guys wanna know the truth?" He let the silence stretch again, that gameshow host. "There's no way in hell I could go back home to my wife without enough cash to get that swimming pool."

The tension exploded into laughter, nearly hysterical laughter—the joke offered us all a way out of that moment, even a path for Kool to save his dignity, and we knew it. Still, Bell milked it, "Honestly, you think you guys are tough, you never seen anything like this woman. She could eat my first two wives for breakfast. She's got a temper like an IED. She's got a mouth like a Claymore…" and so on, until Clay was literally wheezing with tears streaking his cheeks, and Crazy Jay was braying.

Then, in the din, Bell leaned real close to Kool and spoke in such a low tone only the three of us heard: "I have absolutely nothing left to lose, Kool, only a tiny scrap of self-respect. You try to step on that again I swear I will kill you. Do you understand?" Kool nodded, face suddenly pale, and I turned my face away from them so he wouldn't see I'd heard.

Then they shook hands and that's the amazing thing about these alpha male encounters. How happy Kool was to be put back into his place, hopping back and forth like a puppy eager to chase the stick. Bell was good at the man-game. Better than me, not needing to rely on a crushing handshake or other tricks of the body. The laughter had deteriorated into a general hubbub of people wanting to greet Bell, the combat chat scrolling by, forgotten—we were welcoming a wounded soldier home. Only the Major looked worried to see Bell surrounded by admirers; she had come out of her office when the laughter started and now stood on the sidelines, not having heard the joke.

"Major!" Bell shouted. "We gotta young infantry officer here," he pointed to Kool, "with unused aggression. Don't you know an infanteer has to kill at least once a month?" The Major's sigh was drowned in the rekindled laughter. It was against the rules to comfort her. Bell cut through the clamour with a flourish of his hands—he was selling cars again. "That's enough of that, folks. Let's get back to work. Focus your energy on the enemy. Fighting season starts today."

46.

THAT NIGHT THE MAJOR WAS FURIOUS, too angry for touch, striding the ten feet back and forth in the bunker, passing close enough to my face to stir a breeze.

"Who the fuck does he think he is? Spends a whole month napping, then waltzes in and announces, 'it's fighting season now.' Like I haven't been planning operations this whole time. Like the rain hasn't just stopped. Like we haven't seen the fighting pick up in the last week. Like…"

"Major," I said. "Can you please chill out?" But no—she kept striding forward and back. "Give the guy a break? He just got raped."

"Rape is a rite of passage for women at the Military College," she snapped.

Pausing, she turned to face me with the length of the bunker between us. "Jesus, they were hanging off every word he said. I have never had that, not once, in my entire military career. Men have wanted me. Men have obeyed me. But they have never, ever admired me."

"I admire you."

"You're fucking me."

"I admired you before that." She growled and started pacing again. "Can you please listen to me for a second? Bell had to win that crowd."

"You fucking helped him. You're supposed to be on my side."

"I am on your side," I snapped back. "Do you want my advice or not?"

She stopped again. Without looking, ordered, "Speak."

"Let me bring you into the mysterious world of men," I said. "Bell *needed* to crush Kool today."

"Explain."

"I'm talking about the man-game. Our own stupid system of codes and behaviours which are just as complex as the stupid system that governs women. Bell was masterful today: he let Kool off the hook, gave everyone a laugh, brought the rape into the open, and delivered a private threat to Kool at the same time."

"I don't give a shit about your elaborate system of grunts and farts—Bell wants my job—don't you see that?"

I nodded. Held my hands up helplessly. "I think the man-code was written to stop women from becoming you—look what happened to the first

Female Engagement Team, and the pushback against the second. But now that you've happened anyway, you must be stopped at all costs. You must be stoned to death, raped, degraded, undermined, and killed."

She slumped in the sand next to me, back against the concrete wall. "All they need is an excuse to take the FET away from me. That's why I've been saying all those rules. No public affection. No hickies. No love notes. No boners." She nuzzled her head against my shoulder and I sighed as soon as she touched me.

I wanted to tell her I loved her. All I could muster was, "I'm sorry."

47.

WHEN BELL DECLARED THE START of the fighting season he'd willed winter's end; I had seen my last drop of Afghan rain, blinked and missed spring. It was 120°F again in the shade. The locals knew the lesson of bending to the sun—they became reclusive in the day, worked the *wadis* in the late afternoon, and lounged on their rooftops on lawn chairs chatting on cellphones in the evenings. We were the only ones dumb enough to work in the hottest part of the day; at least the TOC had air conditioning, a perk of being an office soldier. The mud puddles dried, leaving the roads on the camp cracked and grooved like ruts from a dragging anchor. Through the drone feeds we saw the river slow—it had surged through the rainy season but within a few days grew brown and murky, then siltier still. Its banks kept getting farther and farther away, like memories of home. Soon it was a feeble stream of mud, stalling and equivocating, flowing the wrong way at times, choking its fish.

The first day of the fighting season started typically: I left the DFAC with heartburn and the taste of cigarette butts in my mouth—I had only eaten cucumbers. I walked past the little airfield where I had once seen a Predator and, over a short fence, spotted a new drone.

It was twice the size and length of its little brother: uglier and lumpier, bulging at the nose for the communications package, and at the rear for the larger engines. Its skin was a cool gray and smooth, lacking seams. This was the Reaper, the size of a jet plane but with its rear fins jutting diagonally upwards, an aggressive posture—like a cobra poised to strike. Still no face, though—it had no eyes and no smile and no expression and no anger, just the impression of a brutish, sloping forehead and overdeveloped jaw. Packed in its chest was not a thrumming heart, but, instead, four five-hundred-pound bombs. That's enough power to flatten a village or gouge a mountain. When it has dropped its deadly payload there is no pilot to feel remorse. Not that grief ever brought anyone back to life. Back in robot grade school, Reaper wore glasses—he could barely see at all. Bull-necked, barrel-chested: he was too strong to care he was blind as he bit the head off the class gerbil. He flushed our goldfish, Bubbles. The boys played king of the castle, and Reaper clawed his way to the top of the playground, and defended his perch so viciously that he killed the game. So he stood there alone on the top of the playground for the rest of the lunch hour, gloating. You were never like the other kids, Reaper; you liked hurting people and you didn't care who. There is no tragic loss in you, no wasted potential for good. Deep down, you were always a mass killer, one who reaps the innocent and guilty alike. You will only ever be a blunt instrument of genocide. So long as the feeblest spark of love or joy animates our species, there will be someone, no matter how small and ineffective, to raise a pen against your ugliness and dub you abomination, horrific blurry-eyed dragon with the breath of the sun.

And so I spat the taste of cucumbers and cigarette butts directly at the eyeless face, watched the fluid trickle, run down, drip. Fuck you, Reaper. I'm never going to be like you. I live for a future where you are scrapped in endless fields of waste and rust, an airplane graveyard of tangled wings. I will fucking dance when the last of you is slain.

Bell was determined to make up for his convalescence—he needed to be twice the man we were. I can still see him, wearing a new uniform since the old had gotten baggy from weight loss, with a pen rammed in one corner of his scarred mouth. He read through all the daily sitreps and SIGACTS of the rainy season, all the discovered unexploded ordinance, the occasional find of a cache of weapons, or drugs. He even plotted them all on the big map, working late into the evening, sticky notes all over the place, so he could see the patterns for himself.

"Here and here," he said, pointing to central Dand and the horn of Panjwa'i. "These are the hot spots. But is it because the Taliban are more active in those areas, or because we are?"

"Both," said the Major, her eyes red from long hours of planning and scheming for the FET. "You know, Bell, I could have gotten the Int guys to print you out a report that does exactly this. Could have saved you some time."

Bell frowned. "I wanted to build it myself, Major, and see the big picture."

"This only tells us where they've been, not where they'll be. What we've got is a dense civilian population who harbours our enemy. The enemy strikes, hides their weapons, and blends back in."

"Anyone who harbours a terrorist is one," said Bell.

I snorted. "Even when they kidnap your kid and start scalding its genitals?"

The Major sounded like she was quoting a textbook, "We attack their base of power by eroding their public support. We achieve that through information operations, our good work in the field, and strategic strikes against known terrorists."

"One big sweep," said Bell, his hand a wave surging from west to east across the map, "that's all we need. This war's not gonna end without drastic action."

The Major clutched her forehead. "Damnit, Bell, we tried that. The Russians tried that. The British tried that. All we do is erode public support and turn the moderates against us."

Bell looked up from the map, his eyes drooping with new bags. "I've been reading, Major. Nothing else to do in the hospital. We think of the Taliban as these masters of flexibility. But some of the cement pads they use for mortar attacks have been handed down from father to son for generations—where's the flexibility in that?"

She argued, "You're not actually thinking outside the box here, Bell, you're taking us backward toward conventional war. This is a counter-insurgency. You're talking Napoleon stuff here: the charge. The glorious charge. It's a fantasy."

Once again Bell raised his volume for the benefit of the eavesdroppers, the soldiers who ringed the room in the workstations. "I know it will be difficult, Major, but I believe we can win this. There's absolutely no reason for us to give up. If we take decisive and effective action, we can end this war."

Steel had entered the Major's voice. "I didn't say anything about giving up, Bell. Quite the contrary. We are in a prolonged war that will involve changing the way people think, training a new police force and Army. It will take generations. This war is not a thing that can be solved with one quick, bloody operation—that stupid idea keeps coming back every few months because it's the only thing we know." Her eyes flickered to me for a second. "The Army has made us into hammers, Bell. But what we need are scalpels. Do you understand?"

"I understand what I was taught in Armor school, Major. In order to win, we need to 'close with and destroy the enemy.' If I was in charge that's exactly what I'd be doing."

"Good thing you're not in charge, Bell," said the Major.

"Well, we'd have killed this little *haji* by now," said Bell, pointing to the drone feed, which had settled on the Afghan teen we'd named and tracked for months. Sahar was on a motorcycle traveling east, and caught behind a jingle truck—broad-shouldered and sometimes gaudy transports the locals used, occasionally spilling surplus sacks or carpets onto the road. "I can't believe you've been following this little punk for the entire month I was away."

"If you had caught up on the Int reports as I suggested," scolded the Major, "you would know that Sahar has been liaising with high-value targets. He's more use to us alive. They also suspect he's becoming radicalized by our surveillance and drone strikes in the area."

"Not to mention he hasn't done anything wrong," I said.

Neither Bell nor the Major answered. They were staring at a second drone feed, on another monitor, a Predator. This monitor rarely showed anything interesting; the drone circled KAF interminably, hoping to dump its missiles on rocketeers who plagued the camp.

"What the hell is that?" said Bell.

The drone paused in its sweep to focus on a section of KAF's northern outer wall—the earth by the wall was disturbed, shifting. The Major, Bell, and I froze, staring at the screen. The soil, still wet and heavy from the rain, bulged. The bulge grew higher and higher, like a bubble of chewing gum, until it broke and a muddy snout emerged. Somewhere between a bear and a human, hair slicked down, with two long tusks jutting from the upper jaw: I knew in a flash what it was.

"What the fuck am I looking at?" said Bell.

"Beats me," said the Maj'. "Any ideas, Jones?"

"Haven't the foggiest." *I told you to dig in the dark, you damn idiot.*

Noah was born. Crawled right out of the muck and ooze, sliming forth by the inch, gasping for air, blinking at the sun in confusion. The tree-trunk neck. The great claws slicing through the earth. The tremendous trapezius. The terrible triceps. The devastating deltoids. The bulging back. As Noah tore at the ground, hauling his lower body from the hole, his lats flared in the sunset like the sweeping wings of a vast, mystical manta ray.

I kept one eye on Bell and the Major because either could turn ruthless at any second, but also to confirm they were seeing what I was seeing—a real live Sasquatch, not a man, not a Taliban, not a fantasy, not a bear, not an insurgent, an actual homegrown monster carrying a flea-ridden blanket like a teddy bear. I felt a growing smugness: not crazy at all, just grown wise.

Finally, Noah had slithered and squirmed his entire bulk through the hole, and stood next to it, working out the kinks in his back and neck. The idiot, despite my warnings, was seemingly oblivious to the many dangers that awaited him on this side of the wall, was breathing the free air and cooing to Lumpy.

"Now what's he doing?" asked Bell, "signalling to his buddies?"

"Stretching," I said. The Major's eyes darted to my face for a second, then away—had I betrayed something?

"If he intends harm to the camp, we have the Rules of Engagement to strike him," she insisted.

"Seems to me he's running *from* KAF," I said.

"Hairy sonofabitch, isn't he?" said Bell.

"You wanna jet?" yelled Crazy Jay. "Two minutes, thirty seconds."

From the Major, "Jones, create a Significant Incident. Call it Possible Enemy Action 01."

"Aye, Ma'am."

Suspicious Fighting Aged Male seen tunneling from under KAF at 1906. Monitoring for Positive Identification with PRED on site. New SIGACT Poss Enemy Action 01.

Checking over his shoulders for witnesses, Noah began to venture into the desert. A decade's worth of barbed wire stretched in front of him, some intact and beautifully coiled, some rusty and discarded piles, some blasted open by rockets. Craters. Mud. No vegetation. A few pieces of blown garbage caught in the wire. He started gingerly, picking his way through the thorns. But then, spotting something, he upped his pace, leaping the defenses, bounding through the ugly desertscape.

The snipers in the towers had noticed the movement. They weren't soldiers like us; they were mercenaries, played by different rules. Long black streaks scored the drone footage as snipers from two different towers fired on Noah. I fought the urge to vomit. *Not a game anymore is it, Noah? Those ain't pistols, little pop-pops I can pull out of your shoulder.* Still, Noah seemed unstoppable—the snipers couldn't lead him far enough—maybe the setting sun was making glare in their scopes, maybe Noah was saved by his increasingly frantic leaps, mini-tumbles down small inclines, use of barbed-wire heaps as shelter, nimble changes of direction. Two shots fired at the same time made a black 'x' on the screen as he leaped over a pit of shit-covered spikes.

"I say we strike him," Bell muttered.

"He's in a restricted area," said the Major.

"But he's unarmed," I said. "Naked."

Noah slipped, fell to one knee. Rolled just in time to avoid a lethal black streak. Scrambled into a shallow ditch with sniper shots slamming into the top. He flattened himself as low as possible. I couldn't hear any whimpers or see the fear in his eyes—I imagined those.

But Sasquatch never pray. At least not in the sad way we do. Pinned down, frightened, Noah began to twist in the soil like he was in ecstasy. His image blurred, became spectral, half-shadow. Curled into the soil, Noah was wracked by horrible contortions, his claws jutting into daggers, teeth bursting from his jaw in new fangs, muscles surging into grotesque overdevelopment, yet lean, horrifically lean, like a starving beast.

Holy hell—the Protector Spirit. Noah wasn't bullshitting; it was real. *Magic is real.* The gasps from Bell and the Major confirmed it.

"If those are knives, then he's technically armed and we can strike," said the Major.

"Maybe those are just his hands," I said.

Fully transformed into the shadowy avatar, Noah waited as sniper rounds pummeled the barbed wire. Then he twisted, crouched, and leaped from the shallow ditch, seeming to fly he moved so nimbly, sometimes running on his feet, sometimes his hands, twisting lithely through tangles of wire, faster, faster. Faster than any human. Faster than a goddamn cheetah. Our drone could barely keep up. Something exploded—black streaks of shrapnel on the screen. *Noah, you're in a goddamn minefield. I told you the tunnel was a mistake, you stubborn fucker.*

Update: Poss Enemy Action 01. FAM engaged from KAF sniper towers at 1910. PRED on sight. Awaiting PID.

Three more landmines detonated around Noah's grotesque and altered body, not slowing him in the slightest. He dodged a sniper round with a laser-quick forward flip. Bell's breath caught, half a gasp. "I've seen that strength before," he whispered urgently. "Felt it, to be more precise—that's the fucker who *took* me. I'm sure of it."

I grabbed his shoulder. "What are you saying, Bell? How can you be certain? You had a goddamn bag on your head."

"Don't fucking touch me," he barked, shoving my hand roughly. Raising his voice, "How many missiles we got on this Pred', Crazy Jay?"

"Three missiles," Crazy Jay yelled, testosterone glinting on his forehead.

"Jesus, Bell." I said. "You can't kill everyone who reminds you of your rapist."

"Permission to fire, Major?" Bell snarled.

"Major, we don't have positive ID on this guy," I said.

"Kill kill kill," chanted Crazy Jay.

"Moves like a soldier," said Bell.

"No PID, no weapons," I said.

"In a restricted area!" Bell shouted.

"Naked, lost!" I yelled back.

"Kill kill kill," chanted Crazy Jay.

> ### The Kill Chant
>
> Yes, it was real. Heart hammers when the killing was close, blood pressure spiking. Hours watching little pixels moving, no explosions—normal to want excitement. No one likes a hockey game where the puck never splashes in the net. Killing was entertainment and religion both, a sacrament, a communion, a ceremony, the surefire way to win.

"Everyone shut the fuck up!" screamed the Major in a voice both hoarse and shrill. It was the ugliest noise I'd ever heard from her.

The Sasquatch was gone. He'd vanished into a culvert, or fold in the ground, or the air. The drone was circling around, zooming out to catch another glimpse.

"Are you happy, Jones?" said Bell. "You just let a killer get away. He puts a bomb in the road and it kills our guys that's on your head."

"We had the ROE, Jones," said the Major.

Update: Poss Enemy Action 01. Engagement complete resulting in NSTR.

"You got a fucking hard-on for ragheads?" Bell asked.

"This is war, Jones," said the Major. "No place for hesitation."

And they went on like that for a few minutes. I folded my arms across my chest. "No weapons. No PID."

"Goddamn sailor." Bell stalked off in disgust.

"Stubborn idiot," my lover's words.

There would be consequences, of course, but I was happy to pay them. My friend still lived.

48.

"JONES. MY OFFICE." There was a time such an order would have thrilled me, but the Major was pissed. She sat behind her desk, grinding her teeth so hard a muscle in her cheek jumped. "I'm going to yell at you for a few minutes because that's what the team needs to hear. We will talk in low voices after." I nodded.

Reprimanding a subordinate who is also your lover is a touchy business, but the Major was a natural, had a harsh drill-sergeant voice when she needed it, and knew all the swear words. "When we have the ROE and PID we strike, Jones. That's the last time I want to see any bullshit from you. We're in a fucking war, not on some stupid cruise in the Great Lakes, you pacifist piece of shit… I've scraped better soldiers off my boots… you fuck up a strike again and I'll waste you myself." It went on and on, searing. I was grateful when it ended.

She turned her computer's monitor toward me. On it, was the video of Noah, pinned down, transforming into the Protector Spirit. She studied my face and spoke in her private voice. "I've never seen anything like this before, Jones. I've been watching the video for half an hour and still can't figure it out. Is it a weapon? Some kind of experimental drug?"

There was no way I would betray Noah, even to her. I shrugged.

"I know you know something about this, Jones. I know you. I know your face. I know your hands. I know the way you breathe. I know when you're lying and I know when you're keeping a secret."

"Well, of course you know I'm keeping a secret, Major."

"Not that secret," she hissed. "A different one. The war is bigger than us—haven't you figured that out?"

"No, it isn't," I said. And I meant it.

The muscle in her cheek leaped again. "You're a pain in my ass, Jones." She played the video of Noah's transformation again. "What am I supposed to do about this?" Then, in an even softer voice, "what am I supposed to do about you?"

49.

A REFRESHER COURSE IN KILLING—that was her solution—not just for me, but for the whole TOC team. When the Major delegated the creation of this training to Bell, my technical superior, everyone knew I was responsible. That I'd let a possible kill slip through our fingers. Kool moaned that he should be "out in the shit" and called me "Haji-lover," but it didn't sting me, so the name didn't stick like "Office Soldier." Bell hauled all the TOC-moles into the presentation room where we usually briefed the General, and projected a PowerPoint onto a wall-wide screen.

Only a few pictures, mostly text-slides packed with bullet points. I knew all this shit already. When you work seven days a week for eight months straight, you don't actually forget the basic skills of the job. But it was useful for Kool and it gave Bell something to put together, his kill-tutorial. One hundred and thirty-seven slides—a bloated monstrosity that washed onto the shore with its legs growing from the side of its head. Next slide, next slide, next slide.

Who can order a drone strike, the approval authority? What is Positive ID, and what does it mean? What are the specific rules of engagement that might apply to us? How do the intelligence folks help determine PID? Does the approval authority change depending on what calibre missile we use? How do we prevent aircraft from entering our airspace when we're shooting missiles? What are the benefits of air strikes versus drones versus attack helicopters versus artillery versus tanks versus sniper rifles versus deathrays from satellites? And most importantly, when we strike and the explosion bursts just so, scooping buckets of earth and throwing it in all directions, with a splash of blood right at the center, doesn't the blast look like a flower?

I yawned so hard I cracked my jaw. I disappeared to shit and admire the graffiti and Bell was still rambling on the same frigging slide when I got back. We were trapped with our heads in vices. Kool was barely awake, even though he'd missed pre-deployment training, arriving late to the party, so lots of this stuff was new.

Bell gestured to the screen, rows of statistics. "The most successful TOCs in the world had a kill-rate of over thirty FAMs a day. Every single day they were using drones, jets, bombers, and artillery. You think any enemy can stand that kind of assault, over time? Not fucking likely."

A thump—Kool's feet sliding off the desk. "Did you just say thirty kills a day?" He looked at his fingers in consternation.

Our mentor's grin cracked his face. "That's right, little brother—no infantry unit can match the kill rate of an active TOC. That's why we do what we do."

The younger soldier's mouth worked soundlessly. From where I was sitting, it was like someone shone a flashlight into the dank cellar of his brain—the creation of a new neural pathway, AKA learning, seemed dangerously close. He teetered on the edge, jaw set in stubbornness, then plunged. A new thought glinted in his eyes: our potential for destruction was greater than a soldier in the field.

He could not disguise his excitement. "So why aren't we doing it? Why are we sitting around like a bunch of office soldiers when we could be killing thirty ragheads a day?"

Bell answered, "You know I've asked the Major that exact question?"

"It's a question of ROE and PID," I said.

"There he goes again," said Bell. "Jones the Haji-lover."

"Yah, shut the fuck up, Jones, you rapist piece of shit." Suddenly, Kool's slouch disappeared. He kept his feet under the desk and took lengthy notes. His hand shot into the air like a rocket whenever Bell asked a question.

"Jones," said Bell. "You fucking yawn again I'm going to put Kool in charge of you. He might not have your experience but at least he's got the right attitude and he's Army." That was unthinkable. I plugged in the coffee pot and stabbed myself in the leg with a pen whenever I started to doze off.

"The fighting season has begun," Bell preached, "no more mistakes."

Long shift, anyway, sandwiched between psychos. But at least Noah got out of it. Any amount of professional disgrace was worth giving him a chance to escape, to be happy. The Major worked late but got one of the signalers to walk her home. The message was clear: pacifists are unfuckable.

In my frustration and isolation, I tried to take up smoking, but didn't have the willpower for it. To head for the chainlink alcove just outside the TOC, every hour on the hour? To plunge into one of the brokeback chairs, all mismatched with stubby legs and one of the cushions gashed, to haul deep on a smoke no matter the pouring rain, stink of the pond, or scorch of sun? I could only make it for three or four smokes in a row before needing a break. But I sat there anyway, remembering the ten minutes I'd spent with the Major resting her head on my shoulder. Just the feeling of touching someone, of comforting and being comforted in turn.

Instead, the taste of ashes. I hated being out of her favor, denting her respect. I missed her in all the ways it's possible to miss a person, so I did something forbidden.

Major,

Because we always begin with these marks of respect and transition to marks of kindness. In the day, we are wearing frosty armor studded with icicles. I always want to look at you but I never do, because love is a discipline.

I will go where you tell me, like a missile. If we are through with our mistake, I understand. But I will never be through with it, not completely. How does one unsee the monsoon rains, that first time, the power of them, the way they steal your breath?

Without you, I will be nothing at all, just a gust of wind carrying snippets of sentences: a weak man, a human, shorn from life raft, roiling in the currents. When I am strong, it is only a game I play for you. I live for your touch. When we are tender, the war disappears.

Major, I am standing at your threshold, holding my hat, and staring with sad eyes—you have seen me through the peephole. You know I should stay out there, even though the rain is pouring down and the sky is streaked with lightning. I am saying, 'please.'

With no signature at all, since her only petname for me so far was "human," and anything else might give us away. I would wait to give her the letter in person. It would be unwise to leave it on her desk, where Kool or Bell might lick it open with greedy tongues. Tomorrow. The letter would burn in my pocket until then: overwritten, hyperbolic, image-bloated, manipulative, true.

That morning, when I finally made it back to the barracks, I tucked the letter in the pocket of tomorrow's shirt, changed into a t-shirt and shorts, secured the locker, and climbed into my rack with a screech of springs. Instead of the relative softness of the thin pillow, my head clunked against something hard—a practical joke, Kool's long-awaited masterstroke? Nay. There seemed to be no malice in the Buddha-shaped object, and when I fished it from the pillowcase, a pear-shaped rock fell into my hand: the speaking stone.

Searching for monsters in the morning gloam—was Noah back or had someone else learned the magic of the stone? And if he was back, *why* the fuck was he back, after all the shit I'd gone through on his behalf? When I poked my head into the entrance of the frog-cave, newly enhanced with better cardboard trails, a bulky blackness filled the rear-most space.

"Noah, is that you, you sonofabitch?"

Noah's voice, deep and wearier than I remembered, "Hey, Jones."

We'd have to keep our voices low so they wouldn't carry through the washroom's thin floor. On the one hand I wanted to give the bastard a piece of my mind. On the other, now I'd seen Noah's transformation with my own eyes. Or rather, the drone's eye, though this distinction was blurring.

I drew close—Noah was cuddled with a sticky Lumpy and laying on one side. Every little squeak of floorboards above and gurgle of pipe made him flinch, twitch. I dragged a piece of semi-clean cardboard and lay down next to him, face to face, a foot away, "What the fuck happened to you, Noah?"

His eyelids fluttered. "So much blood. So much blood."

I scanned him, noticing darker patches in the fur. "Jesus, Noah, are you hurt again?" I started to pat him for injuries.

"Not my blood," he said; I withdrew my hand.

"What did you do, Noah?" I asked. "I saw you transform into… something."

"I took the tunnel," he mumbled, clutching Lumpy tighter.

"I know you took the tunnel—I watched it all on the drone. My bosses wanted to strike—I stalled them."

"Spirit says I should kill ya. Spirit says yer dangerous."

A more urgent whisper: "Spirit can suck my balls—did you not just hear me say I saved your life? Again?"

Noah looked up at me then, and a vagueness in his eyes cleared. "I didn't hurt no one, Jones. Not this time. I didn't wanna come back to this shithole neither." He reached with his lips toward a glistening drop on the pipes that ran over his head. "Needed the water."

I had so many questions to ask him. Like how the hell did he get back on the camp—certainly not through the tunnel? But there was a more pressing issue: "So the Spirit. That shit is real, isn't it?"

Noah rolled his eyes. "Man, you never seen a damn yeti possessed by an evil spirit before?" That made me roll back on the cardboard chuckling, and it felt like old times for a second. His voice dropped even lower, "I didn't want to reach for him—never do—but I was afraid. Sometimes I'm just so afraid it's like I don't gotta choice anymore, ya know?"

I nodded. "I'm glad you're OK, Noah," and patted the bulk of his scarred front deltoid. "I just thought you made it out—had settled into some cave like a Taliban, found a mountainous lady-Sasquatch, ate subterranean mushrooms. You know. The dream."

Noah grinned. "That's ain't my dream, that's yer dream, Jones."

"Thing is, I can't do that again. Stop a strike, I mean. You don't know what it's like in there, Noah. I got one boss who thinks you're a terrorist, the other thinks you raped him. The Spirit is spectacular, but can it stop missiles?"

Noah's brow furrowed, "Whaddya mean ya can't stop 'em? Ya can't just say 'no, don't shoot that guy?' Seems simple enough to me—not like what I gotta deal with. Spirit says yer dangerous. A threat."

I chewed this for a long minute. Finally, "Spirit is right. I am dangerous. But it's not fair to call me a threat—I'm a cog. I threw myself on the grenade last time to protect you and I can't do it again. Bell, one of my bosses, has threatened to put an idiot in my place if I fuck it up again. The idiot will hurt as many people as he can. At least I can make smart choices and only strike the actual fighters, instead of the farmers. And you, my friend, look like a fighter."

Noah scratched his fuzzy muzzle. "You actually chose this shit, didn't ya? At least with me I got an excuse."

I stared at the rotting floorboards above. "I knew from the ships I could make tough choices and work in a team. Who would you rather have looking at you through a drone, finger on the button: a muscle-headed soldier, or a goddamn poet?" Noah didn't answer, just breathed heavily, so I went on. "I'm not a fanatic—this started off being a selfish thing but now my service is meaningful. I need to believe I've helped, otherwise I lived on this base with the rockets and the shit pond, watched people die and get mutilated, sent helicopters after scalded babies, and it was all for nothing."

Quiet after that, and, this time, Noah's bumbling fingers found my shoulder in the semi-dark and squeezed it. "Well, yer trapped here, Jones, but I ain't. I'll miss ya but soon as I can get my hands on a couple jugs o' water, I'm headin' right back to the tunnel."

I was shaking my head. "Engineers are filling your tunnel with concrete right now—Major's orders."

A hard edge: "Spirit says I should kill 'em all, burst free."

He's becoming a voice piece for the Spirit. "Sure, if you want to keep killing people, you can probably bust out of here. You might also catch a bunch of bullets again. But what will you do about the two Predators circling the camp? We've doubled the overwatch since you used the tunnel—yes, I imagine Spirit says you should kill me. Predictable prick. But the TOC will continue to work without me, in fact, it will become even more ruthless, and you'll lose your one ally in the whole fucking world."

In a strange, flat voice Noah said, "Tell me where the TOC is." His eyes had gone glossy again. Had an image of the Spirit descending on the TOC in a fury, tossing signallers into monitors, hewing the heads from Bell, Kool, and the Major. A tight-chested pang.

"Noah," I said. "I want to talk to Noah." *Holy hell, if he's losing control of his monster…*

He blinked a few times, "What? What happened? I say somethin'?"

"Listen up, Noah, you can't kill your way out of this. I know it didn't work out too well last time, but I still think catching a plane is your best bet for getting home. Maximum stealth. Don't take any chances, and try to displace something of a similar weight, ok? They track that."

"Home," he said, tracing a crack in the floorboards above. "Hard to picture, ain't it? Like a movie I saw a long time ago. You think my Mom's still out there?"

"You've got a better chance finding her in Canada than you do in Afghanistan."

A reluctant nod. "I hate waitin', Jones. I hate this cave and the bugs. Tired of bein' bored."

"Why don't you pass a little time and tell me how you got covered in blood?"

He shuddered with the memory, but his eyes lit with the storyteller's gleam.

50.

THERE I WAS, JUST ME AN' OLD LUMPY HERE. SQUIRTED OUTTA THE BASE THROUGH THE HOLE UNDER THE WALL, AND WAS DODGIN' SNIPER SHOTS, BARBED WIRE, AND LANDMINES FOR FIFTEEN MINUTES, THE SPIRIT LEADIN' THE WAY, ME CRAPPIN' MY SHORTS BEHIND THE WALL O' GLASS. WE DUCKED BEHIND THIS ONE LITTLE RISE WITH A PATCH OF TWIGGY GRASS POPPIN' OUT THE TOP. SPIRIT SLICES THE MOUND'S BELLY WITH A CLAW, AND SQUIRMS HIS WAY IN, LETTIN' THE TOP DROP BACK DOWN LIKE A HAT. AIN'T NO MAGIC IN THAT, JONES—JUST SOME OLD NINJA SHIT. SOMETIMES SPIRIT LEAVES ME HOLDIN' THE BAG LIKE THIS, BREATHIN' OUT A TINY-ASS HOLE IN THE SOD.

SPIRIT SAYS I SHOULDN'T BE TELLIN' YOU ANY OF THIS, THAT STORIES GOT POWER. I TELL HIM THAT'S WHY I'M SAYIN' 'EM IN THE FIRST PLACE.

NEXT FEW HOURS THE MOUND WAS LIKE ONE O' THEM SAND-OVENS YA COOK CHICKEN IN. NO WAY I WAS LEAVIN' UNTIL I SAW THE MOON THROUGH MY PEEPHOLE, NOT AFTER ALL THAT ACTION GETTIN' OFF THE CAMP. SO I WAS SWEATIN' LIKE A BANSHEE IN THERE, AND ALWAYS HUNGRY AFTER TRANSFORMIN', NOT TO MENTION ALL THE DIGGIN' AND SHIT. THAT'S WHEN I STARTED FEELIN' THE THIRST CRAWLIN' UP MY THROAT, TONGUE GETTIN' ROUGH AS A CAT'S.

I BUSTED OUTTA THAT MOUND WHEN I SAW MY OL' BUDDY THE MOON— I'M HALF COOKED BY THIS POINT, JONES—STUMBLIN' DOWN A HILL, FARTHER 'WAY FROM 'EM SNIPERS. AIN'T A DROP TO DRINK NOWHERE. I SAW ONE SAD-LOOKIN' CACTUS. I SPLIT THAT BASTARD OPEN NO MATTER HOW THE THORNS DUG IN, BUT IT WASN'T NO GLASS OF OJ IN THERE. NOPE. JUST A DRIED-UP SAC LIKE AN ORANGE PEEL—I CHEWED IT ANYWAY, FOR THE DROPS. DIDN'T DO SHIT.

JUST THE CRUNCH CRUNCH OF HOT ROCKS UNDER MY FEET FOR A COUPLE MILES. THEN I SEE FIREFLIES DANCIN' IN THE VALLEY, AND I FIGURED OUT PRETTY FAST THAT WAS A VILLAGE—YOU PROLLY KNOW THE ONE FROM YER BIGASS MAP. I GOT GOALS, MAN. I'M GETTING THE FUCK OUTTA HERE. GIMME A STREAM WITH CLEAN WATER AND PLENTY OF FISHIES AND I'D SAY GOODBYE TO HUMANS RIGHT QUICK, FIND A CAVE AND HEAL, FIGURE OUT A BETTER DREAM. GET FAT AND HIBERNATE FOR A FEW MONTHS AND COME OUT WITH NEW WISDOM. BUT NONE OF THAT WAS GONNA HAPPEN UNLESS I GOTTA CHANCE TO DRINK A WHOLE RAIN BARREL, AND MAYBE STICK MY HEAD IN ONE, TOO.

I COULD SEE MEN ON THE ROOFTOPS. SITTIN' ON LAWN CHAIRS, GABBIN'

INTO CELL PHONES, LONG SNAKES O' SMOKE CHARMED UPWARDS BY THE STARS. SEEMED LIKE EACH GUY HAD A KITTEN ON HIS LAP OR A DOG BESIDE HIM, SAME AS HOME, BUT WHEN I CREPT CLOSER TURNS OUT THEY WERE RIFLES. "KILL 'EM ALL AND TAKE THE WATER," SAID THE SPIRIT BUT I WAS IN STEALTH MODE, JONES, THE MOST HANDSOME PANTHER YOU NEVER SEEN.

PULLIN' UP THE EDGE OF A BLUE TARP THINKIN' THERE MIGHT BE H_2O UNDERNEATH, WHEN THE ACTUAL DOGS STARTED BARKIN'—GODDAMNIT. THERE WAS A RAIN BARREL UNDER THE TARP AFTER ALL, AND IF I COULDA JUST GOTTEN A MOUTHFUL OF WATER, I MIGHTA BEEN OK—AND *THAT IS ALL I GOT*, JONES. ONE GODDAMN MOUTHFUL, BEFORE THE SHARP TEETH OF A DOG SUNK INTO THE BACK OF MY LEG HERE—SEE THAT SCAR. ALMOST MADE ME SPIT UP THE WATER, TOO, 'FORE I PUNTED THAT MANGY BASTARD LIKE A FOOTBALL, THEN I WAS RUNNIN' AGAIN, DOGS BARKIN', GUNS BARKIN', SPIRIT CALLIN' ME A COWARD AND EVERYTHIN' ELSE HE COULD THINK UP.

YOU SEEN ME RUN NOW THOUGH—I GOT OUTTA THERE PRETTY FAST AND FOUND MYSELF BACK IN THE GODDAMN DESERT, THE DOGS WERE ALL TIRED OUT AND PANTIN', ME THIRSTIER THAN EVER. GETTIN' WEAK. CHEWED ANOTHER ORANGE PEEL O' CACTUS. CLIMBED A HILL, TO GET A BIT MORE INFO, BY THE TIME I REACHED THE TOP I'D GOT REAL DIZZY AND SUNK DOWN TO MY KNEES. "YOU'RE GOING TO DIE UNLESS YOU GET SOME WATER," WHISPERED THE SPIRIT.

SAW A HIGHWAY IN THE MOONLIGHT, AND, MORE IMPORTANT, THE RIVER. USED TO BE A RIVER, ANYWAY, BACK WHEN IT WAS RAININ'. NOW IT WEREN'T SHIT, JONES—YOU COULDA TOLD ME, WISH I'D ASKED YA. JUST A SAD, LONG BED OF CRACKS. NO RIVER. NO WATER. NO FISHIES. FUCK, NO HOPE. "YOU SHOULD HAVE KILLED THAT VILLAGE AND TAKEN THEIR WATER," SAID THE SPIRIT. "NOW YOU'RE GOING TO DIE ON THIS HILL, ALONE."

SEEMED HE WAS RIGHT. I LAY MY HEAD DOWN ON THE CRACKED GROUND AND THOUGHT OF MY SEVEN HAPPY MEMORIES, ONE AFTER ANOTHER, AND I ALMOST GOT THROUGH ALL O' 'EM WHEN I HEARD THIS LOUDASS BOOM FROM THE HIGHWAY, AND SAW A FLASH. LOOK DOWN AND THERE WAS ONE OF YER ARMORED TRUCKS WITH THE BELLY BUSTED OPEN, BURNIN'. A SOLDIER SPILLED OUT THE DRIVER'S SEAT, TOOK THREE DIZZY STEPS, AND DIED.

"THIS IS YOUR CHANCE," SAID THE SPIRIT.

"WHAT THE HELL ARE YOU TALKING ABOUT?" I SAID, MY DRY MOUTH CRACKIN' OPEN LIKE AN OLD WOUND.

"YOUR FRIENDS IN THE CAMP WILL RECOVER THE VEHICLE AND THE BODIES."

"YEAH, SO?"

"IDIOT. DISGUISE YOURSELF AS A SLAIN HUMAN SOLDIER, AND THEY WILL TAKE YOU BACK TO THE CAMP, WHERE THERE IS WATER."

FUNNY THING 'BOUT THE SPIRIT—HE AIN'T NEVER GIVE UP ON ME, NOT ONCE, AND I DIDN'T HAVE NO BETTER IDEA. WENT DOWN TO THAT SMASHED

VEHICLE WITH THE ARMOR ALL DENTED IN AND A BIGASS HOLE IN THE ROAD. DEAD GUY IN THE DITCH. ANOTHER IN FRONT WITH HIS HEAD BENT SIDEWAYS ON THE DASHBOARD. LITTLE FIRES BURNIN' PATCHES OF OIL ON THE ROAD. I CRACKED THE BACK HATCH, THINKIN' I COULD HIDE IN THERE…

WISH I NEVER DID. NEVER SEEN NOTHIN' LIKE IT. GUESS THERE WERE FIVE OR SIX SOLDIERS WHEN THE BOMB STRUCK. NOW THEY WERE ALL TANGLED UP. ANYTHIN' THAT WAS ON THE FLOOR GOT SMUSHED, LEGS ALL TWISTED AND TORN OFF AND BLOOD BLOOD BLOOD ON ALL THE WALLS AND CEILIN' AND THE SMELL OF SHIT AND COPPERY BLOOD AND THE DEAD FACES COVERED IN BLOOD. 'MEMBER IT WAS DARK, ALL THE BLOOD JUST LOOKED BLACKER, LIKE THE NIGHT WAS TAKIN' THOSE THINGS BACK, BUT I COULD FEEL IT ON THE FLOOR, SQUISHIN' UP BETWEEN MY TOES. "HIDE YOURSELF," SAID THE SPIRIT AND I WAS CRYIN', EVEN THOUGH I'D NO WATER TO SPARE AND SMEARIN' BLOOD ON MYSELF AND MOVIN' THE SPARE RIFLES AND PARTS OF 'EM DEAD PEOPLE 'ROUND SO I COULD MAKE A LITTLE SPACE FOR MYSELF TO LIE DOWN, PULLIN' THE BODIES OVER ME TO HIDE HOW BIG I AM. "GOOD GOOD," SAID THE SPIRIT, "NOW DRINK." AND THERE'S A SEVERED LEG NEAR ME THAT'S STILL DRIPPIN' AND THE SPIRIT'S CHANTIN' *DRINK DRINK DRINK* AND I PUT MY LIPS ON THE TORN FLESH. BLOOD WENT IN MY MOUTH AND YOU'D NEVER BELIEVE IT, BUT IT WAS SWEET, JONES, SO SWEET AND THE PERFECT TEMPERATURE… I DIDN'T WANT TO DRINK AT FIRST, BUT THEN I DID AND I SLURPED AND SLURPED AND OH GOD IT WAS AWFUL, IT WAS AWFUL AND I'M SORRY, SO SORRY. I DIDN'T WANNA.

I DIDN'T WANNA.

WAITIN' FOR MORNIN' WITH THE COPPERY BLOODTASTE. TRYIN' TO TAKE ONLY AS MUCH AS I NEEDED. SPIRIT GOT AMUSED. "OH, YOU'RE THE MOST WRETCHED THING I'VE EVER SEEN." AND, "YOU SHOULD HAVE TAKEN THE VILLAGE, LIKE I TOLD YOU." THAT DRAGON LAUGH IN THE DARKNESS AND ALL THE DEAD MEN 'ROUND ME COOLIN' AND BLEEDIN' AND ME GOIN' BACK IN MY MIND TO MY SEVEN HAPPY MEMORIES AND I COULDN'T DO IT, COULDN'T TAKE MYSELF AWAY. I'M STILL THERE. I'M STILL *THERE*.

THEY DID COME, HELICOPTERS AND SOLDIERS WITH THEIR MACHINES FOR HAULIN'—MAYBE YOU SENT 'EM? HITCHED US UP WITH A LURCH. DOCTOR-GUY CRACKED THE DOOR AND PRESSED A CLOTH TO HIS MOUTH, GAGGIN'. I SQUIRMED DEEPER INTO THE PILE, WHICH WAS COLD NOW—COLD 'N' STICKY. BUNCHA SOLDIERS TOWED US BACK TO THE CAMP, BACK HERE. I WAITED UNTIL THE NOISES QUIETED DOWN FOR A SECOND THEN RAN OUT THE BACK O' THE TRUCK SO FAST ANYONE WHO SAW ME MUSTA THOUGHT I WAS A SHADOW. MADE IT HERE TO THE STINKCAVE, PLACED THE STONE AND PASSED OUT.

I'M SORRY, JONES. I AIN'T THE PERSON YOU THOUGHT I WAS. I TRIED SO HARD NOT TO BE A MONSTER BUT IT ALL WORE ME DOWN AND, SO, HERE I AM. TASTE O' BLOOD IN MY MOUTH AND NOW THE SPIRIT AIN'T WHISPERIN' NO MORE. HE'S SHOUTIN'. HE'S ALL I CAN HEAR.

51.

NOAH'S STORY TRAILED OFF and he stared ahead in the gloom of the frog-cave, looking straight through me, seeing nothing. I wanted to comfort him, pat his shoulder—I mean, I'd hosed this guy down and rooted into his wounds; we were pretty damn close—but he had so much blood on him, slicking down the fur of his muzzle, patches of brown and crimson on his arms, legs, and torso.

"I'm sorry, Noah," I said, but he didn't answer, kept staring. It seemed the bloody sacrament Noah endured had strengthened the Spirit's hold.

It was all true, what he said. We *had* recovered a blown-up vehicle the night before, finding **6X US KIA**, and recovered the Lieutenant from the road, and the Master Corporal from the front seat, via helicopter. A catastrophe. After a relatively bloodless rainy season, it was clear the fighting had recommenced, and we were already one point behind.

So that evening, when I arrived for my shift, I was surprised to find the TOC blood-drunk and celebrating. Block-headed Clay was handing out cake on paper plates. Crazy Jay warbled to country music; Kool slapped us all on the back, even me. Bell was showing a video to everyone who came into the TOC, with all the glee of a boy boasting of a captured frog: "Did you see my kill? Did you see my kill?" The lines of pain and exhaustion etched into his face after his rape had softened; he strutted across the room shaking hands and laughing. Killing was making him whole again.

The festivities never touched the Major; she stood in the midst radiating frost and wearing her battered helmet with her arms folded across her chest. When Clay offered her a slice of cake she barked, "Get that away from me," and ignored the hoots and boos. I searched for her eyes, but she didn't give them to me—I wanted to hand her the letter.

Bell sidled close, "Jones, my man, have you seen it? Watch that screen, Big Fella—I'll show you how it's done."

A young man was digging in a culvert, broad daylight, cheeky. He wore the loose-fitting robes that look like pyjamas to us, called a *perahan*. Behind the grit-covered sandals, a spool of wire and the classic red gasoline jugs of Home-Made Explosives.

"Sloppy, wasn't he?" said Bell. "Didn't take five second for Intelligence to give us Positive ID. Then he was fucked, our little Judas, weren't ya, buddy?" Bell asked the now-dead man.

The Major approached, "Bell thinks it's funny to undermine my direction to give our targets a human name."

He scowled, "Someone's gotta think of morale, Major."

"Killing is not a goddamn sport," she said.

"How did you strike him?" I asked.

Bell answered, "40mm rounds from a jet… Now shhhhh—watch that screen!"

The jet fired a volley of shells. The first round exploded near him and he was thrown one way, pieces of his *perahan* tearing off. A second round hit and hurled him another way. "See here, Jones, his shoes go flying." The third round landed and Judas hadn't. Then he was a shrapnel pincushion, a body being flung. "You can almost see the life come out of him here," Bell paused the screen. The blast had ripped Judas' clothes off completely, and his skeleton was showing in places. He levitated in the air with his eyes closed and a peaceful expression on his face.

The other two bombs landed. The apostle disappeared in the explosion. When the dust settled, he was gone, spirited away, ascension. "That's how you fucking do it, Jones," Bell crowed. "No trace. No doctors, no medical bills, no police babysitters, no jail time. All you need to clean this mess is one guy with a mop."

The Major's voice dripped with bitterness, "Because when we destroy them completely, we can pretend they weren't people, right Bell?"

A drone without weapons, the long-sighted Heron, still spun around the crater in the road, a kind of vigil. This scan was routine—a Battle Damage Assessment. It was not symbolic; often Taliban would return to the scene of a strike to reclaim the weapons, and we would strike again. I watched as six women, faceless as drones in their burqas, arrived at the crater, but I couldn't hear them, despite the frantic hand motions, and one woman slumping onto her knees. They were collecting the remains of the body into a basket.

Shouts pulled Bell away and the Major and I stood side-by-side watching the BDA as the basket filled up.

"Look, Jones, we've killed someone's son. We've hurt the very women I've been trying to help."

"We had the ROE and the PID," I said, and the words sounded as hollow as they look.

"Another village lost."

We stood in silence for another long minute, watching. Then, I whispered,

"But we're still alive, aren't we?" and I handed her my letter like it was official correspondence, a brag sheet for the yearly Progress Evaluation Report. She made it disappear into her combat shirt and I didn't even burn with shame—our love had always been a thorn that bloomed in massacres. *Perverts.*

Soon, Bell's shift ended and the Major disappeared into her nook, grumbling loudly that the Colonels were undermining her Female Engagement Team project. Logistical difficulties: the recruiting and training of female soldiers; the hand strength required to cock a 50cal machine gun; designing special body armor to protect women's sensitive breasts, and; most importantly, how the inability to pee standing up necessitated frequent stops of a convoy, increasing the chances of ambush. She was writing a withering response—it sounded like punching the keyboard.

I arranged the deployment of an engineering team to patch the hole we'd made in the road. They'd leave at 0630, under the sun, escorted by an Explosive Ordinance Disposal unit—our friend the adorable robot—in case the road was mined. Wasn't long before the basket filled up and the women left the scene of the strike but I kept the Heron on Judas's grave for an extra hour. Look how efficient we've become—we can kill and dig the grave at the same time. Fifty years of war in Afghanistan, the Russians, the Brits, and all of us digging graves, leaving scars on the earth and the people.

I thought I could make a *difference.*

The lingering on the grave site was partly grief, partly curiosity, partly bearing witness, and partly self interest. I wanted the Major to see I was grieving a human life—because grief is a weapon, too. In the corner of my eye she opened the letter, read the message, and smiled. I knew I would walk her home that night.

The Chief barked "Room!" and the TOC-owls and I snapped to attention; Clay minimized his game of Pacman with the subtlest of gestures.

"How's everyone doing today?" asked the General in his too-loud voice. I

The General

Be suspicious of anyone who tells you Generals are monsters—this is an oversimplification, a civilian fantasy. Let there be no mistake: no one worked harder than the man in charge. A force: only a few hours of sleep each night, hammering himself in the gym, constant excursions to the FOBs, liaison with Afghan officials, family life a shamble—how can I lampoon such a martyr? It would have been easier if he was a moustache-twirling villain, escaping on a helicopter, screaming promises of revenge. But our General had studied leadership and spent decades in combat zones; I admired him.

made the mistake early in my tour of answering this question, and answering honestly, with less-than perfect enthusiasm, and the Chief nearly bit my pinky finger off my left hand. Now I know the question is rhetorical, the appropriate reaction is to wait at attention and smile with your whole face, and radiate joy at the General's presence. This was the answer he needed.

"At ease, troops." We relaxed our postures, and nothing else. The General glanced at the monitor; the drone was chasing the tail of a long empty road. "I heard you guys got some action today? Our man Bell is back in the saddle, doing the work of the war?"

I said, "Correct, Sir. We struck a target, an IED emplacer, at minute 1649 in the vicinity of Mushan. We received Positive ID from Intelligence, lined up a jet, and the Major approved the strike. The strike consisted of five 40mm rounds, which neutralized the target completely. We conducted a Battle Damage Assessment with a Heron, resulting in NSTR." Nothing Significant to Report. At some point every SIGACT dissolved into these four words.

"NSTR? Is that what you call it, Jones?" The Major emerged from the nook. "We just watched the women of the village collect that young man in a basket and you say NSTR?" She turned to the General. "Good evening, Sir."

"Good evening, Major," boomed the General. "I was just popping in to congratulate Bell on his successful strike today. I owe that man a handshake."

"Bell is gone for the night, Sir, but I'd be happy to bend your ear about other matters. This strike only highlights the fragility of our support. We need more female engagement at the village level. If you read my proposal—"

The General batted away her words with a flippant gesture. "Later, later. Had a long day, Major—been all over the battlespace. Show me the video, Jones."

I nodded to Crazy Jay; he loaded the video onto the big screen and Judas was alive again. He was trailing out a spool of wire. The first bomb landed and launched him into the air. Then he was juggled by the next two explosions, before the last two rounds obliterated him completely. The dust settled and Judas was gone—how many times had we killed him?

"Did his shoes come off?" asked the General. "That's the most incredible thing I've ever seen. Again, Jones, and slow it down this time."

I nodded to Crazy Jay. Judas was alive again, but slower. His movements, as he trailed that spool of wire, lacklustre. A black glittering streak. The first round landed and burst. For a second, Judas was standing unharmed and nonchalant, a mere yard from a deadly blast. But then pieces of his clothing started ripping off and smaller black streaks cut through him and his feet left the ground and his mouth opened. The second round exploded. The two forces pushed his body in different ways, twisting it around. The shrapnel ripped the clothes off his back. The third round landed, blasting from beneath; Judas was actually completely upside-down at one point. "Pause it," said the General. Judas was frozen in the air, one leg bent the wrong way at the knee, his neck twisted around, slipping his heels from his sandals like a debutante dangling her toes in the pool.

"Have you seen enough yet, Sir?" said the Major.

"No. Play it in reverse. Slower."

Judas was naked in the air above three bursting clouds. He slipped his sandals back on, turned his face forward, and straightened his broken leg. He somersaulted and a black streak sucked out of the ground and took one of the exploding clouds with it. Clothes flew onto his back. He twisted like a dancer. Another black streak flashed into the sky, inhaling the bursting cloud. Judas landed gracefully on the ground, his clothing flew onto his body and he trapped a cry of anguish in his mouth. Then he was standing invincible next to an explosion for a moment; it seemed he had a change of heart and gave up on war altogether, because he turned and lazily spooled in the wire. Next he would tuck his weapons away, have lunch with his family, and enjoy twenty years of peace.

"OK, twice-normal speed this time," said the General.

"Sir—" I said, beginning to protest.

"Do it," he ordered.

The bombs landed again and Judas was flung around and his shoes came off and his neck broke and then he was buried in explosions and ripped apart and hurled up and down the street so far it was like he had disappeared.

"One more time, Jones, fast again."

"Stop it, Jones," interjected the Major. "Sir, with all respect, what does this prove? We've lost the village—you haven't even seen the women picking up his pieces."

"Don't countermand me, Major. This is what winning looks like. I spent my whole day dealing with politicians who'll knife me the second I turn my back. We have an enemy who strikes and then turns invisible. You're only beginning to understand how muddy these waters are. And here we have a good clean kill of a definite adversary. So play the fucking video, Jones."

Judas was spooling out a wire; a jet launched five high-explosive rounds. Suddenly, he was a dancer, then a gymnast, his shoes flew off somewhere, then his hands somewhere else, and finally there was a dark spot on the road where he had been.

"Aaaaaah," said the General; his rigid spine relaxed by an inch.

52.

THE NEXT DAY, I KNOCKED ON TICTAC'S DOOR for our workout and he grunted in greeting.

"Come in, Jones, come in." He was shirtless again, and the M-KRAK was working since he was visibly bulkier but increasingly shredded with striations and ugly veins: a musclebound inmate on a desert prison-planet.

The girls of the pornography wallpaper were no longer intact. TicTac had cut off the pieces he liked and aggregated them like Frankenstein's monster. So one woman's legs joined a second woman's abs, a third woman's arms, a fourth woman's breasts, and a fifth woman's head. The eyes were still crossed out, but the sticky notes had been removed. Now there were no "axe wounds" to disguise—TicTac had carefully pruned the genitals, stitching the legs closer together, letting the clippings pile on the floor.

TicTac had assembled paper-women until the basket overflowed with spent magazines, until the ground was covered in body parts, except for a few trails where he'd kicked the path clean. Then he'd kept building, usually by adding limbs. One six-armed Shiva with dead eyes waved from near the clock. A three-legged woman (two strong legs, one lean) ambled near his bed like a centaur. Arms and legs sprouted from unnatural places: the small of the back, the face, the stomach. He'd birthed one six-headed hydra-lady and arranged her heads on sinuous necks, the forearms and calves of other models, all joining a central trunk—the ripped abs of a male bodybuilder.

Spinning through his room in growing horror, seeing Judas again. Peering at a two-torsoed chimera with the eyes gouged out, I thought of the recent reports that the Tazer rapist had slashed his victims' eyes. *Is he the rapist? Why else would he fail that tire flip when the cops were watching?*

"You know you're fucking sick, right?" I said.

TicTac shrugged. "Aren't we all, Jones?" Empty cans of M-KRAK cluttered beneath the desk. Amidst the tatters of photos, his garbage can frothed with spent syringes. So he'd added steroids to the brew of exotic testosterones as well. He noticed me notice: "You done snooping, Pervert?"

"How many more chemicals can your liver take?" I asked.

"Oh, is not permanent. A week? Two? Watch my gains and you will be jealous."

"Don't let anyone else in here—they'll take you to the asylum."

"Sounds like upgrade. Do they have good gym at asylum? Will I be allowed to make sex again? Can I drink beer if I want?"

"Just keep your shit together, TicTac." *Eighteen rapes, seven of them fatal. Will he be taking them apart next, like Judas?*

"Don't be such a *pussy*."

Usually I love leg day: how densely the quadriceps musculate, splitting into four squat heads. I was never pushed by a breeze, no matter how fast and bitter it rolled down the *ghar*. To be immobile, unshakeable: it was reassuring amid the TOC's pressures. But I spent that whole workout fantasizing about crushing the Coachbag's head with a dumbbell, or wrenching the bar down hard when he was in the middle of a heavy rep. *No, it can't be him—TicTac is my friend.*

When I looked around in the gym the soldiers were coming apart. They unravelled like string and splattered the weight racks. I could fast forward or rewind it all in my mind. Stuck in the moment, like Judas, the moment of

Coachbag's Corner: Leg Day

Is ArmaLEGadon now, bitches. Yes, that is why ground is shaking. No, is not brontosaurus. This is leg, bunched and massive beneath barbell. No, is not breath of dragon. This is steam shooting off muscles. Oh, Little Man, you need spot today? No! No spot for skinny man on leg day—I am squeezing alligator to death between thighs. "What about now?" you ask in girl-voice. Still no—I am axe-kicking moon.

The leg is biggest muscle in body and easiest to develop. After good leg day, walking is impossible—so much lactic acid in body you take wheelchair—eat many banana. Today we begin with squat because is most important and you must hold in my spine because only sissies use fag-belt. You see today little Army pussies leave us alone—that is why I am Coachbag—I have trained them all. We will stack so much weight, barbell will bend.

These runts have not found turning point of pain, when it starts to feel good. Most could push out three or four more reps of each set, but they are scared to fail and seem weak. This is how we know small man is small, because he is coward. Yes, is true. We do deadlift next, is same as pulling tree from ground, and good for hammies. For grip: try overhand for left and underhand for right this time.

Next we go heavy on legpress and take all weight from gym—these bitches are not using anyway. Is disgrace—weights are lonely. They say, "Please, please, can a real man lift me? I am tired of being almost-lifted by girls."

dismembering. I knew I was fraying. Blood surged into my legs and arms; vision narrowed. Profound urge to scream, an ogre roar that would set everything straight, would break the spell. But I didn't scream, not at all, just brushed some skinnies from the leg press machine, and stacked the weight in a shaking rage as TicTac verbally abused us all.

His stew of ability-enhancing pills and the testosterone of twenty-seven animals had skewed his voice; it was getting shriller and shriller. "This is it, Jones!" he shrieked. "Maximum weight, maximum effort, maximum gain!"

We started with 1300 lbs, to warm up. TicTac hammered twelve full reps, bringing the weight all the way to his glutes before hooting and slapping the safety clasp in place.

But I did eighteen.

"You motherfucker Jones—yes! Lift that shit, look at you!"

1400 lbs. The bombs landed; the men of the gym wore peaceful expressions, were floating next to explosions. I rewound and they were searching helplessly for weights. "Go lift some dumbbells," screamed my companion, the banshee. TicTac did nine solid reps, his legs shaking, clutching his knees to keep them steady, breathing like he was in labor.

But I did fifteen.

"Yes! An animal, Jones, a beast!" We absorbed two more plates from a guy on the bench press—he was just a shattered ribcage anyway.

1500 lbs. The most I'd seen anyone do. TicTac couldn't lower the weight fully, and had to grip the handles next to the seat, arch his back, and bellow like a wounded elk. His last rep, his fifth, the weight inched upwards, legs shaking as he croaked, "Don't help me, Jones, you goddamn cocksucker."

But I did twelve.

This time his mouth was sealed with envy.

We scoured the battlefield for the remaining two 45 lbs weights. Bones crunched under our feet and our legs steamed.

1600 lbs. About 750 lbs on each bar, plus the weight of the mechanism. A new personal best; TicTac would not attempt it. I sneered and wedged my feet against the footplate, gripping the handles on either side of the chair. "You help me if it looks like I'm going to crush myself," I told him and he nodded. I pushed, unclasped the safety, and the weight rose, inch by inch, as my legs quaked. I would lift until the soldiers stayed whole, stopped blasting apart. I lowered that ponderous weight, growling like a bear, until the footplate was near my glutes. A moment of horrible fear—the weight was unbudging.

TicTac found his tongue and screeched, "You got this! You got this!"

The weight moved—I was lifting it, pressing it up. I let the roar escape then, and the soldiers flew back together and the weight surged upwards and my mouth was dry and I was Christ, literally Christ, lugging my cross to Golgotha, except there were no three collapses, no tears, no face-wiping, whole new stations of the cross where I swung the crucifix and clubbed three Roman soldiers before they filled me with arrows and then, and only then cried, *why God have you forsaken me?* A new new testament, rewritten, except this time Christ was strong? I'm slipping again, but you can imagine it, can't you?

An ominous crack: *are my bones breaking?* The rightmost tower of weights, less than a yard from my head, shifted. Another cracking noise—the weld failed, and the entire tower of iron, fifteen 45 lbs weights, tumbled.

There wasn't much time to think about it, none actually. I was pinned in the chair by the remaining 800 lbs, couldn't lift my feet. Resting the weight on the safety mechanism would have taken an entire second I didn't have. It was the strongest moment of my life—I was completely helpless. The instant that weld broke, TicTac tensed, flexed, launched, feet lifting from the ground. It was a classic hockey player bodycheck, like smashing a door open with your shoulder. He rammed his body into the falling weights, the two incredible forces colliding mid-air in a spray of plates and a colossal grunt. As TicTac flew overhead, I covered my face with my forearms. He crashed into the ground on the other side of me with the weights clanking and clattering around him. Two plates struck my forearms—both headed straight for the eyes.

My legs were trembling badly. I pushed the weights off my arms onto the floor and slid the safety catch into place, gasping, my arms aching and bruised. I rolled off the chair onto the floor, slumping on one knee. The bench-press skinny and a few other gym rats ran over to help.

"You all right, TicTac?" I asked. He was laying on the floor with about eight weights around him, like my Dad passed out in spent beer cans.

"Nope. You?"

"Not remotely."

We groaned to our feet, TicTac swooning badly. He waved away a member of the gym staff who approached with a medical kit. Slung an arm around my shoulder, and we stumbled to the rear of the gym, committing the ultimate breach of gym etiquette by not clearing our weights, through the double doors, toward our friend the giant tire. There we collapsed, counting our bruises, the poo-dust thick on the tongue and the sun merciless, at least 110°F.

In that graveyard of tires, heaps of chain, and sledgehammers, TicTac would accept no gratitude, dismissing my thanks with a motion of his hand like dissipating a stink. We were tired and hurting and laughing at everything.

"Remember that time you broke leg press machine?" he said.

"Seems like something I'd remember."

TicTac's chortle expired in a fit of painful coughing.

"Goddamnit. How many reps you think you would've gotten?"

"At least a hundred."

"Fucker, stop making me laugh."

In the wake of the workout, I could think back to Judas' death without wanting to crush a throat. But I couldn't forget who I was sitting next to. *All the victims said the rapist was superhumanly strong. Irresistible.* I had to know.

"Why are we doing this?" I asked. "Why are we getting strong?"

TicTac looked at me, a bruise spreading across his cheekbone, blood on the corner of his lips. "You nearly die on leg press and now you are philosopher? Ah, you want serious answer, don't you? I can tell by your face."

TicTac spat blood into the dust. "I know when you had bad day with drones because you are barbarian after. Me, I am barbarian every day and is for same reason. We want to be stronger because we are ashamed of how weak we were in past."

I chewed that; eventually he spoke again. "Is not complicated. Behind every strong man is weak boy. Maybe I was weaker than most. Couldn't stand up to Dad's rage—I tried. He'd just drill one knuckles into top of my head and that was enough to get me crying. Then I couldn't do anything to help my mother. He kept at her, first thing in morning, last thing in evening, throwing her onto ground, slapping her, punching her belly, kicking her. You know, he must have called her whore fifty times a day? I don't know what person can do to deserve that. Worst part was pictures. All over house. Them in front of Taj Mahal, Eiffel Tower, kissing on little boats in Venice. Beautiful young couple in front of pyramids—their love took them all over." Muscles leaped in his neck and the sound of grinding teeth. "I couldn't do anything, Jones, even at end, when Dad kept kicking until she stop moving. I turn her over, her eyes full of fear and she wasn't breathing. I throw myself over her like shield because he wasn't finished but she was already gone."

It seemed for an instant he was shaking with sobs, but no. He was gripping the edge of the tire and squeezing the rubber so hard his veins were popping. When he spoke again, his voice was deep and cold as a mass grave: "I hate all men for being tyrants. I hate all women for enduring them. Most of all I hate that weak boy I was, after, when I crawled under Dad's newspaper to be held when I missed my mother."

I wrapped my arm around my friend's stony shoulders and squeezed. A truck loaded with soldiers drove past. I told him it wasn't his fault. This was my friend, a person, someone who'd saved my skull minutes ago. *Eighteen rapes, seven of them fatal.*

I must strike him from the shadows, like a drone.

53.

ALMOST DREAMED. MOONLIT NIGHT. KAF. Concrete barriers and ditches full of rusting barbed wire. Halima was there, barefoot in the dust, scarecrow smile and one eye. She turned and ran and I followed after, couldn't let her go. A crunch of gravel, a jolt of electricity and my muscles bunched uncontrollably. A sizzling of membranes. Wisps of smoke from burnt brain tissue. Dropped to my knees, so much for strength. A black bag enveloped my head, or the moon. Irresistible fingers zap-strapped my wrists behind me. I was waiting to be hauled into TicTac's fuck den, where I would be lucky if my heart gave out. Then it was laughter, laughter, Halima's laughter, and I jolted upright in my rack gasping.

Woke and wrote the memo below, which I planned to hand up the chain ASAP.

I didn't do it to save victims nineteen, twenty and twenty-one; operating a drone is not noble work. I was prepared to be TicTac's bosom-buddy, laugh at his jokes, and provide him that perfect spot he craved, even while setting in motion these machinations—anything to avoid the bag. I even did the unthinkable.

When Kool walked into the room, hours later at the end of his shift, he nearly overdosed on joy. "Sweet fuck—are you doing what I think you're doing?"

I was. Gestured to my rusty pistol, the tiny oil containers and swabs of white cotton spread over a blanket. "It was time," I said. "Having some trouble taking it apart, though. Any infantry magic for me?"

Kool's ecstasy quadrupled, a smile brightening his dour but chiselled chin. He dropped a bag near his bunk; I cleared the weapon and handed it to him.

Clutching his heart, "Oh, you poor, poor 9mm, what has this fucking sailor done to you?"

"I didn't do anything to it."

"Exactly, Jones! Your pistol's fucking seized with shit-dust—you'd get charged for this back at the Battalion." Kool placed the muzzle of the gun against the metal bed frame and stomped the pistol-grip until the pieces screeched apart. "This is the rustiest weapon I've ever seen," his voice hovered between disgust and wonder. "Now you can clean it, though. And don't let

June 2011

Military Police (through Chain of Command)

<u>SUSPICIOUS BEHAVIOUR FROM CAPT TZACK</u>

Ref: A. Convo with MP "Harold" 14 Jun 2011.

1.   In accordance with ref A, this report outlines suspicious behaviour from subject individual. Knowing the MPs are searching for a physically strong soldier in connection with the Tazer Rapist attacks, Capt Tzack (AKA TicTac) hid his strength while surveilled by MPs during a workout with LAV tires.

2.   Further, the subject individual's behaviour has grown extremely dominant and violent, including verbal abuse, and throwing a heavily laden barbell at a junior officer in the gym.

3.   More, the member has converted his room in the barracks into a photo-shrine of many nude women who have had their eyes disfigured like recent victims of the Tazer Rapist. Used syringes and packages of illegal supplements are in evidence as well. I propose these premises be searched immediately.

4.   For your consideration, Sir.

M.J. Jones
Lieutenant (Navy)
MARS
Senior Duty Officer
Task Force Kandahar

it get that fucked up again. When you respect your weapon it'll fuckin' save your ass."

He sat on his bed and started expertly dismantling his own pistol, pulling out the cleaning gear, while shaking his head. "Jesus, Jones. What the fuck are you gonna do against a Taser Rapist with a rusty pistol that won't shoot? You figure you're strong enough to take a Taser—you ain't."

"I get it, man, I suck. I'm a pisspoor soldier."

"No, you don't fuckin get it, Jones. The more muscles you got the worse the Taser feels. Your shit just seizes up. Add a little more oil to that rag— you're gonna need some serious love to get that thing working again."

"You felt it before?"

"Yah. We were training with Tasers in case we ever needed to do riot control shit. Sergeant said you needed to earn the right to use it." His fingers danced, oiling and wiping each cog and spring. A moment of reluctant respect for the warrior-like way he treated his weapon.

"You guys are hardcore," I said. "I definitely never got Tasered in the Navy." I waited for the stupid Navy joke to come, but it didn't. He was frowning over his 9mm.

"I miss the Army," he said, pulling a wad of cotton through the barrel of his pistol with a metal stick. "Things made sense there."

"What the hell, Kool? You're literally in Afghanistan. How much more Army do you want?"

"You don't fucking get it, Jones." He uncrumpled the wad of cotton to check for carbon. It was clean. "This isn't a real tour. I'll get a medal, sure, but no one will respect it. All my buddies got sent out into the *real* shit."

For a second all was quiet but for the tiny vials dripping oil onto cotton scraps. Kool continued, "I won't even get the chance to explain how much this place sucks. Sailors. Air Force fags. Rockets. No fucking. Shitting my guts out from the meatloaf. Not to mention the goddamn Taser-rapist."

"Yeah, plus we have to watch people die all the time."

"That's the only good part, Jones. That's making a fucking difference. And now that Bell is back, and the fighting season has started up again, I'm going to make a big difference. A huge difference." He pulled the cotton ball through the barrel again. Inside, it gleamed like a mirror.

54

"HAPPY CANADA DAY, MAJOR." In the evenings I'd gotten back in her graces, tender in the bunkers, stroking her hair and chasing her pleasure with a stubborn tongue.

"Thank you, Jones, Happy Canada Day."

"I wish I could kiss you right now. I wish I could kiss you whenever I liked."

"Shut up, Jones—you know that's impossible. And keep your voice down. This is not a date—we are two professionals attending a concert together. Do you need to repeat the rules again?"

"I haven't forgotten the rules."

"No one can know about us, Jones. Not a single person."

But how could I refrain from getting excited on our national holiday?— easier to bottle the sun. Started way back when Beavers ran the show. Their tremendous dams built across the St. Lawrence River created the great lakes. In those mighty fresh waters, the beaver grew huge and happy, the size of buffalo, but playful, industrious. Sasquatch would ride them into battle, using them as landing craft for beach raids, and stowing their spoils in underwater dens. It all went to hell eventually, but without those beavers, the fashionable hats they made for Europeans, there'd be no Canada. So every year, we gather wearing painted whiskers and large, flat tails. I made up the part about the tails.

We worked through all the holidays and this was no exception, but the main headquarters in Canada, combined with a regiment of volunteers and civil servants, arranged for entertainment: a raft of celebrities. There was a boy band, a chainsaw juggler, a French-Canadian comedian, and a hockey commentator famous for his big mouth and loud jackets. Soldiers crammed helmets on celebrity heads and wrapped the famous torsos in body armor, before stuffing them into the belly of a cargo craft—the same harrowing flight the rest of us took to Kandahar, with the lights turned off so we couldn't be targeted with rocket-propelled grenades, knuckles white on the webbing of a cargo net.

The hockey buff's suit could have made peacocks feel drab; when the Chief guided him into the TOC, we turned our monitors away as if we were jealous children, killing was candy, and we had no intention of sharing.

The boy band I instantly disliked. I mean, the camp was mostly heterosexual dudes, so why not send us a girl band? Plus I got stuck behind the band in the line at Tim Horton's, where I waited for my daily tower of caffeine. It was a long queue, but the lead singer needed to take a selfie with each of the ladies who worked the counter. He flirted with them and probably made their week, but I just wanted the coffee and those dandies were getting in the way. Their fame offended me; they were a soft, arty folk who never really bled for their craft.

The Major and I joined the entire Canadian contingent at the concert: there were at least a thousand of us, all wearing our tan-patterned uniforms, or at least the tan t-shirt and shorts, and our pistols. The stage and sound system had been hoisted in front of the Canada House bunker, where we gathered for the General's "fun run," kitty corner from the gym; the logisticians had busted their balls to make sure it was perfect.

What I remember were all the things missing, once the music started. There was no dancing. There was no singing along. No beach balls. No pot smoke. No Frisbees. No young couples gyrating or kissing. No long, loose hair. Just a thousand soldiers staring grimly at the band, rocking in tune with the music. The grimmest, dourest concertgoers in the history of concerts; indeed, in the history of music. The Major and I stood in the middle of the mob, not touching unless we jostled each other, not speaking except polite indifferences, not looking at each other except glimpses I stole.

We were allocated two beers a month, which we received from a clerk already opened and had to drink on the spot. I remember how the beer cut through the crust of poo pond on the tongue, washed it clean. But for some reason (a fridge failure according to the rumours) there would be no beer this month. This cranked the crustiness of the throng by another fifteen percent.

Of course, the band squirmed under the pressure of our hard eyes—we were an impossible crowd. The Major swayed to and fro, holding her helmet tucked against her breast like a child, her hair tautly bunned. I stood beside her as the band hit its stride and performed their biggest hit: I remember a few lyrics and how it felt to hear them.

Ain't it good to be alive?

If a genie appeared in that second and offered me a magic carpet home, I would have refused. For my lover was mere inches away, the furrow of her forehead eased by pleasure, and we would make love that night—I was sure.

It feels so good to breathe the air.

No matter the stink of the poo pond, the sting of sand, the 120°F heat—I would take all of it for a hint of lemon, the surprise after kissing to find her vanilla gum in my mouth. I was close enough to smell her and no one was looking.

A pint of beer raised toward a better day.

Alas, there is no beer this day, you fops. But there is the fleeting feel of knuckles brushing—happiness only ever lasts for a single second, doesn't it, no matter the hours of craving. She knew it too and that was why we clutched in bunkers.

The gift of love is there for everyone.

Yes, but such a fragile thing, so easy to squash, like a lotus. It exists even for brutes and killers like us. A thousand loneliness monsters in their cages, rocking. Our hands were fully straight, our forearms pressed together and our fingers rubbing and tangling.

Let's find a star, a star to call our own.

A pair of explosions; the band glanced around confused, as huge glowing orbs rose from the camp into the sky like dual moons. "Is it a rocket attack?" I yelled in the Major's ear. "No. That's one of ours." Our biggest artillery-piece firing chunks of glittering stars, white phosphorus. We joined hands in the gloom and density of the crowd, everyone was staring upward.

Ain't it good to be alive?

Yes, goddamnit. The thrill of risk, the rush of defiance, of loving anyway. We held hands as the two moons, on their graceful and deadly path, arced over our heads, exuding sparks, and lighting the sky—what other stars would make sense for *us*? For one, astonishing second we were almost unashamed.

55.

AROUND THAT TIME WE LEARNED that Special Forces ninjas had killed Osama bin Laden. They'd kicked his door open and shot him in his bed. In the TOC, Bell wore a conical party hat as we huddled around the big map during the turnover. I passed him the memo I wrote about TicTac; he promised to read it later. Wasn't sure how he'd take it.

Otherwise, business as usual: an unarmed Heron circled a compound where Sahar squatted on his haunches chatting with two long-bearded men. They huddled in a courtyard behind a mud wall; the Heron was peeking in.

"Those two," said the Major as she approached the map without glancing at me, "have ties to known insurgents in Kandahar, according to Intelligence."

Bell cracked his knuckles. "I told you he was a terrorist."

"Could be they just talked on the phone once or twice," I said.

"We still don't have Positive ID," said the Major. "Look at him now."

Sahar was chattering with excitement, pointing at the skies, at the Heron. The eyes of the older men followed Sahar's finger.

"What do you think he's saying?" I asked, mostly to myself.

We sometimes played a game in the TOC where we would dub in the voices of the people, same as you might watching a movie on mute. Bell took the bait first, affecting an effeminate voice as Sahar spoke. "I'm a dirty little terrorist, yessiree—I can't wait to kill ISAF troops—allahu akbar!" A few soldiers chuckled from the outer desks and drifted closer for the game.

One of Sahar's older companions spoke next, and I provided the voice, "This morning my wife begged me to give her more food. I asked her, 'who let you out of the cellar?'"

Clay jumped in when Sahar opened his mouth once more, "Since the foreign troops already think I'm a terrorist, wouldn't I be safer if I just became one?"

"Stop it—all of you." The Major ended the game. "These are people, not puppets."

Situation: Troops in Contact. 2x Fighting Aged Males, Small Arms Fire from defensive position on a convoy.
Action: Alpha Company returning fire. Request overwatch.
Location: 41R QQ 132 599
Time: 1857Z

Eighteen miles away. We pulled the drone off Sahar and sent it west. Our soldiers loved having a drone on site even for routine shoot and scoots but they hated when we "took their kills." To the south, a many-missiled Predator angled northwards. They would meet in the middle, south of Kandahar city. The Major often insisted that we take a drone with strong vision along with its more dangerous brethren. Helped establish PID.

"Brutus and Cassius," said Bell. "That's what we'll call them." We hadn't even seen the two Taliban yet, only heard about them from the SALT report.

"More famous betrayers," I said. "First you name one of the targets Judas, and now this?"

"The benefits of a classical education." Bell shrugged. The Major and I stared at him. "Hey, at least they're human names. I'm following my orders."

"The letter of them, anyway," said the Major.

The Heron arrived first—there they were in color: two Fighting Aged Males in their twenties, each holding an AK47 and wearing robes. They hid in a trench on the top of a scraggly hill, dun and ruddy, overlooking the road. A landscape of rugged boulders prevented any obvious approach to their position except for a single winding path, impossible for our soldiers to traverse without coming under fire. As Cassius reloaded from a white bucket of bullet-cartridges, Brutus popped from the trench and fired a few rounds. Neither rifle had a shoulder strap; neither chin a beard. A platoon of our own guys were pinned down in their tan-patterned cadpat, webbing, rifles and helmets. A rocky finger jutted near the base of the hill but our soldiers were avoiding it.

"They put IEDs on obvious places where soldiers would seek cover," said the Major. "Lost men to that trick on my first tour."

The Predator stalked closer, the lonely boy with the armful of bombs, searching for playmates. In its eyes the hill, the promontory, the uniforms, the bucket, the rifles—everything was gray. Chunky with pixels. Cassius, now a gray shape, rose from the ragged dip in the ground. For a second the end of his rifle lit with a brighter pixel-spark.

"That's fucking Positive ID right there," said Bell.

"Are we killing soon?" yelled Crazy Jay, straightening in his chair.

"Launch the missile," said the Major, her hands gripping the edge of the big map, eyes wide and focused on the screen.

The moment of waiting, the way it stretched. Through the Heron, beige-garbed Brutus was yelling in excitement as white-clad Cassius reloaded. The soldiers clutched their tan helmets, waiting for the blast. Edges of a white bucket. Finger of stone, the ferrous rock. Then, in the trench, between the two famous traitors, a flash and a billow of smoke as the missile struck.

Bell, Crazy Jay, Kool, and all the other TOC-moles burst into applause and cheers, like their favorite team had kicked the ball in the net. I felt a surge of energy like I wanted to join in and clap.

"Killing is not a fucking sport," screeched the Major in a high, hoarse voice, the one we rarely heard, whose ugliness was piercing.

Through the Predator, the gray cloud settled and resolved into the gray earth. Brutus the gray-garbed and Cassius the gray-clad were still alive, although both had patches of darker pixels on their bodies. Brutus' patches were on his chest and his mouth was a black hole. Cassius' patch was at the end of one leg and the darkness of those pixels was spreading to the other pixels nearby, like a virus.

"Ah, let the troops have a little fun, Major," said Bell. "It's good for morale."

"This isn't supposed to be fun, Bell."

Through the Heron, the devastation was clearer. The missile had blown the trench apart and the men were tossed ten feet from each other. Brutus's beige robe was stained red at the chest. So stained were the white robes of Cassius, between ankle and knee. Brutus was trying to scream but he was running out of breath as he rolled on his back on the reddish earth. Cassius was calling out for someone, it seemed. He was on his back, too, and dragging himself toward Brutus. It was like his leg was getting longer the more he moved, until it was longer than possible, and then it was clear it was in two parts, and the foot wasn't coming with him.

Bell thrust his hands deep into his pockets, like the old days before he was raped. Now Brutus was dragging himself toward Cassius as well and they were calling for each other and stretching out their hands which were stained red, redder than the earth. But it was easier to look through the Predator, where the Brutus-blob stretched a blocky pixel-limb toward Cassius. And Cassius stretched a limb of gray pixels toward Brutus—they reached for each other but were too weak to crawl closer.

"Do you think they're brothers?" I asked.

"When you're dying, everyone is," said the Major.

They couldn't touch. On the Heron, you could see they were looking at each other, and reaching with red hands. They weren't trying to staunch the bleeding. They weren't shooting back at the tan-clad soldiers advancing on their position. They were both stuck in that obsessive cycle of dying, fixated on that one last thing, to clasp the hand of a brother, because dying is lonely. *You're not alone,* I wanted to say, *we're here, we're watching, you're not alone.* And Brutus's leg had gotten longer and longer and it was grotesque the way the leg had stretched in the beige pants stained red. And it was easy to tell when Cassius died because his hand fell limp and a bright red rose burst from his mouth, but mostly from the face of Brutus who wasn't going to get his last handshake after all and he slumped defeated on the red earth with his too-long leg and the blood blooming all around him.

Or maybe they were two gray blobs, lying side by side, their gray hands nearly touching in a dark puddle of pixels. They had fallen asleep. Two brothers on a gray bed.

56.

WE SENT THE PREDATOR SOUTH to scan the roads and kept the Heron on site for the BDA. Nobody wanted to stick around after that last twitch, not even the Major. Yet the SOP was to keep watching the area for an entire hour. Shoulda seen those pricks run out of there—day shift makes the mess; night shift mops.

I stood frozen in front of the screen for the whole hour as the Heron circled. It was like the image was a screw and each rotation of the drone drove the memory deeper. Brutus and Cassius reaching for each other but never quite making it, trapped forever in the moment of need, an ugly version of the Grecian urn with the two lovers nearly kissing.

After, I brooded in the smoker's pit behind the chainlink fence, painfully aware that the pistol in my holster was clean and functional. For the first time since I was a junior officer at sea, I had the urge to kill myself.

No freezing ocean to slip into this time. Didn't matter how happy I was with the Major the day before. The need was so strong the gun was in my hand before I realized—people don't understand how quick and powerful the impulse can be. Cold metal of the pistol grip, thumb flicking off the safety. Staring down the glittering barrel, not a single crumb of carbon. One quick shot, a bang I'd never hear, smell of gunpowder. There was no going home and people would keep dying day after day and I'd have to watch it all without being able to do anything. Or maybe there was no home, I'd just made it up, there was only this, had only ever been this, and that was the worst thought of them all.

But no. Back then I lacked the courage to try. Put the gun away and got off shift and walked to the DFAC for some chow. There was a huge willow in front of the mess, one of the few trees on the camp, and home to hundreds of starlings. Continuous muttering from the trees. A British soldier was standing near the tree, clapping. Each time he clapped the whole murmuration flew up, juggled around in a whirling zigzag, and settled again on the branches. And I thought that I would never clap like that, because the birds seemed so serene sitting there, and what if one of them got hurt in the juggle? Or worst-case scenario: what if they tired of the interruptions and found a new tree? But I didn't say anything to the soldier, and watched the air show for many minutes, complicit.

57

I MENTIONED WE WERE ENTITLED to two beers a month, but I didn't stress how much they mattered. That soldiers kept calendars counting down the days to their next beer. Like cigarettes in prison, beer became currency in a black market of chocolate, muscular supplements, and porn. The fridge failure at the concert was more than an inconvenience: it was a stock market crash. I needed a brew bad; the edges were fraying.

Getting back to the beerless cell I shared with Kool, a grating noise resonated from the washroom, across the hall—had the pipes burst? But when I peered in it was the same old shit: swirling cottage cheese in the scuppers; toothbrush spray on the mirrors; that sagging corner lower than ever, its surface wet-seeming and mushy. The sound: a rusty chainsaw gnawed the heart of an oak, punctuated by the pleasant whistle of a piccolo. The noise came from *beneath the floor.* Loud enough for anyone to hear.

Fuckfuckfuck. *Noah, are you trying to get yourself killed?* I checked the hallway for witnesses, smiled vaguely and waved at Clay (he was always bearing witness, too) then bolted from the barracks through the rear door.

Beer cans everywhere. Hundreds of them. Like a frat party, or a port visit, or Valhalla. For a single, delusional moment, I thought they were full, glinting, shining with perspiration. But this was a trick of the war—they were spent, their dregs boiling away and dissipating with a metallic stink. Footsteps at the door—I couldn't be caught in this situation, too much heat, the wrong kind—I braced the door jamb so the soldier within would think the door was locked. A grumble, and the footsteps moved away.

Still. He could just leave from the front and walk around the building if he cared. Sweat on the palms. No time to think. I plunged into the frog cavern and the normal stench had been replaced with potent alcoholic fumes, so strong I slipped in the muck, and grew an instant headache. Countless beer cans floated on top of the slime. There he was, lying on his back, damn near filling the whole basement now, his face inches from the ceiling above, snoring like a tyrannosaurus.

"Noah! Noah! Wake up!"

He snored on, blissful. In the murk of the frog cave, its glittering snotsicles, his foot twitched. He was dreaming of chasing butterflies, maybe. I punched him in his huge chest and hissed right in his ear, "Noah, you need to wake up. You goddamn asshole—you're in danger." He thumbed his nose. This close, the stink of booze made me dizzy. Revelation dawned.

Motherfucker drank all the beer.

Something burst in my prefrontal cortex and blood streamed from my eyes. My teeth lengthened into fangs. "You sonofabitch," I growled. This was worse than the Cheezies. I plugged his nose with one hand and jammed my elbow hard into his thick throat. The snore trickled to a gurgle. His chest heaved.

Finally, his eyes popped open, wide open: confusion and fear. He batted me away like a mosquito and I splashed into the muck amidst the spent cans.

Noah massaged his throat with one hand. "You tryin' to kill me or something?"

"Save you, actually, you worthless prick. You were snoring so loud everyone on the base could hear you. You've left beer cans everywhere."

"Really?" said Noah. He groaned. "That can't be true, Jones. 'Worthless prick?' What's got into yer shorts?"

"Look at all the fucking beer in here, Noah. Turn your stupid head."

He swivelled his face with a low moan. "That might have been me."

"Sort yourself out, Noah. I got my own problems. I can't keep saving your ass. Help me clean up the cans outside, you giant bastard."

As I left the cave a mini-snore started and I threw an empty beer can at his head. "I'm awake! I'm awake!"

Can you imagine if the Chief walked onto the scene as I was stuffing empty beer cans into a garbage bag? He would have had my nuts in his steely grip. I must have crammed a hundred cans into the bag, while dodging veritable lakes of Sasquatch piss, ears primed for a crunch of gravel. Once, near the end of the clean-up, I did hear someone coming, and dove into the bunker with my clinking trove. Two thick-jawed soldiers walked past thinking they were unobserved, holding hands.

Noah didn't lift a damn finger to help. He eventually squirmed out of the basement and collapsed in the bunker, oozing a snail-trail on the concrete as he slid down. The sweat was pouring off him as he downed bottle after bottle of water.

"You're a real piece of work, Noah. How is this going to help you get home, you sad fucker?"

"Do ya have to speak so loud?" he whispered, sucking his cheeks for moisture, and dabbing his brow with Lumpy, the blanket, nearly black with filth.

"You're damn right I do," I said, enjoying his winces. "You put me in danger and you drank all the soldiers' beer—they only get two a month. Do you think you're the only person suffering on this base, you selfish prick?"

Noah didn't answer. Just dripped miserably and rolled his head from side to side.

"What, are you going to tell me the Spirit made you do it?"

"No, Jones, it ain't the Spirit. Spirit's laughin' at me, too." He belched and grimaced from the taste. "It was the dark."

"You're afraid of the dark now?" I stood over him, forearms crossed.

His eyes grew vague, distant. "I keep thinkin' 'bout that truck where I hid with the dead soldiers. Now I'm back in this little basement," he threw a pebble against the wall of the bunker limply, "and it's like I'm back there, hidin' in the guts again, drinkin' blood from the leaky legs. I need to get outta here, Jones. But everythin' I tried hasn't worked for shit."

The Sasquatch's shoulders shook and my anger cooled a few degrees. Normal enough, I suppose, after a trauma, to drown it. "Doesn't make it right," I said. Though I did remember I was older than my friend in human years. That I'd spent a decade in the Navy as an absolute drunk, one of the worst—passed out in a few gutters myself. Humbling. "After my Dad died, I spent six months drunk and each morning I felt the way you feel now," I said, slumping down next to Noah in the bunker, and lowering my voice. "I imagine, when we go home, most of these soldiers will get as drunk as they can, and some will stay that way."

Noah belched painfully. Whispered, "I kept thinkin' 'bout stoppin', but it was like 'one more, one more.' And then—surprise—the beer'd be in my hand already. The concert was goin' and I was the only one not there and that seemed to make it OK, but it weren't. Wanted to save a whole case for ya, add another happy memory to the list. But I only managed to save one."

I looked up. He was holding an unopened tallboy in his hand. *Is he offering it to me?* His hand was forward, the can in the hand, the hand partially opened, the hand and can uplifted? *Yes, yes! He is offering it to me!*

I snatched the beer and it was pisswarm from the sun and the heat of his hand but it was still a cup of ambrosia, the liquefied bones of fairies and cockatrices; I guzzled it like the parched sailor I was. Noah groaned at the glug-glug. Said, "I think I'll stick to tellin' stories from now on," and I laughed, having made similar promises many times.

58.

JESUS, JONES, I AIN'T IN NO SHAPE for this right now—look at me, barely alive. Still, yer the closest thing I got to a buddy in the world even if yer a damn miser with yer beer. But I'm glad to have a friend anyway, since I never had no friend growin' up. Kids at school let me know I was different.

I was always starin' out the window wonderin' if my real mother was out there. At first the kids were scared o' me but then one o' 'em had a comic book with a picture of a Sasquatch—once they had a name for what I was they weren't afraid no more. I was the biggest kid in the class but at least I weren't the ugliest—lotta inbreedin' in Wawa. Also sometimes the kids would go swimmin' in the lake and get "the itch" all over—they'd come to class covered in red welts, squirmin'.

Worst thing by far was the principal. That was Mr. Richards, the name you heard me sayin' after I got shot. He was this tall and skinnyass creep who wore jackets with wide shoulders. Walked around with a long metal ruler, slappin' his hand like he was waitin' for ya to shit the bed. Kids were terrified o' him—they'd get sent to his office and come out white-faced 'n' tremblin'.

Funny. I spent most classes not understandin' shit. Wishin' the teacher would talk a bit slower so I could follow. When the kids learned I wouldn't fight back they had a field day. No, they had five years o' field days—hittin' me with sticks, wedgies, spittin' on me, callin' me the worst names they could think of: Stankass and Hairball and Mutant and Abortion. The girls were as bad as the boys. Meaner with words. I never fought back. A thousand times I wanted to reach for the Spirit and squash 'em all. But I never did, Jones. I ain't no monster. Just a slow learner, and life's fulla lessons. Or maybe it's the same lesson over and over.

Wasn't long before I started gettin' in trouble. Smoking packs of cigarettes in the parkin' lot. Skippin' class to hang with those hard folks under the railroad tracks. Buyin' beer for my classmates and not even getting' invited to the party. Goin' pants free in gym class.

Stayin' out all hours of the night, comin' home drunk and stoned at five in the mornin'. Spent a lot of time in Mr. Richards' office. Still don't mean I deserve what I got, though.

You wanna know the truth—the whole story? For the fan club, I guess. Cover yer ears, Lumpy. Truth is I was skippin' class cuz I was afraid of Mr. Richards. I dunno how it was for other kids but for me detention was worse than this place. Motherfucker had a voice like Darth Vader. I'd show up in his office tremblin' and he'd tell me to take my clothes off and I did it cuz *fuck clothes* but also cuz I hadn't learned to say no. But he taught me, Jones. He taught me with that metal ruler flashin' down and those skeleton-fingers grabbin' me and worst of all were the words: "stupid, ugly, unruly, giant boy," as the ruler's goin' CRACK CRACK CRACK.

After detention, it was so raw I thought it was gonna fall off. I remember not bein' able to look at myself half the time. He always made me promise not to tell anyone, 'specially Donna.

Don't get me wrong, Jones, I had some happy moments, too. 'Member sittin' on the couch with my human mom, watchin' cartoons and her laughin'. 'Member watchin' squirrels playin' leapfrog on the power lines. Found a five-dollar bill and bought a bag o' candy, once. Cooked 'n' ate a chicken in an open fire with a homeless guy under the bridge. Smoked two joints and giggled for hours at the way the tree branches swayed overhead, thinkin' they was relatives, long dead. Pushed Donna's car outta the snow so she called me a hero. Made a fort, in the woods, up in a tree, and no one could come near me without me knowin'.

Seven happy memories—that ain't bad, right? 'Specially for someone with an ancient murderin' spirit whisperin' in his head. Some people only got one or two good memories. Wheneva I start thinkin' 'bout my Mom, wanderin' through the woods lookin' for me still, or me gettin' killed here under these barracks, or Mr. Richards and that ruler flashin' down, I pull my seven happy memories off the shelf, one at a time, polish 'em, and have a look.

Well, there's more to the story. Mr. Richards got what was comin' to him, maybe I did too, but that's enough of this sad shit for one day—talked too much, now I'm shakin'. I'm gonna think about happy memory number eight for a while. That time we were chattin' in the bunker, you gave me a meatloaf, 'n' I lifted up that stone, 'member?

59.

Dear Mom,

Thanks so much for your last letter. It was exactly what I needed. This gig is wearing me down and the updates about the kids at your school are the best. Some days I don't want to get out of bed but I always do. The work is hard, the gym is hard, eating is hard, the weather is hard, the people are even harder. I just want to lay in a lawn chair for a month, drinking from a coconut.

I always admire your patience in teaching, especially those special-needs kids. If I was in the classroom, there'd be some reckoning. Lesson 1: No Santa Claus. Lesson 2: You're adopted. Lesson 3: Tsunamis. Lesson 4: Plagues. Lesson 5: Landmines. Lesson 6: Loneliness. Lesson 7: Suicide.

And that's just week one, but I could keep up the pace, Mom. I've learned so much now, I'm practically a Bodhisattva. Maybe when I come home I'll write a book about all my insights, with daily meditations, and they'll have to carry my lucre in sacks. Only the finest of retirement homes for you, Mom. Silk pillows for you and the cat, and muscular attendants to change the sheets every day.

I like the kids but the cat-updates are my favorite. Kicked through the screen, rampaged through the night, lost half his ear, and dragged two bird corpses on your pillow? Well, at least it wasn't rats. If I was there I'd give him extra treats for his ferocity. We males are supposed to be fierce, right? Yet even when we bust free we're still in cages.

Thanks again, Mom, for your tender messages. I will try

to respond to them faster. If you can, please send more
peanut butter. Also toilet paper. That stuff literally
saves my life.

Matthew

60.

IT WAS FOOLISH TO HOPE that Noah's antics with the stolen beer—his horrible snores, the clattering of cans—would not be noticed. Diligent dayworkers heard the clanking and sawing and called in a technician. You'd think if there were proper plumbers on KAF we would have a more sophisticated sanitary system than a lake of shit. But this is a riddle for a cleverer mind than mine.

The technician arrived with his utility belt and toolbox of many wrenches. I cracked the door to watch him; he took one sniff of the washroom and jerked his head back liked he'd been clubbed with a brick wrapped in a sweaty jockstrap. Then he backed out waving his hands in front of his face, as if he was swarmed by bees. Outside, in the fresh air, he pulled a cell phone from his pocket and made frantic calls. Then he returned to the offensive zone, but only to stretch a piece of yellow tape across the door: BIOHAZARD.

How did it feel to know a location I'd frequented daily for months, literally eight feet from my rack, was declared hazardous to human health? Well, the feeling got worse when six soldiers dressed in HAZMAT suits marched in the front door. They seemed exactly like martians exploring our toxic environment: they walked in clunky, exaggerated motions. Their breathing was labored and deliberate.

"You need to find another washroom, Sir," said the first alien.

"Keep your door closed while we're working," cautioned the next; I ignored him.

A third positioned himself outside the shitters. It was waving a device that measured particulates in the air, or a ray gun. The faces of their biohazard suits were expressionless, like drones. I needed to get a message to Noah, but the hallway was full of these bizarre sentries, and how do you sneak past someone when you can't tell which direction they're looking?

The spacesuits may have protected these beings from Noah's toxic spores, but they limited visibility. One stepped too close to the soggy corner, and his whole leg went through the floor. His two comrades hauled him to freedom, with a few curses. They checked his suit for rips, then peered into the hole.

A few months ago, they might have seen the glittering eyes of hundreds of frogs staring back. An entire ecosystem of slippery hoppers, hungry for mosquitos. And this would have been better by far than to see Noah's two startled orbs. Like the first time I discovered him, those watery blue eyes, tired and sad, like mine.

The nearest man screamed, literally fell onto his ass, and started skittering away backwards. The next nearest guy must have seen Noah, the sheer hulk of him, the bulge of his shoulders and arms. This, coupled with the rumours of the Taser Rapist's enormous strength, and the assumption that he lived in hiding, were enough. The cry went up.

"T-T-Taser Rapist!"

"Taser Rapist!"

"Taser Rapist, get your weapons!"

"Taser Rapist, shoot him!"

And in the din of yelling, one voice that I hoped he would hear, that I hoped *only* he would hear, "Run, Noah!"

Soldiers, nightowls, started to spill from their rooms, rubbing their eyes and groping for their pistols. "He's out back!" yelled one of the men in a biohazard suit. I charged out the back door, just as Noah burst from the cellar in a spray of slime and soggy wood. *All the world's a stage,* I thought, aiming my pistol at my friend.

"Put your fucking hands up!" I shouted, then mouthed, "RUN."

Noah was near our bunker, looking back over one shoulder. He blinked at me in confusion. *No time.* Other soldiers were coming through the door with pistols in their hands—I fired near his feet CRACK CRACK to get him moving, and the look he gave me was so wounded, his eyebrows sagging to his cheeks. I'd stopped on the back step, blocking the path for at least three soldiers milling behind, and made such a show of aiming and pointing my pistol that I kept bumping them, preventing any aim.

"Get out of the way, Sailor!" someone yelled.

Noah's face hardened. He turned toward us where we clumped in the doorway, clenched his hands in fists, lifted them above his head, and roared.

Sprays of saliva rocketed from his mouth, his tongue bright pink in the chasm of his maw. Noah's roar was deafening and deep enough to jar my intestines. He was glory: ten feet of bulky man-ape, his lats and traps blocking the sun, his arms as big around as my waist. I damn near bolted and I *knew* Noah; the rest would be scrubbing their shorts.

Noah sprinted down the gravel path where I'd swept his blood. I ran after, firing ineffectually. *Maybe I can still help him, if he doesn't move too fast.*

Glimpses only—I cursed my shitty cardio and beefy thighs. Noah bounded through the camp, leaping coils of barbed wire and hurtling concrete barriers. He leap-frogged a tank. Soldiers were spilling from every building, firing pistols and C7s, hollering, "Taser Rapist!" at max volume. Shots flew willy-nilly. I slumped against a bunker to catch my breath. An armored car attempted to train its 50cal machine gun on Noah; he dropped his shoulder, slammed the car, and tipped it onto its side. I gasped, dry-heaved, sprinted. An infanteer aimed his rifle at point blank range; Noah grabbed his face in one meaty palm and tossed him into a scrawl of barbed wire.

I heard it first. The curious sound of a flying lawnmower. Then I spotted the Predator in the air—the Major and Bell had joined the hunt. Noah had ducked into a bunker when snipers in the towers started to fire; he was bleeding from his leg. I could see a proper company of infantry coming up the street in a Light Armored Vehicle with a 25mm cannon on the top.

I gathered my breath and yelled, "Watch out for the drone, Noah!" and our eyes met for a single second. *Fuck you if you can't see I'm trying to help.*

Noah did what his people always do when they are afraid and hunted— he reached for the Protector Spirit. He snarled and dropped to his knees, as his bones popped and lengthened, his tawny pelt grew spectral, his jaw unhinged, and his claws lengthened into dripping black daggers. Tendrils of shadow wisped about him, darting and probing, and his eyes flared with ruby light.

My mouth went dry. *He told me to run.* With two running steps and a flick of the wrist, Noah hurled a one-ton concrete slab into the air, spinning. It flew with deadly and horrible grace, smashing the side of the LAV like a rocket propelled grenade, showering a group of soldiers with sharp shards. Sniper rounds streaked nearby. Noah leaped amongst the dazed soldiers, swinging his mace-like fists, knocking soldiers to the ground. Rifles fired; the shadowy armor sparked. Noah grabbed a soldier by the webbing, knocked the rifle from his hands, threw the hapless bastard over his shoulder, and bounded onto the top of a twenty-foot wall.

My last glimpse of Noah. He was swinging the hostage in a bewildering arc—to confuse the snipers, I assumed. But the Predator got too close, Noah bounced into the air and grabbed hold of one wing. Drone, soldier and Sasquatch plummeted out of view.

There was a splash.

I ran past clusters of dazed and bloody soldiers. A few wrecked vehicles sending up plaintive smoke signals. More soldiers arrived by the second, the whole hornet's nest provoked and gathering at the poo pond.

A single wing jutted from the oily surface, about two feet, and slid deeper. Soldiers set up a cordon along the edges of the pond in yellow tape. A final burble from the drone's engine as it coughed and suffocated in the evil-smelling stew. No sign of the hostage, or of Noah. Just a few waves radiating from the drone as it slunk lower. The little sailboat someone had launched as a lark was swamped and capsized. The clever signs on the shore, "Area Fifty-Poo," were shit-splashed, defaced.

Ah, Noah, you poor bastard, I thought, tears and smoke stinging my eyes. *You deserved better.* I wandered the shore until an infantry Captain told me to get out of there. *He was my best friend,* I wanted to say. I stuck a knuckle into my eye instead—these soldiers would not understand if I wept.

The infantry were still standing guard when I left for work a few hours later. They were still clutching rags to their faces, waiting for some sign of the Taser Rapist or the kidnapped soldier, as the drone sunk lower and lower and eventually disappeared. We lacked the tools to properly dredge the pond. And perhaps the stomach.

A drone was destroyed and no one would grieve. A soldier was killed and his family and comrades would grieve. A Sasquatch was killed and I would grieve. But it ended the same as all incidents, when I closed the SIGACT later that night on my shift.

NSTR. Nothing Significant to Report.

61

HE ONLY HAD EIGHT HAPPY MEMORIES and now he's gone. In the TOC I painted a grin on my face—most everyone was celebrating the death of the so-called Tazer Rapist. Bell was fuelling the illusion, striding the TOC with confidence, slapping backs and cracking jokes, seeming to have shed ten years: the lines on his face had lessened, and his stoop straightened. My face hurt from smiling. *He was my best friend.*

Bell briefed me on the SIGACT during our handover, he and the Major and I standing around the big map, and we played the video uploaded from the crashed drone: transformation, brief rampage, and the hostage-taking. The sudden lurch of the camera—that was when Noah grabbed the wing. Then a short, wobbly flight as the drone drove eye-first into the murky pond.

"Feels good, Jones, feels mighty good." He tapped his delicate fingers on the map.

"How do we know this guy was the rapist?" I asked.

"Oh, that's the guy all right—you think I'd forget him?"

"You had a bag on your head."

"Bell insists on treating this as a victory even though we lost a man," said the Major in a voice of deep fatigue. "Apparently, only Canadian casualties count."

His laughter boomed. Words bounced off his shield of confidence. *Killing is making him whole again.* "What I know is that the guy who attacked me just drowned in a lake of shit. He got exactly what he deserved, and I hope he took his sweet time with it, too."

My plastic smile cracked. *Oh God, Noah.* "Can you explain why you think he's the rapist?"

The Major again, "Bell has convinced himself." She paused the video, the moment when Noah grabbed the soldier as a hostage, their size disparity was most clear. "This is definitely the thing from the tunnel," she said, "but honestly Bell, you'd be dead if that was your attacker."

"He'd have to be that big to get the drop on me, Major." Bell chuckled, raised his volume. "This is a moment to celebrate. The streets are safe again."

The Major's voice was thin with irritation. "We also lost a drone, Bell—they don't exactly grow on trees."

"Well, if we'd fired when I said, we'd still have one."

"We didn't have PID, Bell, you stubborn prick." The Major whirled and stormed away, the door of her office nearly leaping off its hinges when she slammed it.

"Must be her time of the month, eh Jones?"

I was done with the conversation, too. I wasn't buying Bell's Superman act and I kept picturing Noah's last moments with shit flooding his nose and mouth. "Did you even read the goddamn memo I wrote?"

Bell's eyes darted left and right. "Sure, I read it, Jones. And I passed it along to the MPs that afternoon. But, like I said, it's old news. We got the guy."

"You can't unrape yourself by killing someone, Bell."

That shut him up. For a minute, anyway.

"You know that bitch has got to go, right?" he asked. "We were looking right at the guy, had a clear shot, and she didn't take it. Now we've lost a drone and a man and it's her fault."

"He had a hostage. I'm assuming that's why she didn't fire."

"That guy's still dead, Jones—get your head out of your ass." Bell rolled his eyes. "I know you're soft on her, but she's held us back. Target Engagement Authority is wasted on that bitch, and she's gotta go. It's past time."

He kept muttering to himself, drinking a black coffee, until late in the night. A Corporal walked the Major home. I scribbled for a bit in my journal before stepping out, claiming I was grabbing a midnight meal, and left Bell in the TOC. I walked, half-dazed, through shadowy streets, and picked up a lumpy plastic bag from the barracks. When I reached the shore of the poo pond and took off my bush cap, the moon was hanging fat, low and luminous.

"Are you in there, Noah? Are you still alive, old friend?"

But the pond said nothing. Subtle black waves licked the shore.

"Noah, if you're in there let me know, you sonofabitch."

But the pond was mute.

"Damnit Noah," suddenly I was shouting, "it can't end like this! I won't let it. Do you fucking hear me, Noah?" I threw a stone into the pond; it splashed with an oily plop and sank.

The ripples subsided, and the pond said nothing.

I scrubbed my eyes, caught my breath, and pulled a crumpled note from one of my bottomless pockets, and read it in the moonlight, aloud.

Here, in this most unlikely and unlucky of graves, lies Noah. He was a storyteller and a strongman and my best friend. When I met him he was sad and hungry and thirsty. We used to chat in the bunker for hours. Noah seemed like a happy guy even though the world was always unkind, and people always treated him like a monster. He deserved better than all of this.

I'm here today to say goodbye and make two promises. Noah once asked me where the untold stories go when we die. He said he didn't want to die but being forgotten was the real death. So my first promise is this: I'll never forget you, Noah. I'll never forget the stories; I won't forget your eight happy memories, and sometimes I'll take them off the shelf and look at each one.

Noah had a dream. He was going to be a great tree planter, the ferry that rowed his people across—but who will ferry him? So for my second promise, when I get home I'll plant a tree for you, Noah. It's a small thing. But I'll plant the tree in the middle of the forest, with plenty of other trees to talk to, and the birds will come, and squirrels will chatter in the branches. Your tree will never be lonely. No one will hurt it or call it cruel names. It will have a gentle life.

I didn't know Noah that long but I loved him anyway. He was kind and wise in his fashion. I've never figured out what the word "human" means but I think Noah was human in the best way.

Noah, old friend, I don't know what happens next. I don't know if there is a heaven for brutes like us. But I think there is an end of suffering. I think there is such a thing as peace, and we all deserve it, and you more than anyone.

I pulled Lumpy from the plastic bag and laid it on the shore next to the murk. I let the pond take the note, then I blubbered wretchedly for about five minutes. The pond said nothing, except for a single, large, malodorous bubble, which rose from the depths, settled on the surface, and popped.

When I got back to the TOC, I caught a furtive Bell scurrying from the Major's office. His hands trembled like he was carrying live explosives. Mumbling some excuse, he flitted past, without making eye contact. It seemed he'd searched her papers; her desk was a mess of plans for future operations, notes on her subordinates, and a few letters from children drawn in crayon. Even more dodgy, the filing cabinet—the one that never closed right after the Major clubbed it—had been popped open; apparently it wasn't locking right either. Nowhere did I spy the love letter I wrote her, the one I assumed she threw out.

If Bell has the letter… Well, it would be incredibly tempting. Proof of fraternization. An end in sight to Bell's emasculating sojourn, the indignity of working for a woman, especially one so aloof, renowned, and desirable. *Impossible. The Major must have thrown it out.*

62

STILL, BELL'S BEHAVIOUR WAS OFF. When he showed up for the handover his uniform was rumpled and his eyes were baggy as if he hadn't slept—plus, he stank of stale cigarette smoke. Back at the barracks, his favorite table, the one where he'd been nabbed by the rapist, was topped by a heaping ashtray. I could half-picture him stewing there, sitting with his feet up on the other chair, pistol in one hand, the end of his smoke glowing like a firefly. *What is he plotting?*

And, later, after a few hours of sleep and a workout, I arrived at work a bit early, sunset, to enjoy the graffiti. Waiting in line at the meagre canteen for a Diet Coke, I heard familiar voices rising from the smoker's pit.

"She's hard not to notice, isn't she?" said Bell, his voice was used-car-salesman velvet.

"Oh, please," said Kool. "The things I'd do to her pissflaps. I'd fuck her so hard she'd explode like a missile."

"Wow," Bell purred. "You're that good, eh?"

"Bell, I am the goddamn shit. My dick is dynamite. She'd squirt like a fucking geyser."

"She is an attractive lady," Bell admitted. "You see her in her PT gear, during the funrun? Those legs?"

"I fucking saw, Bell. That athletic ass? I only fuck hot chicks, Bell. No fatties. No old babes. No hairy armpits. No darkies. No little furry moustaches."

"It's important to have principles." I crept closer to the chainlink fence to eavesdrop; Bell continued. "But do you think she's into you?"

"She hides it well, but yeah. She wants to fuck. They all do."

"I don't know, Kool. She seems pretty distant. Cold as ice, even."

I could imagine Kool's face fall: his ego was a house of cards. "Maybe she's a lesbo."

Bell chuckled. "Oh, she's definitely *not* a lesbo. I know she's fucking some guy on camp right now."

"What? Who?"

"The more important question: why isn't it you?"

I needed to warn her—Bell knew something, was actively conspiring.

Escalation of Force

The war wasn't all homemade bombs. Let us not forget the suicide bombers, the donkey-bombs, the bicycle-bombs, the goat-bombs, and the fearsome SVBIED—suicide-vehicle-borne-improvised-explosive-device—notorious for the biggest blast. Is that man in the bulky coat trying to blow himself up? Or just carrying his groceries? If you wait until he pulls the trigger, it's a bit late, no? The explosive power hid under a burqa, or wedged into a baby carriage. The size of the blast. Women, children, the elderly, beasts of burden, even poets and gentle artists, the handicapped, nuns, saints, doctors, aid workers, the homeless, nurses, florists, chimneysweeps, scientists, lion-tamers, acrobats, cripples: all were weaponized.

The "solution" is space, controlling it. Fences and checkpoints and well-trained guards. You are a twenty-one-year-old soldier guarding a depot of assault rifles. An eleven-year-old boy starts walking toward your checkpoint. At twenty yards you play the tape, which was recorded in both English and Pashto: "You are approaching a military zone. We are authorized to use deadly force. Cease approaching this location immediately."

The boy keeps walking. He is smiling, but smiles were weaponized long ago. At fifteen yards you might consider the laser dazzler. A hand-held or rifle-mounted device that disorients and blinds the "target." This is particularly effective when the target is driving a possible VBIED. Hard to keep your truck on track when you can't see.

When the boy is twelve yards away, consider a non-lethal sonic weapon. A hand-held device, shaped like a megaphone, it's called the infrasound emitter, or the shit-your-pants gun. This is the notorious riot-suppressing device that rings at the perfect frequency to shake your bowels, causing them to spasm uncontrollably. When that brown note chimes, the boy may clutch his stomach and collapse to the ground, in pain but alive. But these weapons are scarce, and you may not have been issued one. Yet all soldiers get a rifle or pistol, and at ten yards you will likely draw your weapon and point it at the child. It's normal to be afraid, even of a young boy. "Stop. I am authorized to shoot," you might say, in your firmest voice. But the boy does not understand.

You fire a warning shot. This is a contentious step because the warning shot so often skips off the ground and kills a bystander. You're already dabbling with lethal force at this point.

Five yards. The boy is reaching into his pocket for a candy or a trigger. If he is a bomb you will definitely be killed. Last week your friend was killed by a suicide bomber. You miss your mother. You wish you were somewhere else. If you're killed then the Taliban will get all those assault rifles you're guarding. The consequences to innocent people will be tremendous; recently they splashed acid in the faces of girls heading to school. Duty. Fear. Kindness. Anger. Training. Compassion. Racism. Loyalty. Fear.

Do you shoot?

But by the time I got into the TOC, Kool was already harassing her. He'd recently exchanged his baggy uniform for a tighter set, and, as he chatted with the Major, he had one foot on a chair, to accentuate his bulge. His hip was hinged open at a grotesque angle and he was leaning toward her. Suddenly, Kool was interested in the Female Engagement Team—wanted to know all about it while bending low over the coffee pot to show off his glutes. She had wariness painted all over her face. I tried to catch her eye, but we only shared a single, microsecond-long look of worry—I suppose when things were most precarious, the rules were most important.

Kool had the gall to touch her hand, smiling like an idiot. He had the sleeves of his combat shirt rolled up all the way to reveal his spindly triceps. Heat flushed my cheeks—I turned away; Bell was starting the handover briefing.

The Major was pissed. "Damnit, Kool. I'm tired of your bullshit—what's gotten into you? It's well after your shift, I know you don't care about the FET—go home!"

He obliged, grudgingly, maintaining an unblinking stare as long as possible, before turning and strutting from the TOC. I recognized the behaviour; Kool used to brag about his exploits at the Military College. Showing up at the door of known "skanks" late at night, pushing his way into their rooms, and screwing them senseless. How many marked women had succumbed to that intensity, that unflappable confidence, back at the college? It was hard to sift the truth from his boasts.

I stood next to the Major in silence and she muttered from the side of her mouth, "I can't find the letter."

"Are we fucked?" I muttered back.

"No, just me," she said.

63

COULDN'T SHIELD HER; she didn't need one anyway. Doesn't mean I didn't fret for the next few hours, methodically closing the day's SIGACTS and tearing the sticky notes from the big map. The Major kept rolling the FET-boulder, pretending that everything was fine. We could not break routine; that would betray us further. We could not climb through Noah's tunnel, dodge the sniper-fire and landmines, and start a new life in one of the villages we'd been surveilling for nearly a year. Had obligations. Duty.

The Major donned her helmet and asked Alice, the signaller, to walk her back to the barracks; minutes later, Alice returned, mystified. Apparently, Kool had been lurking in the smokers' pit, and he pounced on the Major, offering his gallant company on the journey home. I gnawed my fingernails. An hour later, a phone in the TOC rang, and the signaller in front jotted a quick note, then posted into the combat chat.

MEDICAL EVACUATION REQUEST
Location: Kandahar Airfield, bunker in vicinity of Canadian Women's Barracks
Radio frequency and name: Cell phone
Number of casualties and severity: 1 critically injured, bludgeoning injury to face
Special Equipment required: None
Patient requires litter or ambulatory: litter
Security of pick-up site: Secure
Method of marking pick-up site: Front door
Patient nationality and status: Canadian soldier
Chemical biological or nuclear threat: None

Holy hell, it's her. "Listen up everyone," I shouted. "We've got a critical injury. One of ours." Spines stiffened. Games of Pacman and Bubbles disappeared from computer screens. "Clay, jump on the phone to the hospital." He nodded, and I ACKed the 9-liner, opened a new SIGACT, and plotted the location on the big map, as I'd done hundreds of times before. *If Kool is responsible for this I'm going to tear off his arms.* The Military Police jumped into the chat.

Update: 1x Canadian soldier arrested for questioning after attacking another

with a helmet. 3x witnesses. Ambulance has arrived for injured soldier. Major facial trauma.

I should have known the better soldier would come out on top. The hospital and I wrote Ack. The picture was getting clearer—still blurry, though. Mutters from the other soldiers in the room—everyone had heard the rumours of how the Major had once beaten a man to death with her helmet. The TOC-moles straightened up behind their monitors, waiting for info to come down the chat. Clay asked, "What the hell do you think happened, Jones?" but I stonewalled him, updated my SIGACT slide for the morning briefing, and nibbled my nails. From the hospital:

> **Update: 1x Canadian soldier with facial/dental injury confirmed as Lt Kool. Downgraded from critical injury to non-critical. En route to emergency dental facility.**

I'd gone there once for a root canal. *Finally some good news.* Sounds like Kool's injuries weren't life threatening. Another report came in about a routine UXO found just outside of Bazar-e-Panjwa'i—we'd send an EOD team in the morning. Then back to the waiting, the slow-motion car crash of the worst SIGACTs. It seemed clear the Major would be sent home. The FET would die. And she and I were done. Another hour with the belching coffee pot. From the military police:

> **Update: 1x Canadian Major released after questioning to await trial. Status: relieved from duty.**

If she was displaced from the TOC, tectonic plates would shift and grind. Leadership would fall to Bell. Bloodthirsty Bell, who thought every Afghan was a terrorist, who wanted us to kill thirty times a day. Or maybe they'd catapult a new Major to rule us, a straight-spined soldier with a rugged jaw. But no, I wanted her, our Major, our Valkyrie with her code of honour. *You've never seen how the machine can turn on someone, especially a woman.* She saw all this coming. It was all my fault, my stupid selfish letter where I called her by her rank like an idiot—she even said no notes.

A fumbling at the TOC door, and Kool spilled in, transformed. He was battered and busted, his uniform torn in three places; his face swollen and misshapen. He stumbled four steps into the TOC, punchdrunk, and waving his pistol.

"That b-bith did this to me," he spat a mouthful of blood.

Then you got what you deserved. "Why did they release you from the hospital? You're a wreck," I said. It was clear a bunch of bones in his face, his pretty cheekbones, were shattered; his head looked like a deflated sack.

"I went to the damn hospital. The thunt of a doctor didn't want to treat me. No pain meds, not even an xth-ray. I'm futhing infantry—I deserve proper t-thare!"

"The doctor said you were fine?" The troops in the TOC were drifting from their desks to gaze in horror at the roadkill who'd dragged himself in. "What did the dentist say?"

"That bith said I was fine too!" He clutched at his mouth, cursing, as blood spewed out. "How than I be fine when I got my futhing teeth smashed?"

He fell onto his knees, whimpering. Touched his swollen cheek with two fingers—tears sparkled in his eyes. "Thall me another ambulance, Jones. Send another 9-liner. I'm not OK—why won't anybody help meeee?" His voice melted into a piteous wail, and he hugged his pistol to his chest.

"Everyone get back to your desks!" I shouted hoarsely. I knelt on one knee in front of Kool. "Look at me. *Look* at me."

He stopped blubbering long enough to glance upward. The way his eyes skittered off mine—I knew. "You tried to rape her, didn't you?"

"She wanted to futh, Jones—gave me all the signs."

"And she beat the shit out of you with her helmet, didn't she? Then the female doctor and dentist refused to treat you, right?"

"They said we were in a war. That there were *real* soldiers to look after." He wept harder. I saw into the wound that was his mouth; his teeth were broken shards. "She made me *ugly*."

How many people are going to die because of your cock? And mine? "Get the fuck out of my sight, Kool. Sort yourself out and be back on shift tomorrow morning at the normal time. Don't get blood all over the goddamn room."

64.

RUMORS OF THE MAJOR'S fury spread through the camp like herpes—three female soldiers in their barracks had been roused by the yelling and crashing. Kool had shouldered the Major into a bunker on the walk home, and tried to *take* her there. As the women rubbed sleep-grit from their eyes, grabbed pistols and gathered in front of the barracks, they saw the Major burst from the bunker with her shirt torn and eye black. She was hammering Kool with her helmet, his forearms feebly protecting his face, the air full of crunches and squelching. Apparently, she kicked him so hard in the balls he literally left the ground. He collapsed and she straddled his chest, smashing down with her helmet, screaming out a different man's name with each strike. The three women had to drag the Major off the LT, else she would have left his brains splattered on the ground.

The DFACs were buzzing with the news, as was the queue at Tim Hortons; the whispers grew in strength like desert winds sweeping the camp. How the names the Major screamed were all the men who'd tried to rape her since she joined the Army. How Kool picked himself off the ground, cursing and crying, "fucking sthanth!" and "goddamn whores," insisting he'd done nothing wrong. He demanded that the women who clustered in front of the barracks carry him to the hospital. But no one lifted a finger; most of these women had served with the Major on past tours.

A tap had been turned—compassion itself dried up. While the men rallied behind Kool's story of an unjust attack, the women had endured too much. Their whispers found the paramedic's ear: she refused to give Kool so much as a Tylenol, instead, probing gloved fingers into his battered gums. The other paramedic "lost" his recovered teeth. The whispers outpaced the ambulance, finding ears down sanitized halls. Kool arrived at the hospital with half a bloody towel rammed into his mouth. The female nurse made him wait and wait. He tried to complain and she scolded him. "Sir, in case you have forgotten, we are in a war. There are many soldiers with worse injuries than yours. We will treat the life-threatening injuries first, then the doctor will see you." But the waiting room was empty, and there were no gurneys rolling in the halls, no nurses bustling with gauze.

When the doctor finally admitted him, she investigated thoroughly, poking at the swollen cheekbones with a tongue compressor, and shining a light into the bloody pit of his mouth. "Seems to be healing perfectly."

"You stupid bith," Kool protested. "Lemme talk to a man."

"Did you not understand that you're at war?" asked the doctor. "The oldest war? There is no other doctor. There are no second opinions, and I am not your Mommy. Go back to work."

An unhinged glee fed the rumours—it was impossible to discern the truth. They say the dentist was equally savage, refusing even to file down the sharp edges of his broken teeth. The miserable creature that Kool had become, his face misshapen and asymmetrical, invoked no pity. It was as if by torturing Kool the women on the camp could undo the decades of abuses they'd suffered, rewind the stoning of Halima, even reverse the oppression of the Afghan women.

But the women were shrewd: on paper they appeared to be giving Kool the finest service. It was no one's fault if his follow-ups were delayed due to operational priorities time and again. If what pain medicine he was allowed was a mislabelled drug that caused impotence. If the dental facilities on the base were simply not sophisticated enough to restore his smile. Far as I know, he barely made it past the waiting room, even when his gums started turning green from infection, and he developed piercing and continual migraines.

To the nurses, dentists, and doctor's credit, they kept him alive, barely, but he suffered a social death when the "sthanths" in the barracks spread a web of rumours that the Major had refused Kool's advances because his manhood was miniscule. After that it was laughter. Laughter. Laughter. Always behind him, in front of him, beside him, around a corner, floating down from a second story.

"What the futh's so funny?" he roared at two giggling corporals. "I'm an offither. You will show me respeth." They put their heads together and laughed harder.

I made a study of his pain. As his roommate, I got to watch him deal with his new normal—every time he spat into the sink it was bloody. He lost the heart to smile in the mirror. His mouth was an empty sack, craggy with bloody stalactites and stalagmites, and a rank stink of infection. In the DFAC, I continued my survey; he couldn't chew; but went through the motions anyway, ordering trays of eggs and cucumbers and stirring them with a plastic fork. When he attempted to sink his raw tooth-shards into a soggy cucumber cube, pain rattled his jaw so intensely he nearly vomited.

Did the wheels of justice grind this miserable wretch, too? Half-heartedly. Since there were no witnesses for the rape attempt, but several for the Major's helmet-attack, the investigations focused mainly on her—they even photographed the filing cabinet she bashed, proof of her instability. Although he was permitted to finish his tour, Kool's pay was badly docked; the General himself wrote a warning on Kool's permanent record, and denied him the office-soldier's medal we all expected at tour's end.

Truth be told, most men on the camp who heard his story believed him—they should never have put a woman in charge, just a matter of time before she snapped—but he was still the lowest form of man: one who'd been beaten by a woman. In the gym, ceaseless humiliations. The Coachbag, who I continued to lift with nearly every day despite my suspicions, would flick the miserable LT in the jaw with rocky fingers to shoo him from the weights.

Kool came to the TOC popping Tylenol like Skittles and shouting at everyone who phoned him. Still, he could not take time off work; there was no one to cover his hours. He was too proud to ask for medical leave, and Bell, who was acting-in-charge while the real Major awaited trial, wasn't the sort to grant it.

An earlier version of myself would have been delighted to see Kool's fall, but I no longer teased him, nor sought revenge for his attack on my lover; he was suffering enough. The Major warned me that "the machine" could turn against women, quickly and brutally. But the machine that turned against Kool was ruthless, too.

It was the lesson of the drone all over again: we needed to kill in order to feel we were making change, winning. The women of KAF needed to disgrace Kool for the same reason.

I will be the fool who dances in the thunderstorm.

They will say I'm crazy for feeling compassion even for monsters, but that was just a thing I learned in the war. And it was getting worse. I was feeling it all the time, for everyone. I couldn't shut it off.

I imagine Kool had a moment. A rock-bottom moment, a belly of the whale moment. A moment he forgot he was newly ugly, and smiled and flexed at himself like he did in the old days. And his muscles were wasted from not eating, and his smile was horrible fangs and barbed wire. He realized that he was ugly, the ugliest of us all. Gone was his great pride, his beauty.

But I wish he was still beautiful. Because afterwards the only thing he had left was killing.

65.

AFTER KOOL'S ATTEMPTED RAPE, I didn't see the Major for several days—we were down a person; my shift expanded. There was no way to talk to her, even to send a message, and I still felt the need to hide how much I cared, even though the letter seemed forgotten. Eavesdropped a few hints here and there at the gym, or in the barracks. Once I sat in the bunker where I used to chat with Noah and held the speaking stone. Another time I visited the bunker where the Major and I made love, numbly polishing the button I'd torn off her shirt that first time.

I knew she was awaiting trial, was at the mercy of the General's schedule. I know for sure she reported to the Colonels during this period, and I had a good sense of what that entailed.

My shift started soon. Bell was running the show with his shark-mouthed minion. I sank low into the torn car seat in the smoker's pit, remembering the feel of her fingers when she rubbed lotion into my palms. Through the chain link fence, I saw her disappear into the Colonels' demesne. *Wish I was a fly on the wall for that* I thought, sleepily. I may have dozed.

Crick crick crick chirped the pens, noisy crickets. The Colonels paused, each tilted his head to the left as he reread the last sentence. A knock at the door. "Enter," said the Colonels, in one voice.

There were two military policemen wearing red berets; they escorted a woman into the room. She wore a dented helmet with blood stains. Her chin was high, despite bruising on her cheek, and her bearing was straight.

"Reporting as directed, Sirs," said the Major.

"Take her weapons," said Colonel #1. Though the arrival of a striking young woman into the room had increased the butt clenches by seventy-five percent, the Colonel's voice was dusty and bored, bureaucratic.

"Roger, Sir," said one of the military policemen. The Major handed him her pistol and holster, as well as a knife from her belt, and signed a document the other policeman produced.

"All her weapons," droned Colonel #2.

The policeman blushed, "Ma'am, if you don't mind?" She removed her helmet and handed it to him.

The TFK Colonels, part 2

Semi-dawn in the frontal lobe, behind twenty-three locked doors and daily changing codes. Four identical desks, and identical stationary. Four empty inboxes and bulging outboxes. Another hard night's work for the Colonels, who allowed themselves a single hour of sleep, and only if the work was done. Behind each desk was a metal locker where the Colonels slept upside-down, like bats, strung by the feet. Even dozing, the Colonels maintained their rigid discipline: methodical ass clenches, fifteen a minute.

Sometimes Colonels dream. They dreamed upside-down things. They dreamed about chasing butterflies in the midst of burning villages. The way the wind feels in the hair while skiing down slopes of tangled bodies. They dreamed of throwing themselves onto live grenades to save a flower. They dreamed of systematic worlds, where everything was carefully bureaucratized, where babies were marked with bar codes, and the elderly were boiled down to nourishing gruel. You could tell which Colonel was having the most exciting dream because that locker would be brighter than the others and radiating heat.

Morning. The Colonels have unclasped their claws, righted themselves, and purged their dreams. Tired-eyed staff officers, Captains and Majors, have retrieved the burgeoning outboxes, and replaced them with heaping inbox stacks. Crick crick went the pens of the Colonels. They wrote sentences, then reread, in exact sync with each other. Conveniently, their writing was indistinguishable. Only the names on the rubber stamp varied from memo to memo. This was the work of the war: orders, direction, change.

1. Order 400 helmets

2. Plan a sweep operation in Panjwa'i

3. Arrange the investigation of a malfunctioning grenade

4. Change tagging system for human remains

5. Chastise junior officer

6. Request increased funding for helicopter operations

7. Deploy a team to mentor Afghan security guards

8. Order the whitewashing of the toilets

9. Arrange a trial for an officer's assault on a subordinate

10. Extract information from a detainee

"That's no trouble, Master Corporal, you're just doing your job." Free of the helmet, her blonde hair, contorted into a silky bun.

The Colonels pretended to work for another few minutes. Only the occasional glance at the Major, who stood at ease with her arms behind her back, betrayed the ruse. For it was like a bright-winged bird had flown in through the window (there were no windows), carrying an exotic zest, and opened its beak to sing dazzling arpeggios.

Were loneliness monsters at play here? Perhaps. This is assuming the regimented hearts of the Colonels still pumped blood. Had they forgotten their own families, their growing broods of ex-wives, the old-man pleasure of dandling upon a hoary knee one's monthly alimony checks? Did they still remember their own unloved or unborn children: undisciplined, vibrant, sloppy, grotesque and unfathomable?

But they do not need words to speak, the Colonels, these martyrs of discipline. Their assbrations produce subtle subsonic patterns in the air, which a discerning ear can read.

This is the one who was fucking, wasn't she? hummed Colonel #1.

Damn near beat a man to death, thrummed Colonel #2.

Terrible for morale, buzzed Colonel #3, *Absolutely disastrous distraction.*

Look at the rack on that one, opined Colonel #4, who was a tad slower than the others.

"Am I to wait all day for my orders, Sirs?" asked the Major in her frosty voice, like *they* were the ones about to go on trial.

Oh, she's a spicy minx, isn't she?

The General will have some fun with her.

Great for morale. Fantastic, actually.

Heheheehehe.

Colonel #1 stood and handed the Major a PROTECTED B folder. "Good luck, Major," he said, like he didn't give a shit either way.

The Major turned on her heel and strode out. Promptly, the Colonels stood and locked arms, hands to elbow, standing in a circle. Their asses vibrated, faster and faster—a staff officer carting an armload of maps heard a high-pitched whine. But the Colonels themselves were blurring in a nimbus of light. This particular staff officer, a young Captain, was unaware of the Colonels' powers; he watched with dropped jaw. In the middle of the man-circle, the nimbus grew to a miniature sun. In the glare it was impossible to tell where one officer ended and the next began—they were fusing. Coiling and flattening, stretching and elongating. A many-snouted beast. The staff officer covered his eyes under a sheaf of memos—the light was too intense.

When the room dimmed the Colonels were gone. In their place was a four-headed anaconda, thirty yards long and as big around as a fat canteen. Its eight eyes glittered with cunning and green light. Four forked tongues tasted the air. The staff officer fled in a flurry of stationary. The Colonel-snake slithered up the wall and disappeared into the vent.

No, that isn't real—I'm slipping in and out again. I knew when I went back, I might go back.

Fine, this is how it was.

I was nodding off in the smoker's pit, just like I said—the sun was setting on top of the walls. The Major rushed from the Senior Officer's building like it was full of snakes. A storm: the walls could barely contain her. The fury that was always under the surface, the rage that transforms a helmet into a mace, she wore it on her face. Would she pause to enter the code on the outer wall? Or merely charge straight through?

Neither. She spotted me through the chain link fence of the smoker's pit, and nothing softened. I called, "Good evening, Major," in my business voice.

"Is it, Jones, is it a fucking good evening?" she snapped. She had a fading bruise under one eye, and carried a PROTECTED B folder in her hand.

There was moisture in her eyes; the icicles were melting. She drew closer to the fence, and I stood so we could chat through it.

"I've missed you so much," I said, in our private voice. "All you all right?"

A foul taste twisted her mouth. "No, I'm not *all right*, Jones. They're putting me on trial for gross misconduct and assaulting a subordinate. Bell and Kool have both submitted written statements, one pleading his innocence, the other my incompetence." She scanned left and right for eavesdroppers. "And they've got a copy of your letter, too." *Of course Bell would pass that one up the chain.*

"I didn't want any of this to happen, Major," I mumbled. "Goddamn I was stupid—even after all the times you said 'no notes.' I feel terrible. How can I help?"

"You can't, Jones. They're throwing me to the wolves, just like I told you." Her fingers twisted around the metal wire of the fence. "Bell is taking over the TOC, and the trial will be a sham. I'll be disciplined and sent home in shame. My medals will be stripped and I'll never have another decent posting in my whole career. Obviously, I'll have to explain it all to my husband, so my marriage is pretty much broken, too. And the FET…" She choked up. The moisture in one corner of her eye pooled, grew fat and swollen, then spilled down her cheek. But I could not hold her, not even touch her fingers through the fence, not here.

"I came here to help women, Jones, and I failed. Do us both a favor and leave me alone. Don't visit me, don't write me, don't talk to me—"

"Please stop," I said. "I can help."

"You can't help—this is all your fault!" she spat. "Your stupid fucking letter. I told you not to write a goddamn letter. How many times did we go over the rules? No hickies, I said. No notes. No public displays of affection. No social outings. I made you repeat them over and over." Her fingers slipped from the fence and she stepped backwards, checking to see if anyone heard her outburst. Her voice dropped lower, "They told me I could make a difference. They told me I would be a *leader* and I believed them. They told me I would go to war and be a hero and help people. I put up with all their shit, fifteen years of harassment, and the FET was going to make it worth it."

A muscle in her cheek was leaping. We waited for a soldier to pass. She said, in nearly a whisper, "It was a lie, all of it. None of us are heroes—look." She held up her hands to indicate the smoker's pit, the blowing sand, the barbed wire spools adorning concrete walls, the shit smell and the setting sun. "Can you believe I killed for this and called it honor?" She laughed then, not the garden-party laugh, but a cutting, hard sound. "I would have kept doing it, too, but I even threw my lies away, and this is all it took."

She held up her hands again, pointed toward me, saggy and sad-eyed poet, my uniform baggy, my hanging belly, pockets stuffed with books and toilet paper, moonburnt owl of the TOC, the furthest thing from a soldier that ever was one. I was only a half-step ahead of my shame. *Ogre.* My cheeks burned and finally her eyes softened and she stepped back to the fence.

"Things will change around here, and you will be pressured to kill. I hope you have the strength to say no, when it matters."

"Can we talk?" I sputtered at last.

"No," she said, turning away. A flicker on her face, something flitted past. She was wearing her regrets, making new ones. "You ruined my life."

66.

A DAZED, GUILT-RIDDEN AND TREMBLING HUSK stumbled in the smoker's pit, collapsed into the broken-backed chair, and held his head in his hands—it was made of iron, or something heavier. The Major was shattered; Bell, empowered. *Soon the killing will start and it's all my fault.* The way our dreams leave sharp edges when they break: the Female Engagement Team throttled in the womb. The way crashed ships rot and leave their ribcages behind, like dead whales. The way the bunkers weren't for making love after all, just a place to hide from rockets. The wind swept in hot enough to tear the flesh from your skeleton. Thirsty clouds drank the river. The Major, humiliated, and Noah drowned in a lake of shit. *There is nothing left for me here.*

Fixed a coffee with shaking hands in the little storeroom outside the TOC. Those little Three-in-One packets that taste like powdered shit. Baby Bel cheeses in their wax coffins. One cupboard was full of Target Engagement Authority. No, that was just tea.

Inside the TOC, where the Major was gone. Her dented helmet, gone. Her heaps of paper, her plots for the FET. Bell was sitting in her chair. Not grinning, nor gloating, but serenely turning pages of a manual.

"Did you hear what happened, Jones?"

"I'm still piecing it together." A second of cunning. "Did they ever find the lucky bastard?"

Bell snorted, leaned forward in the chair, scarred grin splitting his face. "It's quite regrettable. The Major wasn't all she seemed. Breaching the no-frat policy is serious business. The General decided to remove her from this position, and here we are." He stretched his hand toward me, a slippery tentacle. "Congratulations, Jones. We're all getting bumped up a spot. I'm the new Major, and you're the new Bell, and Kool is the new Jones."

"Room!" barked the Chief. Bell and I, Kool, and the other TOC-bats, sprang to attention.

"At ease, troops," said the General, smiling like a sphinx, dogtags flashing at his throat, eyes invisible behind the sunglasses. He strode to the big map and stared at all twenty owls in turn, where they sat behind their computer screens. "Listen up. Y'all are probably wondering what's going on. Maybe you heard that your previous boss had a double-life and made some mistakes.

I had high hopes for the Major—impeccable reputation. Top of her class at RMC and captain of the soccer team. Three tours in Afghanistan and a medal of bravery. Incredible potential, all wasted on a ruthless attack on her own subordinate." The General nodded to Kool. "Sometimes it *is* hard to tell what's right, and the people we trust can hurt us the most. But we're going to keep fighting. And we're going to win."

His clenched fist indicated we were so close to victory; his eyes betrayed nothing.

"Now I don't want to tell y'all I told you so, but I made the fraternization policy for a reason. Seems I need to explain myself, yet again. Here goes: the Army wants you to be lonely." He paused, dramatically, to scan us. "It's true. Back home, if you have a family, you need to be gentle with them. And we can't afford that here. It's a sacrifice. We are hard people doing hard work— the destruction of the enemy. And how can you be a destroyer, when you're tucking your kid into bed every night? This is not a vacation and we are not here for love. Maybe you start loving one person, and the chemicals chew on your brain for a bit, and pretty soon you're loving all people, even the ones you see through the drone. That doesn't work for me, for the Army, or for Canada. You have to hate the enemy, trust me. Do y'all understand?"

Shouts of HUA, and frantic nods, and even some clapping. The General gestured to Bell, "Come on over here, Captain." Bell walked to the General— his back had never been so straight. "Now I've been meaning to do this for a long time. Almost since I met the man. I knew this guy was a proper soldier, a real killer, and an upright officer. You've got a professional here— loyal, honest, and competent. He's also tough as hell, isn't he?" Mutters of assent. Glancing around the room, I saw Clay shaking his head, but Crazy Jay looked beatific.

"It's my great pleasure to promote this Captain and make him a Major. I'm confident the TOC-team will be in good hands." From his pocket, the General produced a tan-colored rank slip-on, and tore off the two bars of Bell's old rank, replacing it. The TOC-owls cheered and clapped, like they did when we killed someone with a missile. I clapped along and could barely feel my hands touching, I was so numb. "Anything to say to your new team, Major? What should they expect?"

"Thanks, General, thanks so much. It's a real honour," said Bell. As he spoke he paced the room, rubbing his palms together. "I've been thinking for a long time that things could be improved, streamlined. That a few small adjustments could really ramp up the kills. The last Major was naive about war. She used to get us to name each target, so that we'd look at them different. Now, we'll give them names of people we *want* to kill." Wild roars and soldiers slapping their hands off desks. Bell was working through his plan on his fingers. "The last Major was greedy with the Target Engagement Authority—she wanted all the glory. But I'm more generous. I'll be delegating the authority to strike. Now the Senior Duty Officers, Jones and Kool, won't need permission to do the business. More killers means more dead Taliban, right?"

Time slowed in the way of nightmares, sounds stretching and the walls melting like chocolate. Bell was claiming to give me an *authority* to kill, but in the doublespeak of the war, it was actually an obligation. The worst part of the moment was the General, radiating power, his sunglasses scanning the room.

Bell's voice rose and fell theatrically. "There comes a time in a boy's life when he becomes a man. Back in Canada, this meant getting laid. Here in Kandahar it means killing ragheads. I've got two fat cigars on my desk for my Senior Duty Officers when they bust their cherries." Kool, from across the room, shook his fist at me, like we were competing; the other soldiers laughed. Bell, still counting on his fingers, reached the thumb. "Last thing. We got about four villages that have been thorns in the General's side. We're gonna blast them back to the stone age. We've got all these great toys," he pointed to the drone feed, "but we haven't had the will to use them. Until now."

"Great, Bell. Absolutely fantastic," thundered the general in the midst of the applause. He outstretched his glorious hand for a shake. "Unlock the drone. You have my full support."

67

THE NEXT FEW DAYS PASSED in brutal weight-lifting sessions and time in the TOC—the new Major worked as hard as the old, bags under the eyes drooping. He pored through manuals, staring at the big map, tracing his finger down roads that our drones relentlessly scoured.

"So if I'm the new Bell, why am I still on the night shift?" I asked him.

He glanced up, "Can you imagine Kool in charge, making decisions, all by himself? We need your experience here," and returned to his contemplation—he had learned the knack of dismissing people wordlessly. Also acquired a bunch of gray hair and a cool, calming aura that not even reports of renewed Taser Rapist activity could fray.

"Did you see this report, Major?" I said. "Another victim." A laundrywoman found two soldiers snagged and dragged, hooded and torn, on the east side of the camp.

Crisp response: "Jones, I've already processed your memo. If nothing has come of it that's because you were wrong—deal with it."

"Easy for you to say. You don't have to work out with the guy."

Saw the old Major in the Canada house bunker near the shelves with the boardgames and the chessboard with the missing rook. A ghostly figure in an issued sweatshirt, too hot for the heat, but the only clothing you could disappear into. The notorious maniac who nearly clubbed a man to death—she seemed to melt away whenever I glanced at her, or when men approached to chat, or when I thought about her too hard. I turned away and fell into a book.

"Two milk, one sweetener, just the way you like it, Jones." I arched my eyebrow over the Major's peace offering. Noted, with a pang, her face was paler, pinched and rubbed raw around the eyes. I waved to the seat.

"What happened to the rules, Major? No public outings was one of them."

"Doesn't matter at this point, does it?" She sat, chewed her lip. "Don't get any ideas, Jones, I just came over to apologize. Not sure if I'll be around much longer—my trial with the General's coming up in a few days." She sighed, her hand started to stretch toward mine, but stopped. "I shouldn't have said you ruined my life. I'm an adult and I made my own choices."

I wondered if I could ever want her again. *Probably*. "It's ok," I said. "Completely understandable. Really." I tried to smile.

"You know Kool got what he deserved, right?" Two soldiers entered the bunker, walked toward a foosball table, and she didn't even glance at them. "We almost made it to the barracks when we reached that bunker where you and I first… He hauled me in there by my wrist, threw me against the concrete wall, and raised a finger in my face. 'You're fucking,' he said, as if that meant I owed him. I told him to leave me the hell alone. He told me I was *his* for the rest of the tour. All my parts—he listed them. Then he started taking off his belt."

"I know the rest," I said. "You smashed his face with the helmet until your sisters pulled you off him. Is it true what they say? That you were screaming names as you beat him?"

The tiniest nod. "Lucky for you, Jones. Now all the attention is on the beating, and not on the affair. Unlucky for me, though. Now all the attention is on the beating, and not the rape attempt." She drummed her fingers on the tabletop. "I can still do this, Jones. Maybe the General will listen to reason. Maybe I can find a bit of justice, and keep the FET alive."

I didn't say anything. Thought of the ten minutes with her head on my shoulder. Eventually, though, "The General promoted Bell yesterday, Major. They're talking about 'unlocking the drone.'"

"Ah," she said, falling silent, staring at her knuckles. "They've forgotten about me already."

"I'm sorry."

"I'll tell you where you can shove your pity, Jones."

They were one-foot-in-front-of-the-other days. Let the momentum pull you. Keep your pistol holstered, Soldier. They say talk to the padre if it gets too bad, but I didn't; I figured I'd be misunderstood. One event sticks out from the fog: blood and confusion on the boardwalk, the big one, with the sutler shops and volleyball court in the middle. Because I was still on the night shift I slept through the whole thing, and had to piece it together from police reports, eyewitness accounts, and my handovers from Kool and Bell. Eight soldiers playing volleyball between the wooden-slatted walkways heard a scream. A scream that cut off halfway, that ended in a gurgle. The soldiers, Americans, grabbed their rifles from the sand, ran after the noise in their blueish city-patterned combats, and saw *something*.

One private claimed he witnessed a great shadowy figure bounding away.

A second reported an impression of dripping black claws. All confirmed that the stink of the assailant was without equal—an astonishing boast for these noses, hardened by months of enduring the poo pond.

None recognized the soldier they found, both face and body bloody next to a tan-colored jeep. He had been clawed and hammered, pulverised, it seemed, by repeated slams against the ground. There was shit everywhere—thicker than the blood. Shit in the claw wounds and on the shredded uniform. Shit sprayed on the windows of the jeep. Giant shitty footprints that led straight to the poo pond. I saw them myself.

When military policemen followed the trail, they found the uniform of an English soldier, torn and rancid, but no body. Again, they cordoned the poo pond, enduring its hideousness by pressing cloths to their faces. Those without facecloths frowned bitterly as the hot wind poured off the *ghar*, stirring the cauldron, mysterious bubbles frothing. We still lacked the equipment to plumb the pond. Some of our explosive disposal teams had divers from the Navy, but this option was abandoned—the divers, who had detonated boobytrapped IEDs for months, taken fire from AK47s, lost friends in roadside blasts, refused flatly to participate. They didn't have their scuba gear, and visibility was impossible in that treacle anyway.

The poo pond won. After six hours of suffering on the shores the policemen declared NSTR. But I had my suspicions there *was* something significant down there: an angry shit-beast, a monster, a friend.

68.

WE WERE BECOMING WRETCHED VERSIONS of ourselves. Or so testified Kool's bloody toothbrush when he left it exposed; his sharp teeth kept slicing open his gums. He had been parting his lips in a continual shark-like grimace—I suspect it was painful to close his mouth. Rarely did we overlap, each the other's shadow, just the hour here and there when Bell sent him home early—time Kool spent practicing his quickdraws and squeezing non-existent zits into our shared mirror, gouging his fingernails into his face and twisting until his cheeks were checkered with red wounds.

"You see what that bith did to me?" he asked, mid-squeeze.

"Now you're ugly on the inside *and* out," I said.

He kept rooting into his face for another minute. "What's your futhing problem with me anyway, Jones?"

I laughed. "Hey, remember that time you got me sent to jail because you told everyone I was a rapist?"

"I still think it's you."

"And then you tried to rape our boss?"

"I told you that whore wanted my thoth… wanted the dith. Wanted it bad."

"Do you really think I enjoy sharing a room with a rapist hypocrite piece of shit like you?"

Kool turned his ruined face toward me, withdrew his nails from a lesion on his cheek. "You gotta futhing beef with me, then bring it," he said, his pistol appearing in his hand. Those days he no longer needed to practice his watching-someone-die face—it was his permanent expression: blank eyes and a bloody smile.

"Do the world a favor and shoot yourself with that gun."

The other time we overlapped was during the handover; in the TOC we'd melted our plowshares and crafted swords. Next to one of the drone monitors, Kool had hung a chalkboard with a drawing of a turbaned skull and the words 'Kill Tracker.' The next day there was a single mark, a slender finger of chalk-dust, Kool's first kill.

"Holy futh, Jones, it was amazing. It was just lithe a movie. We thaught a raghead running in a field by FOB Masum Ghar tharrying a rifle. Bell named him Susan, and man did we ever futh him good. I said 'fire the missile'—I got to say it—and the Pred dumped four on him. The raghead was running and ethplosions were bursting around him…" Kool trailed off, his eyes slipping into reverie. "It was just lithe a movie."

A newly-minted man. The defeated slump of his office-soldier posture had straightened, the cloy of cigar smoke still sticking to him. "It was just lithe a movie," he mumbled once more, staring inward.

"Have you met Roadkill?" asked Bell, who appeared from the nook, slapped Kool on the back, and joined us at the big map. "We had a great kill this morning, Jones—shoulda seen it. We can all rest easier knowing there's one fewer piece of shit in the world. Roadkill is a fucking hawk who keeps our soldiers safe. He's one vigilant sonofabitch."

Kool, hearing praise, turned and smiled that carious, broken grin.

"What a pleasure to give this warrior a cigar at lunchtime, Jones. A real pleasure."

Now in the old days, I might have told Bell to fuck himself. But he was a Major now, deeply in the favor of the General. The wheels of power had turned, propped him up, that rank on his chest, the whole system of gears and regulations and laws and discipline and conditioning underpinning his words.

"Major, I'm perfectly happy with Jones. You can't just rename us so we act the way you want."

"I deserve that futhing name," yapped the shark-mouthed goblin. "I was thilling people this morning while you were sleeping like a bith."

"Jesus, Major," I said. "Look what you've done to him. Don't be a tool, Kool."

"Roadthill!" he snapped. "It's my futhing name, it's my *thoice*."

"Do you really want to be Roadkill?" I asked. "We need to go home in a few months. You think there's a place for Roadkill in Canada?"

"Gentlemen, Gentlemen," Bell intervened, "no arguments—we need to have our shit together in front of the troops, OK? Jones, I'm just trying to boost morale a bit. Make it fun. The work is hard enough without us all being a bunch of sourpusses. It's cool that you don't want to play—you're a serious man, serious about your work. That's great. We need that. It's fantastic, really. But let the troops have their fun as well."

I bit off a sharp retort. Swallowed. Bell flapped his moist hands at the drone feed: there was Sahar, my old friend, wearing white man-jammies and loading many-hued prayer mats into the back of a jingle truck. Zooming out, he was running back and forth from the rear of the truck and a mud-walled compound with two grape huts.

"Here's another guy who takes his work too seriously," said Bell.

"Prayer mats?" I asked.

"Yes, but what's in the prayer mats, Jones? The Taliban have learned we strike when they openly carry weapons, and this is the result. AK47s, RPGs, rockets—they wrap them up like sushi. And look how many prayer mats he's moving."

Sahar's labors grew; he was leaping on the rear of the truck to stuff the prayer mats above his head. "Hundreds," said Roadkill.

"Exactly," snapped Bell. "Enough to arm the insurgents in an entire province. Weapons that will be aimed at the faces of women and children, or worse, at Canadian troops."

"But there's no proof," I said.

The new Major tsked. "Working on it, Jones. Intelligence guys will be going over this footage. If there's one bulge that's out of place on these prayer mats, we're gonna fuck this guy in the ass with a missile."

Roadkill cackled as Sahar finished toiling, wiping the sweat from his brow with the back of his forearm. He sat on a rock and rested in the shade. A wind stirred his robe. With shark-mouth on one hand, and the wide-mouthed gameshow host on the other, Sahar didn't seem like much of a monster.

The drone's orbit over Sahar's head was getting tighter; the bullseye on his face, clearer; I had dodged the killing as long as I could, run out of excuses. Knew there was a chance I'd have to push the "big red button" and someone would die. "I hope you have the strength to say no when it matters," the last Major had said. That I might be strong enough to resist the pressure, the chants of *kill kill kill*, stand up to the General himself with a firm "no, Sir," the way she would've.

But strength was just a game I played for her. I couldn't stop TicTac; I couldn't save Noah; I couldn't even keep it in my pants. Sahar's shadow stretched long and cruel across the road like the Protector Spirit. Just because it felt like a nightmare doesn't mean it wasn't real. *If I am dreaming, why am I so tired, and how do I open my eyes?*

"Wake up, Jones, get yourself a coffee or something. Forget about this pissant. You and me and Roadkill gotta talk about tomorrow's Op. Look." Bell pointed to the big map, where a zigzag of red arrows, showing troop movements, fissured the villages, roads, and the single, dried-up river. "This is my fucking masterpiece, gents—seven phases of absolute glory. I've been dreaming it up for months as the skank-Major was working on her bullshit. We know that Nakudak is a Taliban bed-down, right? The only reason these guys survive is because they're shielded by the locals. You shield a Taliban, you are a Taliban, am I right?"

"HUA!" barked Roadkill, his bloody grimace.

I piped up, "We know the Taliban intimidate the locals. 'Let us stay here or we'll kill your family'—isn't much of a choice."

"Please, Jones," said the Major, "Don't be so black and white about things. There is always a choice, OK? Always a choice to side with the good guys, to do the right thing. Now listen up." I gritted my teeth as Bell pointed to a series of long, narrow arrows, all pointing to the town. "First thing is the Special Forces. They're flying in on helicopters in the night, kicking down the door of five insurgent compounds. They're gonna waste all those pricks."

The fattest arrow: "We are clearing from the north, from Masum Ghar. We've got three companies of infantry and tanks. As the Special Forces pull out, the infantry will be here," a poppy field just north of the town.

He pointed to a short, squat arrow, aimed toward the town from the east. "Artillery. Once the Special Forces are out of there, and the troops in position, we light up the sky." Bell cackled and slapped his hand on the map. "Talk about shock and awe, gents! The Taliban will be shitting their pants. And here's the *piece de resistance:* flamethrowers. Yes, flamethrowers—we're going full World War One. Those guilty fucks are gonna start running out of their buildings then they'll all come through here." He stabbed the map with his finger, a narrow crevice between two mountain ranges. "Canalizing ground. And we'll have a Reaper standing by."

"I'm pretty sure Russia already tried the massacre approach, Bell."

"Major!" he shrieked. "You will call me Major, Jones, you insolent fuck. Get your head in the game. Operation VULTURE starts tomorrow night."

He smiled that too-wide smile and put his hands on mine and Roadkill's shoulders, squeezed. "It's gonna be quite the show."

69.

<u>Phase 1</u>: Soldiers departed from Forward Operating Base Masum Ghar. At 1800, three armored vehicles with steep-slanted hulls started groaning their way to the south, troops staggered leftrightleftright following behind. There were grumbles, and last-minute cigarettes, and the Counter-IED team stuck their plastic explosives in rattle-resistant cases. I arrived in the TOC—Roadkill briefed me on the day's SIGACTS and the progress of the Op. Bell was gleeful; he had six phones in his nook and he could use them all simultaneously, like an octopus, arranging and managing and massaging.

<u>Phase 2</u>: The sanitized language of the combat chat marched down the screen, gaining speed, as the updates from the operation rolled in. It was necessary to feel as little as possible, though we all held our breaths as we waited for the reports. Four teams of Special Forces ninjas gathered on the KAF tarmac at 1900—each ninja carried six pistols, a rifle, and fourteen shuriken. They pounced into their helicopters and lifted into the air, buffeting the barbed wire of the camp with sand and tossed garbage. For thirteen minutes they loaded their many weapons; some sharpened their katanas. At minute 1914 the helicopters floated over five mud-walled compounds, beating their hummingbird wings. Five ninjas crept down five dangling ropes, dropping silently onto the roofs. Then they shimmied down the chimneys, bursting into the bedrooms with muted *pop pops* of silencers, or the *swish swish* of a katana. These were the known insurgents in the village; fighters who might help rally the people. As the helicopters flew back to KAF with the bloodstained ninjas, someone brought Bell a Styrofoam container of meatloaf, same as the ones I brought for the Sasquatch. Bell ate with nearly as much relish as Noah used to, smacking his broad mouth as the reports rolled in: **5x KIA, 6x KIA, 4x KIA, 5x KIA, 4x KIA.**

"Why aren't they specifying if the Killed in Action are Fighting Aged Males or Local Nationals?" I asked.

"It's a clearing operation, Jones, not a circle jerk."

<u>Phase 3</u>: The troops from Masum Ghar arrived in their tanks at the RV north

of the village at 2000. The sun had shattered into tiny particles. The soldiers smoked again. One young officer napped briefly in his vehicle's turret, before a grizzled Sergeant poked him with an iron finger. Diesel and propane tugged the noses of soldiers as they attached flamethrowers to their backs, muttering soothing noises, stroking their draconic throats.

"Where the fuck's the illum?" Bell barked into a phone. "Launch the fucking illum already. We got troops on the ground and a guy can't see his dick out there."

Phase 4: 2007, two minutes late ("cocksuckers," Bell spat) the artillery fired, the glowing orbs tracing long meteor-arcs, dispelling darkness and erasing the stars. The soldiers butted their smokes when they saw the illum—showtime. They toasted, clinking the tips of their flamethrowers. Dawn hit the village early. I imagined one grandmother started wailing, her instincts honed by fifty years of massacres, but I felt nothing; I was going to a cold place. The villagers, men mostly, were running from their homes wearing robes and rifles. Some had AK47s, others carried heirlooms from the Brits and Russians.

> **Situation: Troops in Contact reference Op VULTURE. Approx. 20 FAM TB, SAF in village.**
> **Action: Soldiers responding with 25mm rounds and flamethrowers**
> **Location: 41R QQ 157 332**
> **Time: 2010Z**

"It's happening now, Jones. We're gonna flush the shit out of those fuckers."

"Clay, confirm we have medical helicopters standing by for possible Canadian casualties?"

"Affirmative."

Phase 5: The huts were mostly mud but napalm doesn't need wood to burn. An Afghan ran from his house with an antique rifle. The turret of an armored vehicle's 25mm cannon stared back, then blew up his house. **4xEKIA.** One stubborn family refused to leave their home. Soldiers knocked twice with grenades through the window. **5xEKIA.** A human candle. The flame devoured his beard and made him a boy again. He spun twice and collapsed, sputtering. That was a life, **1xKIA.** Everywhere the *raprap* of bullets, the *woof* of grenades, the *whoosh* of the flamethrowers, tracers slashing the night with their ricochets, the arcing illum rounds overhead, the *crack-boom* of the 25mm cannon, the popping of fires in the night, and screams.

"Beautiful, ain't it, Jones?" We were hovering over the battle. Two pairs of gleaming eyes.

"No. It's horrible."

"Oh, you got that cold killer shit going on, Jones. Face made of fucking wood. I see how it is with you, Sicko."

Phase 6: The villagers fled from the village, just like Bell planned; our soldiers held the northern gate. Most of the houses were burning; some blasted open like eggs. Old men dragged themselves on gnarled sticks. Women with loose hair pulled children by the hand. A few scared boys, too young to fight but too old to be carried. One or two FAM tried to herd these village remnants, perhaps thirty of them, through the southern gates. Our soldiers lit more cigarettes. Some trembled.

Phase 7: The Reaper circled. He doesn't feel, has never felt. In his eyes the villagers were just a scattering of disparate pixels. In his eyes it wasn't killing, it's just turning pixels a slightly different color, restoring stillness to a chaotic world.

"These aren't soldiers, Major, these are just refugees."

"All insurgents or future insurgents, Jones. This is a Clear Op. We're wiping Nakudak off the map. We're teaching a lesson to these people. This is what happens when you shelter Taliban."

"It's not right."

"We have the Rules of Engagement, Jones. And the PID."

So we did. The Clear of the village was authorized at the highest level. I had no choice. I had no choice. I had no choice.

"Drop the bomb," I said.

"Oh, you're a cold son of a bitch, Jones. Ooooh. Gives me the fucking shivers."

The Reaper's bomb doors slid open, and a five-hundred-pound bomb detached from its moorings and plummeted toward the villagers. They were packed close where the road narrowed between two rocky ridges. The younger were helping the elder ones, half-carrying them. The bomb was in the air, spinning over and over. The people were just gray pixels, merging and melting into each other. They were just gray pixels, flickering with motion, their faces coarse and square-seeming, their mouths dark patches on lighter head-shaped blobs.

The refugees were between the ridges. The screen flashed and we couldn't see anything. Slowly, slowly, the colors darkened, and there they were, the people. They were the same gray pixels as before but now they were all in a dark crater in the road with all the pixels rearranged. The edges of the ridges had been reshaped. Here or there, a gray mass twitched. I could see a few of those darker black patches that had been mouths before. **30xEKIA.**

<u>Phase 8:</u> No. I am safe now on the edge of a mountain. I am watching myself through a drone feed. Cold wind blows from the summit. The mountain has frozen all my limbs but I am still alive, trapped in a tremendous icicle and I can't turn my head. Did I say trapped? That's not the right word. The right word is safe. Safe in my icicle.

"Perfect fucking timing, Jones, you psycho."

70.

THE BATTLE DAMAGE ASSESSMENT: the Heron circled the burning village for six hours; through the drone I watched blasted and smouldering buildings collapse, windows leering like the eye sockets of skulls, a single hungry dog wandering for scraps. The soldiers holding that north gate, they switched to night vision goggles once the illum rounds expired, set sentries, and settled in for the night. But the thing I remember most was the pit, the grave I smashed in the road—it was worse as the sun began to rise, under the Heron's better camera, edges and colors returned and the pixelated blobs became people again. How far they were scattered, how bloody the road.

How bloody the road, how far they were scattered. I am still down there in the tangle—the writing is taking me back. I'd not forgotten I'm a killer, a deadly cog with sharp edges, and now you see me too. They told me I could make a difference—how mighty I was in those days, so dangerous. When the bomb tumbled from the Reaper, do you know what I felt?

Excitement.

Yes, excitement. Tinged with pride. Pride at killing, at killing well.

Shame found me after. Shame, the legacy of veterans: it slashes our tongues, leaving us mute. Shame on parade in November, Remembrance Day, with the snow pelting my dress uniform and medals; shame transforms cripples like me into noble statues and we stand vigil in stone, voiceless and uncomplaining veterans, pure symbols without pain.

I stared at that village, that knot of bodies, for six hours, until the Heron needed to refuel, and the soldiers had sifted the rubble, counting bodies—we had lingered long enough. At long last I closed the SIGACT and peeled my eyes away. **Update: SIGACT at 2010Z related to OP VULTURE. A COY and HERON conducted BDA resulting in 85 EKIA. SIGACT is closed at 0545 with NSTR.**

71.

Dear Mom,

Thanks for the message. I haven't responded as much as I should. I've been very tired, a tired that doesn't go away with sleep.

I still like your stories of the kids in your school, though. Their precocious questions, their way of cutting to the heart of things, pigtails and shoestrings. I can picture all twenty-seven of them in their plastic seats, shooting rubber bands and sticking their gum under the tables. To think they will all grow old, know suffering, hurt people, die…

I have stopped believing in things. People. That we are inherently good creatures capable of living in harmony. We're not honest but if we were, we'd rank ourselves just below the beetle. Long-horns, sharp mandibles, poison. The sort that chew through their dead to reach the top.

I have stopped believing in home, too. Imagining my old bedroom with the books and the elephant piggybank, everything seems so alien. I have learned terrible wisdom in Kandahar; now I'm a stranger to myself.

Was I born here? I can't remember.

Matthew

72

NOTHING SIGNIFICANT TO REPORT. I wrote that lie many times in the weeks that followed. They blurred so badly that sifting through is like digging in a bucket of crushed glass. Cucumbers and protein shakes and egg-paste omelettes. Dreams of Halima and Judas and Cassius and Brutus and the pit I dug in Nakudak. After my first kill I could still act, solve problems, banter, but otherwise I might spend two hours after my shift just staring at the floor, not sleeping. Outside of the TOC, people would call my name three times before they'd get my attention. Increasingly, I had the feeling I was watching myself through a drone, not in my own body at all.

From this ruin, I can sift a few intact memories. One, the day after Op VULTURE I met TicTac at the gym and we went heavy as fuck on our shoulders. I didn't even greet him, just automatically provided a (minimal) spot, then grabbed weights of my own. He was lifting topless amidst the clanking iron. His torso freakishly colossal after months of steroids and hardcore training, veins and striations snaking his upper body.

"You are upset again, aren't you, Jones? I love it when you are upset." Just being near him made me angry: TicTac's bald head oozed sweat; his eyes shone with the confidence of many rapes, many midnight hunts for armed soldiers on the base, many eyes slashed, asses destroyed.

"Shut up and lift," I grunted. *My friend the rapist.* My machinations had failed—I would need to betray him again, harder. Loaded another plate onto the barbell for shoulder press. Did I really kill thirty people yesterday? Better by far to think about weightlifting, the next set, holding perfect form despite the shaking of the muscles, how to modify my grip for maximum gains, the perfect angle of the elbow, deltoids.

"Go, Jones. Go, Jones," TicTac prodded between sets, eliminating rest. As the weights got heavier this changed to, "Try, Jones. Try, Jones," until all three heads of the shoulder were bloated with blood, straining against the skin.

Another memory. The day after the big strike, we held a party in the TOC; someone was throwing a foam football and the unclassified computer was playing music: Ke$ha was back on the playlist. There was a cake. Bell himself served the slices to the troops. Morale soared.

"Betcha never had a party like this *under the old Major*, eh Jones?" Bell winked, his mouth moist, as he passed me a slab. Maybe he knew about her and me after all, the sly old badger. "One sec, Jones, we're not ready." He dug into a baggie and dropped a cherry on top of my cake. Then he raised his voice so all the TOC-owls could hear.

"Congratulations, everyone, for a very successful operation. OP VULTURE resulted in eighty-five confirmed kills. That's a good pile of dead Taliban; you've made a lot of people safe. The General is happy, the soldiers on the ground are happy and I'm proud of all of you." Roadkill and Crazy Jay hooted and cheered at this. Others, myself and Clay, clapped mechanically. Bell continued his speech, "We had a guy last night pop his cherry." *The fruit on my cake.* "Jones over here, he doesn't do shit halfway. Thirty fucking kills on his first strike. We got a cold, calculating bastard on our hands here, folks, a proper weapon." I stared at the floor. "I'm just glad he's our bastard. And I'm proud to give Jones a new name—please give a warm welcome to the newest member of our team, Killjoy."

Everyone clapped and cheered for me, but I kept my face still. Killjoy. My war name. The chocolate cake tasted of corpses. I should have said something but I didn't. Strength was just a game I had played for her. Once I was an imaginative boy with twelve invented friends. Now…

Killjoy. The name burned into my skin.

After. Sitting in the Canada House bunker holding my head. An unopened book. The old Major plopped a coffee in front of me, slid into the chair. Still wearing that sweatshirt. To think I held her once.

"Thrown to the wolves, Jones, just like I said." She was small in her sweatshirt, a half-pint. Mouth twisted in a bitter sneer. "My 'trial' was a goddamn fiasco, just like I thought. Just an excuse for the General to show someone his kill-shrine."

That got me listening. Sipped coffee. "His what?"

"Oh yeah—the General's got a screen in his office and it's just drone strikes playing over and over. All the strikes of the last year, Jones. He was just sitting there watching the video when I came in. I guess I didn't matter enough to hide it—forgotten, like I said."

So the strike on Nakudak, that was for…

"I thought we'd talk about Kool's rape attempt, but we didn't even go there. First thing he did? Pulled out your letter. Talked about how he was 'this

The Chain of Command

One morning we killed a pregnant woman. Shot her with a tank. We were trying to fire at Taliban fighters, but the tank was shooting from pretty close range and the round skipped over the heads of the guerillas and disappeared into the top of a hill. But the round blasted through the hill without detonating, then dipped, in its arc, down a valley coated in poppies. At the bottom of the valley the tank round struck a mud hut.

Said the gunner, "Hey, what do I know? The LT told me to push the button. People were firing at us. I pushed it. I sleep like a baby."

Said the LT, "We did everything right! They were shooting at us? How was I supposed to know the round would go through the hill? I'd make the same choice again if I had to."

Said the Major, "Well, don't look at me; I didn't push the button. I just wrote the patrol schedule for the platoon."

Said the Colonel, "Terrible shame what happened to that lady. Captain, make a note: 'increase information operations to her village.' We'll claim the explosion was caused by a Taliban's IED."

Said the General, "Do you have a video of the pregnant woman being hit by the tank round? Yes, have it delivered to my private quarters ASAP."

The entire system was built to turn death into porn. The *chain* of command, the way it binds you.

close' to approving the FET before it all went down. The amazing potential.

"I had to help him build his kill-porn collection. Then he told me he could make all the charges disappear, if I had the will—are you even listening to me, Jones? Do you want to guess what happened next?"

I flipped the pages of *The Brothers Karamazov,* to feel the texture on my thumb. I wanted to be there for her but I was still in the numb, cold place.

"He unzipped his fly. That's right, Jones. Fifteen years of service and three tours and a goddamn medal of bravery—what am I good for? Taking a shot in the throat. I told you. I fucking told you, Jones. You've never seen the machine turn on a woman before. I spent the last year trying to make a team that would engage with women, help pull them out of the fucking stone age, and this is what I get as thanks."

I looked up—I'd never seen her so frazzled, even when dropping bombs on people. Hair had escaped her bun and a pimple had sprouted on her cheek. *I wonder if she sucked his cock.* The thought came unbidden; I was too numb to feel shame.

"Say something, Jones. They're sending me home with the luggage next week. Full dishonor and they stabbed the FET to death in the crib. Everything is falling apart and I don't have much time left. My husband hates me and I didn't even get to help the *women.* I don't know what to do—I'm lost. Fucking say something, please." She pushed the book aside and grabbed my hands, forcing me to look in her eyes.

It was like I was watching the encounter through a drone feed, and I was hovering above the young couple circling, and I couldn't feel anything for either of them.

"K-killjoy," I finally stammered. "They named me Killjoy."

73.

THE FIGHTING SEASON RAMPED UP. I remember smoking the cigar that Bell gave me for killing those people. I inhaled so fast I puked in a graffiti-covered stall. After, I was sweaty for two hours. Bell's idea of PID was different than the old Major's. Any Fighting Aged Male was a target. That very day I noticed a **FAM carrying an AK47 south of Mushan and killed him with artillery. 1xKIA, with BDA resulting in NSTR.** Roadkill's chalkboard death count got higher and higher, scuffed and crossed out. I didn't keep such a tool—too nostalgic, out of character. I remember his bloody snarl, his jealousy when **two FAMs forded the Panjwa'i river, carrying AK47s. I had a PRED on scene and struck the targets with two missiles, resulting in 2xKIA and NSTR.** A "squirter" is when a target survives a strike and pops out of the cloud like a slippery watermelon seed, running full tilt. It's good to have a second means of attack in these times. My advice to Roadkill: "Layer your shit. Have an alternative means to strike in case the first fails." Roadkill and Killjoy. Sometimes it felt like we were living for the turnover, a competition, who could hand the other a bloodier sack of meat. One day I **deployed a bomber in response to seven FAMs crossing a field with RPGs, resulting in 7xEKIA and a BDA of NSTR.** The General was so impressed he watched the movie six times and shook my hand. I squeezed it hard enough that he must have known I was still alive. "Good strength," he said, "but don't forget your cardio." After, my hand was tingling with the General's magic. I could do all kinds of tricks except bring people back to life. But new respect from the TOC-weasels; nods when I entered a room, complimentary buckets of Tim Horton's coffee. The arousal of killing. Like when I **deployed a combat helicopter to strike five FAMS moving in tactical formation toward Nakudak at minute 1937Z.** The breath quickened. The vision narrowed. Blood pumped. Balls twitched. The troops chanted "kill kill kill!" and how do you say no to that? Look how happy you can make them with a mere "fire the missile," or "drop the bomb," or "strike the target." The helicopter buzzed thrice with mighty machine guns that scored the road, **resulting in 5xKIA. A HERON conducted the BDA resulting in NSTR,** and the targets collapsed with dramatic flourishes; the audience cheered as the bullets tore them; my face was a work of stone. Through the drone feed it was obvious: war is art; we were all just actors playing our parts, the killer and the victims both.

74

THE SHIT-BEAST HAD STRUCK AGAIN. Emerged from its lair like a scatological Grendel, wreaking and reeking. In its wake, the bodies of two Canadian soldiers, logisticians, were torn and crap-blasted, left half-eaten and shit-smothered near the boardwalk. I dragged myself from the routine, out of the numb place, spilling from the TOC under the moon, until I stood once more on the shore of the poo pond. At my feet, the eggplant-shaped speaking stone. A relic of kinder days, back when the old Major and I trysted, when Noah and I were bunker-friends, allies of the meatloaf.

But the pond was mute. Just the buzzing of flies. Pair of discarded boots. Two or three miserable-looking cacti. Lumpy, right where I left him. After the drone's crash, no one resurrected the clever shore-signs. The poo pond was no longer our little joke to ourselves, that anxious place where forbidden things stewed. Now it showed us our own lies—we could not bury our shame; it would always return, dangerous and irrepressible.

"Are you in there, Noah?"

But the pond said nothing.

"I keep getting these reports, Man. That there's a monster living in there. That he comes to the surface to feed. They say the monster is impossibly huge and strong and I think, 'Hey, I knew someone like that… except he was gentle."

A bubble popped. Otherwise, stillness.

"If I knew you were alive, I could bring you some meatloaf, and you could stop eating people. We could talk about you moving somewhere else, somewhere dry… I could hose you down again."

Three more bubbles. I waited a full five minutes, aware that my midnight-meal window was dwindling, that I might be losing my mind.

"All right fine, Noah, you cocksucker. You want the truth? I'm not here for you at all, I'm here for me. I need a friend. I've become something terrible, killed whole villages." Four bubbles popped in quick succession. "I never asked you for anything, Noah, and I saved your life twice. Now I need your help, so stop hiding like a coward and get out of there."

The pond started to bubble furiously. It frothed and splashed, bucking against its shores. I backed up several steps to avoid the murk drenching my boots. But there was no avoiding the activated stench molecules, which divebombed the nose anew. A broad dome-shape rose in the center of the pond, the vast shoulders and downcast head emerging first, followed by a towering torso—blocky under a thick shit-sheath. The creature grew taller as it marched toward the shore, two, three, four, five yards tall, sewage streaming off the legs and muck-covered fists.

The ground shook like a tank rumbled on it. I nearly turned and fled—no idea if it was Noah or the Protector Spirit in there, and either could be hostile. What use would my little pistol be on such a monster?

But it stopped, just shy of the shore, its feet disappearing into the poo pond. Then it stretched its huge claws above its head on the great pistons of its arms, I assumed to pluck me off the ground and cram my head into its mouth, but no. The shit-beast unballed its fists and scraped the gunk from its eyes.

The eyes were Noah's, but they had grown ancient and wise from too much suffering. He huffed, clearing his sinuses, and took a long and ragged breath. His deep voice had gotten even lower, the sound ice makes when it scrapes the hull of ships. "Ya got some nerve askin' me for help, Jones. Does it look like I can help ya?"

He'd never been a rose but now his awesome funk was of a different magnitude: he had marinated in the poo pond's sediment. I plunged anyway, "I killed, Noah. Lots of people. I killed them when I knew they were innocent. I want to stop but I can't."

Noah spat a black tar that struck a cactus, withering it. "So? Everyone kills. I been killin' since Mr. Richards. And I killed them hunters who came after me. And I killed two soldiers the night we met when they opened the hatch on the plane and I jumped out at 'em. Spirit makes it easy. I don't even have to say yes—I just hafta not say no.

"Look at ya. Yer sad because ya finally got yer hands dirty. I've eaten twelve people since I been in this pond. I wait in the dark, same as in the back of that truck when I hid under them bodies, drinkin' blood. 'Cept now, I'm breathin' through a tube until I get so hungry I hand myself over to the Spirit, and by the time the Spirit hands the power back, I gotta belly full of guys like you. Spirit says I should kill ya now. He says yer the biggest threat to me. He's prolly right."

"But you never listen to the Spirit, do you, Noah?"

He laughed then, without mirth. It was such a low note my insides quaked. "Sometimes, I listen. Sometimes the Spirit keeps me safe. And eatin' soldiers is makin' me *strong*, Jones—stronger than I ever been. Seems like I ain't supposed to be happy but least I got that."

A menacing step forward, Noah's voice dropped lower, dragon-like. "Spirit says strength's gonna unlock his magic and set me free. It's meat gonna help me now—kind that comes in boots 'n' helmets. By the time I outgrow this pond I'm gonna be a *force,* Jones. I'm gonna be an army to myself—ain't nobody gonna push me 'round no more, ever.

A burning feeling in my eyes. *There's not much Noah left in there.* "What about your dream, Noah? The great tree-planter? Keeping the stories alive? You're trying to tell me we're both monsters now, that there's nothing we can do about it?"

Noah grimaced; a blob of muck fell from his face. "Gotta new dream now, Jones. I ain't plantin' trees cuz I ain't no ferry. Best thing I can do for my people is stay alive 'n' hurt as many of ya as I can. Too late for stories now, Jones. Forget all the ones I told ya. Stories don't make nothin' better. Stories is just lies so we like ourselves more. Look at ya. Just a buncha little wheels in one big machine in this evil fuckin' base. Pinnin' medals on the chests o' killers and cowards."

He plunged a hand into the pond, rooted, and flung a slimy object at me. I tried to dodge but it struck me in the chest—more soft squelch than pain. It was an arm, a slender arm, wrenched off at the shoulder, gnawed and skeletal in places. Bile rose in my throat. Noah said, "Stories can't bring people back to life," then he turned and lowered himself back into the murk.

75

NEXT MORNING THE WALLS REACHED THE SUN, shadows shaped like tombstones. To wake and think, *I will kill today* and still ram your feet into your boots. Easier to stop thinking, to simply act, move yardsticks, be a proper cog. Imagination, booze and love: none of these escapes were potent enough to withstand a year in KAF. Only the riddle of steel remained.

I paused at TicTac's door. *Should I go straight to the police now? No, it's chest day.*

Once again I heard the strange sibilance of something heavy being dragged. TicTac cracked the door. "Come in, Jones. Come in." Weren't his eyes baggy, my friend the Taser Rapist? Which hapless soldier preyed upon last night, which bunkers lurked in, what screams bottled?

I stood in his ever-evolving pornography cathedral as he chugged a viscous green liquid from a canteen. The girls had lost their bodies. Decapitated heads covered the walls and ceilings, staring eyelessly.

"Is it finished?" I asked.

"Stop perving on my ladies," he answered, between gulps of green froth, the thick veins of his front shoulder apparent even through the tan t-shirt.

There, on TicTac's nightstand, I finally saw it, and my last doubts that he was the rapist dissolved. He'd grown so powerful he no longer cared about discovery: his Tazer with a much-scored handle. His love toy and murder weapon and second cock, magic wand with the spell of paralysis. The way he stared at me, unblinking, forehead creased all the way up his razored scalp, left no doubt he knew I'd seen it. When his voice emerged it was his normal, slightly high-pitched tone, "You do not look surprised, Jones—just tired. You have known since I drop tire, clever man."

I nodded. *And who's to say which of us is worse?*

"And you have not betrayed me—a true friend."

My fingers ached for my pistol, but we never carried them to our workouts. *If I can get him to the gym, there'll be witnesses. I can call for help.*

TicTac stood. "Is good. I am sick of hiding." He shrugged off his shirt and pants. One of the photos on the wall had a string attached—an eyeless mask that he pulled onto his face. He clutched the Taser in his right hand. "Now you see me as I am," he said. "Look, look!" he demanded. "See what

Coachbag's Corner: Chest Day

Of course we are lifting! Is chest day, no? Poseurs and dbags beware—no longer shall we make a joke of chest with silly pec dances for giggles of girls. This is complex muscle that provides depth and width to upper torso. Today we work whole chest, starting with bench press. We work upper, middle, and lower with presses, flyes, dips, pullovers and the pec dec. We use barbells, dumbbells, cables as well as body weight. Today we focus on form—every rep must be perfect, path of weight through air must be beautiful.

You know when you struggle with heavy barbell on benchpress, but push through sticking point in triumph? That is how it feels to show you who I am. To talk freely about how I spend nights—like Bell. Oh, Jones, he was my favorite little piggy, my rump roast! I marathon-fucked him—and as you know, my cardio is excellent.

And now, every Sunday evening he wait for me on same chair. He is girlfriend. I toss him bag and he put on own head and we take little stroll to dented truck and he spread legs, no ropes. I am little more gentle than first time, but not so gentle, Jones. I only use Taser once or twice.

Do you want to know secret of Taser? Lean close, I will whisper. When I am inside a man and I zap him, his ass clenches tight like fist. It is great pleasure. But what is better is that man nearly always cums. You have no idea how much joy I have given. I am like Santa Claus.

we have achieved together."

His musculature was devastating and horrifying; veins tangled everywhere, even over his abs. From traps to calves he was freakishly bulky and completely without fat. All the supersets and protein shakes and negatives and half-reps had paid off.

TicTac spun, posing, his features hidden behind a beautiful woman's face. "What do you think, Jones? Tonight we go together. You will drag little piggy and watch me in action. Is good step in friendship—I will be your coachbag in new thing, too."

He stroked his hardening cock with his free hand. "And if you go to police you wear bag next. You know you cannot stop me."

Unlike the Afghans I bombed each day, who seemed so like me, here was a proper villain, an obvious one, easy to hate. And that's why the Taser Rapist happened, I think. Because we needed him so badly.

"Triceps need a little work," I said. "We lifting today?"

As TicTac prattled, I scanned the gym, searching for deliverance. Same old church, barn-sized, the mirrors along the walls, and the machines and weight racks arranged in rows, the broken legpress machine at the altar. I scanned for police, a way out, tried to catch the eyes of two staff members in matching t-shirts. Failed. Two other soldiers worked out separately and doggedly—TicTac sneered at a welterweight soldier, who was shoulder pressing a mere 65 lbs.

It wasn't a typical day but it was a typical workout: benchpress, heavy as possible, to tire the chest. We'd worry about finesse and pinpointing the different sections of the pec later. "Go Jones. Go Jones," said the Coachbag. 225 lbs felt like a joke, an extension of the warm-up set. I did fifteen reps and TicTac twenty. 275 lbs is a solid weight because of the way it looks on the bar. Two big plates of iron and one demi-plate per side. I did ten reps and TicTac did fifteen. "Watch your fucking grip, Jones." 315 lbs. Three plates a side plus the weight of the bar. I lifted six and TicTac did twelve. "Four hundred today, Jones. Is big day." I stepped up to 350 lbs and did four, but TicTac increased to 400 lbs for eight. I'd reached my limit, but TicTac shouted, "Fuck it!" and we threw 420 lbs pounds on the bar. On the fourth rep his muscles faltered, failed. *Now's my chance.* He needed my help; instead, I struck, wielding a 100 lbs dumbbell in two hands like a club, I smashed him in the stomach.

Rusty iron met rocky abs. TicTac struggled with the barbell still in his hands, losing breath. I smashed him again. He kicked out, catching me in the side, while twisting his body. The barbell clattered down where his head had been, blood bubbling from his lips. His kick knocked my breath out and launched me into a rack of pre-fitted barbells. *Hits like a goddamn elephant.* Two barbells clanged onto the ground, bouncing and jarring. "He's the rapist!" I shouted. "I've seen the Taser!"

TicTac gasped, spat blood. "After all we've been through together, Jones? You betray me on chest day? MY PERSONAL BEST?" His voice got higher and higher pitched, more demonic, ending in a horrible shriek. Two soldiers who had been running toward TicTac to help him stopped, began backing up, as TicTac reached onto the dumbbell rack and hurled a 65 lbs weight overhead, same way we'd tossed the medicine ball.

CLANG—I deflected with a 45 lbs plate. A 75 lbs dumbbell whistled in the air; I blocked it with the plate but it struck my fingers, splitting the knuckles badly. An 85 lbs weight struck like a catapult—I blocked, but the force was so extreme my shield smashed my forehead. A 95 lbs weight came in low, smashed my stomach; I tripped over a bench and collapsed on the floor groaning, clutching my belly, and gasping to breathe. *He's too strong. It's impossible.*

"Look at the mighty killer," said the Coachbag, holding a barbell like a bo staff, a blood stain on his t-shirt. "He is a great terror to the women and children in the villages, did you know?" The welterweight mustered his courage, attempted a tackle; TicTac swatted him with the barbell with contempt. The man crumpled onto the floor like a pile of laundry. The other soldier fled through the back door, near the leg press.

"Get help!" I called after him.

Struggled to my feet and grasped a barbell, leaning on it like a cane. Blood dripped down my face and over my split knuckles. It had all led me here—an entire life of stinking weight rooms, of rugby fields and boxing rings, of playground bullies and the ones at home too. *I should have been a poet. Never got a chance.* If I could just delay him a little, long enough for police to arrive with a bulletstorm, then this whole insane saga might stop. I coughed, buying time, catching my breath. Soon as I heard TicTac start to laugh, I whirled my 45 lbs shield at him like a discus, then charged with the barbell, roaring.

He batted the discus aside, but lost time, and I landed a lucky blow on his triceps. Kicked over a weight bench. Finally a good, clear enemy. Swung again, and he blocked with a huge clang and sparks. No finesse—we whirled those 45 lbs rods around our heads in brutish arcs, the clumsy dance reflected in the gym mirrors. Again the barbells struck, rang like church bells, dented. He landed a blow on my quadricep and I laughed in his face—wasn't I the one who broke the leg press?—but my arms were growing leaden, the swings slower, and the inevitable happened.

Lunging with the barbell like a spear, he struck me right in the solar plexus, blasting the air from my lungs, and I flew backwards, crashing once more into the rack of pre-fitted barbells. The weights tinkled and rattled, and I collapsed beneath the rack, sucking air and bleeding, muscles burning with lactic acid. TicTac wasted no time—seized the rack low from the other side, deadlifted powerfully, and the whole rack crushed down, more than a thousand pounds, barbells pinning my hamstrings and glutes and back and even one on my neck, squishing my face into the ground. Pinned, I tried to move and something crunched in my spine, and I gasped, would have screamed, choked instead.

You're fucked now, Jones.

My one free hand flapped. Blood pooled under my nose. One eye crushed shut; the other could only see the gym-floor. *Like being run over by a tank.* I could see his sneakers, my friend the Taser Rapist, the Coachbag. His voice, overhead, breathless: "I should thank you, Jones. Now there is no going back to fake life. I can only be true self—yes, is gift."

My world was shrinking. The blood from my nose stretching out like a river. The Coachbag's shoe. The rest was blackness. The barbells settled, shifted, and I groaned. *Where were the police?* I mumbled something. Tried to get up. Failed. Thought of Noah, trapped in his pond. I thought of words he said to me once. "Seems like everyone who ever knew me betrayed me in the end."

TicTac's shoe crunched down on my fingers. "What is it you are saying, Jones? Say it. Don't be such a *pussy*."

"The shit beast," I croaked. "In the poo pond… stronger than… both of us." Darkness fell.

76.

WOKE WINCING, a flashlight blasting in my eye, my shoulders spilling over the edges of a narrow bed. I had three headaches at once: pain by the right temple, above the left eye, and in the brainstem. A hospital light glowed feebly above.

"You're awake," said the doctor, a woman in her forties wearing spectacles on a sharp nose.

"I preferred being asleep," I said, groaning as awareness grew of my many welts.

"Will he be all right, Doctor?" The Major's voice. I shifted and saw her, perched on a three-pronged stool. Red-eyed and stray hairs escaping the bun. *She visits me the way we used to visit our victims.*

The doctor picked up a clipboard, read from it: "Five cracked ribs, extensive bruising, two broken knuckles, and a serious concussion—you should have heard the things he was rambling about. Monsters and beautiful women."

"I have a rich inner life," I said.

"And a serious head injury," said the doctor.

"Should have seen the other guy," I quipped, and it was almost smooth, except for the cough that shook the cracked ribs in front and back. Then I whimpered and a tear escaped my eye. *I hate for her to see me like this.*

"He escaped, Jones," said the Major. "The police are sweeping the camp for him. They didn't find the Taser in his room, but they did find a British soldier gagged and stuck into a trunk. He was still alive, though barely." *TicTac, you sick fucker.* "Doctor, if there's nothing else, may I speak to the patient in private for a minute?"

"Of course, Major," said the Doctor. "Tell him to take a few days off from the gym." As she walked away, over her shoulder, "They'll need to rebuild it anyway."

Once the doctor shut the door, I stretched my hand for the Major, but she was too far to reach.

"This isn't a social call, Jones. My baby is dead. I kept fighting for it even when I knew my career was over, when they were all laughing at me." She was talking quickly, words spilling. "I'm just here to say goodbye. I've been doing a lot of thinking. Thinking about Kool and the General, and the FET and my husband and Halima, and how I never wanted to be a mother at all, I just wanted to help women. Been thinking about all the lies the military told me over the last fifteen years and trying to imagine a new life—could you see me as a civilian at this point? After all the things I've done?"

"A teacher," I said. Wanted to close my eyes and sleep, or slip into the numbness again, or float away on a drone. Yet here was a person in pain, someone I love. I was kind once—might be again. "A kindergarten teacher with bangles on your wrists."

She smiled the saddest smile and her steely fingers found mine, squeezing. Her elf-fingers in my ogre-palm. "Welcome back, human," she said. "But it's too late. How can I look after two dozen kids when I don't even give a shit about my own? When I close my eyes, all I hear are women screaming. All I see are the faces of men who've tried to rape me." She grimaced, but the expression eased into a sad smile. "I fought for women, Jones. And I failed. It was the only thing that mattered."

She squeezed harder, her callouses on my callouses. "I know this isn't the best time, Jones. But I wanted to say goodbye."

"They finally got you a flight?"

"Something like that," she said, and kissed me.

77.

IN A DIFFERENT WORLD, nearly being smashed to death beneath a rack of pre-fitted barbells would have been a great excuse to miss work. In the cracked bathroom mirror, I grinned at my own expense. With the stitches on my forehead, I looked like a zombie extra on a B film. Popped some Ibuprofen and tried to bathe despite the bandages and welts.

No compassion from my colleagues when I arrived at the TOC, limping. Nor had they forgotten my new name. Roadkill was snapping and scowling, his mangled mouth still untreated. "You're futhing twenty minutes late, Thilljoy—what the hell happened to you? Get tharried away with a wanth?"

Bell joined us at the big map. "You look like something the cat dragged in, Killjoy."

Despite the headache and dizziness, I told them all about TicTac, the Taser, and the battle of the ogres. They already knew some of the story through the MP reports. I didn't mention to Bell that I knew he'd become complicit in his own recurring rape—how do you broach that topic? Still, the way his gaze lingered on me suggested he knew. All said, Bell took the update fairly well. Just clutched the edge of the map with his delicate fingers, trembled violently, and aged about four hundred years.

"There's more, Killjoy. Absolute fiasco in Kandahar this morning—tell him, Roadkill."

Roadkill yapped the memorized report in a mechanical voice, **"This morning at minute 0715 in the vithinity of Thandar Thity, we retheived reports of a VBIED blast, resulthing in 5xKIA and 8xWIA. Afghan sethurity forces and embedded units responded with Small Arms Fire to 6x INS who attathed with AK47s."**

"But it was a load of horseshit," Bell interjected. "A goddamn distraction."

I glanced at the shark-mouthed kobold, who continued his report, **"During the Battle Damage Assessment we disthovered that approx. 300 Insurgents had esthaped from Thandahar Thity prison through a tunnel. All units informed to ethpeth a higher level of Insurgent athivity. The tunnel has been sealed and an investigation ordered. Inthident is thlosed at minute 1544 with NSTR."**

"Right under our fucking noses, Killjoy." Bell slumped ever lower, aged another fifty years; I hadn't seen him so defeated since he was raped. "All the detainees we took under the old Major… I told her it was better to kill them, but you think she ever listened to me?" Bell stroked his chin; he hadn't shaved that day—the Chief would have his nuts for that. "It's the story of Kandahar, Killjoy. For every step you take forward, you take a dozen back."

"So it never mattered at all," I said, dazed. "It really is fruitless."

"Oh, I wouldn't say fruitless, Killjoy. Remember that sometimes the war gives us little gifts. About fucking time, too—I need a *win*." His cold grin split his head in half.

"What sort of gift?"

"The positive identification sort of gift." A grandiloquent gesture of his hands. "Watch that screen!"

It was Sahar through the Predator's feed. Last we saw, he was loading a jingle truck with prayer mats. Intelligence suspected the mats were stuffed with bazookas and AK47s. They spent three days doing whatever it was they did: poring over the footage in super-slow motion, zooming in and out, dickering and dithering over pixels, irregular folds, patterns of stitching. Are the prayer mats a bit stiff, or stuffed with deadly hardware?

"INT gave us PID this morning," said Bell. "That is a confirmed terrorist right there, Killjoy. Look at that sonofabitch."

Sahar was driving the jingle truck northeast along the rutted highway, stunted shrubs dotting the *wadis* and cracked earth. The occasional abandoned fencepost. Motorcycles zipped past the jingle truck; cars queued behind. "He's heading right for Kandahar city, Killjoy. And what's in Kandahar City? Hundreds of newly escaped Taliban. And what do they need?"

"Weapons," I said. Sinister Sahar, hiding behind the windshield of the jingle truck, where the glancing sunrays obscured his face.

"You know what you gotta do, Killjoy," said the Major. "We have the ROE and the PID."

I knew, goddamnit. Wasn't I the monster who dropped the 500 lbs bomb on those villagers in Mushan? The ones scrabbling for safety. But those were strangers—too many to name. This was Sahar, who I'd been watching for nearly six months. Met his family. Saw him make that adult choice to take up arms, same one I did, except we drove him to it with our ravens.

Roadkill: "Maybe our little sailor doesn't have the futhing stones?"

But he's just a boy. Never kissed a girl. Can't read.

KILL KILL KILL When Crazy Jay began the chant, it was deep and somber. As it continued, it grew in resonance, as more voices joined. *KILL KILL KILL*

Bell asked, "Whatcha waiting for, Killjoy?"

"Pattern of life," I said. "We strike now, we might hit one of those other vehicles."

Waiting to be convinced. Waiting to wake up. Waiting to disappear.

KILL KILL KILL

If they had the ROE and the PID, why had Bell waited for me?

KILL KILL KILL

Damnit. Sahar stopped the truck and climbed out, the waiting cars zoomed past.

KILL KILL KILL

I remember he was mostly pixels, anyway, and gray. A stunted shrub on the side of the road—an ideal place to take a leak. I might have done the same.

KILL KILL KILL

"Strike this futhing Taliban piece of shit, Thilljoy," said Roadkill.

"Don't worry—Killjoy knows exactly what to do."

Was he even a person? Or a dangerous terrorist who caches deadly weapons in symbols of faith? Had a face like a person though, if you could see through the pixels. A young man, handsome, maybe. In Canada, he would be a schoolboy still. It's not my fault we were born on different sides.

KILL KILL KILL

Maybe he'd be a doctor. Maybe he'd save someone's life one day. Fuck it, maybe he'd farm the ground, and put some food on the table. Maybe he'd just have a decent life, with more than eight happy moments.

KILL KILL KILL

He had driven for a long time, and after pissing, walked a few steps from the puddle, reached high into the air, and then toward his toes, to stretch his back, the way I would.

KILL KILL KILL chanted the whole TOC.

"This bith ain't gonna do it."

"Whatcha waiting for, Killjoy?"

I couldn't say. Certainly I was no virgin in these matters. Tension rising in the air, like it always did before a strike. That sense of waiting. *KILL KILL KILL* went the chant. Something was pushing back. Something was stopping my mouth. Something was wrong.

"We've got the ROE, Killjoy."

"Yes, that means we're allowed to strike, not that we have to."

"We also have the PID."

KILL KILL KILL echoed the chant. *NO NO NO NO NO* screamed a voice inside my head.

"Fire the missile," I said.

"Attaboy, Killjoy," said Bell. And we waited those four seconds for the missile to strike and Sahar was still touching his toes, alternating between them, a solid lower back stretch and wasn't he nimble and strong and fit in that moment, almost human?

Sahar disappeared in a blossom of dust and we cheered. A smoke cloud obscured the screen. The truck was on fire. The smoke was drifting away. I held my breath, clenching my hand so hard it started to bleed again.

He was on his knees, praying; prayer had cocooned him in his last moments in an impenetrable bubble. No, that wasn't what happened. The prayer was too urgent; he was rocking back and forth, his hands in his lap. The drone was circling around.

"Where's your futhing God now?" said Roadkill. But I had stopped believing long ago, grown wise.

Sahar was fishing from his knees. The casting out and the reeling in, who'd taught him this? Curious and jarring in the desert. Difficult to see clearly through the dust and smoke, but he must have been struggling with a proper mackerel, and couldn't get that fucker into the boat, needed help, someone stronger. Sahar was not used to fishing; his country is landlocked. I could show him.

No. The drone circled round. No. He was not fishing. He was not praying. He was neither fishing nor praying Sahar what have we fucking done to you the drone was circling round no I said no everything was gray and the long gray spools the long gray ropes of him had spilled out the guts have spilled out the intestines all over the goddamn ground and he wasn't fishing not praying he was trying to hold himself together again trying to stuff himself back together and he was stuffing half the desert into himself and the black pixels of flies and the black pixels of his mouth and this wasn't praying not fishing I said no I said no—

"Fuck, you're a cold bastard, Killjoy," said Bell.

"Looth how futhing disgusting he is," muttered Roadkill.

My voice from a long dark tunnel. Someone else's voice. "He's injured. No threat anymore. We can send a helicopter, recover the weapons."

"Not a fucking chance, Killjoy. You blew him up in no-man's land. We send a chopper, the Taliban shoots it down."

Still fishing, but the stuffing was getting slower and slower. The chant died when the missile struck and revulsion dawned: Sahar gave us a window into our own bodies. In the back, Crazy Jay puked into a basket. Sahar's eyes were just two pixels. I couldn't hear the prayer he was screaming. But the fish got snagged on something, a root or rock. Sahar tried to free it with flicks of the wrist. He was caught in the *habit* of dying, the repetition of it. I must collect my teeth. I must touch my brother's hand. I must finish hoeing the field. I must remove my boots. I must collect myself again. I must die whole.

"Lemme know how the BDA goes, Killjoy," Bell's skin was green-tinted. "I'll be in the office."

"Should we strike him again and finish it?"

"Negative. We don't have the ROE for that."

It seemed Sahar was giving up. The wrist flicks were getting weaker and weaker. Beaten by a root. But no. The gray coil was slippery and the game began anew and Sahar returned to the stuffing and coiling, but the more he stuffed the more fell out.

"Can we pull the drone away?" said Crazy Jay, dabbing his mouth with a napkin.

"Negative," I said. "We have to keep watching. "

Sahar had lost all his strength, could no longer fish, his head lolling side to side. There were darker pixels all around him, and on his chest. He was saying something. He was yelling something. Something important. I strained to hear him but the drone has no ears.

Wet-eyed Crazy Jay yelled, "Just die, Man. Just die already, OK? Please die."

But Sahar will never die. He will live forever, trapped in his final moments. Every time he comes near to death, I rewind the video and play it all again.

We sent a platoon of soldiers to Sahar's location to confiscate the weapons and conduct a Battle Damage Assessment. He was splayed all over the ground. The soldiers rooted through the jingle truck, heaping the prayer mats on the road. The mound grew higher and higher, like a ghoul's barrow. They did not find any weapons hidden in the too-starchy prayer mats, their many hues in the last rays of the sun. With the moon waning, the soldiers returned to the Forward Operating Base. **1xKIA with BDA resulting in NSTR.**

78.

HE WAS INNOCENT. Just like I thought.

None of my colleagues—the ones who chanted *KILL KILL KILL*—could look at me. My eyes were for Sahar, the drone circling round and round as Bell and Roadkill went home to the barracks for the evening. I stayed and watched the BDA until the soldiers left, then kept watching as night fell, the splash on the road that had been Sahar, the abandoned jingle truck, and the heap of prayer mats. I didn't brew the coffee, didn't search the roads for IED emplacers, didn't even prep the Daily Situation Report. Just watched. Eventually, the PRED got low on fuel, and I had to send it back to KAF. *I won't forget you, Sahar.*

A foolish promise. I got it backwards. It was Sahar who refused to forget me.

From then on, whenever I blinked, or shut my eyes for any period, the image of Sahar wrestling with himself would flash into my mind: fully in color and beseeching for help. More, he appeared in the waking world, always at the height of his injuries. Half the time it was as though I saw him through the drone: gritty, pixelated, and mute. The rest of the time he appeared as he was, the same as the rest of us, except torn open.

How do you escape from someone who lives in your head? I keep expecting him to fade, but he doesn't; he follows me everywhere; he followed me back to Canada. A ghost.

79.

MY BODY STILL ACHED WITH BRUISES and cuts and I deserved it. Took pleasure in paying penance. Sahar appeared and perched on the desk just in front of the drone-feed, his entrails sliming on the floor. I labored over a PowerPoint slide for Sahar's death—this was required for the morning brief. I wanted it to be perfect, a cairn. Alas, the slides were written in the sanitized language of the combat chat—no poetry—and it would be barked by Roadkill at the morning brief at 10:00.

After the strike, the evening was slow. Mostly just waiting as Sahar explored the TOC, staring in bewilderment at the drone feeds and combat chat, attempting to strike up a conversation with Clay and the other TOC-moles. A whole system of science, manned by killers, arrayed against you. His eyes were wide in wonder.

The shift ended. *Come along, Sahar.* We walked home together and I pointed out the DFAC, and the tree with the starlings in front, and the bunker where the Major and I had made love.

Next day in the TOC: frantic reports of a disturbance. Drifted on a drone to the poo pond, where a dark shape was emerging, two-and-a-half times the height of a man. Smooth and contoured in the shit-sheath. Thick-set with the gunk of thirty-thousand soldiers. Noah wore a hose as a belt, into which were tucked six or seven rockets, Unexploded rockets from the pond, I figured. Sahar clapped for the monster.

Shame had brought Sahar back to life, but it only made Noah stronger. He had scarcely emerged when a jeep passed and the driver turned his head toward the shit-beast, gaped, and **crashed the jeep into a ditch of barbed wire, resulting in 1xKIA, the passenger, who wasn't wearing a seatbelt**, who crashed through the window and into the barbed wire. He coughed violently, through a wound in his chest. Disgusting. **The driver and the passenger in the back engaged 1x shit-beast with SAF, which proved ineffective.**

The shit-beast was faster, swiping his mighty arm in a spray of suffocating stench. Doused, gagging, the soldiers lost precious seconds as their bullets plunked harmlessly into Noah's protective coating. He leaped among them, tearing, snarling. Ripped the door off the jeep, the arm from one man, the other, the leg, **resulting in a 1xKIA and 1xCAT A WIA.**

Bell shouted, "What the fuck is that? Crazy Jay, we need a drone with missiles, ASAP. Killjoy, you handle the medevacs."

"On it, Sir."

"Roger."

Noah was headed straight for the boardwalk, that capital of commerce, with the six shops that popped up to feed off the soldiers; TGI Fridays where sweat-stained grunts with hard-eyed stares collapsed into booths. The queue grew long and bitter outside of a Green Beans coffee shop. An American soldier strummed a guitar, while a singer's mouth flapped open and shut. The Afghan book-peddler wondered why he couldn't move his stock; poetry is dead, sorry. The creature was coming for all of them, the great teacher with harsh lessons.

The shit-beast arrived and started hurling unexploded rockets like spears. The first struck the guitar, smashing the chest of the strummer in a twang of broken strings **resulting in 1xKIA.** A waitress at TGI Fridays slapped a watery pizza on the table. She glanced upward as the second spear smashed the coffee queue, **resulting in 6xKIA, a spray of blood and several wasted coffees.** Even hardened soldiers scream when nightmares come to life. Noah hollered something, as he threw a third missile-spear through the window of TGI Fridays, where it splashed on a soggy pizza; the fickle mechanism detonated. The restaurant exploded—soldiers, waiters and cooks toughened by fifty rocket attacks, one civilian reporter scribbling in a notepad: **25xEKIA with serious fires and risk of secondary explosion. Firefighters en route with INF attached. ETA 6 minutes.** Survivors stumbled onto the boardwalk, coughing, and the building went up in the smoke.

"Goddamnit," said Bell. "Can't see shit in all the smoke—can't get a clear shot."

"Kill. Kill. Kill," suggested Crazy Jay.

"No more chanting," I said.

The fourth rocket smashed the bookstore, pounding the shelves of gold-gilt Korans, and perforated the merchant with splinters **resulting in 1xKIA.** A fifth spear shattered a milling crowd of thirty-or-so soldiers, **resulting in 8xKIA as survivors engaged 1x Shit Beast with ineffective SAF,** little *pop* *pops* that couldn't penetrate the muddy defenses. Noah strode in, flinging, clawing, and screaming. Grabbed a soldier by the face and used him as a club, steel-toed boots serving as the business end, **resulting in 12xEKIA including the bludgeon, which 1x Shit Beast flung across the boardwalk, where it struck the UXO in the bookstore, resulting in a secondary explosion and 6xWIA**. A cloud of torn poems fluttered like moths.

"Yay!" shouted Sahar, his injuries forgotten in the excitement.
"Killing is not a sport," I hollered.
"Who the futh you talthing to?" demanded Roadkill.

Troops arrived in their armadillos. Dozens of infantry, with bits of brush strapped to their helmets, firing toward the monster. In the midst of the burning boardwalk, Noah stood with his head downcast, the bullets sinking into the mud. Seemed to be shuddering and shaking. Seemed like huge forces battled in his body. One force compelled him to leap toward the soldiers. The other insisted he stay and endure their stings. He hollered and growled, furrowing his chest with his claws, and digging into the muck of his face as if to tear out his own brain. The claws twisted deeper and the bullets sank into his crust, and his mouth was cracked open in a scream.

Noah buckled, fell to his knees, transformed. Shadowy tendrils burst from shoulders and back, snapping and coiling. The arms doubled in length; his claws grew into swords. Jaw broke three times and fused back gaping, his maw filled with rows of razors. Noah was back behind the pane of unbreakable glass, a passenger in his body, all the while snarling as the bullets struck the mud. The shadows combined into another layer of armor; the torso-shape twisted longer, leaner, faster.

"You're too close," I said. "Remember what happened before."
"He's right," said Bell. "Pull the drone out to 200 yards."
"Leave him alone!" Sahar shouted.

We backed the drone farther away, afraid, a lazy loop of the burning boardwalk. Noah was a shadowy thing, dance-killing among the screams and chaos and fire. The occasional single frame of clarity. The ticking of the kill-count. A flash of grisly black claws. A superhuman leap. The monster guzzling marrow from a cracked femur. Throwing a grenade back at some infantry. The final rocket exploding a recon vehicle. An engine block flung like a frisbee.

But the Protector Spirit couldn't kill the soldiers as fast as they flooded the area, couldn't dodge all the shrapnel from bursting 25mm rounds, or absorb the powerful .50 cal machine gun fire fully with his shit/shadow shield. Drops of black blood on the ground, seeping through the poo layer. All the hornets of the many nations were responding in diverse shades of camouflage. Noah was swinging a great wooden pillar he'd torn from the boardwalk; he always said when the Spirit took over he couldn't shut his eyes.

A curious thing happened.

Noah surrendered.

There were nearly five hundred soldiers closing in when Noah dropped his maul and lifted his hands into the air. Fifteen feet tall and covered in shit and blood with smoke billowing around him and shadowy tentacles writhing. Crushed soldiers were heaped in all directions.

Perhaps there is such a thing as too much blood. Perhaps the ancient Spirit had glutted, reached its threshold of killing. Perhaps noble Noah won out, wrestling control back of his body. Perhaps goodness will prevail, the impulse for life overreaching our systems of murder and hatred. Perhaps innocence will save us all.

The soldiers gathered closer, bound by the ROE not to strike a surrendering opponent, no matter how much devastation wreaked. Sweaty brows and pinched, worried eyes under helmet rims. Closer and closer they inched, until the soldiers surrounded Noah, aiming rifles at his face and vitals.

How would they tie his hands? How would they cage him? Never got to figure it out before Noah opened his mouth and roared. A shocking low note that shook the drone, like the grumbles of calving icebergs. *RRRRRAAAAAAAAAAAAAAAAA*. We could hear it all the way in the TOC.

All the soldiers, the Americans and Canadians and Italians and Brits and Romanians, clutched their stomachs and groaned. The Bigfoot was tugging their bowel-strings. *RRRRRRRAAAAAAAAAAAAAAAAA* the roar continued, growing louder and deeper and stronger. Noah dropped his hands and clenched them into fists. The roar lowered another octave, another octave; spittle flew from the mighty mouth, and then he hit it.

The brown note.

The stomach-clutching soldiers collapsed onto the earth, hundreds of them, defecating madly and violently, clawing at the ground, shitting and vomiting and vomiting and shitting. Because dignity is a casualty of war, too. Soldiers wailed like neglected babes, tears streaming, firing a few feeble rounds at the creature when they could look straight.

In the chaos of that crapaclysm, the Shit-Beast strode through the licking flames and smoke, slaying with vicious swipes the unlucky few who could not crawl away fast enough. A towering rampage of shit and muscle. Noah became a *force*, just like he said. When the smoke thickened, the monster disappeared within the cloud, shadowy and silent, flitting away.

80.

WE ALL LOST COMRADES THAT DAY—everyone was grieving and dazed. I needed to talk to her, the old Major. Maybe I could catch her before her flight, and we could grieve together like we used to. Found myself in front of the women's barracks. I would tell her I killed Sahar and pay the penance of a slap, maybe. I told him to wait outside—he looked up, only as tall as my shoulder, uncomprehending.

Wandered down the dark hall of the women's barracks, shining my sailor's pocket light on the doors to read the names. The faint scent of lemon wafting from the washroom.

A shot rang out, a muffled crack.

I pushed open her door and shone my little light. I had always wanted to visit here, like a proper lover, but not like this.

Is she sleeping?

No. She was still at her desk, though no light shone, slumped far in her chair, her blonde hair freed and streaming down almost to the floor. One hand hung limply, the other clutched a pistol in her lap. A sudden clawing at my throat; I flicked on the lights.

No—not like this. No. No NO NO NO. Rewind, damnit—rewind!

She was wearing her arid-patterned uniform. Her pale hand dangled in a red pool. Blood was just starting to clot in the hair, a trickle from one corner of her lips. Otherwise, her face was untouched: the high cheekbones, the mouth hanging open slack, the eyes staring at nothing. Blue eyes, blue like glacier ice. Still piercing, still clever. Fading pimple on the cheek. A freckle on her collarbone. Tiny scar under the eye. When I dropped to my knees and rested my head on her shoulder, there was still warmth.

I should have known—she tried to tell me. Goddamnit, that visit in the hospital—she was saying goodbye. I checked her pulse, listened for her breath. Nothing.

I stroked her hair, blubbering. Tried to rub warmth into her fingers. I whispered, "I'm sorry, Jen," until my voice cracked and my eyes flooded and I told her that I loved her. I slid onto the floor beside her, still holding her hand, and sobbed into my sleeve.

Jen. She'd told me her name was Jen, right before we first made love. That was the only time I'd used it. But in that moment, I used it without thinking. She would forgive me the breach, I think. Death doesn't give a shit about names. *We're finally friends.* I shook and laughed and wept on the floor.

81.

I HUDDLED WITH MY DEAD LOVER, until I felt a comforting pat on my shoulder. When I looked up—it was Sahar, his face twisted in compassion—I screamed.

The sound of the gunshot drew a neighbor in about two minutes, a helpful hornet with broad shoulders, a Master Corporal. She called the ambulance and stroked the Major's long hair and kissed her forehead. "You don't want to be here when the police arrive," she said, not unkindly, and I thanked her thrice.

Stumbled back to my cabin, kicked off my boots, and wrapped myself in wool, whimpering the Major's name. Everywhere I looked was like staring at the sun; everything scalded—I ripped off my bandages so it would hurt more. As blood soaked into the sheets of my rack, I became wise, eyes rolling back and lips fluttering soundlessly. There is no life without pain and the best of us will always die. Survivors befriend their shame, live in the rotting garden of dead loves.

I was flitting in and out, watching myself through a drone. Sahar was playing with my boot laces, next to the cabinet. Halima was staring at me from the mirror. A single picture of a sailboat on a lonely sea. A reminder that every apple has a fishhook. The tank always crushes the flower. Each of us is a wretch of loneliness; everyone is always a stranger.

There is no point to suffering, no lesson, no payoff. Only hard wisdom, better left unlearned. The Major became wise in the end, too.

82.

WORKED OUT ALONE. No one had seen TicTac since we brawled: smashed mirrors in the gym, dents in the walls, and the soldiers' stares—finally people watching me instead of me watching them all the time. Loud moans for dead friends on the boardwalk. A mutter or two about the skank who shot herself in the barracks the day before; we shoulda never let women into combat zones: bad luck. Slipped headphones on and took the workout outside where Sahar bore witness as I flipped the giant tire down the ruined boardwalk, salt-sting in the still-fresh wounds on my forehead and knuckles, and tears running down my face. Sahar had never seen someone like me before, beef-fed, a giant, and he clapped his bloody hands noiselessly.

Arrived at the TOC with the stack of coffees. Roadkill was standing in front of the big map, quickdrawing from two pistols on either hip. Lightning. Face a mess of blotches from where he'd massacred non-existent zits. Mouth snapping open and shut. When he spoke, it was the metallic tones of the combat chat, "**Update from the attath on the boardwalk, ThillJoy. 1x unknown INS attathed ISAF forthes with rothets and hand-to-hand—**"

I tried to hasten him, "Yep, yep, I saw," but he pushed on.

"**—resulting in 60xEKIA and 55xEWIA from ethplosions and smothe inhalation. 1xINS utilizcd a sonith wcapon rcsulting in approx. 250xWIA CAT C thasualties. All base hospitals at thapathity. Awaiting final thasualty numbers. Ramp theremonies ongoing. NFTR ATT.**"

Not a single word about the Major. Like when she pulled the trigger, she erased herself.

"Been a hell of a shift, Killjoy," said Bell, approaching the big map and taking a coffee from the stack. Bell was about six hundred years old by this point. A desiccated skeleton with the skin hanging off. An old lich with his organs stowed in a phylactery. Hadn't shaved in days—his stubble was coalescing into a thin, pale beard. "Never did get our shot at the thing. Too many people. Spent the whole day moving casualties."

Roadkill spoke, "Watching people die without being able to futhing do shit is the worst."

Bell: "Yah. Like the woman who hit the IED in the marketplace."

I remembered. "Double amputee. We sent a helicopter for her, but the men of the village didn't let the medical team get close."

"That was back before you got here, Roadkill," said Bell.

"Same shit."

We stood in silence and were comrades for an instant. Bell tried to say something, couldn't. Eventually, though, "Still plenty going on tonight, gents. Got about twelve ramp ceremonies happening—the whole base is on parade, sending their folks home. Roadkill, go get some rest—I got a few more things to take care of."

Roadkill nodded, barked out a few more lines of combat chat, then left. Bell spoke in a weary voice, "Six of those casualties last night were Canadian, Killjoy. We got a shit-ton of admin between lining up flights, talking to padres, passing info, dealing with RFIs from the headquarters in Canada. You can imagine the questions they're asking. Motherfuckers never see a day of combat, sitting on their damn thrones back in Canada, asking stupid questions. One of those pencil-pushers caught a whiff of the Shit Beast and then the phones exploded." A death-grip on his coffee seemed the only thing keeping Bell going. "Don't use the term 'shit beast' if you need to talk to HQ. Use the term, 'unknown insurgent.' Got it?"

"Got it, boss."

"One more thing, Jones." I raised an eyebrow at his use of my actual name. "One of the ramp ceremonies tonight is likely to have poor attendance, due to the circumstances of death. I'll cover for you if you want to go."

My throat swelled shut; I nodded. Bell's eyes were ancient and sad.

83.

RAMP CEREMONY. Moon. The old Major's torn-off button in my palm. Normally every soldier came out to these, stood on parade, as pallbearers carried the casket with the flag folded on top. My love was in a box, several hundred yards from a small-bellied cargo plane. No bagpipes to keen for *her*. No ceremony at all.

The Sergeant organizing the move chewed a moist cigar and wore a red patch on his upper sleeve. Otherwise, there was one other soldier beside me; he had his bushcap pulled low over his eyes. Somber Sahar stood a bit removed from where we clustered near the plane. Whatever troops were loyal to the Major must have been at a different ramp—or maybe they were never told about her last flight.

"Can you believe it, Sir?" the Sergeant growled around the cigar. "I get stuck with Tits McGee who wasted herself when there's actual dead heroes to send home."

"You didn't know her, Sergeant," I said.

"With respect, Sir, you'll forgive me if I don't get misty-eyed over a suicide. Especially one who never even left the camp the whole tour. I mean, I'm not Special Forces, but how stressful can it be working in an office?"

I gritted my teeth. "Let's move this forward. I need to get back on shift."

The Sergeant brandished a clipboard. "Well, all the padres are dealing with the *real* casualties—so this won't be much of a ceremony. If you two could grab the casket and stuff her in the back of this plane it'd be great. Lemme know when she's in there so I can check her off my list."

Walked the few hundred yards to her casket, simple wooden box, no flag draped over. No boots polished; no crisp salutes. No planes flying overhead, dipping their wings. No great sage to share wisdom and give our grief a voice. No bagpipes to wail into the atmosphere.

The other soldier said nothing, kept his face hidden. Strong though—the two of us hefted the coffin by ourselves, without lurches. Even walked in step with our cargo, he in front, me behind. Sahar followed our small procession six feet back, holding his guts like a bouquet.

I could at least *imagine* she got the death she deserved. Hundreds, thousands of soldiers standing in somber ranks with rain shining in the floodlights. Jesus himself leads us in prayer, jewels dripping from his lips. When he's done, the bagpipes start with that low moan and then explode into sound.

Shuddered with the weight of the casket and a half-sob. The other soldier cocked his head, listening, but said nothing. Not fair how any of this went down. How she'll just become a story tossed around messes and galleys: the promising Major who turned skank and blew herself away when she got busted. None of those people will ever know her as the Valkyrie who stormed ramparts, as the voice who gave our victims human names, who kissed my nose and called me poet.

I don't need a crystal ball to predict how the military will handle her suicide. First, they'll dump her body into the well of shame. It will bubble up, a few days later, as a crude joke. Then, she'll become a weapon again; they'll say the Female Engagement Team was a madwoman's delusion, and the killing will continue, same as before. Then she'll be forgotten, the final death.

Noah said that stories can't bring people back to life, but I will. I have to; she told me to act with my highest integrity. She'll be a hero with a steel arm and a helmet-fist. She'll be the only one with the courage to not kill. She'll be tender, but only in bunkers. Her laughter will chime again and again: birds escaping a cage.

We reached the ramp and, tilted upward, I felt her weight shift inside the casket. A tiny noise of sliding from within. I whimpered and swore I'd bring her back to life.

84.

FLOODLIGHT SWITCHED OFF as the Sergeant raised the hatch of the plane, and I couldn't see the casket and then the hatch clunked shut and she was gone.

I took four steps onto the darkened tarmac to breathe, Sahar at my elbow.

The other ramp ceremony, a mile down the runway, was still going. Faint bagpipe—too far to hear the drone.

"You loved her, didn't you?" said a man's voice, slightly high-pitched, familiar. I looked up; the other soldier in the procession had followed me. Under the moonlight, I saw his name was Jones as well, and he wore his uniform baggy. "I am sorry for your loss."

The soldier pushed his bushcap higher, revealing a bald head, relentless stare. Veinshadows and moonglimmers on his throat. He pulled a Taser from his pocket, pointed it at my face. I raised wary arms into the air. "It is not lie," said the Coachbag, as he unclipped my pistol from the holster, stepped back a few feet, and tossed it, skittering, across the tarmac. "A funeral is very important thing for grieving, no? I had to go to my father's, when I was just boy."

"After you killed him?" I asked.

TicTac's face twitched. "He got what he deserved. And you will too."

"Did you see his eyes?"

The twitch became a spasm. "Not seeing the eyes—that is the problem." He waved me forward with the Taser. "Now we go on little walk, Jones. Somewhere more private. You go in front and I follow behind. You cannot outrun me, let alone bullet."

That much was true. I shuffled to the north, as directed, scanning for someone who could help me, a soldier, anyone. Somber Sahar trailed after us, adding dignity to this procession, too. *He is my son, now.* We reached the edge of the tarmac and gravel crunched underfoot as we skirted the pond, continued. Took shortcuts between the concrete barriers, treading secret and meticulously kept paths in the barbed wire.

I was trying to escape in my mind and be with her. But it wasn't working. *Her pale hand dangling over a red pool.*

"What do you want, TicTac?" Sahar walked at my side, wrapped a moist friendship bracelet around my wrist.

"All I ever wanted was friend to spot me perfectly on benchpress, with minimal help. You did not break my heart when you hit me with dumbbell, but you did break few ribs. And tonight I have been friend to you anyway, for it was grief that made us close."

"I always appreciated your friendship, TicTac—" I stumbled, nearly fell into a coil of daggerwire. TicTac grabbed my sleeve in his invincible grip.

"And I yours, Jones. Tonight we are brothers—I even wear your nametag, look. But tonight is also breakup. Not to worry, though. Before end you will know tremendous pleasure—this I promise." Sahar was listening, rapt, mouth hanging open, as we pushed deeper into a concrete maze. "I am *so* generous, Jones. I am practically Easter Bunny. Now sit."

We had reached the junkyard in the north of the camp where mangled cars had been erected like fences, a dense maze of broken-down vehicles, scraps of IED blasts, stacks of ruptured tires, shattered windshields, twisted nests of rebar, scattered frigate-sized droppings with fingerbones. I was facing the dented truck where we found Bell, not far from Noah's tunnel. Coils of bloody rope. "If you do not want to taste Taser, you will sit." TicTac repeated, and began to strip, tearing off the shirt with my name, kicking off his boots, never taking his eyes from me. *Her blonde hair freed and streaming down almost to the floor.* I sat on the dented trunk of the truck.

Bulging pectorals in the moonlight: naked except for the Taser. "I didn't want this, Jones. I wanted to finish my tour, jump on plane home. Now I am trapped here." A dark chuckle. "I am like rat who has outgrown maze." A sour wind blew from the poo pond. He donned his paper mask of a woman's face with the eyeholes cut out, the page creased and supported by a string that ran behind his ears. *Now.* I leapt toward him, swinging a beefy fist. Sahar gasped.

Sparks. The muscles of my chest and shoulders contracted and expanded uncontrollably, explosively. A dart stuck out of my chest with two wires attached, trailing back to the Taser. Paralysis. I gasped, choked, fell to the ground and drummed my heels helplessly.

Sparks. My abs tightened, seized. Radiating shockwaves. A tendon in my neck cramped, twisting my vision skyward. Tried to clamp my teeth on a moan, failed. Tried to send my brain away on a drone, failed. Pain dragged me back to the body.

Sparks. Quadricep clenched so hard I thought it would tear off the bone, twisted me sideways onto the hood of the truck and flipped me back to the ground; I convulsed and gnashed my teeth. My heartbeat was agony, pumping electricity, skipping beats. *Blue eyes, blue like icebergs, and the blood clotting in her hair.*

"You listen close to last lesson from Coachbag, Jones." TicTac was reaching into a backpack and withdrawing a black, cloth hood. "This is not rock-bottom. You can always suffer more." He took a step toward me with the bag in one hand, the Taser in the other. I tried to move but it was like being pinned under the barbells again. Face pressed into the dust, blood in my mouth. Sahar lay down beside me with a peaceful expression—*yes, Sahar, I deserve this, all of it.* A step closer, a step closer, a step closer—I could only stare at Sahar. Needed to meet his eyes. Had to stare deep into his human eyes so I wouldn't forget them when the bag came down. *Would he ever forgive me?*

A growl from a nearby bunker. A horrible low growl a buffalo-sized cat might make. All the hairs of my neck stood up and my bowels loosened. Yes, child-like terror, no matter the relief. TicTac's eyes widened, darting from cranny to cranny in the stacked cars and bomb-blasted vehicles of the junkyard maze. He stepped back, scanning. "Is this your friend, Jones? The so-called strongest in KAF?"

My hero in shades of hubcaps and fenders and twisted rebar; the junk-wall came alive with a second growl, the vast man-shape of Noah, armored in scrap metal with fists wrapped in barbed wire. A colossus. Beneath the armor, the poo crust was scaling and stained red in places. Ratty orange fur poked through the fissures. The poo pond had taught him patience and the taste for flesh—he bounded toward TicTac howling, slapping the Taser from his grasp with a fierce backhand.

TicTac deftly rolled backward, landing on his feet, trying to claw the mask from his face. Noah leaped, driving his enormous power and weight into a single punch. Connected with a boom and squelch; TicTac soared fifty feet and tumbled into the junk wall, flailing.

I could move a little. Sahar and I slid farther back from the combatants, wormed behind a stack of tires. *Get behind me, Sahar. I'll protect you, if I can.*

"We're done now, Jones," growled Noah. "I got no more debts to yer world. Everyone left is meat. Tried to play it gentle but that was just blood in the water for you sharks. Never wanted to be no monster. But how do you stop it once you start?" *I wish I knew.* TicTac was pulling himself from the wreckage. Noah's voice grew stony and his eyes blazed, "Spirit says I should kill ya both."

"The shit monster speaks." TicTac stood, propping himself on a six-foot staff of rebar, his jaw dislocated badly, jutting to the side. He snapped it back in place. Drooled. "So proud. Does your mother know you live in lake of shit?"

Noah tilted his head. "Yer gonna insult me, Pervert? What, yer gonna try to fuck me with yer tiny human dick? Didn't ya hear what happened on the boardwalk? You can't beat the Spirit—no one can." He stooped and grabbed a length of chain connected to a concrete stump that must have weighed 500 lbs. Noah swung the stump around him, building speed, until it blurred. Invincible, skin tough as bark, his muscles filling the whole page, spinning a comet around his head. *He's Mack, back from the dead. A hero.* I burrowed deeper into the tires.

The Coachbag in a wrestler stance, holding his rebar rod, looking for an opening. When Noah's slab hit the junkyard walls it didn't even slow, just collapsed metal or blasted over cars. Hubcap shrapnel sprayed TicTac, who dodged nearly flat as the boulder whistled overhead, then charged with the rebar rod.

The shit-beast grunted, adjusted his grip on the chain, and the stump struck meat. A glancing blow, still strong enough to hurl TicTac headfirst into the junkyard wall.

He stumbled to his feet with blood running down his forehead and the Taser in his hand. Fired.

The darts struck stomach flesh and Noah bellowed, the chain slipping from his fingers, the stump crashing into the wall.

TicTac reloaded, fired again. Noah's great muscles heaved so hard his bones popped and a few of the ropes on his armor snapped—the contractions were literally knocking him off the ground. Reloaded, fired. The Sasquatch howled, gnashed his teeth. Smell of burning hair.

"You goddamn coward!" I yelled. "You know you can't beat him strength for strength!"

Fired again and again, the junkyard sparking as if wizards battled, until Noah collapsed at first onto his knees, then onto his stomach, and lay panting.

The Coachbag tore a length of barbed wire from Noah's helpless fist, and wrapped it around the Sasquatch's neck. Pressed his knee against the base of the spine, and pulled upward with his leg-arms bulging.

Blood sprayed from under the wire. Noah's eyes darted wildly left and right, until tears flooded them. He pawed impotently at the ground as I struggled to my feet, searching for the Taser, for the rebar rod, something. "Do something, Sahar!" I shouted.

Shadow lightning marked the Spirit's arrival; dark tendrils burst from Noah's shoulders, snapping at his assailant like serpents. I started backing away; TicTac pulled the wire even harder, grinding his knee into Noah's spine.

Under the armor, the Sasquatch's body was stretching, burning with ghostly fire. The claws twisted long and sharp and his bones creaked and popped. Suddenly he had enough air in his lungs to growl and SPRONG—

the wire snapped; the Spirit flung TicTac to the ground, stooped low, and slashed him open with two swipes of his vicious claws.

A blood-bubble burst at the corner of TicTac's mouth; he convulsed violently once, arching his back. His eyes were wide open and horrified. Sahar knelt next to him, took his hand.

Then the Spirit turned to me and leaned so close I could smell the soldiers on its breath. The great maw of daggers and the burning yellow eyes. The muscles, vast yet so ripped they seemed emaciated. The arms dragging low on the ground and the lingering stench of the pond. My knees shook; the rest was paralyzed. This was the monster that had corrupted gentle Noah and turned him vicious. Who would prey on soldiers and Afghans until it was a god again. Mouth gaping open, it raised its black blades high—the moon shone between the claws—and slashed.

I blinked awake—expecting to find myself in a sanatorium, the padded walls covered in glyphs, or in the hospital with tubes rammed up my nose, or in hell being turned on a spit by imps, finally making amends for the blood I'd spilt. But no, it was real—I was still in Afghanistan, with only a few minutes gone. Sahar was whispering in my ear, stroking my cheek, and the Major was still dead. Tiny pieces of white paper surrounded me, fluttering like snow.

Gingerly, gingerly, I felt for wounds. The creature had rent my combat shirt, leaving a jagged tear. I explored it with my fingers, keeping my eyelids pressed, found no sticky blood. It had been a low blow, intended to gut me, make me another Sahar, perhaps.

That hadn't happened. When the claws should have shredded my flesh, they struck something else. Something both soft and strong, a thing of my people. Of the forest. With trembling fingers, I withdrew the rolled-up silk my mother used to pad the morale boxes, the three-ply toilet paper that always bulged in my pocket. Now, a devastated spool. Not even the claws of a furious god could penetrate to its cardboard core. A toilet paper of such softness, such unnecessary decadence, such velvet richness, that even tender Canadians would dab with it. *Their gentle, uncalloused asses saved my life.*

Sahar started noiselessly chuckling. When I looked over, he was making balloon animals with himself. "Are you gonna be here for the rest of my life?" I asked him, but he didn't answer, was too busy making a rabbit.

TicTac was dead with his ribcage cracked open, his muscles finally relaxed, and the fear etched into his face. I climbed to my feet and stumbled from the junkyard maze with my whole body aching and could see the Spirit down the road, moonlight glinting on pieces of junkyard armor, swinging his claws and gorging on soldiers. Fingered the rip in my shirt as the claws flashed. This madness had gone on long enough, had hurt enough people. It would be up to me to end it. "Come along, Sahar," I said. "I'll need your help."

I shuffled my bruised and wearied body down the road toward the TOC, pulling out the Taser dart still stuck in my quad. Not a strong runner on the best of days and this was the worst. Made it to the outer door of the Canadian compound and had to input the code three times before the door swung open. Caught the scent of lemon and nearly screamed. Stumbled past the graffiti-covered washroom, the General's office building. Inputted another code in another door and burst into the TOC.

Roadkill gnashed his broken teeth. "What the futh, Jones? Bell thalled me bath in when you didn't show up for two hours. You don't thinth I need my beauty sleep?"

"Tie him up," I said to Sahar.

"Who the futh you talking to?"

"Fine, I'll do it myself." I grabbed Roadkill by the spindly triceps. Squeezed. Predictably, his other hand shot for his holster. I headbutted him straight in the jaw, using all the strength in my back to drive the blow. A few more teeth clattered on the ground and Roadkill fell limp in my grasp. I hauled him to the Major's office, and flung him against the filing cabinet.

Bell was standing by his desk, all bones, and murmuring *muh muh muh* to himself. A withered immortal with long white hair, long white beard. Horrible ancient eyes. In his hands, the memo I wrote that reported TicTac's dodginess—he'd never passed it up the chain.

"We were all so happy back then, Jones." He held up his skeletal fingers helplessly and the memo dropped. "Frank the Tank, the Bear, the girl and I. Softness and hardness together." I wedged a steel-backed chair under the doorknob, trapping him and Kool both.

"All right, Team, listen up," I shouted. The TOC-moles perked up. "We gotta visual on the Shit Beast. I need all possible assets. I need drones, I need jets, I need artillery. I need everything."

"One Predator on station," said Crazy Jay. He hadn't cheered a strike since Sahar. "I'll work on the jets."

We swung the Pred east from Dand district and in a few minutes KAF was in black and white. My home for the last year, its high walls and barbed wire crenellations. A plane took off carrying dead soldiers. "There!" I shouted, pointing to a breach in the wall, the monster striding through, out of the camp, into the minefields.

"I don't see shit," said Crazy Jay. Sahar was dying in his lap.

"You don't see him?" I said, pointing to Noah. Picking his way through barbed wire emplacements, dodging mines.

"See who?"

"Fire the missile," I said.

And it was like Noah knew, that he had seized control of his body long enough to look up at me, at the drone. He was standing in the bottom of a trench, with poppies growing from the sides. The shadowy creature turned his palms upwards as if to show me he was unarmed.

The missile struck. Noah disappeared in a cloud of smoke. No one cheered.

"Fire the missile," I said again. "Fire all the missiles." Even as the dust was settling from the first blast, the second missile struck. Throwing the dust up again. Inside the cloud, a deeper shadow writhed. The next two missiles burst. But it wasn't enough to stop the shadow, not nearly enough.

"Artillery. Is it ready?"

"It's ready to go, but are you sure you didn't get him?" said Crazy Jay.

"Fire the artillery," I said. "All of it."

God-hammers struck the earth. The whole minefield was being flipped over; the artillery rounds packed a bigger punch than the Pred's little missiles: great gouts of earth like the spume of volcanoes. Some rounds struck directly on the writhing smoky mass. Others dug foxholes, battering the soil.

"What about a Reaper?" I asked. "Need one of those. Definitely."

"One minute," said Crazy Jay. "I can get one in a minute."

"Keep the barrage going until the Reaper's online," I said.

Was that a limb? Something flailing? Noah and his demon wrestling with each other in the smoke. One wanting to flee and live and kill again, the other wanting to just die, and stop the hurting, and sleep. Between the bursts of artillery Noah pounded and slashed at himself, half-spectral. One clenched fist, one dripping claw.

Through the gritty, pixelated camera of the Reaper, I could almost see Noah *more* clearly, a deeper black within the gray. Roadkill had awoken and was hammering the door of the office. Someone was yelling, "Stop him!" Sahar was draped over the radios.

"Drop the bomb," I said.

"What's the target?" asked Crazy Jay.

"Shut up and do it."

A 500 lbs bomb tumbled end over end. It was shaped like a tremendous eggplant with shark fins. The writhing black splash that was Noah disappeared in a torrent of flame, a titanic explosion that dug a great wound in the earth. But no, there was still a black tint to the middle, a little more monster still in there.

"Get the fuck back to your seat," I growled at Clay. He was moving toward the Major's door, trying to free the other officers.

Behind me, Crazy Jay was on the phone, "Can we get some help down in the TOC, Killjoy has lost it."

"Fucking traitor," I spat. "Drop the bomb. Drop all the bombs."

"Jones, there's nothing there!" shouted Clay.

"We have the PID and the ROE," I said. Sahar was crying without sound, top of his lungs.

The next three bombs landed, in increasing spurts of earth and fire. Surely Noah was just particles now. The black spot wrestling in the center of the maelstrom was fading.

"More bombs," I said. "Where's that jet?"

"Stop this immediately," said the General, throwing open the door.

"Are you listening to me, Jay?" I said.

"Killjoy's lost it," shouted Clay.

"Fire the missile," I said.

"There's none left," said Crazy Jay.

"What is he shooting at?" said the General.

"Drop the bomb," I said.

"There are no bombs," screamed Crazy Jay.

"Son, you need to sit down. Have some water. Take a breather," said the General.

"Get your fucking hands off me," I shouted.

"No one's touching you, Son," said the General.

"Shoot the laser," I said.

"Incapacitate this man," ordered the General.

Clunk. Sharp pain in the back of my skull and a blast of vertigo. Tried to spin around, too woozy. Clunk again and the sound of coconuts colliding. Fell to one knee. "Go down, Futher," growled Roadkill, fresh blood on his lips and holding the butt of his pistol like a club. *Idiots—can't you see I was setting you free? Setting us all free?* Clunk again, forehead. Pain. Vision narrowed and the floor was cool on my face. Sahar sidled behind me, the big spoon. The door to the nook—kicked open.

I had fallen off the edge of the world; grown so wise everyone thought I was crazy. A salty peanut on the floor, inches from my eyes. Beyond it, the drone monitor where the Reaper still circled Noah's grave. A giant, bomb-blasted pit, the size of a lake, visible from space. A few shrubs with broken spines along the shore, twisted and contaminated by the Spirit's particles.

The surrounding lands, a mess of scree and boulders. No birds circled.

Staring at that pit, a moment of perfect, scorching clarity. This would be our legacy. Not the schools, not the roads, the pit. We sent noble warriors like the Major to champion the Afghan people, but the bomb lake was all we accomplished in a year of murder, amputation, nightmares, massacres, shame, suicide, loneliness, rape, madness, and grief. An empty lake with jagged edges where nothing grows.

85.

I NEVER LEFT THE WAR—none of us do—just took the battle down corridors of decompression, counselling sessions, and onto the page.

Every morning I sit and build this shrine to my fallen love: a temple of words. It doesn't matter that stories can't bring people back to life, I spend weeks placing a single brick, anyway. At least now I can turn the page and see my idea of her, hear her laughter when it flies in an open window, beating its wings.

Every afternoon, Sahar bursts into the room and smashes my temple. He has full run of my dreams and the space behind my eyelids. He has perfected his rope tricks, dreaming new ways to remind me how he died, that he was innocent. He arrives for me when I'm grocery shopping, at the dentist, or driving a car. I owe him his life back.

No, Sahar—now is not the time. I'm trying to write. I'm trying to say something meaningful about war and service and the things we gave up. I want to say something about the people I loved who are gone. I'm trying to say something about sanitized language and how words need meaning. I'm trying to say that veterans are not statues, not perfect, not voiceless; that we bleed and shit and grieve. I want to say it perfectly, so that my losses matter.

I said stop it, Sahar. Yes, that's a very nice trick you have there, but I've seen it a hundred times. No, your guts are not a lasso, that's not how it happened. No, you can't skip with them either. Just let me work—all I need is a few hours. You stay in your corner, Sahar. That's Crispy's bed but you can lay there. You can just lay there and wait for it—no, you never listen, have never listened.

Shut up, Sahar, I'm trying to write. I don't hear what you're saying no matter how loud you yell it—is that a prayer? Do prayers go higher when you yell them?

GO INTO THE FUCKING BOX, SAHAR. GET INTO THE FUCKING BOX! Climb up the little ladder and get to the top bunk, don't get your guts stuck on anything—there you go. No, I am not OK. None of it is OK. Open the box, buddy. I know you don't wanna go back in but I need a few hours to write.

Now put your foot in. Get your guts together and get in there. Good. Good. Now close it. Yes, Sahar, close the lid.

MEDEVAC

9-Line REQUEST	DTG:	UNIT:
	.... D	

1	**Callsign & Freq**	(1)
2	**Location (Grid of HLS)**	(2)

	Number of Patients / Precedence	(3) P1 .... P2 .... P3 ....
3	PRIORITY 1 (to be at R2 or R3 within 60 mins)	PRIORITY 2 (to be at R2 or R3 within 4 hrs) — PRIORITY 3 (to be at R2 or R3 within 24 hrs)

	Special Equipment Required	(4)
4	A - NONE — B - HOIST — C - EXTRACTION EQUIP — D - VENTILATOR — E - OTHER	

	Number of Patients / Type	(5) S .... W .... / E .... O ....
5	S (Stretcher) — W (Walking) — E (Escort) — O (Other, give details)	

	Security at HLS	(6)
6	N - NO ENEMY — E - ENEMY IN AREA	
	P - POSSIBLE ENEMY — X - ARMED ESCORT REQUIRED	

	HLS Marking Method	(7)
7	A - Panels — B - Pyro — C - Smoke (colour?) — D - None — E - OTHER	

	Number of Patients by Nationality / Status	A .... B ...... / D .... E .... / G .... H ....
8	A - UK / NATO Military — B - UK / NATO Civilian — C - Non-UK / NATO Military	
	D - Non-UK / NATO Civilian — E - Detainees / PW — F - Embedded Interpreter	
	G - Civ Cas caused by FF — H - Child	

9	**HLS TERRAIN / OBSTACLES**	

(ACK)nowledgements

UNDER THE WORKING TITLE *DRONES*, I wrote this book as a shrine to fallen friends and homage to our victims. Little did I know that in the ten years since I served in Afghanistan, the meaning of the word 'drones' would change, and these war machines (we could pretend 'unmanned' meant 'unpiloted' when it served us) became children's toys, and the sport of photographers. Though the old title was overtaken by events, it did give a window into the text: soldiers are not drones, not worker ants, but individuals. This, I think, helps explain the storytelling, poetry, boxes, and other devices which so often interrupt this story. Soldiers bleed, are not made of stone; we even dream.

This book would not have happened without the generosity of the Canada Council of the Arts. Their bursary arrived just as I became convinced that no one would ever give two shits about my work, pulling me back from the brink of bitterness. It also allowed me to offer compensation to some of the earth's greatest writers and editors: Malik Ameer Crumpler, Janne Cleveland, Corinne Labalme, Amanda Dennis, Reine Arcache Melvin, Nina Marie Gardner, Rachel Kapelke Dale, Helen Cusack O'Keeffe, Albert Alla, and Nafkote Tamirat. They, alongside the talented writers of the DWG workshop in Paris, were instrumental in my transition from a veteran who writes, into a writer who veterans.

My most sincere gratitude to every friend who stuck by me after I was diagnosed with PTSD, years after the war. To Halima, who cracked the vase, and Sahar, who smashed it. To Jane, my therapist, who admitted our sessions were the most fun. To Phil, James and Chuck at Double Dagger for making this opportunity happen. To Tracy Crow for championing the book so diligently. To the faithful loggers who met weekly in the bois de Boulogne or the parc de la Villette, so I wouldn't atone alone. To family and friends who sent me those morale boxes with the peanut butter and rolled-up silk. To the 145 humans on my mailing list who endured monthly my overwrought spam. To Kate, who supported, encouraged and inspired me in Nicaragua, China and those first few years in Paris.

My final thanks to all the friends who found me in the pit, breathing through a hose, who forgave my long-stretching shadow, and bid me climb.

ABOUT THE AUTHOR

Matt Jones is a Canadian poet, novelist, storyteller and veteran who has published in *Arc*, *F(r)iction*, and many other places. Today, Matt writes and teaches in Paris: leadership at the *École militaire* and creative writing at SciencesPo. He edits prose at The Wrath Bearing Tree, co-hosts the by-donation WriteTime workshop, and organizes fitness enthusiasts who use trees as barbells: the Log Club.

Follow his work at www.matthewjamesjones.com

DOUBLE‡DAGGER
— www.doubledagger.ca —

DOUBLE DAGGER BOOKS is Canada's only military-focused publisher. Conflict and warfare have shaped human history since before we began to record it. The earliest stories that we know of, passed on as oral tradition, speak of war, and more importantly, the essential elements of the human condition that are revealed under its pressure.

We are dedicated to publishing material that, while rooted in conflict, transcend the idea of "war" as merely a genre. Fiction, non-fiction, and stuff that defies categorization, we want to read it all.

Because if you want peace, study war.